CURIOUS TOYS

ALSO BY ELIZABETH HAND

Cass Neary Novels

Generation Loss
Available Dark
Hard Light

Wylding Hall
Errantry: Strange Stories
Radiant Days
Glimmering
Illyria
Saffron and Brimstone: Strange Stories
Chip Crockett's Christmas Carol
Mortal Love
Bibliomancy: Four Novellas
Black Light
Last Summer at Mars Hill and Other Stories
Waking the Moon
Icarus Descending
Aestival Tide
Winterlong

CURIOUS TOYS

A Novel

ELIZABETH HAND

MULHOLLAND
BOOKS

Little, Brown and Company

New York   Boston   London

Mulholland Books / Little, Brown and Company
Hachette Book Group
1290 Avenue of the Americas, New York, NY 10104
mulhollandbooks.com

First Edition: October 2019

Mulholland Books is an imprint of Little, Brown and Company, a division of Hachette Book Group, Inc. The Mulholland Books name and logo are trademarks of Hachette Book Group, Inc.

The publisher is not responsible for websites (or their content) that are not owned by the publisher.

The Hachette Speakers Bureau provides a wide range of authors for speaking events. To find out more, go to hachettespeakersbureau.com or call (866) 376-6591.

The quotation from John Ashbery's *Girls on the Run* is used by permission.

The quotation from Henry Darger's *In the Realms of the Unreal* is used by permission, copyright 2018 Kiyoko Lerner/Artists Rights Society (ARS), New York.

A brief section from this novel first appeared in a slightly different form in *Conjunctions: 71, A Cabinet of Curiosity* under the title "Henry's Room."

ISBN 978-0-316-48588-3
LCCN 2019937208

10 9 8 7 6 5 4 3 2 1

LSC-C

Printed in the United States of America

For my mother, who suggested that I write a story with Henry Darger as a detective, with love and gratitude for a lifetime of books, and reading

Suppose, now, that in a room of watching others coquet with Death, you should toy with her yourself. With infinite ingenuity, the amusement park offers you opportunity.
—Rollin Lynde Hartt, "The Amusement Park,"
Atlantic Monthly, May 1907

We aren't easily intimidated.
And yet we are always frightened
—John Ashbery, *Girls on the Run*

CURIOUS TOYS

Chapter 1

An accident, not his fault. Wouldn't stop bouncing, set her on fire and policeman choked him, big hands yes your fault, not an accident don't you lie to me. He ran and here he was, keeping her safe, keeping them all safe. Won't happen again he was watching now. It was an accident.

Chapter 2

Riverview Amusement Park, Chicago, August 1915

THERE HE WAS again, smoking a cigar in front of the Infant Incubators. A white man not much taller than Pin—and she was small for her age and looked twelve, rather than fourteen—but too tall to be a midget. Something stealthy and twitchy about him: every few minutes, his head would twist violently and he'd punch the air, fending off an invisible assailant.

There was no attacker. Crowded as the amusement park was, Pin saw no one anywhere near him. The young mothers dragging their kids into the Infant Incubators building to escape the heat stepped off the sidewalk onto the Pike to avoid coming within two feet of him. He was a dingbat.

She ran her sweaty hands across her knickerbockers, removed her cap to fan her face. She'd seen the weird little man at the park often— three or four times a week he'd be standing near one of the rides, always watching, watching. He never seemed to change out of the same soiled work clothes. Trousers, shirt, a dark-blue canvas jacket.

Heavy boots. A white boater hat with a stained red band; sometimes a bowler.

Today it was a boater. He never rode any of the rides, and never seemed to partake in any of the attractions. Once she'd seen him outside the Casino Restaurant, drinking a glass of beer and eating a sausage. A few times he'd been with another man, older, the two of them like Mutt and Jeff in the funnies: one tall and skinny, the other short with that grubby mustache and dinged-up boater.

But lately the weird little man was always alone. And all he ever seemed to do was watch the kids go in and out of the Infant Incubators, hop off and on the Velvet Coaster, clamber into the boats that bore them into Hell Gate or the Old Mill, then back out again.

He knew Pin was watching him. She could tell by the way his eyes slanted when he cocked his head, pretending to look in the other direction, the way Mr. Lerwin used to look at her younger sister, Abriana. But the dingbat wouldn't know that Pin was a girl disguised as a boy. No one knew, except Pin and her mother.

He talked to himself, too. One of these days she'd sidle up close enough to hear what he was saying. But not this morning. She tugged her cap back down, felt in her pocket for the Helmar cigarette box Max had given her half an hour ago, along with a cuff to the back of her head.

"Don't you go dragging your feet like last time," he'd said. "I can't afford to lose business."

"It was raining. Lionel ain't gonna ditch you."

"It's not raining today. Go."

He raised his hand in warning. She darted out of the dressing room and heard him laughing behind her. "Run, rabbit, run!"

She spat on the pavement, kicking at a squashed stogie, spun on her heel, and headed for the exit gate. When she glanced back over her shoulder, the dingbatty little man was gone.

Chapter 3

MAX ALWAYS GAVE her fare to the movie studio or the other places where she delivered hashish cigarettes and dope, though only enough for one way. She never stopped asking him for the nickel, even though that risked getting smacked.

"What about the fare home?" She sat in his dressing room, a makeshift shack even smaller than the one where she lived with her mother, tossing her cap into the air as she watched him get ready for work. "Just another nickel, you got plenty."

"The hell I do. Tell Lionel to give it to you. That's his end of the deal, not mine." Max leaned into his makeup mirror, drew a comma in black kohl along one eyelid. "You're too lazy to work, boy, I'll find someone else."

Before she could duck, he grabbed the cap from her hand and tossed it toward the back of the room, where it fell beneath the cracked window. Pin retrieved the cap, then stepped to an overturned barrel that served as a chair. Scattered photographs lay atop it, old French postcards that showed the same young woman, dark haired and wearing a black schoolgirl's uniform. Her waist was grotesquely small, tightly corseted beneath the uniform. Corsets were going out of fashion; these pictures had to be at least ten years old.

Looking at them made Pin feel slightly sick. The woman's tiny waist made it look as though she'd been cut in two, the halves of her body held together by a strip of black ribbon: if you pulled at it, she'd fall apart. Pin quickly gathered the photos and shoved them onto a shelf covered with similar photographs, then settled on top of the barrel to gaze, mesmerized, over Max's shoulder into the mirror.

She'd never known a guy who wore makeup. She'd heard of fairies, of course. Ikie and the other boys in the park sometimes pointed them out to her at night. To Pin, they looked like ordinary men. A few were dudes, flashy dressers who wore spats and striped waistcoats and nice shoes, but she'd seen plenty of dudes fondling women in the dark rides. Some fairies looked like workmen, others businessmen. Some might be with their wives, or even children.

"How can fairies have kids?" she'd asked Ikie.

He shrugged. "Hell if I know."

Once in the Comique, the park's movie arcade, she'd seen a pair of young men standing together in front of a Mutoscope, dressed like they were headed for a dance hall. The men took turns peering into the viewer, and for a fraction of a second their fingers had touched—deliberately, one finger caressing the other before the hand was withdrawn. The sight had filled her with an emotion she'd never felt before: a cold flash, neither dread nor fear yet partaking of both, along with a pulse of exhilaration, as though she sat in the first car of the Velvet Coaster as it began its plunge down the tracks.

Max wasn't a dude, or a fairy, as far as Pin could tell. She followed him sometimes around the park, always careful to keep a safe distance, half hoping and half fearful that she might see some proof that he was…something. Some look or touch, a foray into the Fairyland woods and picnic ground, where men were rumored to meet.

She never did. Other than the occasional knock to the head, he never laid hands on her. Offstage he wore shirtsleeves, no cuffs or celluloid collar, and plain dark trousers, indifferently pressed. He had vivid yellow-green eyes, the color of uranium glass. He dyed his hair blond, but that was for the act, like the makeup he painstakingly applied before his first performance and touched up during the day.

His mustache, too, was fake, and only half a mustache. He was Max and Maxene, the She-Male, half man and half woman, appearing at irregular interludes in the last tent on the Pike, just past the Ten-in-One. Not a real freak, but a gaffed freak, like most of the others.

According to Clyde, the Negro magician, Max had been an actor before he arrived in Riverview early that summer. "He played Romeo at the Hudson Theatre. Shakespeare."

"Romeo?"

Clyde had given her a sharp look. Pin thought he was handsome enough to be an actor himself—tall and broad chested, with beautiful chestnut-brown eyes. "You think it's funny he played Romeo?"

She shrugged. "Sure. Look how old he is."

"He was younger then. They said he was going to be the next Karl Nash."

"Why's he working here, then?"

Clyde shook his head. "What I heard, some little gal broke his heart. That's the way it goes. He's just doing this to get by. He'll find work again when he wants to. Real work."

Max used her to deliver drugs only a few times a week. Pin wished she had a more reliable source of cash. Like Louie, the kid who worked as a sniper, putting up signs around Chicago that advertised new shows at Riverview. He got three dollars a day for that, plus streetcar fare. Or the boys who worked as shills and made twenty-five cents an hour, winning big prizes in fixed carnival games while the rubes looked on. The rubes never won, and they never saw the boys slipping through the back doors of the concessions to return their prizes—child-sized dolls, five-cent John Ruskin cigars, glass tumblers.

And only boys were used to deliver drugs across town. Hashish and marihuana were considered poison, like arsenic. Heroin was worse—Pin had to get it illegally from a druggist on the North Side and bring the glass bottle back to Max, who measured the dope into tiny tinfoil packets, twenty for a quarter. Pin dreaded those trips, especially since two policewomen arrested a druggist on North Clark for selling heroin and cocaine to another delivery boy.

Max had a few regular clients—Lionel, a writer at the movie studio; a woman who performed abortions in Dogville; a Negro horn player who played jazz music at Colosimo's Cafe, a black-and-tan joint, where black people and white people could dance together. The rest were onetime deliveries: students at the university, musicians, whores, vaudeville performers at the theaters along the Golden Mile. Her run to the Essanay Studios was Mondays and Fridays, usually. Lionel made good money, twenty dollars a story, and he pitched three or four scenarios a week.

She knew the work was risky, but it never felt dangerous. If she'd been a fourteen-year-old white girl roaming the South Side or Packingtown, sure. But no one blinked to see a white boy the same age sauntering along the Golden Mile, or ducking in and out of theaters, or Barney Grogan's illegal saloon, hands in his pockets and a smart mouth on him if you looked at him sideways.

She seldom saw Max smoke hashish. Instead she watched in fascination as he applied his makeup. He made a paste from cold cream and talcum powder and used this to cover the left side of his face; then carefully mixed cigarette ash, pulverized charcoal, and dried ink to make kohl and mascara, which he applied with tiny brushes and a blunt pencil to his left eye.

"Why don't you just buy ladies' stuff?" she wondered aloud.

Max laughed. "What do you think they'd say to me in Marshall Field's, I went in and asked for some face paint and rouge?"

"The actors at Essanay use makeup. Charlie Chaplin uses makeup. And Wallace Beery."

"Do I look like Charlie Chaplin?"

After he'd painted his cheeks and lips, he dabbed the edge of one eyelid with adhesive, then affixed a fringe of false lashes made of curled black paper. Last of all, he put on a wig of blond curls. It was only half a wig, like his face was only half a woman's. The right side had Max's own bristly stubble on his chin and neck, a web of broken capillaries across his cheek. Blond hair slicked back so you could see where the orange dye had seeped into his scalp. Outside his tent, a banner depicted an idealized version of the real thing: the She-Male's face split down the middle and body divided lengthwise—natty black suit and shiny shoes, yellow shirtwaist and hobble skirt, the hem hiked up to display a trim ankle.

"Gimme a match," Max ordered. He tapped a cigarette from a box of Helmars, its logo depicting an Egyptian pharaoh. Pin lit the cigarette for him, and he turned away, leaving her to stare at her own face in the mirror, a luxury she didn't have in her own shack. Snub nose and pointed chin, dirt smudged across one cheek, uptilted soot-brown eyes, a chipped front tooth where she'd gotten into a fight. A scrawny boy's face, you'd never think otherwise.

"Look sharp." Without turning, Max tossed her a Helmar cigarette box, barely giving her time to catch it before he threw her a nickel. She snatched it from the air and he laughed. "Nice catch, kid."

She grinned at the compliment, pocketed the nickel, and headed out on her run.

Chapter 4

THE TWO OF them always slept in the same bed, in the back room of a long, narrow apartment where you could hear people coming and going all day and all night, though they were forbidden to enter the room where the children lived. He was afraid of the dark and clung to her the way he'd seen grown-ups do in the other rooms; like the pictures he saw years later of people hanging on to the sides of lifeboats and bobbing planks as the *Titanic* sank behind them.

His sister didn't mind, even when she got sick, though her coughing kept him from sleeping. He'd cover her mouth with his hand, and she'd angrily slap it away, though as the weeks passed the slap seemed more like a reflex, like when she turned in bed and her arm would flop across his chest and she didn't even know it. Sometimes he didn't know it, either, until he woke. She died like that, in her sleep. No one checked on them for two days, maybe they knew and were afraid to have it proved true, maybe they just forgot. He lay beside her in the dark, frightened, then gradually comforted, by her silence, how still and smooth her face looked. It didn't distress him that her cheeks and arms were cold to the touch. He pressed the thin fabric of her pinafore across his face and bunched the skirt between his fingers. It soothed him. When they finally came into the room and found them and took her away, he wailed uncontrollably until one of them returned and slipped a doll beneath the filthy sheet. It was wearing his sister's nightdress.

"Here, sweetheart," she whispered. She smelled like spoiled milk and coal-tar soap. "You can play this is her, all right? She don't need that shimmy now." He'd lost that doll years ago, and what remained of his sister's nightdress, a greasy scrap of fabric no bigger than his hand.

Chapter 5

FRANCIS BACON REMOVED his helmet and mopped his forehead with a handkerchief. The park had opened only an hour ago, and already it was so hot that several people had visited the infirmary complaining of heatstroke, and a kid had fainted outside the Ten-in-One. Served them right for coming out in this weather. If he didn't have to report for work at the park's station house, Francis would be down by the riverside or in a dim saloon, drinking a glass of beer.

In the grove behind him, a small crowd had gathered to wait for Riverview's giant cuckoo clock to chime eleven. Francis replaced his handkerchief and helmet, withdrew his pocket watch, and counted the seconds until he heard a mechanical whirring, followed by cheers as the cuckoo clock's automata emerged. They performed their hourly dance, bowing and twirling, a half-dozen brightly painted figures half as tall as he was, until the metal cuckoo bird emerged from a pair of doors and made its grating cry. Francis set his watch back in his pocket and headed toward a water fountain.

A line had formed, women mostly. Francis took his place behind them, doffing his helmet and stepping aside to let a young woman go in front of him.

"Thank you, sir," she said, and smiled from beneath a stylish straw toque. Francis watched as she bent over the fountain, a spray of droplets spattering her white shirtwaist. No beauty, but she had a nice figure and wore the shorter skirts that were fashionable this summer, her ankles visible beneath the linen hem.

"You're very welcome." He smiled, winking, and she blushed before hurrying to join her friends. Maybe he could find her later in one of the beer gardens.

He stepped up to the fountain, drank, and returned to his rounds, watching for pickpockets, jackrollers, lost children. It was early for drunks, but sometimes you'd see someone who'd been up all night elsewhere and ridden the streetcar to Western Avenue in hopes of keeping the fun going. But mostly, he gave directions to the washrooms and water fountains.

Francis had been a real cop years before—detective sergeant at Robey Street station. That was before he got involved with the notorious murder case involving Pietro Divine, the killer for the Black Hand. Francis had found incontrovertible evidence linking Divine to seventeen missing persons, including five members of the same family, mother, father, and three small children, their skeletal remains discovered in a gravel pit in an abandoned Little Hell brickyard.

He'd also uncovered evidence of corruption in the police department, linking several high-ranking men to the Black Hand. Francis testified against Rusty Cabell and the captain over at Dearborn Street, despite being warned that the judge was also in cahoots with the Sicilians. The case got thrown out of court. Cabell was promoted to captain at Robey Street, and Francis got tossed from the force.

That had been more than three years ago—around the same time that Bill Hickey, a former colleague of Francis's, had taken over as head of the amusement park's police force. They ran into each other at a saloon a few weeks after Francis's dismissal.

"Come work with me, Francis," Hickey urged as he peeled a hard-boiled egg. "Pay's good. Two dollars a day. Three if you work till midnight and close the place."

Francis had stared stonily into his glass of beer and refused to reply. Hickey shook his head.

"You got snookered, Francis, I know that. But you need a job, and it would be good to have another policeman working with me—they're detailing everyone from the force to the Loop these days, or Little Hell. Half my staff are night watchmen from the meat plants, they don't know a bunco artist from their auntie's arse. It'd be a favor to me, Francis."

Francis snorted. "Misery loves company." But he took the job.

The amusement park was seasonal work, but it paid well, and it was better than walking the haberdashery floor at Marshall Field's, which is what Francis did during the rest of the year. The stray kids who ran around the park called him Fatty, but Bacon was tall and well built, with auburn hair and very light grey eyes. The summer sun had burnished his ruddy skin and streaked his mustache gold. Come fall, he'd be wearing an ill-fitting suit and escorting light-fingered men and women back out onto State Street.

"Hey, Bacon."

Francis turned to see another Riverview sergeant hurrying toward him. O'Connell, the lanky young man who worked at the station office. He stopped beside Francis, flapping his hand in front of his face. "Jesus, it's hot."

"You ran out here to tell me that?"

"Nope. Lady said her reticule got stolen, over by the incubators."

Francis made a face. "Isn't D'Angelo over there?"

"Nope. Hickey's got him at the Velvet Coaster, they got a big crowd, and Hickey don't want things to wind up. Kind of a fat old lady, she's waiting in the station. Hickey says check the incubators first, then come talk to her."

"All right." Francis sighed and walked toward the Infant Incubators.

Chapter 6

PIN HADN'T ALWAYS lived at the amusement park—only since her mother, Gina, started working there as a fortune-teller. Pin had been born when her mother was the same age as Pin was now, her sister, Abriana, two years later. Back then they lived in a tenement in Little Hell, the Sicilian slum on Chicago's North Side. Over the years Gina had told Pin that her father was dead; had moved back to Italy; was mining gold in South America; had run off with the woman who owned the Chinese laundry in Larrabee Street.

Until one day when Pin asked about him, Gina slapped her so hard her left ear rang for an entire day. She never brought it up again.

Little Hell was overshadowed by a huge gashouse, which belched flames and fumes that blotted out the sun. Day and night, red-neckerchiefed men shoveled tons of coal into the furnace, then doused the glowing coals with water from the river. The resulting gas was stored in huge tanks, their cylinders rising during the day, then dropping overnight as the gas was piped into the surrounding tenements for lights and heat and cooking. As a very young girl, Pin had mistaken the furnace's deafening thunder for that of approaching trains.

The women from the Relief and Aid Society complained constantly about how their white uniforms turned black as they approached Little Hell. They never drew near to Death Corner, where the Black Hand gangs that ruled Little Hell dumped the bodies of their victims beneath a dead tree twisted as a corkscrew. Pin had stopped counting the number of murders when it reached a hundred.

They had left Little Hell in May, when Gina started working as a Gypsy fortune-teller at Riverview. She also worked at the park's vast ballroom, teaching customers the latest dance crazes—fox-trot, turkey trot, grizzly-bear hug, bunny hug. Before, she'd sewn ribbons onto women's hats for a milliner in State Street. But hat sales had dropped after Christmas and never picked up again, and the shop closed in April.

There was no money for the rent. For a week they'd eaten nothing but coarse wheat flour boiled in water.

The night before they fled their tenement, Gina had locked the door to the room. Pin didn't know why she bothered; they had nothing to steal. The floors were bare dirt and the walls patched with cardboard; you could punch your hand right through. There was a hole she used to spy on the family who lived next to them, a scrawny man who used to climb on top of his wife on the kitchen table and, sometimes, his daughters.

Putting a finger to her lips, Gina dropped to her knees in front of the sofa and dragged out a burlap sack Pin had never seen before. Her mother rummaged through it, pulling out a pair of knickerbockers and a white cambric shirt.

"Get undressed and try these on. Mrs. Puglia gave them to me after her son ran off to Montana."

Pin stared at her, dumbfounded, until Gina threw the clothes in her face. Pin grabbed them, tore off her pinafore and chemise, and kicked them across the floor. She pulled on the knickerbockers and shirt, fingers shaking so she almost couldn't button them. There was no mirror in the room, but her mother's expression told her what she needed to know.

"Am I...?"

Gina nodded.

Pin bit her lip so she wouldn't cry. For as long as she could recall, this was all she'd wanted. When she remembered her dreams, she recalled being neither girl nor boy, only flying, nothing between her skin and the wind. She hated waking up, even more so in the last six months since she'd first menstruated and her mother had explained, or tried to, what the blood on her drawers portended. Childbirth, babies—the end of freedom. The end of everything.

Being a girl was like a huge scab she couldn't scrape off, no matter how hard she tried. As she stood there in her new clothes, her mother produced the shears she used to trim ostrich willows. She grasped a handful of Pin's unruly curls and began to cut.

At last the snicking of the shears stopped. Pin ran a hand across her cropped head, then took a few deep breaths so she could feel the air moving inside this strange new creature, herself. Her mother handed her an elastic truss, designed for a small man.

"Your titties are so small, you hardly need this," she said. "But wear it anyway. You have to stay safe. We're not going to use our real names—I don't want anyone knowing who we are."

"Why?"

Gina slapped her, hard enough Pin's eyes sparked. "You know why! If anyone asks, your name's Maffucci. Not Onofria: Maffucci."

Pin turned so her mother wouldn't see her tears. "What about yours?"

"Maffucci, the same as yours. Of course it will be the same. I'm still your mother." She pulled Pin close and embraced her for a heartbeat, Gina's breath scented with Sen-Sen and schnapps, then quickly pushed her away. "In the fall it will be different. Till then, you need to stay safe."

Safe? Pin bit her lip to keep from arguing with her. No one was ever, ever safe.

Chapter 7

PIN CAUGHT THE streetcar to Uptown, clutching her cap as she pushed her way past the straphangers to poke her head out a window in the back. She closed her eyes and pretended she was by the lake. She'd been there only once, the summer before her younger sister, Abriana, disappeared. The boys from Riverview went sometimes, but she couldn't take the risk. It was hard enough to keep her shirt on when everyone else peeled theirs off in the heat to go swimming, and to feign being pee-shy when they urinated in the river.

She drew her head in as the streetcar's bell jangled, signaling her stop. Its wheels threw up sparks as it screeched around a corner and slowed. She pushed her way to the door, jumped off, and hurried across the intersection, dodging an automobile.

Essanay Studios took up a whole city block, its name above the entrance with its distinctive logo, the profile of an Indian chief wearing an eagle headdress. Outside, the building looked like a factory. Inside, the heavy air smelled of drugstore perfume and cigarette smoke, cleaning fluid, greasepaint, and a peculiar, sweet odor that came from the long spools of motion-picture film. Sometimes she heard hysterical laughter or sobs in here, or a dog barking. Once a man had raced past her, stark naked except for a towel clutched to his privates. Another time she'd ducked into a closet as a dozen policemen strode down the hall, only to realize they were in costume.

She halted when she reached a row of doors. She pushed open the one that bore a sign with the names GLORY and VALERIE on it, revealing two girls in shimmies. They stood side by side, perusing a clothing rack.

"Hi, Glory."

Glory, the smaller of the two, turned to greet her, baring big white teeth in a smile. "Hiya, Pin. C'mon in," she said absently, and continued her inspection of the costumes. She wore a silk teddy bare, a sleeveless chemise that clung to her breasts and barely grazed the tops of her thighs. Like Pin, she was slight, just under five feet tall, and deeply tanned, with an olive tinge to her smooth skin, thick black hair, and striking sapphire-blue eyes. She had a mole on her chin that she covered with powder when she had to go in front of the camera, and she smelled of cardamom and sugar and toasted almonds—her aunt Inga often sent her to work with pastries to share.

Lionel jokingly referred to her as Princess Glorious, or the Spanish Princess, and Pin almost believed it. Small as she was, Glory could command a room. She wanted to be an opera singer, not an actress, but the studio paid her well—thirteen dollars for a week's work as an extra, whether they used her or not, with Sundays off. Only sixteen, Glory looked older, especially when she tilted her head and regarded Pin through narrowed eyes. She regularly got cast as an imperious matron or headwaitress.

She held up a faded-blue satin gown with half-moon stains beneath the sleeves. "What do you think, Pin? Suit me as a banker's wife?"

"Sure." Pin took off her cap and fanned herself. The tiny room was hot enough to melt wax. "That color's nice with your eyes."

The other girl, Valerie, grimaced. "God, it's ugly. You have such nice things, Glory, why would you even want to wear it? It makes you look thirty."

"I'm *supposed* to look thirty." Glory reached for a pincushion and gave Pin a sideways glance. "You looking for Lionel? He's down in the studio. Here, hold this for me."

Glory shoved the mass of blue satin into her arms. Pin wrinkled her nose. You'd think the fancy clothes they wore in the movies would smell of perfume and eau de cologne. Instead they reeked of tobacco smoke and perspiration, and sometimes of scorched hair, if whoever'd been wearing them had stood too close to a spotlight.

"I'm heading out." Valerie pulled a mohair bathing suit over her chemise and plucked a smoldering cigarette from an ashtray. "They want pictures for that Sweedie movie they did at the lake. Newspaper advertisement. See you later, Glorious. Bye, Pin."

Valerie swanned from the cubicle. When she was gone, Glory rolled her eyes. "She is *not* going to get her picture taken. Guess who's here?"

"Who?"

"Charlie Chaplin. Spoor's trying to sweet talk him to stay with the studio—they're all down on the stage. Lionel's with 'em, even though he can't stand Charlie. Probably the only reason Lionel even came in today is that he's waiting for you. Don't you ever worry about bringing that stuff here? Or anywhere?"

Pin flushed and Glory laughed, reaching to stroke her neck. "Ow, you're hot!"

Pin forced a grin. She lived in terror that one of the Riverview boys would figure out her secret. Far worse if Glory did, with her white teeth and rouged mouth and all that soft black hair. But Glory's attention had already returned to the satin dress. She held it in front of her. "Too long?"

Pin could clearly see Glory's nipples through the pink charmeuse of her teddy. "N-n-no," she stammered. "It looks just right."

"Okay, thanks."

Glory stepped into the dress. Pin hoped she'd ask her to button it, blushing again when she realized the buttons ran down the front.

"I better go," she said at last.

"Bye," replied Glory without looking up.

Chapter 8

LIKE FLOATING. HE could see the different parts and move them around. Cut off the top of the big flower and move it around. Cut off the other one and move it here, the girl's head too. After his head hurt goddamn it to hell he hated God yes he said it Hated Goddamn it close your eyes damn it he said I told you what did I say to you

Chapter 9

THEY WERE SETTING up a scene when Pin arrived. She found a space along the wall where she could observe the frantic goings-on. Pin was fascinated by the cameramen, watching as they cranked the handles on the old Pathé cracker-box cameras, which were always being repaired with tape; adjusting their speed, then replacing reels and processing the film, and finally taping bits of paper to indicate where the splices should go, once the film went to the girls who worked as joiners. An older cameraman named Billy Carrera had taken a shine to Pin, patiently answering her questions when he took a break. He put her to work sometimes, asking her to retrieve a fallen prop or climb a ladder to move one of the heavy arc lamps. He boasted he could calculate how many frames were left on a reel, not just by how many times he'd turned the crank, but by hearing each individual frame click on the sprockets inside the magazine. He taught Pin that people could read only a single word per second, which was why you shot title cards slowly, a foot of film for each word.

"It's all numbers, kid," he told Pin. "Three hundred feet for a five-minute short, a thousand feet for a one-reeler. Seventeen minutes. Can you do the math in your head?"

She bit her lip, thinking. "Sixty?"

"Congratulations! Now go make a movie."

She watched as he strode across the set, pausing to check the placement of the Mazda lights.

"That number three needs to be hotter," Carrera shouted. "We need it on the girl who plays the doll. Make it look like a moonbeam."

The set was the interior of a toy shop. A wall of shelves held cheap celluloid dolls, all unclothed. Doll heads covered a long table in the middle of the set, along with hammers and other tools.

A tall figure sat beside the table, smoking. He wore a dress, a mobcap, and high-button boots that must have been a size 15. This was the comic actor Wallace Beery, in character as Sweedie, the Swedish housemaid who was the star of a popular series of slapstick films. Pin tried to recall if Lionel had written this scenario. Sometimes he made up ridiculous scenarios on the fly, or stole them from the *Saturday Evening Post* or *Cosmopolitan*.

And, like Pin, Lionel read adventure tales avidly. He loved gruesome accounts of true events—the cannibals of the Donner Party, the recent *Eastland* tragedy here in Chicago.

"*That's* what people want to see," he told her one morning when she'd met him at a vacant lot near the studio. He'd given her the money for Max, hidden as always in an Omar cigarette box—Lionel smoked Omars, Max Helmars, that was how she could tell which box held the dope cigarettes and which the money for them. Then he lit one of the hashish cigarettes, right there in broad daylight.

"Dead bodies," he went on languidly. "Not those idiotic Sweedie flickers. Dead bodies and blood. Want some?"

He held out the cigarette, but she shook her head. "Max'd kill me."

"Max doesn't have to know."

She glanced around nervously, then grabbed the cigarette and took a puff. It smelled like perfume but burned her throat and gave her the spins. When she handed it back to Lionel, he pinched it out and put it into his cigarette case, slid his hand into his breast pocket, and withdrew a small book. "Look at this."

It was a flip-book—photographs of a naked woman, bound and blindfolded. Pin gazed at them, both repelled and curious. Another time, he showed her a small volume with a cover drawing of a woman tied up with so much rope she resembled a parcel with hair. Once he'd passed her a book with pictures of naked men and appeared to wait a bit nervously for her response. Pin thumbed through the pages, but the words were in another language. She looked up at Lionel.

"Is it French?"

"Of course," he said. "What d'you think?"

She stared at the photographs, recalling the two men she'd seen at the Comique. At last she handed the book back to him. "They must've been cold, standing there with no clothes on."

Lionel had laughed. He claimed Max's hashish helped him think.

But if this toy-shop flicker was his scenario, Pin didn't believe he'd thought much. She watched as Beery grabbed a hammer and tapped at a doll head so hard it broke. Everyone in the studio laughed, and she took advantage of the moment to search the crowd for Lionel.

She sighted him on the far side of the crowded room. Slipping past several actors dressed as policemen, she hopped over coils of wires and other equipment until she reached him.

Lionel looked down and elbowed her. "Hiya, kid. This is one of mine."

Pin furtively dug the box of hashish cigarettes from her pocket and gave it to him.

"Thanks, kid," Lionel murmured, and slid the box into his pocket. He was old, almost thirty, medium tall, but he slouched. Even though he only wrote photoplays, he dressed like an actor: beautifully pressed trousers and shirts, his dark hair beneath his boater slicked back and smelling of Lilac Vegetal. He looked rich, which Pin figured he was, if he could afford to spend three dollars a week on hashish.

He nudged her again. "See who that is?"

Lionel cocked his head to indicate a man in the near corner, posing for a publicity photo with two girls. The girls were maybe twelve years old but costumed to look younger, in matching buttercup-yellow dresses embroidered with white daisies. Enormous yellow bows perched on their dark curls like butterflies. Close by stood several cameramen and a man in a business suit—Mr. Spoor, the *S* of the *S and A* in Essanay Studios, like Bronco Billy Anderson was the *A*.

Chaplin draped an arm around the shoulders of each girl, lowered his head, and pulled them close to him, grinning for the photographer.

"Charlie Chaplin?" marveled Pin. "He came back?"

"Just for a visit. Too cold here, he says."

"It's not cold now."

"Wait a few months. He asked your gal Glory to lunch with him at the canteen. She turned him down, so he asked her pal Valerie."

Pin watched Chaplin mug for the camera, playing with his hat, a boater, not the bowler he wore in the movies. He was much smaller than he looked on screen, and much younger, slender and tan, with tousled black hair, his face clean shaven. Of course she knew the mustache was only greasepaint, but it was still surprising how boyish he looked without it; also to see the color of his eyes, a brilliant lake blue.

The photographer lifted his head from his camera to adjust the tripod and signaled Chaplin with a finger: *One more shot.* Chaplin dropped his arms and hugged the prettier of the two girls, burying his face in her ringlets.

"Smile, Maria!" yelled the photographer.

The girl squealed—Chaplin must have goosed her. He kissed her on the mouth, slid his hand across her rump, and pushed her away, laughing. He lit a cigarette and turned to Spoor, said something to him as he gestured at the girl. The two men laughed.

"Maria and whatever your name is!" Carrera yelled impatiently. "The door, girls, the door!"

The two girls scampered to the back of the set. Maria, the one Chaplin had kissed, fell. She pushed herself back to her feet, examined her dress, and cried, "Now it's torn!"

"Nobody cares!" yelled Carrera. "Keep going!"

Both girls disappeared behind the painted plywood walls as Chaplin was hustled from the room.

"Here you go, kid." Pin started as Lionel handed her the Omar cigarette box containing Max's money. "I'm heading home. Don't stick around," he added, and walked off.

She peeked inside the box with its image of a pharaoh and saw three rolled-up dollar bills. No nickel. He'd stiffed her for the streetcar fare back to Riverview again. Pin swore under her breath. "Goddamned piker," she said.

Chapter 10

She returned to Riverview, sweaty and out of sorts. The truss she wore beneath her shirt chafed at her painfully in the heat. She ducked into the shadows behind Max's tent to adjust the elastic, then stepped over to lift a canvas flap and peer inside.

A dozen men stood at the foot of a makeshift stage—to judge by their yeasty smell and unsteady balance, most of them already drunk. They watched as Max turned, displaying first a man's profile, then a woman's. Electrical bulbs with pink gel shades bathed the room in sunset light, an effect heightened by the haze of cigar smoke that hung above the small audience.

"Cat got your tongue?" one of them yelled. "Say something!"

"A lady doesn't speak until spoken to," purred Maxene.

Pin was always amazed at how the illusion persisted. She knew Max was a man dressed—half dressed—as a woman, yet the combination of pink lights and shadows, and Max's own peculiar magic, really did summon a woman up there on the stack of wooden crates covered with a muslin sheet.

Maxene lifted a delicate hand to adjust the limp ostrich feather sewn to a saggy lump of felt that served as both derby and cloche. "And a gentleman always says *please*."

Maxene arched her neck, turning so that Max regarded the onlookers. *"Please,"* he repeated in Max's own deeper voice, "or else."

He tapped the waxed curl of mustache held on with spirit gum, and the men laughed. At that moment, Pin glimpsed a strange flicker in Max's green-glass gaze. He stood with his eyes half closed, as though recalling some distant memory, and for a fraction of a second she could imagine that he once really might have played Romeo. Then he turned his head slightly sideways again, displaying Maxene's face, and his expression shifted once more: no longer a woman's disdain, but violent hatred for the crowd of men.

She quickly dropped the canvas flap, unnerved, and hurried around back to Max's dressing room. She let herself in, noticing that the photographs of the wasp-waisted girl had been tossed back on the barrel, alongside a glass of some murky liquid and a dead mouse, its head crushed.

Averting her eyes, she brushed aside a shawl, opened the drawer where Max kept the Omar and Helmar cigarette boxes, and added the Omar box that Lionel had given her. Later Max would check for it and count the dollar bills inside. She knew better than to steal from him. She'd seen him deck a would-be pickpocket outside the Casino and leave him moaning in the dirt.

And Clyde told her that, back in New York, Max had knifed a man who'd propositioned him. "Never mistake a fella dressed as a lady on the stage for a fairy" had been the moral of that story. "Not if he's bigger'n you."

She left the trunk and went to Max's dressing table, where a glass ashtray held spare change. She picked out two quarters—her arrangement with Max, if he wasn't around to pay her. As always, she considered pocketing a nickel to cover her fare back, but decided against it.

She grabbed the silver flask that stood beside a bottle of laudanum syrup. She'd tried it once, but it made her sick to her stomach. She preferred beer, or schnapps. She gulped a mouthful of whatever Max's silver flask contained, something so harsh it brought tears to her eyes. Turning to leave, she saw Max in the doorway.

"Checking the wares?" He cuffed her head, but lightly. He sounded more amused than angry. "You make the drop?"

She nodded, one eye on the door in case he came at her. But he just pulled off the blond wig and tossed it onto the dressing table.

"That stuff'll give you the willies." He reached under the table for a bottle, poured a small amount into a glass. "Here, take a snootful of this."

Pin drank it, grimacing. Max laughed. "Well, you'll learn."

He took the glass from her, filled it, and downed it. "'Shallow draughts intoxicate the brain; drinking largely sobers us again.'" He lit a Helmar and glanced at the ashtray. "You take your pay?"

Pin nodded. She was working on an empty stomach: the whiskey, on top of whatever had been in the silver flask, made her woozy.

Max regarded her through eyes slitted like a cat's. "How much?"

"Two bits." She shifted uneasily.

"Ever take more when I'm not here?" She shook her head. "Why not?"

"Scared to," she admitted.

"Good answer." He picked up a dime and flipped it to her. "Go buy yourself a meal. I'm hungry just looking at you."

Chapter 11

CHAPLIN HAD TO sweet talk the girl, Valerie, into joining him for lunch at a hash house a few blocks from the studio. He'd asked her friend Glory first, but she'd just looked him up and down, her nose wrinkling as she pronounced, "You're too old for me."

Even with Valerie, it took a bit of doing—she wanted to eat at the canteen, where everyone would see her with him.

Out in the street, he was just another young dude smoking a cigarette, boater tipped jauntily as he took her arm and steered her through the restaurant to a table in the back. But she was amiable enough once he poured her a glass of beer, and even friendlier after she'd drunk two and he ordered her ice cream. He slid his hand beneath the white tablecloth, found her knee and pushed aside the folds of cotton, ran his fingers along her cheap silk stockings up to the warm skin plumped up between her garters and her cotton bloomers. She clicked the long spoon against her teeth as she stared, expressionless, at the strawberry ice melting in its metal bowl. He closed his eyes and thought of the buttercup-yellow-clad girl on the Essanay set, that sweet yellow bow on her dark ringlets and her smooth skin, no rouge save a dab on her lower lip so she'd resemble the large dolls in the toy shop.

"How old are you?" he'd asked her.

"Twelve," she'd replied. "I was twelve in June."

"When you're sixteen I'll marry you," he'd whispered, and she giggled.

He moved Valerie's free hand beneath the tablecloth and squeezed his eyes shut, as though the light hurt them. When he opened them again, all the ice cream had melted, so he ordered another dish for Valerie and one for himself. After they finished eating, he paid, walked her outside, and turned to go.

"You're not coming back to the studio?" she asked, disappointed.

"I have an early train tomorrow."

"Are you going back East?"

"Nope. California. I'm done with New York. Done with Chicago." He lit another cigarette, tipped his hat, and strolled off in the afternoon sun.

Chapter 12

Pin felt wobbly along the Pike. She'd been thinking about food all morning. An ice-cream cone or a slice of pie, maybe a wienie. Or she could go to the canteen where the park employees had their meals, brown bread and some sort of German stew. The sixty cents in her pocket could last her till tomorrow—longer, if she was frugal, and still leave her enough to visit the Comique.

But now the air shimmered with heat, and her stomach churned at the thought of food. As the house-sized German cuckoo clock near the Blue Streak chimed, Pin strained to count the hours above Ballmann's band playing "The Washington Post March."

Three-fifteen. Day halfway gone.

She yawned and wandered toward a stand of rhododendrons, lay on the grass, and closed her eyes, waiting for the world to slow down.

She felt better after a few minutes. She got up and walked to the water fountain by the Infant Incubators, stood in line, and, when it was her turn, drank until her stomach felt like a balloon. She stuck her face in the spray, soaked her cap, and clapped it, dripping, back on her head. An old man gave her a disapproving look.

"Whatcha gawking at, Mister?" Pin sneered and shoved past him, right into Fatty Bacon.

"Hiya, Pin. Where's your friends?"

Pin swiped water from her face. "Dunno. I been gone all morning."

Fatty Bacon gazed down at her from beneath the brim of his helmet. "Lady said her reticule got stolen, over by the incubators."

She started to sprint off, but Fatty grabbed her shoulder. "A reticule, and two stolen wallets," he continued. "Captain Hickey says there's been a rash of 'em. You seen any pickpockets, Pin? Or any other bunco?"

"Nope." She yanked her arm, and he let go of her. "I told you, I don't know."

"What about your friends? Anyone got more spending money than usual? Mugsy?"

"Ask him yourself. Everyone's broke."

"I'll take your word for it." Fatty removed his helmet and blotted his forehead with a handkerchief. "Heat makes people nutty. Seen anything funny?"

Pin puffed her cheeks out, pretending to think. "Yeah," she said at last. "A feller by the incubators. Short feller with a mustache. He looks suspicious."

"Yeah? What's he look like?"

"I told you. Short. He wore a boater."

"That'll make him stand out in the crowd."

"I seen him before. He watches the kids going in and out. I think he went off to the Tickler," she added, lying.

"Really?" Fatty turned to gaze at the long line in front of the Tickler's entrance. He sighed, glanced down, and adjusted Pin's cap. "Regards to your mother."

She waited until he was out of sight, then spat and walked in the opposite direction.

Chapter 13

*T*HE *L*ITTLE *G*IRL'S *Sewing Book*. Pink dress and matching bow on her pretty pretty head, dark ringlets, sewing a lace handkerchief as her dolls looked on. Three of the dolls were naked, that was naughty, and he looked away but only for an instant.

One doll had three smaller dolls of her own. A toy bear, too, but he snipped that out and squashed it in between his fingers and threw it away dirty paper. He cut very carefully around the girl, very carefully don't slice her hand, the one that held a needle so tiny it could not be seen. There were daffodils in the window and he cut them out, too, and got the paste and pasted them onto the girl's hair so soft such pretty pretty hair such

Goddamn it oh goddamn it oh fuck the filthy bastard white paste on her face and in her little eyes and it was ruint now all ruint oh fuck he didn't mean to

Chapter 14

Pin wandered along the Pike, hoping she might run into Ikie or Joe Bean or even Mugsy Morrissey, who was dumb as a switch but could recite the alphabet while burping. She wanted to tell someone she'd seen Charlie Chaplin. Her only currency with the boys she ran with was the stories she told them. Stuff she read in the papers or stories she made up, based on the movies she watched in the Comique.

But everyone she knew was at work. The boys all had fathers employed by the park, men who repaired the merry-go-round when it broke down, repainted the flames on its dragons and swans, recalibrated the gears if it ran too fast or slow. They operated the roller coasters and dark rides, took money for the rigged games of chance, chanted the bally for Clyde's magic show and the High Striker, the Casino Restaurant and Palace Ballroom and Woodland Cabaret. Mugsy's father ran the Velvet Coaster, and Mugsy worked with him, a job Pin coveted—people riding the coasters lost coins, wallets, eyeglasses, jewelry, false teeth. When he wasn't sniping, Louie cleaned the stables at the racetrack. Ikie worked backstage at the Sunny South minstrel show and helped out as a ticket taker for Clyde, who was his uncle.

Pin stared at the crowds, remembering her mother's words back in their tenement room. *You have to stay safe…In the fall it will be different. Till then, you need to stay safe.*

Yet here were all these people, all of them paying to be *not* safe, to pretend they'd fall off a cliff or drown, or be snatched at by ghouls in the dark.

She stopped to watch the Velvet Coaster begin its ascent, riders already screaming with anticipation. Pin could follow the cars' progress with her eyes closed: with every clank and shudder the screams grew louder, until they became a single terrified howl that died into relieved laughter as the cars returned to the shed to be unloaded.

"Move it!"

Someone knocked into her, a beefy man in work clothes, his face puffed with drink. Pin kicked him and watched as he staggered, then fell. Before he could stumble back to his feet, she was gone.

She ducked in and out of the throngs of line lice, kicking up dust as she scanned the ground for coins or feathers, hatpins, cigarettes. A boy she knew had once found a silver powder box on a ribbon. She spied a pink carnation fallen from a dude's buttonhole, grabbed it, and stuck it into her own buttonhole. It smelled like Glory, sweet and slightly dusty.

A wave of longing overcame her. She imagined standing next to Glory, taking turns at the Mutoscope; but would an actress even want to see a moving picture?

And what if Glory wanted to see where she lived? Almost everyone Pin knew at Riverview lived elsewhere. Near indigents, like Pin and her mother, squatted in makeshift shelters so they could save enough to pay for a tenement room during the winter months. Pin and Gina's tiny shack—constructed of plywood and plaster lath, painted to look like a log cabin—was a castoff from the Sunny South minstrel show, where colored actors danced the cakewalk and sang "Dixie" for audiences made up of white immigrants from Germany and Sweden and Ireland. When Ikie learned where she lived, he'd stared at her with open contempt.

"You living in a slave shack? What the hell's wrong with you?"

Since then, she avoided the shack except as a place to catch a few hours of fitful sleep. On nights when Gina worked as a dance teacher—ten cents a dance, no hugging—Pin lay alone on the pallet they shared.

Once her mother didn't return until late the next morning. Abriana's disappearance had been like this, a splinter of worry that grew septic as it worked its way through Pin's body: now, as then, she paced to keep from throwing up. When her mother did return, eyes sunken with exhaustion, her dark hair unbound beneath her straw Panama, all she said was "I met a friend."

Pin wouldn't show Glory the shack for cash money. Just the thought made her hot with shame. She trudged along the Pike, pausing to buy a slice of watermelon from the watermelon man, ate it, and tossed the rind into the trash pail. Food made her feel better. She wiped her fingers on her knickerbockers and decided she'd go to Hell Gate.

Chapter 15

Back in his room, Lionel lit up one of the hashish cigarettes Max's boy had delivered and inhaled deeply. He'd left Essanay in a rage after yet another argument with Spoor.

"What is this garbage, Mr. Gerring? Women buried alive, skeletons in tombs—" Spoor had tossed the pages of Lionel's most recent photoplay back onto his desk.

"She gets saved," Lionel protested. "It'd be perfect for Bushman."

"Bushman would follow Chaplin to California if he ever got a whiff of this. Garbage," he repeated in disgust.

"It's from Edgar Allan Poe."

"Dieter's already working on Edgar Allan Poe. 'The Raven,' lots of spooky stuff. And where's the love interest? That's what the ladies want to see. Something funny and exciting. *Brewster's Millions,* why didn't you come up with that one before DeMille?"

"Because George Barr McCutcheon already did, years ago. In a book."

"No one wants to watch a story about a murderer."

"He gets captured! We see him brought to the gallows in chains!"

Spoor's face crinkled in distaste. "No one wants to see that, either, Gerring."

A week earlier he'd pitched a flicker inspired by *The Tales of Hoffmann,* which he'd seen before he fled New York. He'd been especially intrigued by the segment featuring a life-size toy, an automaton that could dance and sing. Lionel had typed up a photoplay, six scenes, all but the last set in a toy shop.

"You've got something here," Spoor had said. "I like the toy shop, the dolls, too. But it's too spooky. And kissing the doll, that just strikes me as peculiar. Maybe these…notions…are accepted back East, Mr. Gerring, but not here. I don't want to see any more girls buried alive, or men fondling kids dressed like dolls. Spoiled my dinner, reading that. Made me think of my own little girls."

Lionel didn't bother pointing out that half the movies shot in Chicago and New York starred girls under sixteen, or women cast because they looked like children. Or that some of the most successful moving pictures of the last few years were what Spoor called garbage: *The Body in the Trunk, Dr. Jekyll and Mr. Hyde, The Skull.*

Spoor handed the sheaf of typescript back to Lionel. "But it's a funny idea. I mentioned it to Wally, it's a good fit for him. Write it funny. Get it to me by Wednesday, we can begin shooting next week."

That had been just over a week ago. *Sweedie's Tell-Tale Toys* had already opened and was raking in the nickels. There'd been no point in arguing. Lionel got paid a hundred and fifty dollars for a Sweedie scenario…

But he'd felt a chill at the way Spoor had paused before enunciating the word *notions.* Because it was true, back in New York he had been able to hide his tastes even while indulging them; had learned to recognize men whose expressions, at once avid and fearful, mirrored his own. He knew his stories and photoplays were efforts to disguise his desires—obviously futile efforts, to judge from Spoor's icy stare. He had grabbed his pages and left the studio, choosing to walk rather than take the streetcar, in hopes that his anger and fear might burn off.

They hadn't. Thus, the hashish.

He took another puff, then hid the photoplay in a drawer along-side the notebook where he wrote down his ideas, leaned back in his chair, and gazed at the stained ceiling; its pattern of cracks and bulges gradually transformed into a counterpane and a girl floating in the air, a girl who fragmented into hundreds of Kewpies, their tiny hands and tiny feet pattering against his face like rain as they melted away, one by one.

Chapter 16

DARK RIDES LIKE Hell Gate or the Old Mill weren't popular on hot afternoons. Visitors preferred the Thousand Islands, where they rode outdoors in canoes, or the Scenic Railway, which wasn't a railway but a coaster that whizzed past painted backdrops of the Alps and North Pole. The line for the Thousand Islands stretched almost to the park's entrance, dozens of crying babies and fighting children, parents at the end of their rope.

Hell Gate towered above the opposite end of the midway, the only attraction devoid of the red, white, and blue flags and bunting that fluttered from every other building in the park. Hell Gate's ominous white pavilion looked more like a church than a ride: a church with an enormous red devil perched on its roof.

The devil was plaster and lath, but Pin's mother still crossed herself every time she walked past. It had black horns, a leering mouth and enormous eyes, immense bat wings that shaded the ride's entry like a black umbrella. Horace, a sour man who'd served in Cuba during the Spanish-American War, ran the dark ride. When an imperious suffragist once confronted him about the lack of flags on the pavilion, he spat in the canal and said, "Ain't no American flags in hell, 'cause there ain't no Americans there."

Today, only a few dozen people waited in line beside the canal. Pin removed her cap and flapped it at her face. Goddamn it was hot. Squinting, she tried to see who was behind the ticket booth: Larry, a bespectacled college boy, one of the only Negroes at the University of Chicago. Larry read the same kinds of magazines that Pin liked and passed them on to her when he'd finished reading them.

She strolled over to where Larry slumped behind the HELL GATE 10 CENTS sign, immersed in the latest *Adventure* magazine.

"Hey, Larry." Pin peered over the railing. "Any good?"

Larry held up an illustration of a man in a loincloth stabbing a shark with a knife. "So-so. Not as good as that Yasmini story."

He set the magazine aside to take two dimes from a pair of high-school girls wearing flared skirts instead of the hobble skirts that had been fashionable for the last few years. "Watch your head inside the boat, ladies; Horace there will help you."

He watched the girls walk off, their skirts barely grazing their ankles, and whistled softly. "They're about fryin' size," he said, and turned back to Pin. She twisted her head to read the title of the story he'd been reading.

"Can I borrow that when you're finished?"

"Yeah, sure." Larry folded the magazine and stuck it in his back pocket, eyeing several more girls as they approached the booth. "Come by later, I'll be done by then."

With a mocking salute, she ambled off, idly watching as the line for Hell Gate grew longer. People her own age or a few years older waited for the rowboats to appear, one at a time, alongside the loading area. Three young couples amused themselves by kicking each other's feet. The boys wore boaters and sailor suits, the girls blue-and-white sailor dresses and Panama hats. One boy grabbed a girl by the shoulders and pretended to push her into the canal.

She shrieked, and Pin whispered a curse. She hated girls who acted like sissies, and hated even more that boys liked it. Sometimes Ikie and the others would grab some girl's hat on the Pike, just to make her scream. Pin refused to join in.

"What if that was your sister?" she said once to Ikie.

"You ain't got a sister, why d'you care?" he retorted.

She replied before she could stop herself. "I used to have a sister."

Ikie laughed. "*Used* to! *Used*—"

She punched him and ran off before he could retaliate.

"*Billy, stop!*" The girl in line for Hell Gate shrieked again. With a scowl, Pin stalked toward a small rise, a man-made hill where a stand of tired-looking sycamores provided some shade.

Up here you could catch the wind, even on the hottest days. Pin sat on the grass and shut her eyes against the sky's blue glitter. After a minute, she opened her eyes, turned, and looked back down at Hell Gate.

Two more people had joined the line, a man and a young girl. The man wore a boater, like just about every other dude at Riverview, a suit, and a bow tie. The girl wore a buttercup-yellow dress, her dark ringlets spilling from beneath a floppy yellow bow nearly the size of her head.

Pin frowned. She recognized this girl—she'd seen her at Essanay that morning, one of the two costumed to look like twins.

Pin shaded her eyes. Was the man Charlie Chaplin? From this distance, she couldn't tell. He gestured toward the canal, then leaned in to whisper in the girl's ear. Ahead of them, the last of the three couples waited as Horace used his boat hook to pull a boat toward the wooden walkway. The boat rocked slightly as the boy stepped in. He took the girl's hand, pulled her onto the seat beside him, and slid his arm around her shoulders as Horace pushed them off.

After a few minutes another empty boat appeared. Horace snagged it so that the man and the girl in the yellow dress could step inside. The man sank onto the plank seat, and instead of sitting beside him, the girl settled onto his lap. Horace pushed them off, straightened, and wiped his forehead, leaning on his boat hook as he waited for the next customer. He pulled a stogie from his pocket, lit it, and began to smoke.

A strange sick heaviness weighted Pin, like one of the nightmares after her sister, Abriana, disappeared. Abriana had been born backward, their mother said. The woman who'd come to help had pulled the baby out by her feet as Pin watched. She was only two, so she didn't remember, but she'd heard Gina tell the story so many times that she'd never been able to get the image out of her head. Later, when their mother explained to people that Abriana was slow, Pin thought it was because her sister's feet had been injured when she was born.

As she got older, Pin realized that *slow* meant Abriana would never, never learn to read or write, never remember the rules of ringolevio or stickball or even checkers. She'd never learn not to talk to strangers or follow an organ-grinder, no matter how often you told her. Pin would beat up other kids who called her sister numb in the head, though sometimes Pin felt like saying the same thing herself.

You couldn't tell by looking at her that something was wrong; not unless you watched the way her smile seemed disconnected from her eyes. That was something else their mother said: that Abriana had been born smiling, the way that Pin had been born dissatisfied. Abriana might have been born backward, Gina said, but Pin had been born sideways.

Her sister couldn't go anywhere alone. Pin had to constantly watch that she didn't eat herself sick with sweets. Abriana would mash her face against the window of the German bakery on Kingsbury Street, in hopes that the owner would give her a cruller. She smiled at Jack the shoeshine man, who gave her penny candy, and the old lady who ran Ionucci's Grocery, who chased them away with a broom because she thought Abriana scared off customers.

Abriana, too, had been wearing a yellow dress, her Easter dress. Pin searched until she spotted the boat that held the girl from the movie studio. The man had slipped his arm around her and hugged her close to him, his hat tipped so Pin couldn't see his face. She watched as the boat bobbed along the spiraling canal, pulled by the man-made current in ever-tightening circles as it moved toward the center, until at last it reached the chute that gave the ride its name, and plunged out of sight.

Chapter 17

Don't be afraid, he murmured, moving his hand from her silky hair to the even-softer folds of her dress, a buttercup held to the sun. *Don't be afraid, none of it's real, pretend they're toys, that's what I do.* The fabric bunched between his fingers, nothing softer than that, not skin or hair or their mouths. *Hush now, I mean it, be quiet, no one can hear you.*

Yes, that one was scary.

There, now you've done it. What did I tell you?

Chapter 18

She might have dozed there on the knoll, lulled by heat and the strains of ragtime from the bandstand. The flicker of sun and shade on her eyelids made her think she was in the Comique, watching Charlie Chaplin and the girl with the big yellow bow. The girl was her sister, how had she forgotten that?

Abriana, she said, and her sister nodded. *Where did you go?*

I'm right here, said Abriana, and got very small. Chaplin started dancing, one hand held out to Pin. She reached for it and jolted awake.

She was sitting cross-legged on the grass. Overhead, leaves stirred in the hot breeze. She blinked, her mouth tasting of grit, rubbed her eyes, and stood. Where was she? A glance down the hillside and she remembered: Hell Gate.

A dust devil whipped along the sidewalk. Something moved at the far end of the pavilion, where the boats returned from their underground journey and the passengers disembarked. A skinny stray dog, one of the trained terriers from the dog-and-monkey show, cut loose because it bit someone.

The dog nosed at the wooden boardwalk as a boat approached along the canal. Pin recognized two of the high-school kids from earlier. Horace stepped from the pavilion, put out his foot, and stopped the boat so they could scramble out. The girl clutched her Panama hat, her hair wild about her shoulders. The boy grinned at Horace, took the girl's hand, and pulled her after him onto the Pike.

Horace leaned on his boat hook and watched them go, then pushed off the empty boat and turned to wait for the next one. A few yards away, the skinny terrier paced back and forth, pausing to scratch at the dirt. Horace threw a rock at it, and it ran off.

After a few minutes, another boat appeared and halted when Horace set his foot on its prow. A young couple, Pin recognized them, too. The girl slapped the boy's hand when he tried to help her from the boat and hurried off without waiting for him.

Pin plucked a long piece of grass and chewed the white pith at the bottom. Pieces of her dream came back to her, and her heart constricted as she remembered that her sister would have turned twelve this past April. Pin had forgotten her birthday. So had their mother.

Tears pricked at her eyes. It was her fault that Abriana had disappeared—Pin had stopped in a vacant lot near the gasworks to play a round of mumblety-peg, which she lost. When she turned, Abriana was gone. Lily Mikowski, a girl who'd been observing the game, said Abriana had followed an organ-grinder down the alley. He'd been playing "After the Ball," Lily remembered that. Abriana was never seen again.

No one blamed Pin: they all blamed her mother. Gina *did* blame Pin, screaming and cursing for hours that first night. In the days that followed she fell into a strange rapt silence, as though she were sitting in church during the Easter vigil. Gina never blamed her again, but Pin knew the truth. Even if no one else knew, even if no one but Pin and her mother remembered Abriana, it would always be her fault.

Pin wiped her eyes on her sleeve and looked back down at the pavilion. Here was the next boat, the one that the man and young girl had entered.

She hesitated, then hurried down the slope. If the man was Chaplin, she wanted to be able to tell Max that she'd seen him. The boat slipped along the black water, the last bars of sunlight striping it as it slowed. Horace continued to smoke, his back to the canal. The boat rocked as the man in the boater hat hopped out onto the raised wooden walkway and strode rapidly down the Pike. Pin frowned. Where was the girl?

Horace dropped his cigarette in the canal, turned, and used his boat hook to snag the empty vessel and pull it toward him. He glanced inside, set his foot against the stern, and pushed, watching as the boat floated on to join the others that awaited passengers at the opposite end of the pavilion.

Pin turned toward the Pike. Now that the sky had begun to darken, with the promise of cooler air, a line had formed in front of Hell Gate. Nearly every man she saw wore the same straw hat and white shirt and ice-cream suit, the exact color of its pastel stripes impossible to discern at a distance. She saw no sign of the girl in the yellow dress and matching hair bow. Like Abriana, she had disappeared. It was like she'd never been there at all.

Chapter 19

Pin spent the next ten minutes searching the park, looking for any sign of the girl. Finally reaching the Grand Lagoon, she gave up. She stood and stared at the Hippodrome reflected in the shimmering water. It was supposed to be a marvel, its angel figurehead even taller than Riverview's Eye-Full Tower and supposedly visible beyond the city itself.

Sighing, Pin turned and walked back toward Hell Gate. She'd borrow that magazine from Larry and go find a quiet place to read. As she drew near the pavilion, she glanced reflexively up at the knoll where she'd sat earlier.

Someone stood there, watching her. A man, short, wearing a boater, his head tilted to one side. Was he really looking at her? After a moment he raised his hand, like a cigar-store Indian. Pin looked over her shoulder but saw no one. Tentatively she raised her hand, squinting to get a better look.

Now she recognized him: the dingbatty little guy she'd seen at the Infant Incubators that morning, with his straw boater and mustache that looked like it'd been stuck on with spit. Did the man at Hell Gate with the girl have a mustache? She couldn't remember.

Then he was pointing to a grassy spot a short distance from the Pike, protected from view by a stand of poplars. He nodded at her, turned, and hurried down the little knoll toward the grass. Pin hesitated, then ran to meet him.

Chapter 20

HE LOOKED LIKE Charlie Chaplin. Not the handsome actor she'd glimpsed at Essanay but the Tramp, the weird little fellow Chaplin played in the movies. Though this man wore a boater, not a bowler. Apart from his straw hat, his clothes were all blue. Indigo pants, a heavy cambric work shirt, canvas jacket, everything well worn. A grimy bow tie. He'd wrapped twine around one battered shoe, tying it in a filthy knot. He had very pale, round blue eyes—bug eyes—and ruddy skin. His ears stuck out. He was even shorter than she'd first thought, not much over five feet. Barely taller than she was. She could knock him down, easy.

She waited for him to speak; he looked away uneasily, his gaze sliding sideways. She continued to stare at him, but still he wouldn't meet her eyes. Annoyed, she finally demanded, "What do you want?"

"She's gone." He still wouldn't look at her.

"Who?" He moved his hand, drawing a strange pattern in the air, and Pin felt her neck prickle. "You mean the girl?"

He nodded, gaze fixed on the Hell Gate pavilion. Pin expected him to go on, but he said nothing. Maybe he wasn't just dingbatty but a moron.

Or perhaps he'd been the man who'd taken the girl into Hell Gate. She stared at his hands, which were big, the skin chapped raw, the fingernails broken and dirty. He smelled strongly of sweat and Bon Ami soap. She tried to determine if there were any bloodstains on his cuffs, but the blue fabric was too dark.

It could be him.

She took a deep breath. "At Hell Gate. There was a girl, I saw a girl go in with…someone. A man," she added, watching to see how he reacted.

And yes, one of his eyelids fluttered. He blinked rapidly before nodding. "I saw her, too."

He grunted, like he was imitating a frog. He was much younger than she'd first thought: not more than twenty-two or twenty-three. The scruffy mustache was to make him appear older, but close up it had the opposite effect. He seemed unaware of how odd he appeared: flapping his hand in the air, making those weird noises.

Was he a jackroller? She glanced down to see if he had a blackjack in his pocket. He lifted his head and, for the first time, met her gaze.

"I've been watching you," he said.

She edged backward as he slid his hand into a pocket. But instead of a knife or a blackjack, he withdrew a handmade cardboard wallet, bound with more twine. He opened it with great care and sorted through a wad of news clippings, cigarette cards, scraps of dirty paper. At last he pulled out a small card and handed it to her:

GEMINI CHILD PROTECTIVE SOCIETY
BLACK BROTHERS LODGE
HENRICO DARGERO, PRES.

She read it, puzzled. "Gemini? Are you with the freak show?"

"*No!*" The man shouted so loudly that she jumped. "Are you an idiot?"

He tried to snatch the card back, but she yanked her hand away. "Henrico Dargero? That's you?"

"It is." Hearing the name seemed to calm him. He nodded solemnly. "I am from Brazil."

"Brazil?" She shot him a doubtful look. The words on the card looked like they'd first been written in pencil, then traced in black ink. "You a detective?"

He nodded. "We keep them safe. Girls. Curls. Because."

"'We'?"

"Me and Willhie. Silly."

"Who's Willhie?"

"My friend the night watchman. He's gone to Decatur. Later."

She recalled the tall man she often saw with him, the other half of Mutt and Jeff. She glanced at the card again. *Gemini Child Protective Society.* "Is your name really Henrico?"

He scowled and murmured something she could barely hear. It sounded like *Henry.*

"Who are *you?*" he demanded, as though it had been her idea to meet, and not his.

She hesitated. "Pin."

"Pin?" Henry laughed in disbelief. His deep voice grew shrill as a woman's. "Pinprick? Pinhead? Pinhole? Pin—"

"Just Pin," she snapped. "So you and this night watchman—you're the Gemini? And you find them? Missing kids?"

"Yes. Did you see where he took her?" She shook her head. "Are you sure?"

She shrugged. "I guess. I looked around afterward, but I didn't see her anywhere. Or him. Did you?"

"No." He seemed disappointed, like he regretted having signaled her to join him. "I need to go."

He gestured at the card. Reluctantly, she returned it, and he slid it back into the cardboard wallet. He didn't notice as a scrap of newspaper fell to the ground.

"Do you ever find them?" she asked. "The missing children? "My sister—"

Henry raised a finger to his lips, turned, and broke into a

shambling run, his head jerking back and forth as though arguing with someone. When he'd disappeared into the crowd, Pin stooped to retrieve the scrap of newspaper that had fallen from his wallet. One side was an advertisement for Cream of Wheat. The other was an article about Iolanda Vasilescu, an eleven-year-old Gypsy girl who'd gone missing a year ago:

> When she did not return from the washhouse where she worked, her mother contacted the police. Members of the Gypsy camp immediately began to search for the girl. Iolanda's father, Constantine Vasilescu, berated the police captain, who accused the Gypsies of kidnapping the child and did not organize a police search for two days...

Pin's stomach clenched. She remembered this. The girl had been only a year older than her sister. And, like Abriana, she'd never been found.

Chapter 21

FRANCIS HAD NO luck tracking the pickpocket at the Infant Incubators. No one working there recalled seeing anyone suspicious, except for that same queer little man who was there a few times a week. Francis knew him by sight—shabby and probably touched in the head, always talking to himself. Sometimes he was with another man, tall and gangly as a scarecrow. One of the nurses thought the two guys might be chesters, the way they watched the children in the park. But you couldn't haul off a guy for looking, and anytime the little man saw Francis coming, he took off.

Francis returned to the station house and spoke to the lady who'd lost her reticule. She was obstreperous and middle-aged—he pegged her for a suffragist.

"I don't know what you're getting paid for, if you can't find a common criminal," she exclaimed, smoothing her expensive skirts as she stood. "I'm going to write Mr. Baumgarten a letter of complaint." Karl Baumgarten was the amusement park's owner.

"I think that's a good idea," Francis replied, and steered her toward the station-house door. "He'll be very interested in what you have to say, I'm sure."

He returned to his rounds, keeping an eye out for trouble. There were seven midways at Riverview, all linked by the Pike, and almost a hundred concessions, nearly every one rigged. You'd think people would know better by now, yet fights still broke out when men realized they'd been taken. But today it was too hot for fighting in the late-afternoon heat, and too early for the serious drunks to emerge from the beer garden or Woodland Cabaret.

Sunset found him by Hell Gate. Not many people in line, so he took advantage of the lull to stand in the shade of a pin oak and remove his helmet. He looked around absently—balloon man, hokeypokey cart, lots of high-school kids. No sign of that hooligan Mugsy, who'd end up in prison if he didn't find a job in the stockyards once summer ended.

He set his helmet back on his head and headed for the path that led to the adult attractions—Salome's tent, the She-Male, the Woodland Cabaret, the booth that specialized in art postcards. Past a grassy clearing, the path forked. To the right, you'd end up in Fairyland, the woods frequented by picnickers and trysting couples.

Two small figures stood in the clearing. Francis shaded his eyes and squinted to make them out: here was the strange little man who hung around the incubators, standing beside the Gypsy fortune-teller's kid, Pin. Skinny as a rail, he looked like he hadn't had a meal since Christmas. Francis had heard that he worked as an errand boy for Max, but he'd never known the kid to get into any serious trouble. His mother was skinny, too, but pretty, olive skinned and dark haired. She also worked as a dance teacher at the park; Francis had gone to the ballroom one night in hopes of dancing with her, but she already had a knot of men waiting by her table. She looked barely old enough to have a kid Pin's age.

Francis waited to see if the weird fellow laid a hand on the boy. But they seemed to be merely talking. Then the man handed something to the kid. Dope? That could explain why the man behaved like a lunatic. They talked for a few more minutes, the kid handed whatever it was back to the little man, and they went their separate ways.

Francis frowned. What had been exchanged? If it really was dope, the boy was smart enough not to hang on to it. Still, Francis could think of other things that might be almost as dangerous to a kid— money, dirty pictures, a deck of poker cards.

And chesters didn't prey just on young girls. Last year there'd been a notorious string of murders in Wisconsin, four boys gutted like fish at a remote hunting camp. Francis watched as the little man made his way along the Pike, feinting at unseen attackers. Few men acted furtive without a reason—Francis knew that from his days at Robey Street—but such men were clever. Apprehending them was like engaging in a game of poker where bodies could be cast aside, rather than cards.

He recalled the gun he'd had to turn in when he was fired from the department, and the one that had taken its place, bought for seventeen dollars from a pawnbroker and hidden in his bureau back at Mrs. Dahl's boardinghouse. He'd no cause to carry it with him here at Riverview. That was about to change.

Chapter 22

AT A WIENIE stand, Pin bought a frankfurter loaded with sauerkraut, sat on a bench, and ate while she brooded.

If that dingbat Henry hadn't confirmed what she saw, Pin could almost have convinced herself that she hadn't actually glimpsed the girl from Essanay enter Hell Gate. Or that she might have seen a different girl, and misremembered what she looked like, and the man with her. Thousands of girls crowded Riverview every day, most with their families or girlfriends. They didn't roam freely the way that boys did. A girl on her own was likely a lost girl, one who could fall prey to the mashers who lurked around the park, especially in the late afternoon.

Yet the girl in yellow hadn't been on her own. That man didn't appear old enough to be her father, but he could have been her brother. Maybe she'd left the studio and come to the park to meet him.

Had she then gotten lost in the dark ride? But a lost kid would be brought to the park's police station and kept there until her parents came to claim her. A brass bell outside the building was rung only when a child was lost, or found. In the hours since she'd seen the girl enter Hell Gate, Pin hadn't once heard the bell.

She wondered if Clyde might have been working Hell Gate that afternoon—he often filled in as Satan. With four kids and an adult son attending Wilberforce University, he needed the extra cash.

She followed the Pike toward the Ten-in-One and saw Bernie the watermelon man. He had no customers, so she sidled up to him and asked, "Hey Bernie, you hear of anyone looking for a lost kid?"

"People's always looking for a lost kid." Bernie turned to yell at a middle-aged woman and her husband, "Good evening, madam! Sir! Ice-cold watermelon, right here!"

In the distance, the giant cuckoo clock began to chime. Seven o'clock. It had been around four when the girl and man entered the dark ride. Clyde's first performance was always at eight sharp—unlike Max, Clyde never missed a show due to drink or anything else.

The clock's last chime faded. From somewhere far away came the strains of a barrel organ, "After the Ball." Pin's mouth went dry. She fought a wave of nausea and hurried toward the building that housed the Ten-in-One shows.

Chapter 23

IT WAS DARK when he arrived back at the Workingmen's House. He trudged upstairs to the third floor, then down the long corridor to his room. His nostrils burned as he inhaled the scent of the same lye cleanser he used to mop the hospital floors. For the last few years, he'd lived here. Before that, save for a few stints at the Cook County Insane Asylum, he'd spent much of his life at the Illinois Asylum for Feeble-Minded Children in Lincoln.

But he wasn't feebleminded or insane. Pinhead had thought so; he could tell by the way the boy had stared at him.

DON'T YOU LOOK AT ME I TOLD YOU NOT TO WATCH

And he'd shown Pin the Gemini card! He'd thought he would understand! The others were fools, no one knew how powerful Henry was, how he'd saved all those children.

DON'T YOU LIE I SAW YOU I KNOW EVERYONE KNOWS

He'd seen him before, Pinhead. He knew the boy watched him. And he didn't behave like the other boys he ran with. Pinhead paid too much attention to how they acted, like he was looking for clues. He watched them the way Henry watched little girls.

Henry loved children. Yet as a boy he'd hated small girls, especially babies! When he was four, his mother died while giving birth to his sister. He never knew what happened to the baby.

YOU KILLED HER NO I GAVE HER AWAY NO I DIDN'T SHE RAN AWAY NO SHE DIDN'T DON'T YOU LIE TO ME I SAW HER FOLLOWING YOU THEY STOLE HER I SAW WHAT YOU DID I SAW WHAT YOU DID I SAW SHE WAS JUST A LITTLE BABY I SAVED HER

He'd spent the last nineteen years imagining her face in that of every pretty child he saw.

Other children were afraid of him. In the classroom he twitched and made frog noises and invented rhymes, trying to be funny so the other children would like him. He pretended to throw things, snowballs and baseballs that no one could see. Sometimes he forgot he was pretending. His classmates yelled when they saw him coming.

"Crazy Daisy, Crazy Daisy!"

He'd chase them, throwing real rocks or brandishing the long-bladed knife he kept hidden in a pocket of his dungarees. He skipped school, roaming the streets on his own. He started fires in vacant buildings just to watch them burn.

Finally, when he was twelve, his father had him committed to the Lincoln asylum.

He ran away repeatedly but only escaped for good when he was seventeen. He walked one hundred and sixty-five miles back to Chicago, where his aunt and uncle took him in for a few weeks. His godmother got him the janitor job at St. Joseph's Hospital, mopping floors, cleaning sinks and toilets, emptying pails full of blood-soaked bandages and bits of skin. Every morning, he'd start in the basement and work his way to the top floor. Most days no one spoke to him at all. Not one word.

DON'T YOU LOOK AT ME WAS I TALKING TO YOU COME HERE NOW I'LL BEAT YOU BLACK AND BLUE

There was an elevator at the hospital, but he was forbidden to use it. So he lugged the heavy metal bucket and wringer and a rope mop taller than he was up and down eight flights of stairs. He emptied filthy water in the utility sink on each floor, filling the bucket again on the next. The lye soap burned the skin on his hands until his knuckles bled. At night he'd toss and turn on his thin mattress, struggling to sleep because of the pain in his back and shoulders.

Only Sister Dymphna ever showed him any kindness. An obese woman with a feathery birthmark on one cheek, she was named for Saint Dymphna, virgin martyr and patron of the insane. Sister Dymphna had given Henry a scapular of her namesake. The holy card showed a dainty red-haired girl with a halo. A bloody line indicated where her head had been cut off, then miraculously reattached, as if with red thread. Henry wore the scapular beneath his undershirt, even when he was asleep.

Inside, his room was small and hot as a bakery. A large crucifix on the wall, a single narrow iron bedstead, a small wooden desk and chair. The only window was narrow and overlooked an air shaft. An electrical bulb hung from the ceiling, but it was too bright; it hurt his eyes. He stepped to his desk, opened the drawer, and removed a handwritten manuscript bound in string. He'd salvaged the yellow paper from trash bins on the third floor, where the doctors had their offices.

PUT THAT BACK I TOLD YOU NEVER TO TOUCH THEM I DIDN'T TOUCH HER I SAVED HER DIDN'T I SAW YOU YOU LITTLE BASTARD

He clutched the manuscript to his chest and kicked out at the bad men until they disappeared. Panting, he sat at his desk, set down the manuscript. He waited until he was calm, waited for calm to bloom into anticipation, then expectation. The dim room seemed to brighten as he gazed at the stack of pages, each one a door poised to open.

HERE WE ARE! HERE WE ARE WAITING HERE WE ARE WE WAITED JUST LIKE WE PROMISED!

His breath quickened, no longer anxiety but eagerness. Brave girls, brave General Dargero! He would save them as he always did!

He leaned over the table. His outstretched hands hovered a few inches above the manuscript, the way he'd seen the colored magician conjure white doves from a brick at the freak show. He'd written the title in meticulous block letters, using a thick pencil he'd pilfered from a nurse's desk:

THE ADVENTURES OF GENERAL
HENRICO DARGERO,
OF THE GEMINI AND THE BLACK BROTHERS,
AND OF THE GIRLS ARMY
THAT FOUGHT BESIDE THEM
IN THEIR BATTLE AGAINST THE
CONFEDERACY OF THE
CLAN OF THE AGIVECENNIANS

By Henry Joseph Darger
The author of this exciting story

He ran a finger beneath the string, but didn't undo the knot yet. *Too soon and you're a loon.*

He reached into the drawer, removed a votive candle and a box of matches. He'd pocketed both in the hospital chapel, where he attended Mass every day.

He lit the candle, then untied the string binding his manuscript. He'd begun it four years ago, working on it in every spare moment. He turned the pages, stopping to peruse a picture he'd drawn of an outsize, misshapen hand clutching someone's throat. The someone was meant to be a girl but looked more like a turnip. Not one of his better efforts. He continued shuffling pages until he came to one filled with more blocky writing:

Never had General Dargero encountered such a foe as that evil General Forestor. "My heart fills with pity for those brave Girls" he thought. "How they will escape i cannot imagine. He has defiled this once beautiful countryside and when he lets the floods loose there will be no safe refuge for anyone, Least of all these brave Girls. Brave though they may be they are shockingly outnumbered."

The page needed an illustration. From the drawer he withdrew a cardboard folder that contained dozens of pages from newspapers and magazines culled from trash bins. Pictures of children, all of them girls. Dotty Darling from the *Woman's Home Companion*. Illustrations from *The Little Girl's Sewing Book*. A holy card depicting Saint Joan in armor, leading an army of blond angels. The Kewpies.

He traced their faces with a calloused finger. Only here were they safe. Only here could he truly protect them.

As a boy at the asylum, he'd secretly traced illustrations he found in books. He copied countless pictures of Dorothy Gale and her friends, especially Princess Ozma, the girl who turned into a boy. There was a good illustrated book about the Battle of Gettysburg, too. He traced its fierce generals and brave soldiers and began to combine these drawings with those of the girls from Oz. The girls brandished firearms and sabers. The Scarecrow and Tik Tok took their places among the generals.

All of this came to an end when he was discovered one afternoon by the asylum's school librarian.

"I wondered who'd been vandalizing all those books!" Knocking the volume from his hands, she slapped him so hard he fell from his chair. "Who's going to pay for that, you imbecile?"

He attacked her as she snatched up his drawing, and ended up being beaten with a hose, then left alone in a concrete cell for two days. It was only since he'd arrived at the Workingmen's House that he'd begun writing and drawing again.

He traced Princess Ozma's mouth, but his pencil was dull and the paper kept tearing. In a rage, he balled it up and shoved the picture of Ozma back inside the folder.

DAMN OH DAMN YOU CLUMSY SHIT LOOK WHAT YOU DID NOW YOU'LL GET IT, OPEN AND SEE WHAT YOU MADE ME DO

He slapped himself, trying to calm down; frantically sorted through his papers until he found a scrap of newsprint that felt like velvet, so worn was it from handling. His most precious possession, even more precious than his manuscript: a newspaper photograph of a five-year-old girl, blond, her face bleached out so that only her eyes and mouth could be clearly seen. Elsie Paroubek. She looked otherworldly, elfin, her expression one of slight alarm.

She was no longer alive. His eyes welled; the image blurred as he brought it to his face and pressed it against his mouth.

"Dearest one," he whispered.

He shut his eyes and saw her floating before him, her tiny mouth and dark eyes. He bent over the picture, hands in his lap, and waited for the happy spell to come. Afterward he rocked back and forth, weeping as he prayed for forgiveness. When his grief subsided, he replaced the newspaper picture in the folder and gathered up the pages of his manuscript. He tied them back together with the piece of string, his clumsy, damaged fingers fumbling with the knot, opened the drawer, and put everything back inside.

Last of all, he blew out the candle, set it with his other things, and closed the drawer. He stood and undressed, folding his clothes before pulling on his nightshirt. He knelt beside his bed and said his prayers, fingering the scapular. When he finished, he made the Sign of the Cross and crawled under the covers. Within a few minutes he was sleeping soundly.

Chapter 24

THERE HAD BEEN a girl—Maura, a friend of his sister Ellen's, dark haired and buxom, with freckled cheeks and breasts. A laughing girl. They'd been courting for almost a year when it happened: not the usual fumbling in the dark with a whore, but a stolen afternoon in a hotel room. Lying beside her afterward had been even sweeter than what had gone before.

"Will you marry me?" Francis had whispered.

"Of course," she'd whispered back, her face still wet from crying. Happiness, he'd thought at the time. Two weeks later she was dead, bled out on an abortionist's table. Not his child, of course. Ever since he'd tried to balance it in his head: Would it have mattered? If he'd known the choice was another man's child or her lying in bed beside him now, warm and laughing? Most days he believed he might have lived with it. Other days, he did not. And some days, thinking of her freckled limbs tangled with those of another man, he almost wished he'd killed her himself.

Chapter 25

She had a ritual for nightfall at Riverview, and not even the urgency of talking to Clyde would change it. Unless it was pouring rain, she'd find a spot where she could clearly see the Hippodrome. Once the sun dipped below the horizon, colors bled from the world like dye from untreated cloth. The Hippodrome's pale façade darkened to grey, its shadow angel, more mysterious and sinister: a guardian angel, but whom was it protecting? The fading light tinted women's white dresses and shirtwaists lavender, turned the miles of red, white, and blue bunting into ashy ribbons.

She staked out a patch of grass and stared across the Lagoon. People streamed toward the Velodrome, eager for the evening's cycle races, and crowded into the Waterdrome's bleachers to watch the diving elephants. She made a tunnel of her hands, mimicking a camera's lens, moved around till she found an angle that eliminated the crowds and other buildings, and gazed at the Hippodrome's angel.

The world contracted to what she could see, what she wanted to see. She pretended she was back in the studio. *That light on the Hippodrome needs to be hotter,* she thought, and held her breath.

A cry went up from the people thronging the Pike as the Hippodrome burst into white flame, the angel no longer sinister but glorious: invincible. Every building and ride shivered with light, the coasters' scaffolding and the Gyroplane flaring like a gigantic box of matches tossed into a fireplace, the Bob's chute a shining knife plunged into the Lagoon. The Aerostat's tower, five stories high, blazed like a torch that could be seen from twenty miles away.

Or so she'd been told. Pin had never been that far. She shoved her hands into her pockets and rejoined the crowd. No one paid her any mind. She was just another footloose boy, not big enough to pose a threat unless you found his hand in your pocket. After a few minutes she reached the Ten-in-One building. Garish canvas banners advertised what was inside:

ENGLISH SKELETAL GIANTESS: 7 FEET TALL, 90 LBS!
LOLITA THE SNAKE CHARMER
ESCAPEO, THE MAN WHO DEFIES LOCKS AND BOLTS
IDA, THE LIVING MERMAID! EIGHTH WONDER
OF THE WORLD
LORD CLYDE, THE HOO-DOO KING

There were six more acts, all part of Armstrong's Freak Show, and Pin had seen them all. Gaffed freaks—fakes, except for Mildred the giantess and Flossie the fat lady, who weighed six hundred pounds and had a one-hundred-two-inch waist. The four-legged woman was real, even if she was dead and floating in a jar. And Lolita was very much alive—her real name was Alice—and so beautiful it hurt to look at her, wearing a slithery dress, a pair of poison-green boa constrictors named Honey Bunch and General Villa wrapped around her arms.

Lord Clyde, though, was the big draw. He did only two shows a night, at eight and nine-thirty. By now, someone else would have taken over for him as Satan at Hell Gate. Clyde spent his winters on an island off the South Carolina coast, fishing and crabbing, took the train up to New York City for an occasional show in Harlem.

"I got a good life," he'd told Pin. "No matter I'm colored or a white man, it's a good-enough life."

She went around back and slipped inside the door used by the performers.

The door to Clyde's dressing room was open, and she saw him lacing one elegant black goatskin shoe. In a bamboo cage, a trio of white doves fluttered as she walked in. Clyde glanced up and nodded.

"You staying out of trouble, boy?"

He picked a white feather from his dress trousers and stood. He was the tallest man she'd ever known, also one of the best looking. After each performance, he did a brisk business selling photographs of himself, to Negroes and even some white people. Pin had one tacked to the wall of the shack, alongside a picture of the dead aviator Harriet Quimby:

LORD CLYDE, THE HOO-DOO KING, MASTER OF MYSTIC AMAZEMENT

He'd signed it *To Pin, with regards,* in an expansive, swooping hand. She'd spent an afternoon copying the way he'd written her name, in hopes she might develop a star's signature, too.

"Doing my best," she said. She watched as Clyde straightened his celluloid collar—a new collar for every show, an extravagance Pin couldn't even imagine. Ikie said Clyde and his family lived in a house with four bedrooms and an indoor toilet, down in Bronzeville.

"What do you want, boy?" Clyde shrugged into his jacket, picked up his bow tie, and looped it around his neck. "Cat got your tongue?"

"Were you working Hell Gate a few hours ago?"

He nodded. "I was."

"Did you see a man in one of the boats with a girl? About four o'clock, I think. A white man with a white girl."

"I see a lot of white men with a lot of white girls." Clyde's voice was so deep he didn't need a megaphone. Pin once heard a grown man shriek like a woman when Clyde reared out of the darkness at Hell

Gate and brandished his pitchfork, shouting *Welcome, sinner!* "You talking about a little girl, or a grown woman?"

"No, a girl. Eleven or twelve, wearing a yellow dress. Big yellow bow in her hair."

"You know how many girls in yellow dresses I see every day in Riverview? Five hundred and ninety-seven. And that's just white girls. How come you asking?"

"This man, when he got into the boat, he had a girl with him. When he came out of the tunnel, he didn't. He was alone."

Clyde shook his head. "Hell if I know. You say four o'clock? I left right about then to come back here. But no one came around asking for a lost kid. Did you talk to Horace? Or Larry?"

"I figured I'd ask you first. You were in the tunnel with them."

"Them and one thousand nine hundred and twelve other folks."

He tugged at the tails of his jacket. Clyde was a dandy. Black swallowtail jacket, matching pants with a stripe of black ribbon down the sides. Immaculate white shirt and purple tie, secured with an emerald stickpin, white carnation in his buttonhole.

"How do I look?" he asked, adjusting the stickpin. "Not too flossy?"

"Not too flossy." She peered inside the dove cage, cooing softly at the birds. "I ain't mistaken," she said. "I saw Charlie Chaplin at the studio this morning. The man at Hell Gate looked like him."

"Charlie Chaplin?"

"Yeah. He was meeting with Spoor, they're trying to get him to come back from California. He was with the same girl—Chaplin, I mean. He was kidding around with her on the movie stage."

"You sure it was the same girl?"

She shrugged. "Pretty sure. I got a pretty good look at them at Essanay."

"Huh." Clyde stared at her thoughtfully. "That is peculiar, I agree. Have you told Bacon or any of the police?"

"I told you, I wanted to ask you first."

"I'm not the police, boy." He gave a barking laugh. "Not even close.

That's who you need to talk to. And you should find yourself an honest job, instead of hanging round Max."

"You've smoked his dope."

"I'm not denying it. But women cause more trouble than dope ever did."

"So you don't remember a man and a girl in a yellow dress?"

Clyde let his breath out in an impatient huff, shut his eyes for a moment.

"No," he said at last. "But there was a white man, I remember him because he was the only person riding alone. I saw him in the tunnel, right before I got ready to leave when Lemuel came on—that's who was spelling me. Clean shaven, with a hat. Couldn't tell you what color hair. No girl that I saw. Now I got to run."

Clyde stooped beside her. His fingers grazed the hair behind her temple.

"Forgot to wash behind your ears again," he announced, and handed her a wooden token. "Tell the cops. If she's gone missing, they'll have been looking for her. You shouldn't have waited till now," he added. "That kid's ma will be worried sick." He picked up the dove cage and sauntered off.

Pin inspected the wooden disk. One side was stamped with Hell Gate's winged devil. The other read GOOD FOR ONE TRIP TO HADES. Pin flipped it into the air and caught it. "Thanks," she said, though Clyde was long gone.

Chapter 26

Larry had already left for the day, and the skinny, pock-faced white man named Rubbery Moe had taken over the ticket booth. Screams and nervous laughter echoed from inside the Hell Gate pavilion, along with recorded groans and shrieks from hidden phonographs. Pin craned her neck to see if Horace was still on duty in back. He was. She swore and got in line, keeping an eye out for any sign of the man she'd seen that afternoon.

Clyde had seemed to remember him, too. So that made three of them: her, Henry, Clyde. Yet Clyde hadn't seen the girl in yellow. She must have scrambled from the boat once the trip was under way and tried to run off. But why would she have run? She'd gone with the man willingly, sat on his lap like she knew him.

Unbidden, the image of her sister came to Pin, Abriana smiling as the German baker handed her a cruller, Abriana who trusted everyone who smiled at her or offered her a treat. Pin dug her fingernails into her palm until the pain drove the picture from her mind and she was back in the sticky warm night outside Hell Gate.

The line moved quickly with Rubbery Moe behind the ticket

booth. He used to work the Derby Racer coaster, with its motto Sixty Miles an Hour in Sixty Seconds.

"Ten cents, one thin dime, watch'er heads, ladies, might want to remove your hats. No refunds, the management is not responsible for medical emergencies."

In front of Pin stood two girls, arms linked. One wore a sailor cap, the other a hat with a white froth of willow plumes.

"You might want to keep that on your lap, miss." Rubbery Moe jabbed a thumb at the mass of ostrich feathers. "That's a real nice hat, shame to ruin it."

The girl looked at her friend. "What you think? I should take it off?"

Her friend nodded. "Better safe than sorry."

The two stepped over to the waiting boat, a four-seater. Rubbery Moe turned to Pin. She held out her token. He took it with a grunt, pointing to the plank seat behind the girls. Pin started toward the boat, then asked, "Hey, Moe—did you see a man here today? He was with a girl in a yellow dress, she was maybe twelve."

"I seen a thousand men." He gestured at the line behind her. "I got paying customers. Get in or skedaddle."

Pin hopped into the back of the boat. The two girls turned to stare at her.

"Damn, it's a kid." The girl in the sailor cap looked past Pin, to where a group of young men shelled out dimes to Rubbery Moe. "Say, Mister, how's about fixing us with a couple of those fellas instead of this kid?"

Without waiting for an answer, the two girls extricated themselves from the boat and hurried to join the young men. Moe glared at Pin, now alone in the boat. "You're losing me money," he said, and pushed her off.

Pin quickly hopped to the front seat, grabbing the sides of the vessel as it coasted along the canal's spiraling path. The rank water appeared as thick and black as machine oil. Her boat followed the canal's circular route, slowly at first, then faster and faster as the spiral tightened and the little vessel approached the central chute. In the boat behind hers, the two girls were already canoodling with the boys they'd just met. In front of her loomed the tunnel, its entrance an enormous mouth surmounted by a pair of huge eyes, red and angry looking. Flame-colored streamers billowed around it, blown by hidden electrical fans. From inside, recorded shrieks and moans drowned out the voices of couples in the other boats.

Streamers whipped Pin's face as the prow of her boat slid forward and, for a second, hung over empty air. It dropped in a sickening rush, and she was thrust backward, barely catching herself as she frantically clutched the plank seat. Spray spattered her cheeks as the boat splashed down, hard, at the bottom of the chute. After bobbing precariously and bumping against the wall, her boat righted itself and began to glide through the tunnel.

The din momentarily deafened her. Screaming girls and women, whooping men. Sounds of hollow laughter and clanking chains boomed from phonographs tucked into plywood grottoes. Flashing red and blue lights illuminated wax dummies, skeletons, disembodied skulls, bedsheet ghosts dipped in luminous paint so they glowed like toadstools. An electrical motor turned the waterwheels so the canal flowed past all of them. Devils stabbed a wax policeman with pitchforks. Two turnip-headed goblins tugged at the skirt of a papier-mâché woman, exposing broomstick legs and a bare electrical bulb. Pin gasped as a skeleton dropped from the ceiling, its fingers scraping her scalp before it was yanked back up to await the next boat.

Even worse was a stretch where there were no lights, and hundreds of threads hung down to graze her face like cobwebs. She had ridden through Hell Gate several times this summer: she knew it was all chicken wire and plaster and colored gelatin lights.

Still, it terrified her. It reminded her of the monstrous storage tank in Little Hell—the constant fear of flames or explosions, the vast darkness of the vacant lot surrounding the tank, and rumors of the scores of bodies buried there. Like Bricktown, which bordered Riverview. Until a few years ago, Ikie had told her, plumes of black smoke rose into the sky from kilns, each as big as a house. The kilns had burned night and day: if the wind shifted, fairy floss would melt in your hand.

Here in the tunnel the air smelled cold and chalky, the way she imagined a cave would smell. Large white balloons with skull faces bumped against unwary heads in the boats ahead of her. Spotlights flickered on and off like lightning. Front and back, the nearest boats seemed a safe distance from her own, forty feet or more. Far enough that courting couples could grab a few minutes alone in the dark. Far enough for her to carry out her plan, such as it was.

She stared into the tunnel nervously. She'd seen a drowned cat here once, as bloated as one of the misshapen fetuses they kept in jars at the freak show. From behind her came the unmistakable sound of a slap, followed by muffled sobs. Her boat drifted on, pulled by the current along a curving stretch with no other boats in sight.

Pin remembered this part of the tunnel—the first time she'd come here, she'd nearly jumped out of her skin. But now she knew what to expect. She held her breath and waited for the boom of a thunder sheet, followed by the blinding white flare of a flash pot. In the split second that followed, she jumped from the boat.

She landed on the narrow ledge that ran alongside the canal. Her foot slipped on the slimy surface, but she caught herself before she tumbled into the black water. As the thunder faded into ripples of nervous laughter, she scrambled behind a pile of fake stalagmites.

She had only ten minutes before her empty boat shot out of the tunnel, into the stagnant pool that served as a holding area. Horace would yell at Moe to demand why there was an empty boat, and Moe would tell him it was Pin's. If Horace caught her, he'd slam her against the wall, the way he'd done Mugsy when he tried to steal one of the skeletons. She ducked as the next boat drifted past, the couples inside kissing so passionately they never noticed her. As they receded into shadow, she glanced around.

What she was looking for? A corpse? But someone would have seen a body in the water and called the cops hours ago. Maybe the girl had climbed out of her boat and, like Pin, found her way onto the ledge and gotten lost in the dark. She could have hit her head. Or fallen asleep, though that seemed unlikely with all this racket. Maybe the man hadn't noticed she was gone till he got out at the end of the ride. Maybe he'd hurried off to get help.

Pin rubbed her arms, chilled. The ledge was just wide enough for someone to walk along when it was necessary to change an electrical bulb or adjust one of the spook-house figures. Underfoot, the concrete surface was slick and uneven. She took a step and slipped, banging her knee so hard it brought tears to her eyes.

She hauled herself back up until she was half standing, half crouched, and began to walk crabwise with her back to the canal, hands splayed across the moist wall. She tried not to gag: the air smelled strongly of mildew and sulfur from the flash pot. She moved quickly, ready to duck when the next boat approached. Every flare of the flash pots revealed walls black with mold. She stepped among trash on the ledge—cigar stubs, a Coca-Cola bottle, hair ribbons.

From behind her she heard voices. Another boat. There was nothing here to hide behind, so she bellied onto the ledge, grimacing when her hand touched something moist and soft. Her eyes had grown accustomed to the violent play of light and shadow. She could pick out shapes on the other side of the canal, wax mannequins slumped over fake boulders like drunks in a saloon.

"They had a long night," remarked the man in the boat below her, and the woman beside him laughed.

A few inches from where Pin lay, something scurried. The woman in the boat gasped. "What was that!"

Pin held her breath. "Nothing, sweetheart," the man murmured. "Don't you worry…"

Pin heard the rustle of fabric, a sudden intake of breath. The boat floated on, and she crept forward.

Two more boats passed. Each time she crouched, unseen by their passengers. She wondered if they mistook her for one of the waxworks.

Crimson light streaked the water's surface as the tunnel began to curve. Another flash pot flared, revealing a row of large, flaccid skeleton balloons suspended from the arched ceiling. The canal blazed into a river of fire and plunged back into darkness. The recorded howls and shrieks grew louder.

Pin gnawed her lip. She'd neared the end of the tunnel, where the actor playing Satan attacked each boat as it went by. It would be difficult if not impossible to creep past him unseen.

And her empty boat might already have left Hell Gate. Even if she got out unscathed, she'd still have to deal with Horace. She crouched as low as she could, trying to figure out what to do next. Return the way she came, and take her chances with Moe?

She looked over her shoulder at the seemingly endless dark passage, the dim outlines of rocks and stalagmites and stalactites, shapeless white forms dangling from hooks in the ceiling. Fake or not, the sight filled her with dread. She decided to continue.

As she turned, another flash pot exploded, illuminating something on the ledge a few yards ahead of her. A skull balloon that drooped over the edge, just inches above the water. From behind her came the sound of laughter as the next boat approached.

"Stop it, Walter!"

"You started it, honey!"

"I mean it! Make him quit, Rudy!"

Pin squatted as the boat floated by. When it slid out of sight, she straightened. The flash pot blazed again, brighter than before. She took a step toward the skull balloon and looked down.

It wasn't a balloon but a large doll, one of the fancier prizes from the shooting gallery: a toy the size of the triumphant girl who'd tote it home.

This doll had a stained yellow bow caught in its matted curls. It didn't wear a dress, only a shimmy, discolored with ruddy blotches. The blotches extended to its neck, like a port-wine stain. Its eyes bulged, its lashes like spiders. An ugly toy, the ugliest doll she'd ever seen.

Only she knew it wasn't a doll. It was a girl, a dead girl, staring up at Pin with eyes that had burst like grapes. She smelled like pee but also of something Pin couldn't quite place, lemons and a vaguely medicinal odor.

Pin gazed at her, unable to move. Finally she stretched out her hand and let her fingertips graze the girl's cheek, then the bedraggled yellow hair ribbon. Slowly the head turned, mouth lolling open so she could see a blackened tongue and gums, a glistening sliver like a shard of glass in the back of her throat.

Pin snatched her hand back, the ribbon tight between her fingers. She watched in horror as the body began to move, sliding slowly across the ledge until with a soft splash it fell into the water and floated, facedown, drawn inexorably by the current through the tunnel.

Chapter 27

For a few seconds she thought she'd be sick. She dropped onto her hands and knees, waited till the spasm passed before forcing herself to turn her head.

The girl's corpse had floated to the opposite side of the canal, where a board protruded into the water. The body butted up against it and remained there, partially submerged. It would be easy to miss, just as easy to do what Pin had done—mistake it for a lost doll or one of the flash pots.

She started at the slap of water on a wooden hull. Flattening herself against the ledge, she watched an empty boat slowly round the corner. Only when it floated to within a few feet of her did Pin realize that both its passengers were in the front. A grunting man lay on top of a woman, flat on her back, her long skirt and petticoat pulled up so high they covered her face.

Pin shoved the filthy hair ribbon into her pocket, pushed herself to a sitting position, lowered her legs over the ledge, and, when the boat had almost passed, dropped into the back. The boat rocked as she pulled herself beneath the plank bench, heart pounding.

Faint stirring in front, murmurs, then silence. The rhythmic grunts started up again as the boat approached the turn where Satan waited, the boat's occupants oblivious to the explosions of flash pots around them.

"Ho-ho-*ho*!"

Pin heard a muffled yelp from the front of the boat as a rubber-tipped pitchfork found its mark. By the time the boat shot back out into a dazzle of electrical lights, the man and woman sat side by side, the crushed silk flowers on her hat the only sign that anything illicit had occurred. As they spoke to each other, Pin edged out from beneath the bench, trying to locate Horace so she could avoid him.

She was in luck. Instead of Horace, she saw a lanky figure in overalls, cigarette clamped between his teeth—Johnny Iacono. He was in high school, a few years older than Pin. He usually worked the Thousand Islands but filled in at Hell Gate a couple of nights a week when he needed extra cash. Sometimes he'd buy cigarettes for Mugsy and the other boys, and once he gave Pin a nickel, when she was broke and had gone all day without eating.

She kept out of sight until she felt the thud of his boat hook as it snagged her vessel and pulled it alongside the wooden walkway. The man in front disembarked first and leaned in to help out his lady friend. As they sauntered off, Pin jumped from the boat.

"Pin! What the hell you doing?" Johnny pushed off the empty boat and stared at her. "That better not have been you sent that empty boat through a while ago."

Pin stumbled toward him. "Listen, you gotta listen to me. Someone's dead in there." Grabbing his arm, she pointed into the tunnel. "A kid, a girl. I saw her this afternoon—"

Johnny shook her arm from his. "What the hell you talking about?"

"What I said! There's a girl in there. I don't know if she's drowned or what. But she's dead."

Johnny's eyes narrowed. "Don't give me that bullshit. I got work to do." He looked past her as the next boat emerged into the light. "You better get the hell out of here before Horace sees you."

"I swear to God, I'm telling the truth. You can kill me if I'm lying."

"Jesus, why the hell would I kill you? You're nuts! Get outta here."

Johnny shoved her aside and headed for the next boat.

"Damn it, Johnny, look—"

She dug into her pocket for the soiled yellow hair ribbon. "This is hers. I saw her go into the tunnel this afternoon, but she didn't come out. She's in the water right before you get to Satan, right-hand side as you're heading this way—she got snagged on something. Swear to Jesus, Johnny, just go look!"

Johnny continued to stare at her. Finally, he looked at the tunnel.

"All right," he said, and pitched his cigarette into the water. "You cover for me, I'll go inside and see what's what. But if you're lying, I won't need to kill you, 'cause Horace will." He tossed her the boat hook. "Don't let anyone fall in. I'll be right back."

She spent the next few minutes grabbing each boat and holding it steady as customers disembarked. More than a few of the women were flushed, their clothes rumpled. Several of the men grinned and winked at Pin behind the women's backs.

"Here, ma'am, be careful," she warned, taking hold of an older lady's hand to help her onto the walkway where her husband waited. The woman took her husband's arm.

"Thank you, young man," she said.

Pin peered anxiously into the tunnel, looking for Johnny. When someone tapped her shoulder, she jumped, then turned to see Johnny, his face white as milk.

"You're right. There's someone dead in there. I don't know how you knew about it. I don't *want* to know. I told Horace—all I can say is you better not be here when he comes round."

He snatched the boat hook from her and slapped a magazine into her hand. "Larry left this at the booth for you. You need to stop reading detective stories."

She glanced at the next boat floating toward them. "Isn't Horace going to shut it down?"

"Horace wouldn't shut this fucking thing down if it was on fire. He says he'll go see for himself in a couple minutes. Now scram before he comes looking for you."

Chapter 28

No ONE HAD seen him as he hurried from the amusement park and hopped onto the streetcar, found a seat by the window, and rode to Uptown, hat on his lap. Reflexively he checked his pockets. One held his card case and wallet; the other, the girl's balled-up dress, a bottle of Sydenham's laudanum syrup, and a tin of lemon drops. When the streetcar reached its terminus, he walked several blocks and caught another one headed in the opposite direction. He hopped off a few blocks from the hospital and walked the rest of the way home.

He never took the same route twice. He'd learned that four years earlier, back at Coney Island, and a few months after that in Revere with Deirdre Monahan. The only way to reach Wonderland Amusement Park was by the *Narrow Gauge* from Boston, unless you had an automobile, or walked, or paid an outrageous sum for a taxi. So he'd taken the *Narrow Gauge*. Packed as the train car had been, he'd still worried about being recognized.

And he had been. As he rode the train back into Boston that evening, he saw the same young woman he'd inadvertently locked eyes with on the *Narrow Gauge* that morning, a strong-featured girl with an insolent black gaze and a pealing laugh that was loosed every time her male companion opened his mouth. Another Irish girl, they were always loud and bold. On the return trip from Wonderland she was alone, her color high and hair tousled by the sea wind. He wondered if she and her boyfriend had fought, or if she was a prostitute. She stared at him brazenly enough.

He moved to the back of the crowded train, desperate not to be seen. She followed him. Definitely a whore. He removed his boater and held it in front of his face, turning his back to her, but he could sense her gaze through the crush of passengers. When he climbed down at the station, she stood on the platform, waiting for him.

"Hello." Smiling, she reached for his sleeve. He saw the heart-shaped mark on her neck where she'd been kissed hard, and the purplish cloud of a bruise. "I saw you at Wonderland by the roller coaster—want some company?"

He pushed past her, still clutching his boater to his face. The next day, he caught the train back to New York City. In February he headed south to Charleston, and this past April returned to New York to catch the *Lake Shore Limited* to Chicago. With each move, a trunk accompanied him, along with a large suitcase. The trunk was stored in the luggage car; the suitcase he insisted on having in his sleeping compartment, where he paid to have both berths. He always tipped the porters well for the extra trouble. He had attended Dale Carnegie's class at the YMCA in Harlem and been impressed by bits of wisdom: always repeat a person's name, always tip generously.

Riverview Amusement Park wouldn't open until mid-May, which gave him plenty of time to get settled in Chicago. In the last few years, amusement parks had sprung up across the country, along with nickelodeons and movie theaters and vaudeville houses. The amusement parks had the advantage of great crowds and countless children. He'd been dazzled to the point of nausea the first time he'd visited Luna Park in Coney Island. A summer day with tens of thousands of visitors eating hot dogs and lobster rolls and buttered corn, swimming in the ocean, screaming on the roller coasters—even fucking, in the dark rides.

But he learned to navigate Luna Park and its boardwalk rival, Dreamland, and then later Wonderland outside Boston, and finally Riverview. He'd been amazed to see that they all had the same rides— Hell Gate, the Witching Waves, the Blue Streak coaster, the Derby Racer.

Carousels of course were a dime a dozen, as were the Infant Incubators. They were very impressive, though the little things looked a bit like grubs. When the German who'd invented the incubators couldn't find hospitals that would pay to house and staff his miraculous machines, he'd taken them to Coney Island, then Wonderland and Riverview. A German doctor hadn't invented the Hell Gate attraction, but he wondered if the engineer who'd designed the dark ride at Dreamland had designed those at Wonderland and Riverview.

Now, the wind off the Lagoon brought little comfort as he walked: his clothes were soaked with sweat. He slipped a hand into his pocket to stroke the dress there. His heart stirred, knowing what was ahead, and recalling this afternoon's events.

"What's your name," he'd asked as their boat neared the Hell Gate chute.

"I already told you. Maria," she replied, her tone sullen, and moved from his lap to the bench. He could tell she was growing uneasy, but he knew that, within minutes, the tunnel's terrors would override any mistrust she had of him.

A few more steps and he reached his building. He opened the door and hastened down the hallway, then upstairs. Once in his room, he bolted the door, set down his hat, withdrew the dress from his pocket and placed it on the table, and finally removed his jacket and folded it neatly over a chair. On the wall behind him hung a summer duster, another seersucker jacket, several hats. His shaving things sat on a window ledge: straight razor and brush, a pair of scissors, and a bottle of Lilac Vegetal eau de cologne. He always kept the drapes drawn; he lit the gas lamp, its hiss the only sound other than the occasional putt-putt of an automobile in the street.

He crossed the dim room to the closet, digging in his pocket for the key, and opened it.

There was no light inside, but he didn't need one. The doll stood on the floor, gazing straight ahead. Her socket head and jointed limbs were made of molded bisque, as was the top half of her torso. A wig of dark hair—real human hair—was attached to her bisque scalp, and her blue sleep-glass eyes closed whenever he lay her down on a flat surface.

At forty-four inches tall, she was the largest doll he'd been able to find. The dresses she wore were still much too big, the fabric frayed where he'd cut off sleeves and hems in an attempt to make them look as though one day the doll might grow into them.

The doll had started as a prop, a means of deflecting attention from the fact that he had a collection of girls' worn clothing in his suitcase. At first he'd invented imaginary daughters, but this provoked too many questions—their ages, names, where they lived, why he traveled with their clothes, their mother's name, on and on and on.

The doll, oddly, inspired less curiosity. Of course he kept her out of sight. It was possible to forget where he'd stuffed a dress or pinafore, but not the doll. The doll demanded attention. She demanded to be hidden. Only twice had someone glimpsed her. The first time, he'd been careless in his hotel room and left her on his bed after unpacking. A bellman noticed her when he dropped off an item he'd left in the lobby. The bellman assumed she was a mannequin of the sort one saw in the more expensive department stores, and that he was a salesman.

The other time it had been the landlady at a short-term boardinghouse in Passaic, a nosy bitch always sniffing around for available single men. She'd found the doll in the armoire where his suits hung. Not content with that discovery, she'd pawed through his bureau and come across a stack of folded dresses and pinnies. He'd given her a cock-and-bull story about the doll being a gift for his daughter, which resulted in an argument over why he'd told her he was unmarried. He left that night, despite having paid for an entire week's lodging.

Over time, the doll took on her own life. Or, not her own, but the lives of the girls whose clothes she wore. He couldn't recall the faces of the girls, but he knew the name of each one, now associated with a red-gingham frock or faded, much-worn pinny, a middy blouse or blue serge coat with white crystal-ball buttons.

He tucked one of the doll's ringlets behind a delicate ear. She had been manufactured by the German doll makers Simon & Halbig. He had purchased her three years ago at John Wanamaker. A lady-body doll, not a baby doll, she had smooth swellings to represent breasts. The subtle curves had been unnoticeable beneath her original clothes—indigo taffeta, Belgian lace, satin ribbons, real kid-leather shoes. She was intended as a rich girl's doll, and he'd acted the part of a rich girl's father. Her wardrobe had changed numerous times in the last three years, though her original clothing remained folded inside a pillowcase at the bottom of an oversize straw-and-leather suitcase.

The suitcase had belonged to a man named Richard, who impersonated women at burlesque houses and places of men's entertainment. Richard had befriended him when they shared a weeklong bill at the opera house in Manchester, New Hampshire. "My wife ran off with a preacher in Detroit," he confided one boozy evening. "It's a tough life if you're not in it."

He'd killed Richard after a long bout of drinking in a saloon frequented by the city's mill workers, the night before they were scheduled to leave for Bangor, Maine. He had no particular animus against the man, just curiosity.

And he coveted his suitcase. He'd always had a vague, unarticulated belief that it might be possible to commit a crime with no fear of reprisal, if only one didn't plan it in advance. The other man had consumed nearly a quart of whiskey. The weather was frigid. They'd walked along the river, where he'd taken Richard by the arm, to keep him from stumbling. He knew Richard kept his keys and wallet in the inside pocket of his worsted overcoat. It was easy to slide them out, under pretense of pulling the coat more tightly about his companion, to keep him warm. Even easier, as they approached an unlit stretch behind the mill, to push him into the river.

He left a note to the company manager in the hotel, imitating Richard's handwriting: an unexpected letter from his former wife gave him hope of a rapprochement, therefore Richard was leaving directly to meet her in Saugaus, Michigan. He'd left on the next train for Boston with Richard's belongings, traveling from there to Manhattan.

Now he gently stroked the doll's dark hair. Her sleep-glass eyes gleamed in the gas light. He didn't think of her as a toy, but as a girl composed of his memories of all those other girls.

Those other girls talked too much. All girls did. That was why the moving pictures were perfect for them. Kathlyn Williams or Mary Pickford or Lillian Gish—no matter how many times they were threatened on the screen, they always escaped. Their innocence couldn't be assailed.

He knew that innocence was a fraud. Diminutive and doll-like, Pickford and Gish looked much younger than their years, which was why they continued to be cast as near children. Every performer he'd ever known lied. Chaplin at least was honest. He liked flirting with young girls, and they liked him back.

He embraced the doll. For just a few more minutes, her name would be Iolanda. Her white pinny had been starched and clean when he'd found her, her dark hair covered by a pert maroon bow, now limp. He carried her to the table and laid her on it, facedown; unbuttoned the back of her pinafore and removed it, then the plaid dress beneath. He folded the clothes carefully, went to the corner, and opened the suitcase. A breath of rot exuded from it, despite the balls of camphor sprinkled inside.

Beneath his clothes and other items of his trade was a pile of neatly folded dresses, skirts, chemises. He pressed Iolanda's dress and pinafore to his face, inhaling the scent that barely clung there now. The camphor would quickly overpower what remained. He placed her clothing with the rest, closed the suitcase, and locked it.

He retrieved his scissors and, setting the yellow dress on top of the doll, began to carefully snip away the excess fabric. As always, the dress was too big, but he had grown more adept over the years. He stopped often, holding a sleeve alongside an arm, measuring with his thumb joint, clipping loose threads. A long time passed before he was content with his handiwork. When he was finished, he slipped the dress over the doll's head and stood her on the chair.

The dress ended a few inches above her ankles. Not a perfectly even hem, but a few pins fixed that. The sleeves were just about right; when he folded back the cuffs, you couldn't tell they hadn't been made to order. He ran his fingers across the soft folds that fell to her knees, smoothing them out. He regretted not having kept her yellow hair ribbon. He untied Iolanda's wilted maroon bow and tied it around the doll's waist; straightened and took a step back to gaze at her.

"Perfect," he murmured.

He gathered the doll into his arms. Her body felt stiff and unyielding after the girl's, but that was what he loved about dolls, their quiescence. Even standing upright, glass eyes wide open, they dreamed: lying alongside them, he could impose his own longings upon them, just as children did to their own dolls.

But most of all he treasured the way the phantom presence of flesh-and-blood girls would, fleetingly, animate the face, the limbs. It was like a theatrical performance or moving picture, one that you could enter and leave at will. He buried his face in the buttercup-yellow fabric, breathing in the scents of ice cream and lemon drops and, more faintly, Sydenham's syrup.

"Maria." He murmured the new name, waking her, and carried her into the other room.

Chapter 29

Pɪɴ sʜᴏᴠᴇᴅ ᴛʜʀᴏᴜɢʜ the crowd on the midway. Gone were the families and picnickers. The park belonged to serious revelers now, workers escaping jobs in stockyards and slaughterhouses, hospitals and whorehouses, small shops and the monolithic department store Marshall Field's. Ballmann's musicians had moved to the Palace Ballroom, where some nights more than a thousand couples came to dance. On the bandstand, Ballmann's men were replaced by a ragtime band whose members came from the Sunny South show, eager to cut loose. "Searchlight Rag" echoed from a dance-hall piano, polkas from the beer gardens. At the Ten-in-One, Red Friend belted the same bally he'd been shouting all day beneath his faded-green canvas umbrella.

"Happened right where you're standing, friend—that very spot!"

She found an empty bench and sat, exhausted; squeezed her eyes shut and tried not to see the dead girl's face, pale and swollen as a sponge. Pin wondered if her mother would be working the dance hall tonight. She imagined her pulling a man in a seersucker suit onto the dance floor, grabbing his arms as they swung around in the grizzly bear. A third person joined them, a girl. No, a doll, flopping around their feet. The man stepped on her face, and her mother screamed as the doll pushed itself up and began to turn, its face no longer a doll's.

Pin woke, her heart racing. She lurched to her feet and hugged herself, fighting tears, and continued walking.

She considered returning to the shack, yet tired as she was, she knew she wouldn't fall asleep there. The Kansas Cyclone next door ran the same one-reeler until closing time, accompanied by noisy flourishes from the pianist.

Still, Ikie and the others sometimes hung around the Cyclone. Pin was cautious of spending too much time with them, or anyone, but sometimes her loneliness felt like cold fingers pinching her throat. Ikie and Mugsy and the rest were her age or older, and bigger than she was. At first they'd treated her like a kid brother.

But as the season got under way, the others worked the rides and games for fifteen hours at a stretch, stealing a few free minutes when they could. They were constantly brawling—real fights, sometimes the cops had to break them up. Mugsy stole bottles of beer to share. Ikie flirted with colored girls and, because he looked older, sometimes took them dancing. And they all talked about girls incessantly.

She felt neither girl nor boy but trapped in between. Like an out-of-focus bit of film, one of those fragments where the sprockets didn't line up. She knew what happened to those damaged frames: they got burned up by the projector or edited out and thrown away.

The trick was to stay out of focus, but on purpose. To always keep moving, hands in her pockets and cap pulled down low to make her look tough. After her sister disappeared, Pin's mother gave her a shiv that Pin kept in her pocket. Some nights, waiting for her mother to return from the dance hall, she'd fall asleep on the pallet they shared with the knife in her hand.

"Watch it, you fucking punk!"

A drunk bumped into her, nearly knocking her to the ground. A big guy, suspenders loose over his slack belly. Pin slipped a hand into her pocket to touch the blade, its steel cool and reassuring. She gazed at the drunk, and her eyes went funny: she saw two figures stepping into the boat at Hell Gate, the girl in yellow hopping onto the man's lap. She sucked in her breath. Was this the same man?

But of course it wasn't him. He'd already joined the crowd of stewed monkeys at the High Striker, waiting to try their luck with the mallet. The game was rigged; all the games were rigged. Pin knuckled her eyes, tasted something sour at the back of her mouth. Kept moving.

Chapter 30

It was late when Max finally sat down in his apartment and counted out his day's earnings. Seven dollars and thirty-five cents. A pathetic haul for a Saturday. He stared at the piles of coins, trying to recall where the spare dime had gone; then remembered he'd given that punk Pin a dime in addition to his streetcar fare. The kid's mother must be a whore—fortune-tellers often were, especially if there was no husband in tow. But she could still feed her kid.

Slut, he thought, and poured himself another tumbler of whiskey. It scorched his throat, burning away the memory of Pin's half-starved face, the postcard image of a childlike woman with a waist no bigger than a doll's. Tomorrow was Sunday: the park would be crowded, and by late afternoon men would be lined up three-deep in front of his tent. He'd be able to make up for today's shortfall if he kept his head clear. He finished the whiskey and stumbled off to bed.

Chapter 31

SHE FOUND IKIE and Mugsy in the alley behind the Kansas Cyclone building, sitting on upturned barrels. Ikie waved her over.

"Want one?" He jabbed a thumb at a paper cone of fried potatoes in his lap. "Clyde told me you got a case of the crazies. All hopped up about kidnappers."

Pin wolfed down a potato, staring at the beer bottle in Mugsy's hand. "Gimme some of that and I'll tell you what I saw."

Mugsy hesitated, then gave it to her. "Tastes like piss anyway," he said.

"You would know," retorted Pin, and took a swallow of warm beer. "So I'm over by Hell Gate, and I see this guy. He goes into the tunnel with a girl, she's twelve maybe. He comes out. She doesn't."

Ikie made a face. "You sure?"

"Yeah. This other fella I talked to, he saw them, too—kind of a dingbat, he hangs around all day watching kids on the rides."

"A chester," sneered Mugsy.

"Maybe. Seems more like he has snakes in his boots. But that's not the point. I asked Clyde did he see them, but he couldn't remember. So I go back inside a little while ago and…"

Saying anything more would make it real. She stared down the dark alley. At last she said, "I took one of the boats and hopped out onto the ledge and walked to where Clyde or whoever's doing Satan is."

"You did not," said Ikie.

"I did. That's where I found her. The girl. Dead."

Mugsy leaned closer. "How'd she die?"

"I don't know. She didn't have her clothes on—I mean, the dress, when I saw her go in, she wore a yellow dress. But inside, she only had on her shimmy. And this..."

She slid her hand into her pocket and withdrew the dirty yellow ribbon. "It fell into the canal. Her body. I saw it float away. That's when I ran out."

She waited for them to mock her or laugh. But they just continued to stare.

"Who'd you tell?" Ikie asked.

"No one. Johnny Iacono was working the exit, I told him."

Ikie shook his head. "Why didn't you—"

The clamor of the police station's alarm bell abruptly silenced him. Pin jumped as a man shouted her name.

"Pin!"

Ikie and Mugsy fled. Pin made it only halfway down the alley before someone grabbed her collar and yanked her off her feet.

"I didn't do nothing!" she protested.

"Who said you did?"

Fatty Bacon peered past her, but the boys had scattered. He lowered her to the ground and clamped a hand around her wrist. He looked grim.

"You know what I need to talk to you about. Johnny Iacono said you told him about the body in the Hell Gate. Were they with you?" He gestured at the overturned barrels.

"No. I just got here. I—"

"Wait till we get to the station."

"I didn't do nothing!" she yelped as he dragged her down the alley. "I was the one trying to find her! Ow, leggo, that *hurts.*"

"Why didn't you report what you saw?"

Because you're a fucking copper, she thought, and stared at him with hatred. Fatty's mouth tightened.

"Well, you can make your report now," he said. "Stop squirming, no one's hurting you."

"Says you," spat Pin as he hauled her to the station.

Chapter 32

RIVERVIEW'S POLICE FORCE was housed in a trim brick building near the park's entrance. A dozen sergeants were on staff, most of them part-time constables. Pin had never been inside before. She recited a silent Hail Mary, praying they wouldn't pat her down and find her shiv—or discover she wasn't a boy.

Men mobbed the main room, shouting or talking excitedly. Riverview cops and also Dr. Overcash, who had an office on the premises of the Infant Incubators and often stayed there overnight.

"Francis!" Captain Hickey pushed his way through the room, barely glancing at Pin. "Bring the boy in here."

Fatty poked her in the back, indicating an office. Hickey looked over his shoulder and yelled, "Get O'Connell in here, I need someone to write this down."

The room had a desk, a table in the back, several chairs, and a framed photograph of the Riverview force saluting President Taft, whose bulk was superior to Hickey's, but not by much. The captain leaned against the desk, his face red, and nervously stroked his mustache. He was a stout white man, red haired like Fatty. His hazel eyes

97

glinted behind wire-rimmed spectacles, and instead of a high-domed helmet he favored a fedora, now sitting on the desk.

"Have a seat, young man," he said, pointing to a chair.

Fatty let go of her wrist, and Pin turned to the police captain. "I told him, I was just—"

Hickey held up a meaty hand. "Not till the recorder gets here. You need to wait until you're asked a question before speaking."

Pin sat and stared at the floor, her heart racing. She gnawed her lip, hands shoved in her pockets, while Fatty and Hickey spoke together in low voices. A few minutes later O'Connell rushed in, a young sergeant carrying a small typewriter.

"Sorry." He hurried around the desk and set down the typewriter. "Steiner at Robey Street didn't want to loan it to us. I waited till he got called out, and Wilkes let me take it. Just be sure it's out of sight when Cabell arrives."

Fatty's lip curled at Cabell's name. "Did you tell them what we needed it for?"

"Absolutely not. But they'll be here soon enough. And I keep telling you, if we had our own typewriter, we wouldn't have to—"

For the first time O'Connell noticed Pin. He turned to Hickey in surprise. "Surely this wee lad didn't do it?"

Hickey shot O'Connell a warning look. "We're just questioning this young man. Could you please close the door, Mr. O'Connell?"

The captain turned to Pin and began to speak, not unkindly. "Sergeant Bacon or I will ask you questions, and Sergeant O'Connell will record them on the stenotype machine. That way we'll know exactly what you said. Are you ready?"

"Yes," she muttered.

"First, what's your name?"

"Pin."

"Pin what?"

"Pin Maffucci."

"That's a queer name, *Pin*. Is it short for something?"

"No."

"Who's your father, Pin?"

"Don't got one."

Hickey glanced at Fatty, who nodded. "His mother's that Gypsy fortune-teller by the cabaret. Madame Zanto," he explained. "Real name's Regina Maffucci. This is the first year she's worked here."

Hickey turned back to Pin. "I see. How old are you, Pin?"

"Fourteen."

Hickey raised an eyebrow. "Fourteen?"

"My birthday's in April," she retorted. "April nineteenth."

Hickey looked at O'Connell, who shrugged and tapped the information into the stenotype. "You work here, Pin? I see you running around with your friends. Some of those boys are hooligans. Got a job?"

She avoided his eyes. "I do odd jobs. Help out when someone needs it."

When she didn't continue, Hickey nodded. "All right, then. Why don't you tell us what happened this afternoon?"

She recounted it all from the beginning. Most of it, anyway; some. She didn't mention that the missing girl reminded her of the girl she'd seen at Essanay—she didn't mention the studio at all. Hickey asked most of the questions. Occasionally Fatty would break in, as O'Connell continued to type her answers.

"Sergeant Bacon said you found a girl's hair ribbon. May I see it?"

She gave it to him with reluctance. Hickey turned it over in his hand. He shot a look at Fatty, then set the ribbon on the desk. "Can you describe the man who was with her?"

"He had on a hat. A boater. Seersucker jacket, I think. Or I dunno, maybe it was just a suit."

"Was he a colored man?"

"No. He was white."

"How can you be sure?"

"I dunno. He looked like a white man."

"What color hair?"

"Dunno. The hat."

"If the hat hid his face, how could you be sure he was a white man?"

"He just was."

Hickey drummed his fingers on the desk. "What else?"

She bit her lip, thinking. "He had a mustache, maybe. Red or blond. Or light brown. I'm not sure, he might not have had one."

"Red or blond or light brown. Maybe. Jesus." Hickey puffed his cheeks out. "Got that, O'Connell? Red or blond or brown mustache. Maybe."

"Could be anyone," said Fatty.

Hickey sighed. "What else can you remember, son? There must be something."

Pin closed her eyes. "That's all."

Hickey paced to the window, peered out at the people on the midway. He lowered the shade.

"That queer little man you mentioned—why did you approach him?" he asked, turning back to her. "You said he was a stranger. You weren't up to any mischief like your pal Mugsy Morrissey, were you?"

"You know I wouldn't."

"Then why'd you go talk to him?"

"I seen him hanging around sometimes." Pin averted her gaze from the captain's. She shouldn't have told him anything.

"You said he told you he was part of some society called the Gemini?"

"He showed me a card and that's what it said. Gemini Child Protectors, something like that."

"Did you get his name?"

"No." It was her first outright lie.

"Can you describe him?"

"No."

"No? You talked to this man and you don't know what he looked like?"

"He looked like a regular man."

Hickey frowned. "What about the card—was his name on the card?"

"I don't think so. I can't remember."

Hickey glanced at Fatty and O'Connell. "Gemini Child Protectors—ever heard of them?"

The two sergeants shook their heads. Hickey rubbed his chin.

"Maybe a private agency hired by the parents," he mused. "If this was a kidnapping that went wrong." He returned his attention to Pin. "Why'd you go speak to Lord Clyde?"

"Some days he plays Satan in Hell Gate. I thought he might've seen the girl in the yellow dress."

O'Connell looked up from the stenotype machine. "Clyde's surname?"

"Smithson," said Fatty. "Clyde Smithson. He's the Negro magician at the freak show. Never had any complaints about Clyde."

Pin looked at him, startled. "Nobody has! Jesus Christ."

"Watch your tongue, boy. You said he'd just gotten off working at Hell Gate when you saw him," Hickey went on. "You told him about the missing girl, but he didn't remember seeing her." Hickey stared at her pointedly, and she felt a spike of panic. "If Clyde was working inside the attraction, wouldn't he have noticed if something went awry, and reported it?"

She shook her head. "He couldn't check 'cause he had to get to his show at the Ten-in-One. He had to dress in a hurry."

"So he was changing his clothes when you saw him at the Ten-in-One?"

"No. He already had his suit on."

Hickey and Fatty exchanged a look. Hickey brooded, finally asked, "Why didn't you report this to the police when it happened, Pin? There something you're not telling us? This girl, did you know her? Anything happen between you and her that you want to tell me?"

Pin stared at him, aghast. "What? No!"

Hickey stood for a long time, waiting for her to say something. She clenched her hands in her lap and refused to look at him. After a minute, he turned toward O'Connell. "You got all that?"

O'Connell nodded. Someone knocked at the door and cracked it open.

"Sir, Captain Cabell is here from Robey Street station."

Hickey waved him off. After the door closed, he shook his head. "Goddamn it. Now it'll all go to hell." He pointed at the stenotype machine. "Get that out of here before that son of a bitch sees it. Bacon, ask someone to escort this young man home. I want him in his mother's custody for the night."

"I'll bring him," Fatty replied quickly. Pin scowled. Now the stupid bastard would know where she lived.

Captain Hickey grabbed his hat from the desk. He gave Pin a terse nod of dismissal. "If you hear or see anything else, I'll trust you to let us know immediately. Especially about that man, the detective or whatever the hell he is."

Hickey left. O'Connell followed, the stenotype machine bundled beneath his uniform jacket. Pin stared sullenly at the floor, willing Fatty to leave.

Instead he stepped to the door, motioning impatiently for her to join him. "Well, let's get you home," he said. "It's going to be a long night for the rest of us."

He hustled her through the crowded waiting room. She was almost out the door before she heard a familiar voice shouting from somewhere behind her, demanding to see a lawyer. Clyde Smithson.

Chapter 33

THE PARK HAD closed early, its electrical lights extinguished. Before Pin could run off into the darkness, Fatty grabbed her.

"You heard the captain. I'm to see you home."

She tried to shake him off, but he yanked her upright.

"Now you listen to me, goddamn it!" he exclaimed, and raised his nightstick. "A little girl's been murdered. I don't want anything to happen to you or anyone else on my watch. So shut your gab. If you promise not to run away, I won't keep hold of you. But if you run off, so help me God…"

Pin gave him a cold stare, but nodded. He released her arm. "Good lad. Now let's get you home."

It was late, after midnight. A few custodians still emptied trash bins and swept up horse dung along the Pike. Two city policemen on motorcycles raced past. The coasters and other attractions looked ghostly, except for Hell Gate. The devil atop the pavilion blazed in the glare of spotlights. Policemen swarmed over the boats in the holding area, carrying kerosene lamps and flashlights. A lone figure with a lantern peered into the mouth of the tunnel. Pin glanced uneasily up at Fatty.

"Who's Cabell?"

"Captain of the Robey Street station. Any serious crime here falls under his purview. But we've never had much in the way of serious crime. And never a murder."

They crossed to the other side of the Pike. Passing the Ten-in-One, Pin felt her throat tighten. She wished she'd never mentioned Clyde. She hesitated, then asked, "How did she die?"

At first she thought Fatty wouldn't answer. "She was suffocated," he said at last. "That's what Doc Overcash said. We just called him in the event—in the event that there was anything to be done. We'll have to wait for the official cause of death from the coroner. But it seems that she was smothered."

The policeman set his hand on her shoulder, but gently. "That was an ugly thing for you to see, Pin. A terrible thing." He shook his head. "Where exactly do you live?"

"That alley by the Cyclone. I can go from here."

"I'd like to say hello to your mother. Put her mind at ease if she's been worried about you."

"Probably she won't even be there," Pin said quickly, alarmed. "I can just go on my own. She wouldn't worry, anyway."

"She might if she's heard about what happened."

He steered her down the alley, toward the trash-strewn lot. Something rustled in the shadows, and Pin stiffened as a cat streaked in front of them. When she looked up, her mother stood in the doorway of the tiny shack, holding a kerosene lantern.

"Is that your mother?" For the first time Fatty sounded uneasy, almost shy.

Pin nodded miserably. Her mother looked disheveled and suspicious. After Abriana's disappearance, Gina began to disappear, too. She shrank from Pin, as though her bones might crumble at her touch. Pin wondered how she could stand to be handled by the men she danced with. Alcohol helped, she knew that, and the laudanum syrup she kept in a tin box alongside their mattress.

"Pin? What are you doing?"

She hadn't gone dancing. She'd removed the cheap bangles she favored for fortune-telling, but still wore her Gypsy clothes—a short skirt that fell halfway below the knee, cheap red silk over Rusleen petti-coats. Her shirtwaist was too big, her thick dark hair loosed from the amber combs she usually wore. Her garnet earrings caught the light and glowed—the only truly beautiful things she owned. Pin approached her hesitantly, flinching when she saw her mother's face grow rigid.

"It's all right, Ma," she said as Gina covered her mouth, staring at Fatty Bacon. Stepping beside her, Pin caught the candied scent of soothing syrup and the Sen-Sen Gina chewed to mask it. "There's no trouble, Ma, I'm fine!"

"Yes, ma'am, that's right." Bacon removed his helmet. "Well, no, that's not true." He smoothed his hair nervously. "There's trouble, but Pin here's not in it. I just wanted to make sure he got home safely."

"Safely?" Gina shook her head. She sounded as though she'd swal-lowed a mouthful of honey. "I don't understand. What's not safe? Did they, did they—"

Pin cut her off before she could mention Abriana. "Nothing, Ma! I told you—"

"Don't you lie." Gina grabbed her wrist. "What happened? What did they find?"

He stepped toward them and raised a hand. "You might as well hear it from me, Mrs. Maffucci. Someone was killed on one of the rides today."

Gina murmured something in Italian and crossed herself. "The Blue Streak?"

"No, ma'am." Bacon turned his helmet over in his big freckled hands. "A girl was murdered. In Hell Gate."

Gina cried out and sagged against the doorframe. Pin caught the lantern as Bacon hurried to her side. Together they half carried Gina the few steps to the mattress on the floor. Pin helped her lie down. When she looked up, she saw Bacon staring at her mother with pity.

"It's a terrible thing," he said. "Your boy, he was the one who found her. That's a brave son you have there, not many boys would have done what he did."

Was he mocking her? Bacon caught her look. He tilted his head at the bottle of soothing syrup on the floor, and continued, "I just wanted to make sure the lad was safe. And you."

His gaze flickered across the tiny room, and Pin cringed. A single chair and a metal trunk that held their clothes and served as her mother's dressing table. A chamber pot with an ill-fitting lid. Pin's spare clothes hung from nails on the wall, knickerbocker trousers and a grimy white shirt.

Bacon cleared his throat. "Do you have someone you can stay with, Mrs. Maffucci? Family elsewhere in the city? Your parents?"

Gina shook her head. "Not till fall," she whispered.

"We'll be fine," said Pin fiercely. "We *are* fine."

Bacon appeared unconvinced. At last he said, "Well. I have to get back to the station house."

Gina nodded and brushed a flyaway hair from her face. "What's your name again?"

"Francis Bacon."

"Of course. Sergeant Bacon. I recognize you." She gave him a crooked smile. "I work on the Pike. Madame Zanto, the fortune-teller."

"I've seen you, too." Bacon slid his helmet back onto his head. "I'll try to keep an eye on your place."

"We'll be fine," repeated Pin. Her mother nodded.

"Thank you so much, Mr. Bacon," she said.

He crossed to the door, the floorboards buckling beneath his heavy boots, and left.

"Good riddance," Pin said, and sank onto the mattress. "Are you all right, Ma?"

Gina turned to her, face aflame. Before Pin could move, she'd struck her cheek. Pin reeled backward and hit the wall, so hard the shack quivered.

"*Why were you there?*" Gina tried to grab her hair, but Pin had already scrambled away. "Do you want to die, too?"

She lunged at Pin, but her daughter's hand closed around her wrist. She felt the knobs in Gina's wrist, skin so papery thin it scarcely seemed to cover bone.

"Stop, Ma," she said through gritted teeth. *"Stop."*

Gina stiffened, straining against her. Pin feared her wrist might snap like balsa. After a few seconds her mother's face went slack. Pin released her, and Gina's body seemed to disappear within her shabby clothing as she sank to the floor.

"Why would you do that?" she kept repeating. "Why, why…"

Pin dropped beside her. "Ma, don't," she cried. "Please don't. I'm sorry, I'm so sorry."

Her mother rested her head upon Pin's shoulder. She stroked Pin's hair, pressed her cheek against her daughter's. Pin flinched, and her mother drew back, gazed at Pin's face, and tugged a finger through her daughter's matted curls.

"We need to cut it again soon," she said. "Help me out of my clothes."

Pin hated this task. The metal hooks and eyes dug at her fingers, and she struggled with the buttons on her mother's boots.

"Why don't you just get new ones?" she demanded, yanking off one boot and throwing it into a corner. "These are falling apart. They smell."

"Why do you think?" her mother replied wearily.

For Pin, all that was over. She could pull her shirts on over her head. Her trousers had sensible buttons, the kind that didn't need a buttonhook. Her boots laced up. She never needed to bother with her hair, except to cut it.

"Pin…?" Gina murmured, eyelids drooping. Pin set aside her mother's clothes and helped her lie down. Gina whispered, "Thanks," eyes dark in her sunken face as Pin lay next to her, watched her mother's chest rise and fall. After a long time, her eyes fluttered open to stare at Pin.

"I miss my daughter," she whispered.

"I do, too."

Gina shook her head. "Not Abriana."

Pin drew closer. She began to cry. "Oh, Ma," she said. But her mother was already asleep.

Chapter 34

HE SLEPT SOUNDLY, as he always did afterward; woke and lay on his side to gaze at the form beside him. Early morning sunlight brought out minute imperfections in her face, spots where a bit of grime or soot had permeated the unglazed porcelain. He pushed back the blanket and rearranged her dress, tugging it down to cover her spindle-shaped legs and soft torso stuffed with excelsior. He preferred the cool smooth touch of her bisque limbs and cheeks to the soft places, except her hair. He buried his face in her ringlets. They had a sweet grassy smell, nothing like human hair at all. He wondered sometimes if the company had substituted horsehair, but that would have been difficult to curl.

He roused himself and put on clean clothes, a new shirt and the pink seersucker suit and jacket he hadn't worn in two months. He got a basin and cloth, returned to the bedroom to clean her. When he finished, he picked her up, her porcelain chin on his shoulder, and carried her to the other room. He set her in a chair, carefully arranging her legs so they hung over the edge, fluffed her hair, straightened her dress. Turning, he went to the windowsill and plucked a small round tin from his shaving bag, a pot of rouge. He dabbed a bit on his fingertip, returned to the doll, and ran his finger across her mouth, tracing her lips. With a handkerchief, he wiped off his finger, stood back, and reviewed his work. Mouths often lacked definition in photographs, but he wanted her to look lifelike, not whorish.

Satisfied, he turned and retrieved his camera from beneath the bed. He spent the next few minutes adjusting the doll's limbs, trying to make her resemble the girl as he remembered her, not in the boat but earlier when, replete with ice cream, she'd finally accepted first one lemon drop, then a second.

He finally stopped posing her. He knew from experience that he could lose hours like this, with the same outcome he'd achieved twice already since last night. He had no time for that now. He had scant time to develop his film, and he couldn't afford to squander it.

He shot his photos, a dozen in all, making certain some film remained for later. He hoped he would have another opportunity to take more pictures with a different model in the next few days. He'd hold off on developing the film until then. Back East, he'd purchased a Kodak film tank, a portable developer that had proved invaluable.

He replaced the camera under his bed and picked up the doll, crushing her to him as he inhaled the scent that still clung to her dress, a whiff of vanilla ice cream and lemon. For a long time he stood, rocking back and forth, until he heard the clatter of a milk wagon in the street. He kissed her cool forehead, pulled a key from his pocket, and carried her to the closet. He stood her inside and locked the door.

Only then did he allow himself to retrieve his greatest treasures from the suitcase: a sheaf of photographs nestled within a leather folder. Each one showed a doll—always the same doll, but you would never know it. He had dressed and posed her so naturally that, as he fanned out the photos, it seemed to him as though he held an entire garden of beautiful creatures in his hands.

His fingers trembled as he recalled the name of each girl: Maria, Iolanda, Abriana, Deirdre, and all the others. The Italian girl,

Abriana, had been so pliant and vacant of expression that she might truly have been a life-size doll. Yet her beauty, like that of the others, would have been lost forever, save for these images. The innocent symmetry of the doll's features would never change, never age; never be tainted by betrayal. They were his alone, always.

Chapter 35

PIN WOKE, FOR once, long before her mother. Floating between sleep and wakefulness, she waited for the sun's rays to creep down the alley. A devil's face danced in front of her, twisting into a Kewpie doll's and then her sister's, which was the same face as the girl's in the tunnel, only laughing. With a cry she sat up, looked down to see if she'd awakened her mother.

No. Gina slept through anything. As Pin's heart slowed, she stared at the dingy sheet, the muslin panels Gina had pinned over the windows to provide some privacy, the red utility bag where her mother kept her few cosmetics and fortune-telling cards.

Everything was as it had been when she woke yesterday morning. How could the entire world change, yet her mother still keep her face powder in a stained red bag?

She slid from bed, pulled her boots over her bare feet, and went outside. She snuck into the back of the Cyclone building and made her way to the utility washroom, used the toilet, then washed her face and arms. She drank water straight from the faucet until her stomach bulged, and hurried back to the shack. Her stomach cramped from hunger, an ache she'd grown accustomed to. Drinking a lot of water helped, but not much.

In the distance, the giant cuckoo clock chimed eight. Pin sat cross-legged on the floor and reached for the magazine Larry had given her. She flipped through the pages until she found the continuation of a story she'd started last month.

CHAPTER III: AMONG THE MISSING

"Where is the coach?" he cried. "Where are Jane Mint, One-Eyed Dell, and the Eskimo woman, Kittigazuit?"

She read until she finished the chapter and tossed the magazine aside. She bellied onto the mattress and gazed at the wall, where she'd tacked Clyde's photo alongside an advertising card for Vin Fiz grape soda, with a color portrait of the aviatrix Harriet Quimby, clad in knee-high leather boots, trousers, aviator goggles, and a plum-colored satin jacket with a hood.

On April 16, 1912, Harriet had flown across the English Channel in those clothes—the first woman to achieve such a feat. But because the *Titanic* had sunk the day before, no one remembered Harriet Quimby.

Pin did. She'd watched a Mutoscope of Harriet's flight dozens of times, memorizing Harriet's masculine attire, her knowing smile. Two and a half months after she'd flown across the Channel, Harriet died when her monoplane crashed during a Boston air show. The only time Pin had cried harder was when Abriana disappeared.

Glory loved Harriet, too. The first time Pin visited the film studio, she'd stopped at her room to ask for directions and spotted a color poster of the beautiful woman in plum-colored satin and black leather, standing in front of her plane. A bold signature swooped across the image.

Yours affectionately, Harriet Quimby.

"Holy smokes." Pin barely glanced at the girl bent over an ironing board across from her. "Where'd you get this?"

The girl set down the iron. She seemed unperturbed that a strange boy had walked into her dressing room. "G.M. gave it to me. He knew her—she wrote for the movies before she began to fly."

"She did?"

"Sure. What, you think girls can't write?" The girl gave Pin a scornful look and reached to flick Pin's cap. "Who are you, kid?"

"Pin."

"Pin? What kind of name's that?"

"Nickname." Pin hesitated. She'd stopped explaining it after she got beat up too many times, but this girl was unlikely to beat her up. "They called me that when I was little, 'cause I was small and sharp."

"Sharp? I'll decide that." She leaned against the wall. "I'm Glory. Gloria May, but they call me Glory." She grinned. "Because I'm so glorious."

She stuck out a hand, the way a boy would. Pin took it, trying to think of something clever to say, finally just shrugged. "Pleased to meet you."

Glory dropped her hand. "You looking for someone?"

"Yeah. Lionel Gerring. He's a writer—know where I can find him?"

"Stage, probably. That way." She pointed into the corridor. "Maybe I'll see you later. Or drop by anytime. I'll be around somewhere."

In her room, Pin gazed at the picture of Harriet Quimby but thought of Glory. Maybe she'd invite her to the amusement park one day. Maybe she'd get another chance to hold her hand, on one of the coasters or the Old Mill. Not Hell Gate. She wouldn't go inside there again on a dare.

She did a futile search of the shack in hopes of finding something edible, spotted a tin of lemon drops tucked into her mother's red bag. But the tin was empty. She dug around in the bag till she came up with a dime. Sometimes her mother gave her money for food, but usually she forgot. Pin checked to make sure her mother was breathing evenly, and went outside.

She wondered with apprehension if the park would even be open the day after a murder. But Matthew, the manager of the Kansas Cyclone theater, had already arrived for work. He stood in front of the

Cyclone building, staring, baffled, at a piece of camera equipment in his hands. A projector. He glanced up as she approached.

"Heya, kid. You don't got a pin on ya, do you?"

She shook her head. "Sorry."

Matthew sighed. "Something's stuck in here, but I'm afraid if I try to fix it, it'll fall apart."

"Can I see?"

Matthew squinted at her. "You know about projectors?"

Nodding, she fooled with the projector's gate. She managed to open it and felt inside until she found the culprit.

"Here it is." She held up a shriveled strip that looked like a piece of dried-up bacon. "A piece of melted film got stuck. Someone should've cleaned it out."

She flicked it away and handed the projector back to Matthew. "How old is that thing, anyway?"

Matthew shot her a wry look. "Old."

"I figured." She pointed at the slot the film passed through as the projector ran. "Those older cameras they used to shoot with, the film wasn't, you know, perforated. So they'd punch in the holes after they processed it. But everyone uses different kinds of perforators, and the holes don't always line up with the wheels in the projector. You should get a Bell and Howell perforator, that's what they use at Essanay."

"Bell and Howell, huh?" Matthew regarded Pin, amused but also impressed.

"Yeah. And tell your projectionist that if the film tears, he should clip it out right away. Otherwise it'll burn up—that's how that big fire in Des Moines started."

Matthew hefted the projector. "Thanks, kid. You're the one lives back in the shed there with your ma, right?" Pin saw a flash of sympathy in his eyes. "I'll tell Felix what you said. Bell and Howell, right?" He dug in his pocket and flipped Pin a nickel.

She ambled onto the Pike. It was not yet ten o'clock and already scorching hot. The air shimmered above the freshly raked gravel path, and mist drifted into the Fairyland woods, obscuring the picnic tables beneath the trees. The woods bordered the North Branch of the Chicago River. From the other side of the river, the scaffolding of the Velvet Coaster resembled the gasworks in Little Hell. A small tributary, barely a stream, trickled off from the North Branch, marking the boundary between the amusement park and the abandoned factories known as Bricktown.

You could see Bricktown from Fairyland, and smell it, too, the lingering tang of acrid smoke from the kilns and dung from the horses that used to haul off carts piled with pink Chicago bricks. After the Great Fire, the city banned wooden buildings. Brick factories filled this part of the North Side, with their clay pits and kilns and hobo workers hopping on and off the freight trains destined for the slaughterhouses in Packingtown.

In other parts of Chicago, the brickyards had been shut down by those who objected to the stink and noise, the shifting population of vagrants who worked there. Ikie insisted that the factories in Bricktown had closed, yet its kilns still roared intermittently, belching black smoke and flames. Some nights you could hear voices. Rumor was the Black Hand came to Bricktown in the middle of the night and burned the bodies of the people they killed.

The giant cuckoo clock began to count the hour as the Blue Streak coaster made its safety run, empty cars rattling like a runaway milk wagon. The final stroke of ten had not quite died away when the screamer march "Thunder and Blazes" rang out from Ballmann's bandstand. Riverview Amusement Park was open for the day.

Frowning, Pin surveyed the crowds streaming through the entrance gate. Hadn't news of the girl's murder hit the papers? At the least, she'd thought that parents might keep their younger kids at home, especially girls.

But no—it was just another Sunday. People beelined for the Tickler and Aerostat and Flying Bobs, the Jack Rabbit coaster and Gyroplane. Already a long line had formed for the Hippodrome, where an Italian movie, *The Inferno,* had been showing all month. Mugsy and Ikie had snuck in and claimed there were scenes of naked people.

She wondered what was going on at Hell Gate. She got as far as the terminus for the Miniature Railway and halted.

The dark ride had been roped off, a group of city policemen milling around its entrance. She continued on cautiously, but as she drew near the unattended ticket booth, a cop yelled at her.

"Ride's closed, kid." He made a shooing motion.

Pin waited till he turned away and kept walking, maintaining a safe distance from the cops. Men in shirtsleeves and rolled-up trousers waded through the canal, dragging nets on long poles through the water. Every few minutes, they'd shake out whatever they'd dredged up onto the boardwalk. Pin covered her nose as the wind carried the stink of accumulated muck.

After a quarter hour, a tall, broad-shouldered man in a uniform strode toward the front of the pavilion. The cops stopped whatever they were doing to assemble around him. He wore a dark-blue fedora like Captain Hickey's and had a jowly face, a mouth like a loose seam that flapped as he spoke. She strained to hear him through the din of rides and screams, Red Friend's endless chant.

"Happened right where you're standing, friend—that very spot!"

The man in the fedora raised his hands, as though to silence the calliope and coasters.

"Gentlemen, thank you all for being here this morning. Mr. Baumgarten does not want a panic, and neither do we," he announced calmly, as though used to this kind of gathering. "I assured him we'd patrol the grounds, but do our best not to interfere with the normal doings of the park…"

He must be Captain Cabell, Pin realized, the man Hickey had called a son of a bitch.

"As you all know," he went on, "the commissioner is on vacation in Wisconsin, but he's been notified of what's happened. And we now have a suspect in custody. The child's parents have come forward and identified her. I'll be speaking to the newspapers sometime this afternoon at the Robey Street station. Till then, don't talk to any reporters. Or anyone else."

He took a step back and clapped his hands. "So! Back to work, gentlemen. I'll call in reinforcements as needed. I hope they won't be."

He strode off toward the park entrance. The men returned to dredging the canal, and the cops dispersed. All were armed with billy clubs, and she saw two who carried guns in holsters around their waists.

Pin abruptly remembered she wasn't supposed to be here. As she turned to go, she saw Larry a few yards off, also watching the proceedings. She hesitated, then walked over to him.

"What the hell you doing here?" he snarled.

"Just watching. Like you."

"I'm here 'cause I'm not *there*." He pointed at the empty ticket booth.

"Think they'll open it later?"

"You an imbecile?"

He glanced past Pin, then swiftly walked away. She looked over to see a policeman heading in their direction and took off after Larry.

"Maybe they'll open later," she said when she caught up with him. "Captain Cabell back there just said they already have someone in custody."

Larry stopped to stare at her in disbelief. "You know who that suspect is?"

"No."

"Clyde. What the hell did you tell them?"

"Clyde?" Her stomach turned as she recalled last night in the station house, Clyde's booming voice demanding to see a lawyer. "Tell who?"

"The cops! You were the first one they questioned, they went and dragged him out of his house!"

"Clyde? They arrested Clyde?"

"Of course they did!" Larry looked like he wanted to punch her. "He was the only colored man working there except me, and everyone saw me selling tickets. I thought you and him were friends. What the hell did you say to them?"

"Nothing! Just, I went to tell Clyde about what I saw."

"The body."

She nodded. "But Clyde didn't believe me. Johnny was the one who did. And Clyde couldn't have done it, he was working the ride. Everyone knows that."

"Everyone knows, but no one can prove it. He was wearing a rubber mask and a costume. No one could swear it was him in there."

"But someone must've seen something!" Pin's voice rose in desperation. "Or seen Clyde and recognized him. They could testify."

Larry gave a derisive laugh. "Testify? You read too many stories, kid. That only happens if it goes to trial. And if it goes to trial, they'll send him to the gallows."

"But they couldn't! He didn't kill her!"

"You think that matters? Little white girl's dead, Negro man's within a mile, they'll kill him for it. And maybe now I'm out of a job. And don't you tell me I should go looking at the Sunny South. You ever see any colored folks watching that show? They make the Negro singers wear blackface."

"I never seen it."

"Well, you should go sometime, maybe you'd learn something. Tell you this, when I graduate I'm going to practice law."

Something in Larry's expression shifted as he gazed at her, and for a terrifying instant she feared he saw through her disguise.

"Wake up, boy," he said. "You're not Clyde's friend. Doesn't matter what you did or didn't do. Clyde's hired a good attorney, he's trying to find some witnesses. I don't know what you saw in there, but you better think hard before you start talking about it, you hear?"

He walked away and she hurried after him, holding out the magazine. He smacked it from her hands, then pushed her so she fell onto the dusty gravel. "And don't you follow me, you little fink. I see you again, I'll put your lights out."

Chapter 36

THE PORTER BROUGHT him the newspapers after they'd left Kansas City.

"Like you asked, Mr. Chaplin." The porter opened the door to the private compartment and handed him the *Chicago Tribune*. "I know you wanted the New York papers, but we can't get them out here."

Chaplin tucked the newspaper under his arm and nodded, counted out enough coins to cover the cost, and dropped them into the man's hand. The porter remained as he was, smiling. Of course, he was expecting a tip.

Instead Chaplin gifted him with a huge grin and a half bow, pretending to doff a hat. The porter laughed as Chaplin swiftly closed the door. The man would dine out on that for much longer than he would a dime.

The train had left Chicago late that morning, a good thing as otherwise he might have missed it. It always took him longer to pack his suitcase than he anticipated. His breakfast tray had been delivered as requested. A poached egg, toast and butter, bacon, half a grapefruit. He didn't care for grapefruit but couldn't forgo the novelty.

And orange juice! The bacon was crisp American bacon, not very nice. He peeled the bits of fat from it and left the rest. The coffee had cooled, but he didn't mind that. Coffee was also a novelty.

He settled in his chair, picked up his coffee cup and a piece of cold toast, and scanned the headlines. For the last few weeks, the *Eastland* ship disaster had supplanted the European war in the papers. The vast tourist steamer had capsized at its dock on the Chicago River, killing eight hundred forty-four of its twenty-five hundred passengers. More than were lost on the *Lusitania* back in May, and more passengers than had died on the *Titanic.*

But now, that tragedy was no longer front-page stuff. Unlike the sinking of the *Lusitania,* it couldn't be used as military propaganda. He read of several failed British military ventures in the Ottoman Empire and turned the page.

His gaze fell upon a photograph of a young man, his cheek pressed against that of a pretty little girl in a long-waisted dress patterned with embroidered daisies, a large bow atop her curls.

For Charlie Chaplin, Nothing Amiss with This Miss

The popular moving picture actor made a surprise appearance at Essanay Studios in Chicago, where he made a new friend. Pretty Miss Maria Walewski, twelve years old, is an aspiring thespian. "I hope Maria might work with me someday," Chaplin said. She will make her first appearance in a new Sweedie comedy starring comic Wallace Beery.

Chaplin took another bite of toast, then carefully tore out the clipping and put it in his pocket, further proof of his success and also a souvenir of the pretty child. *I hope Maria might work with me someday.* He'd said no such thing, knowing it was an impossibility. But he was accustomed to reporters putting words in his mouth.

And it was a good sign that the photograph ran prominently on page 3. People were tired of bad news. His most popular moving picture for Essanay, *The Tramp,* had been released four months earlier and was still playing in motion-picture theaters and storefront nickelodeons alike, along with a few others that had appeared since then. The studio also had several films in the can lined up for release, but these would be his last with the studio. He was holding off on breaking that bit of news to Spoor and Anderson.

The train whistle blew as they barreled through another dusty town, half a dozen derelict buildings with horses in a paddock, dogs lolling in the street, a group of children who ran shouting and waving as the locomotive steamed by. A wooden structure with a sign above its door:

ALPINE THEATER
SHOWING THE CAPTIVE

Cecil DeMille's five-reeler, released about a week after *The Tramp,* and a flop. Still, here it was, all these months later, in the middle of a desert. He drew his face closer to the window, to grin and wave at the running kids. Maybe one of them would recognize him.

Chapter 37

LIONEL HATED SUNDAYS. The studio was closed, and while he got along well enough with the folks he worked with, no one had ever invited him to a picnic or Sunday supper. They thought he was strange—no girl, those bizarre scenarios and photoplays he wrote—and they were right. Beery had been warned off the young girls he toyed with at Essanay, but if Lionel's colleagues knew more about his own predilections, he'd be fired in a heartbeat, or arrested.

So Sundays presented themselves as a wasteland. He woke sick and shaken by his indulgences of the night before, exacerbated by constant fear that someday he'd be caught. He knew his taste in stories—his own and others'—stemmed from his tormented desires, phantasmagoric fruit from a tree with twisted roots. He should never have left his room yesterday. He should never have left New York.

St. Olaf's church bells pealed as he lay in bed, sharpening his hangover to a spike driven through his skull. With a groan he stood, pulled on his robe, and paced the room, trying to ignore the disturbing images that fed his thoughts, even now that he was awake. After a few minutes, he sat at his desk and calmed himself by smoking a hashish cigarette. He waited for the heaviness to seep through his body, then read through what he had revised in his latest scenario, hoping to placate Spoor.

Stripped of blood and fire and secrets, the photoplay was dull as wet newsprint. Spoor was wrong. What was the point of a story, or a life, without shadows and unseen things?

He turned to gaze at his reflection in the mirror. Other than his red-rimmed eyes, no one would ever guess what he got up to when he was alone. He ran a hand across his stubbled cheek. Most barbershops closed on Sunday, but he knew of one on the fringes of Bronzeville that catered to men, white and colored, whose business or pleasure demanded they look sharp seven days a week. He dressed in his usual summer attire: white shirt, seersucker suit, red bow tie. He popped his boater on his head, grabbed his pencil and notebook, and went to catch the L to the South Side.

"Settle yourself," the barber said as Lionel walked in. A figure swaddled in steaming towels sat in the chair in front of him. "Be ten minutes. Maybe twenty."

The small shop was crowded with men reading newspapers. Lionel counted six, all colored, along with the man in the chair. He assumed he was a Negro as well. But when the barber removed the towels from the man's head, he revealed a white man in early middle age. Lionel took a seat near an elderly man perusing the *Police Gazette* and opened a copy of the *Chicago Defender*. The barber dropped the used towels into a receptacle, picked up a china cup and bristle brush, and whipped the shaving soap into a froth.

"In a minute, nobody going to know you been up all night, Mr. Demarest," he said. "I couldn't do what you do. I need my beauty sleep."

"Me too, Morris," replied the white man in the chair. There were dark circles under his eyes, and his expression was grim. "But I get the call, I gotta take it."

"Terrible thing, what a ugly thing. Young girl like that." Morris shook his head and began covering the man's face with lather. "They catch him yet?"

"Not sure. The captain at Robey Street station's supposed to talk to us this morning. Someone on the Riverview force told me they'd taken a Negro man into custody."

Every head turned. "Do you know who?" the barber asked.

"No."

Lionel suspected Demarest was lying. The others must have as well: they continued to stare at the man in the chair. The barber set down the shaving mug and picked up a straight razor. Demarest frowned.

"How'd you hear about it, Morris? They held the morning edition. Commissioner's on vacation, but he telephoned and we all have to hold the story till tonight. They don't want a panic."

"I got my ways," Morris said evenly. "Black man I know on the force came in this morning, he said this was almost as bad as when the *Eastland* went down. 'Cause it was purposeful."

"No doubt about that," agreed Demarest. "I talked to a fellow works at Riverview, but he didn't know anything. No one knows anything except a kid's dead."

Morris stropped the razor. "Park open today?"

Demarest nodded, and the old man next to Lionel snorted in disgust. "Baumgarten don't want to lose any revenue," he said to a rumble of approval.

"Opening the park and holding the story just means we'll sell out the evening paper in a hot minute," said Demarest. "Bet they see a lot of ticket sales for that ride."

Morris shook his head. "People are ugly. Now you turn to me just a little, Mr. Demarest, that's it…"

Lionel pretended to read his newspaper until it was his turn in the barber chair. No one mentioned what had happened at Riverview again.

Chapter 38

Sunday was always the busiest day at the park. Today there were cops everywhere, both Riverview's and the city's, acting as though this was an ordinary Sunday, and they all just happened to drop by for fun.

Pin didn't want to run into any more goddamn cops. She wandered along the Pike in the direction of Fairyland, scowling as she dodged in and out of the crowd. She seldom made deliveries on the weekend, except occasionally to students. And Lionel, of course. Still, Max sometimes showed up on Sunday mornings, and there was always the chance he might have work for her. She kicked at spent cigars and paper cones sticky with pink threads of spun sugar, halting when she reached the tent with its lurid banner and hand-lettered sign warning away women and children.

She pulled aside the canvas flap and peered inside. No Max. Something lay on the flattened grass near the entrance, a snakelike twist of red. A neckerchief, the kind worn by the Sicilian men who lived in Little Hell. She picked it up, considered keeping it, then threw it aside. It was risky enough to disguise herself as a boy: she'd be tempting fate if she marked herself as one who might be involved with the Black Hand.

She turned and walked the few steps to Max's shack, knocked on the door, and listened. "Max?"

There was no answer. She tried the doorknob. To her surprise, it turned. She cracked the door and peered inside, calling out again. Still no answer, and no sign of Max.

She stepped inside, closing the door behind her. She knew this was risky—if Max found her, he'd knock her across the room. But since finding the dead girl yesterday, she felt at once more wary and more reckless. She'd seen the worst that could happen to a girl, not once but twice: first her sister, now that dead kid in Hell Gate. But Pin herself was safe. Still, she tiptoed to the shelf where she'd left the French postcards the day before, picked them up, and shuffled through them.

None of the girls were as pretty as Glory. They all looked like they belonged in Armstrong's Freak Show. She set the postcards aside, turned to glance at Max's makeup table, the pots of cold cream and rouge, brushes and bottles of spirit gum arrayed haphazardly alongside the mirror, ashtrays and empty Helmar cigarette packets. A twist of brown hair lay beside a comb: a mustache, waxed and ready to be snipped in two to adorn half of the She-Male's face. She picked it up, pressed it against her upper lip, and stooped so she could see herself in the mirror.

"Ugh," she said aloud. With a grimace she replaced the mustache. Being a boy meant freedom; being a man meant joining an army of monsters and dingbats. She crossed quickly back to the door and left.

She walked toward the knoll where she'd seen Henry the day before. He might be a dingbat, but he was the only person who'd believed what she said about the girl in the tunnel. Didn't just believe it: like her, he'd *seen* it.

The thought made her feel odd. The two of them were strangers, but they shared a secret. She had never shared a secret with anyone, except for her mother.

But that was a secret *about* herself, inside herself. This was a secret outside herself: it made her feel bigger, not smaller.

She walked to the top of the knoll, yanked off her cap. Up here the air didn't torment her with the smells of sausages and frying potatoes and hot taffy. It smelled of sweet grass and leaves, dirt and clouds. She took off her socks and boots, luxuriating in the slippery feel of the long grass against her bare feet, then raised her arms, and for a moment it was as if she were flying.

She thought of Harriet Quimby flying over the English Channel and wondered if she'd felt like this. The world seemed to hold a mystery: Sometimes Pin thought it might be her sister, Abriana, in some far-off place never to be found but alive. Sometimes the mystery was inside her, a sensation as though her heart might explode with joy. Sometimes it moved through Glory, the way she laughed or leaned against the wall in the costume room. And sometimes she glimpsed it at the studio, in the machines that transformed drab brown ribbon into living things.

"Pin Drop."

She turned. Henry stood there, staring at her, but quickly angled his head so that she couldn't catch his gaze. He wore the same clothes as yesterday—too-big dark jacket, pants rolled at the ankle—but a different hat, a cap like her own.

"Did you find the girl?" he asked, and at Pin's nod his eyes widened. "You saved her."

"No. She was dead. I found her in Hell Gate."

"Hate Hell Gate." Henry knelt on the grass and started to pull it up. "Flyweight."

He didn't ask, but she told him everything. He listened intently and gave her the side-eye, as though it hurt to look at her head-on.

"I told them I talked to you, and they said maybe the girl was kidnapped and her family hired you to find her. You and that fella Willhie you talked about. The Gemini. Did someone hire you to find her?"

Henry's brow furrowed. "Yes, they did." He spoke slowly, as though he'd had to think about it first. "Her mother and father hired us to find her."

"Well, why in hell didn't you tell me?"

Henry's face grew red. He clawed at the grass, throwing up hand-fuls. "Because it's a *secret*!" he bellowed, and stumbled to his feet. "A secret, it's a goddamned *secret*!"

Pin backed away as Henry shouted words she couldn't understand—German or maybe just gibberish. He didn't look like a detective: he looked like Morga the Deranged, the gaffed freak who only pretended to be crazy, though Morga really did eat glass.

"You're not a detective," she sneered. "You're a damn liar. A god-damned liar."

"Cursing's a sin!"

"So's lying! If you were a real detective, you would have saved her."

Henry opened his mouth and shut it again. The crazy light in his blue eyes dimmed.

"You're right." His guttural voice broke. He let a fistful of grass trickle between his fingers to the ground. "But I am too a detective."

Pin waited to see if he'd start shouting again. If he did, she'd leave and forget she ever saw him. She held her breath, counting to ten. Without a word, he pulled out his cardboard wallet, removed the Gemini card, and stared at it as though he'd never seen it before.

"We should find him," she said at last. "The killer. You and me. I bet we'd get a reward. They arrested Clyde, the Negro magician—they'll execute him if we don't find the guy who really did it."

Henry shook his head and stuffed the card back into his wallet. He started to breathe loudly through his nose, like he was going to begin shouting again. "They enslaved the Negroes. Now they are making slaves of children. This evil murderer is one of their generals."

Pin made a face. "How could a general go into Hell Gate without anyone noticing? He'd be in uniform."

"You don't need special clothes to be a general. *I* was a general. Be-fore I was a detective," he added quickly. "And an evil general would be wearing different clothes."

"He wasn't a general!" Pin gestured impatiently at the park below them. "He's probably down there right now."

Henry's eyes widened. "Then we should watch the Infant Incubators! A stake out. When you wait for a criminal."

"I know what a stake out is." Pin sighed. "Let's go. You have grass on your head."

"Grass, jackass."

As they trudged down the hill, she asked, "Where do you live?"

"By the hospital, but just a little. St. Joseph's. I work there."

She nodded, only half listening. When they reached the Pike, she scanned the ground, looking for loose coins. No luck, but over by the incubators someone had left most of a wienie in a bun on a bench. Pin snatched it up.

Still warm. She took a bite and held it out to Henry, was relieved when he refused to touch it. She finished the wienie, wiped her hands on her knickerbockers, and noticed that Henry had already moved on.

He'd wandered off to stand behind a tree, half hidden so he couldn't be seen as he stared at the little girls waiting in line for the Infant Incubators. Even from here she could see him quivering, the way that greyhounds did before they were released.

A sick taste filled her mouth. She thought of the man settling into the boat at Hell Gate, the way the girl in the yellow dress had slipped into his lap, how he'd stroked her hair ribbon. Pin watched as Henry leaned forward and his hands moved, not as though he were throwing a ball but like he held something, something he twisted as his mouth silently opened and closed, while a few yards away the children scampered back and forth, laughing in the sunlight.

Chapter 39

HE WALKED THE few blocks to the nearest L stop and caught a train destined for the Loop. He hopped off at a busy part of Lincoln Park. He'd steeled himself to hear newsboys shouting about the murder, but their singsong was all about the hurricane that had destroyed Galveston and a German ship sunk by an English submarine.

He bought the papers, and it was the same. Not a word about the Riverview murder. He felt more disconcerted than relieved. Surely someone would have found the body by now?

He tucked the papers under his arm and walked across Stanton Park, strolled along the sidewalk until he saw a druggist's shop. Most shops closed on Sunday. But, judging by the A-K TABLETS sign propped prominently in front, this one was open.

He felt in his pocket for the gold ring that long ago had belonged to his wife and slid it onto the ring finger of his left hand. He entered the shop, removing his hat with a practiced, weary smile. Behind the counter, an elderly man in a white jacket glanced up.

"What can I do for you, sir?" he asked, with a nod at the open door. "Going to be a scorcher."

"So I hear." He made a show of yawning, covered his mouth so the gold ring caught the sunlight. "Do you carry Sydenham's syrup? My wife's been up all night. The little stranger's teething."

The druggist nodded. "Looks like you kept her company. No fun, no fun at all. Let me see…"

He examined the shelves behind him, frowning. "I know we had Sydenham's, but I believe I sold the last of it. No, none left. I do have this…"

He turned and held up a bottle of Dr. James Soothing Cordial. "Purer than that other stuff—it's made with heroin."

He took the bottle from the druggist and gave it a cursory examination, gingerly stroking his mustache. "Thank you," he said. "This will do just fine. Since you recommend it, could I have another bottle, please?"

"Of course." The druggist retrieved a second bottle. "I used to sell a great deal of this, until the government got involved. Hard to find it these days. It's a shame—babies still cry, don't they? This is my last bottle. Will there be anything else?"

"Yes, please—some lemon drops. Two tins."

He'd lost count of how often he'd had a transaction like this one, but every time it made him break out in a cold sweat. The druggist placed his purchases in a paper sack and handed it to him with a smile. "A nice day for a stroll along the lake with the missus and little one."

Anxious to be gone, he dropped a few coins on the counter and grabbed the items. "What a fine idea. Thank you again."

He hurried back out onto the sidewalk and walked to the end of the block, caught a streetcar, and went to a Weeghman's for breakfast. Coffee, bratwurst, fried eggs. He found it difficult to concentrate. When he finished eating, he felt slightly ill. He considered returning to the druggist's to buy some aspirin.

Yet that might be risky. But why? There were thousands of colicky babies in Chicago, and twice as many parents hoping for relief. No one would remember a man buying soothing syrup and lemon drops.

Still, better safe than sorry. But his nausea increased, along with a lancing headache. He uncorked the bottle of Dr. James Cordial, its sickly sweet smell undercut by something chemical, cherries dipped in kerosene. He poured some into his coffee and drank it. After several minutes he felt the familiar, fizzing sensation, as though his head had been pumped full of seltzer.

He paid for his breakfast and went outside. The shimmering air made him feel as though he walked underwater. Dreamily he imagined Hell Gate's subterranean river flowing beneath the entire city, moving under his feet at this very moment; not just this city but New York and Boston, Dreamland and Wonderland, all those places where he'd found children unafraid of venturing into the darkness with him. His hand reached out as though to grasp another, smaller hand as he crossed the street and headed north, toward the amusement park.

Chapter 40

FRANCIS HAD A bad night's sleep in his room at Mrs. Dahl's boarding-house. Back at Robey Street, he'd grown accustomed to seeing men gutted like carcasses at Packingtown, twelve-year-old girls dead from botched abortions, women whose faces had been melted like candle wax because their lovers belonged to the Black Hand and suspected a betrayal. That's what had happened to his sister, Ellen, his only family since their parents had died of influenza. Ellen had taken up with a man named Lorenzo Filli, who worked at a bakery while extorting money for the Black Hand. After he impregnated her, Ellen con-fronted Lorenzo's wife after Mass one Sunday morning, showing her the evidence of her husband's infidelity. Two weeks later Ellen was dead, her hair and flesh burned away and her violated body thrown from the roof of the building where she and Francis shared a small apartment.

"Leave it," Cabell had ordered him when Francis, mad with grief, began his own investigation of the gang's activities in Little Hell. "Your sister's not cold in the ground, you'll be joining her if you continue like this."

Francis didn't leave it. He knew the only reason he hadn't been killed in the aftermath of his failed investigation and subsequent firing was that his death would have brought more attention to the department's corruption. Or made a martyr of Francis and inspired one of the city's newspapers to delve into the tale behind it. Better that he become a floorwalker and a toy cop patrolling the midway.

Francis showed up at the Riverview station shortly before ten o'clock, bleary eyed and unshaven. He'd rushed from Mass at Immaculate Heart of Mary and was somewhat relieved to see that Hickey, too, didn't look like he'd slept. Francis usually didn't work Sundays. Neither did Hickey. But every man at the park had been called in this morning.

"I want you to go to Robey Street later." Hickey dropped the roster he'd been reading and gazed wearily across his desk at Francis. "Cabell's meeting with the newspapers there around two o'clock. I want to know what he has to say."

Francis's jaw clenched. "Send Paterno. Or yourself. They'll be expecting the captain, not me."

"They're expecting no one." Hickey's voice sounded like his throat had been scraped raw. "Not from here. I can't leave the park, and you're the only real sergeant I've got. You'll know if Cabell is lying. Get a shave and some lunch before you go, and come see me after."

Francis left, glaring at Paterno in the waiting room as he stormed out the door. He couldn't find a barber open on Sunday, and his brief meeting with Hickey had killed his appetite. But he knew a hop joint that used to be a meeting place for reporters as well as cops. The cops had moved on after the saloon changed hands—good luck for Francis, who'd gotten into several brawls with former colleagues since he'd left the department.

The new owner was a taciturn Irishman known as Cue, short for Cue Ball, the weapon he'd used to kill a man back in Boston. He ran the place as a blind pig these days—the cops never bothered him, out of deference to the saloon's legal past—but on Sundays Cue waited till noon to open, so he could attend Mass. A heavyset Irish boy sat on a box that blocked the entry, paring his nails with a shiv while he perused a newspaper. He glanced at Francis, then shifted the box, allowing Francis to enter.

Inside was dark as a confessional. A kerosene lantern gave off just enough light that Francis could see two other customers seated at separate tables, wizened men bent over glasses of beer or whiskey. He made his way through wooden crates and empty pickle barrels to the far wall and rapped four times on a worn panel. The panel slid open and Cue's face peered out. Francis saw the bar counter behind his broad shoulders, and heavy drapes drawn across the window that fronted the street.

"Mr. Bacon." Cue gave a nod of greeting. "What is your pleasure on a Sunday?" His breath smelled of coffee and pickled eggs.

"A whiskey."

Cue turned to fill a tumbler with whiskey. Francis dropped two coins into his hand and downed his drink. Cue refilled the glass, sipped delicately from a china coffee cup. He said, "That was a very unfortunate event occurred yesterday in your park, Mr. Bacon."

Francis winced. "You've heard, then."

"A Polack girl, I was told, from St. Hedwig's parish."

Francis gestured at the newspaper. "It's in there?"

"Not yet." Cue took another sip of coffee. "I was told they're holding it from the morning editions. So as not to interfere with Mr. Deneen's visit with his sister in Wisconsin."

"What else were you told?"

Cue's voice dropped. "That the child was interfered with, and her clothes taken. And they arrested a colored man who works at the park."

Francis nodded. "Clyde Smithson. I know the man—he couldn't have done such a thing."

"I've known of one who did."

Francis eyed him skeptically. "When?"

"Four years ago, in Wonderland. Before I came to this city."

"Wonderland?"

"An amusement park. Like yours, Mr. Bacon. With the Hell Gate and the roller coasters and the freaks. Deirdre Monahan—I knew her sister's husband, Joseph. Joe Neely, we worked together at the docks. A wee girl. She was twelve years old and they found her in the Hell Gate." He lowered his voice to a whisper. "Defiled and her little dress stolen. Joe went off his head with drink, couldn't see the hole in a ladder after that. I won't take a step into your park, Mr. Bacon, and now you know why."

Francis set down his empty tumbler. "How do you know this?"

"Joe Neeley worked beside me for three years, Mr. Bacon, how would I not know? It was in the papers for a month. Anyone with eyes and ears knew her name. Deirdre Monahan," he repeated, and fixed Francis with an iron stare.

"Did they find him? The man who killed her?"

"If they had, I'd be telling you his name."

Cue glanced at the empty whiskey glass, but Francis shook his head. He asked, "This park, it's in Boston?"

"Revere. Was. It closed after that. You can understand why."

"Does anyone know of this? Have you spoken to anyone?"

Cue picked up the china cup. He stared at Francis as he drank the rest of his coffee. Setting the cup back on the counter he continued, "I live a quiet life in this city and do not care to have any more doings with the Chicago police if I can help it.

"But I speak to you as one who values your trade, Mr. Bacon. And I have heard of your own circumstances. I will appreciate you not bringing my name into any conversation you may have about that Polack girl. Deirdre Monahan," he added as he closed the panel. "A name to remember, Mr. Bacon."

Chapter 41

AFTER HALF AN hour at the Infant Incubators, Pin refused to stay any longer.

"It's all ladies and babies. C'mon, let's try the Witching Waves." Henry ignored her, still gazing at the little girls whose dresses and hair ribbons drooped in the heat.

"Men don't come here," she said. "Except for you."

She stalked off toward the Witching Waves. The way he stared at those kids, much younger than the girl from Hell Gate, only five or six years old...

Her irritation edged into unease. Yesterday, she'd seen Henry *after* the girl went into the dark ride. She'd dozed off and, when she woke, witnessed the man with the boater leave the ride without the girl. She'd spent about ten minutes searching the Pike for a sign of the girl before returning to Hell Gate. That was when Henry had signaled her. What had he been wearing?

The same clothes as now, she thought. But what had the other man worn? A suit, maybe seersucker, maybe not. But what if she was wrong? What if his clothes were the same as Henry's? The man had worn a bow tie, she knew that. Henry had worn one, too, she remembered, because it was so dirty.

And they both wore boater hats—that was the only thing she knew for sure. She squeezed her eyes shut in frustration. Why was it so hard to remember something that happened only a day ago? Why hadn't she paid more attention then? It was like every time she told someone what had happened, or thought about it, the image in her mind changed. All she could be sure of was the boater hat.

And the killer was a man; she knew that. And that meant any man could be a murderer.

She opened her eyes and saw men everywhere, drunk or shouting, laughing as they pulled women around: onto the roller coasters, where the women would scream and cling to them; into the House of a Thousand Troubles, where fans would blow up the women's skirts so you could see their drawers; onto the Witching Waves, where men and women would be thrown against each other and the men could grab their breasts, pretending it was a mistake. Her breath came too fast, she fought the urge to run—but run where? Nothing was safe, nothing was safe, it was the only thing she knew was true.

The sun was a hot skillet pressed against her face. She wiped her forehead, glanced back to see Henry twenty or so feet behind her. The instant he saw she'd noticed him, he looked away. It couldn't be him, she thought, why would he have signaled her if he'd been the one who killed the girl? He'd really be a moron to do that.

But she couldn't trust him. She wouldn't go to the Witching Waves; she'd head for the Lagoon and lose him there. She broke into a run, but when she looked back again, there he was, dogging her. She kept on a few more yards, finally whirled to confront him.

"Stop following me!"

"Not following. I'm tailing you." He removed his hat and fanned his face. "You hungry?"

"What?"

"Hungry. You look hungry. I'll get us some corn."

He turned and walked to the hot-buttered-corn stand. She watched him, torn between her suspicion and her empty stomach.

Hunger won. She waited till he came back with two dripping ears and handed her both without speaking. She ate them quickly, before he could ask her to share. When she was done, she wiped her hands on her knickerbockers. Henry stood motionless as a wax figure from the Ten-in-One, again gazing at the Infant Incubators.

"Why do you do that?" she demanded. He flinched but didn't look away. "Those girls—why are you always watching them?"

"Protecting them," he grunted without looking at her.

"Lemme see that card again," she said. "From your detective agency."

She drew up alongside him, her hands clenched. Let him think she'd punch him; maybe he'd run away. Instead he just looked around furtively, gestured for her to follow him to a grove of trees. She hesitated, then joined him. He glanced around again, pulled out his cardboard wallet, and sorted through its contents with exaggerated care. Scraps of paper spilled to the grass.

Trash, she thought with disdain, *he's got nothing but trash in there.*

She bent to pick them up, then froze, staring at a newspaper photo: a black-and-grey smudge that might have been clouds but wasn't. It was the top portion of a picture of her sister.

Chapter 42

Aʙʀɪᴀɴᴀ's ᴛʜɪᴄᴋ ᴅᴀʀᴋ hair was held back by a ribbon that the newspaper photograph had turned to ash. The photo had been taken on Easter, just a few weeks before she disappeared. It was the last time Pin and her mother had attended Mass at Assumption, the Italian church closest to Little Hell. A man from the *Examiner* stood outside the church after Mass and shot photographs of the congregation as they left.

She and Abriana had been crushed when the newspaper photo never appeared. By the time it did, it accompanied an article about a girl who had been missing for two days. She stared at the clipping, words she'd memorized without realizing it.

Police continue their search for ten-year-old Abriana Onofria, missing since April 13, and believed to have been abducted by a vagrant. She was last seen wearing a smocked yellow dress, pink hair ribbon and black shoes and stockings. Members of the public are encouraged to share any information they may have with the police department.

"Why do you have this?" Pin's voice came out as a whisper, then a shout. *"Why do you have this?"*

"Give me that!" Henry tried to snatch it from her. "It's mine, you thieving bastard!"

"Why do you have this? Tell me!" People turned to stare, and she lowered her voice. "This is—"

She stopped before she said, *This is my sister.* "This is someone you don't even know. What are you—"

He grabbed the paper. It tore in two as Henry burst into a string of violent epithets. She punched his arm, hissing, "Shut up!"

To her relief he did. His hands shook as he fumbled with the scrap, trying to stuff it back into the wallet. When he started to walk away, Pin grabbed him.

"Why do you have that? Do you know something? *Did you hurt her?*"

"No!" Henry shouted, and more people stopped to stare.

Pin fought to keep her voice low as again she hissed, "Shut up!" She kept hold of Henry's arm, and after a few seconds the rubberneckers moved on. "I could go back to the police," she continued. "They asked me about you, I—"

He yanked his arm free, his eyes wild. "She was very brave, all of the girl rebels are brave! They fight tirelessly—I have seen them!"

"Abriana—have you seen her?"

His face twisted with fury but also terror. "No! Only Annie Aronburg. And Elsie," he babbled. "But no, not Elsie!"

"What are you talking about? Elsie? Do you mean Elsie Paroubek? Did you know her?"

"Elsie?" He blinked, staring at Pin, and his face crumpled. "We were great friends, you know," he whispered. "Very great friends. We fought together against the generals."

"What generals?"

He didn't answer, and Pin's neck prickled. She'd been almost ten when Elsie Paroubek had gone missing, but she remembered the photo that accompanied endless articles about the five-year-old girl in her coat with the fur collar.

The little girl is described as having long curly golden hair, blue eyes and pink chubby cheeks, with a prominent dimple in each. At the time she disappeared she wore a red hat, a red dress, black stockings and high top black boots.

She stared at Henry, sweat trickling into her eyes.

He knew something. He'd *done* something—that's why he watched children all the time, why he had pictures of little girls stuffed in his pocket. Abriana, Elsie Paroubek—the realization that she'd been talking to the man who might have murdered her sister made her stomach turn. She clapped a hand to her mouth, trying not to be sick, breathed deeply through her nose until she felt calmer.

It might not be true. If he had killed the girl in Hell Gate, would he have had time to run from there, then find her? She didn't think so.

Yet why would he even want to find Pin?

Maybe he knows I saw him go into the tunnel with her, she thought. *He knows, and he wants to kill me.*

But what if Henry was telling the truth, and the Gemini were real, and he was a detective, trying to track down whoever killed Abriana and Elsie and the girl in Hell Gate?

She ran a hand through her cropped curls, looked up to see Henry muttering to himself and punching at the air. If Henry was a detective, she could help him find the killer. If Henry was the murderer, she would need more proof of that.

She closed her eyes for a moment. Taking a deep breath, she walked to his side and pointed to the Lagoon.

"We can look over there," she said.

They continued without speaking. Henry seemed subdued and nervous. She saw him watching her from the corners of his eyes as he kept touching the pocket that held his wallet. As they passed the elephants lined up alongside the Waterdrome, she asked him, "Did you really know Elsie Paroubek?"

"We were very great friends" was all he said.

Chapter 43

He paid his entrance fee and made his way through the crowd. A hot breeze carried the smells of burnt sugar and the yeasty scent of beer. A group of boys scampered along the path, shouting as they kicked up dust. The strains of a polka vied with the ballyhoo from the Great Train Robbery.

"See the bloodthirsty crime! Your only chance to see Tom Mix, the star of the moving pictures live and in the flesh!"

A warm lassitude filled him, a sense that his flesh melted into the air like wax into a flame. Sweat trickled down his neck; he thought of Maria, the girl's head replaced by a doll's. So pretty.

He made a detour around the dunk tank, arriving at a broad avenue that surrounded green lawn and trees. An organ-grinder strolled across the grass, trailed by half a dozen children waving balloons on sticks. A Chinese woman selling paper fans from a tray was doing a brisk business. He stopped and bought one for a penny, but it was useless against this infernal heat. He decided on the German beer garden, which had electrical fans inside.

It was crowded in the beer hall. He went to the bar and ordered a pilsner, drank it, and set down another nickel, waiting as the bartender refilled his glass, then walked slowly through the room.

Couples sat at tables, laughing and talking in German, Italian, Polish, and Greek and Czech. Jungle noises. The girl in Indiana had squeaked some foreign nonsense before she fell silent.

He found an empty table and sat. Waiters in long white aprons carried trays filled with steins. From the garden erupted waves of music from the oompah band, singing, and the thunder of hobnailed boots pounding the wooden dance floor.

He sipped his pilsner. The smell of frying pork nauseated him. He should have asked for a glass of seltzer water. He should have returned to the druggist and bought some aspirin. A few tables away, a father sat between two young girls in matching dresses and floppy blue velvet bows. One of the girls clambered to her feet on her chair, put her hands around her father's neck, and kissed him. Her father made a face, covering his mouth like Chaplin's clown, then pecked her cheek as both girls pealed with laughter.

He watched them, suffused with an ache that was inextricably twinned with a darker longing. For an instant he saw his sister's face, smiling as she clung to him in that filthy room, the soiled mattress where he'd cried inconsolably as he clutched a scrap of his sister's dress. *She don't need that shimmy now.*

"Papa, look at me!" the second girl cried, reaching to kiss him, too. "Papa!"

He quickly looked away before they saw him watching them. The dreamy warmth he'd felt just a short time again dissolved into dread. How could they not notice him? How was it possible he could sit here and not be surrounded by leering, horrified onlookers, the way every other monster in the park was?

It wasn't possible, he knew that, even if he stopped. And he couldn't stop, any more than they could stop beckoning him, with their eyes and flower-garden dresses. The dread ballooned inside him, and the mad thought that he should seize that girl now, no one would recognize him, no one knew who he was...

He fumbled for one of the bottles of Dr. James Soothing Cordial from the paper sack, *A miracle of the modern Medical Profession,* and drew the bottle to his lips. Took one swallow, then another, and replaced the bottle.

He returned to the midway, weaving slightly. The cordial was stronger than he'd anticipated; he'd adjust the dose when he used it on the lemon drops. He licked his lips, gingerly stroked his mustache, and idled along with the crowd toward the Great Lagoon. People mobbed the water's edge, pointing gleefully as boats raced down the Shoot-the-Chutes, the women on board clutching their hats and screaming. Boys leaned out over the Lagoon, splashing one another. He wrinkled his nose in disgust. The water smelled fetid. Discarded watermelon rinds and paper wrappers floated on its surface. You could get sepsis from touching it.

He moved on. He noted a number of policemen in the crowd—Chicago cops, not the dolts employed by the amusement park. He was unconcerned: there were enough Negroes and vagrants and Gypsies to blame for a thousand murders.

He smiled. His head felt as though it had been pumped full of laughing gas. He was invincible, invisible. A white man in a hat and an ice-cream suit.

The path wound past the Great Train Robbery and to the Sunny South, a long sheltered arcade featuring games of chance. He stopped to observe a black-haired girl manipulating the Digger Claw crane, attempting to pick up a Kewpie doll inside a glass vitrine. She looked about twelve, maybe slightly older—she wore a child's dress, faded red-and-blue calico, but the blouse strained against her bosom. Her black lace-up boots were scuffed and almost certainly too small for her.

A crowd of younger children watched her eagerly. Any accompanying adults had no doubt headed to the roulette wheel. The crane's jaws held the doll poised just above the slot, but the girl cranked the handle too quickly. The doll fell and landed beside the chute, and the crane froze in place.

"Bad luck, Gilda!" a boy exclaimed. "You got another nickel?"

She shook her head in disappointment. "No. You?"

"Nah." Shrugging, the boy walked off. The other children continued to stare at the girl, Gilda, as though waiting for her to prove herself a liar and produce a nickel. But after a bit of bantering among themselves, they, too, dispersed to other parts of the arcade.

He waited to see if Gilda joined them. When she didn't, he stepped over and dug into his pocket.

"Will this help?"

He held out a nickel. The girl grabbed it, barely looking at him. "Hey, thanks, Mister!"

She turned back to the game and slid the nickel into the coin slot. He stood behind her, nodding as she turned the crank.

"You need to do it more slowly," he said. He took her hand lightly in his own. "Like this."

A moment of resistance, and then he felt her hand relax as he guided her. The crane's jaws closed around the doll, and he moved the controls a fraction of an inch, squeezing them so that the metal jaws opened at just the right instant and the Kewpie dropped down the chute.

"I got it!" Gilda snatched the celluloid doll from the tray. She turned and beamed up at him. "Thanks, Mister!"

She had a pretty face, large dark eyes and a small mouth, baby fat in her cheeks and chin, crooked front teeth. A dimple—he'd never found a doll that had one. Her black hair hung in a thick braid halfway down her back, tied with a scrap of red grosgrain ribbon. She smelled of sun and dirt, like newly turned earth in a garden.

"Where'd your friends go?" He looked around, scanning the arcade.

"Oh, they just ran off." A lisp made her sound younger than she was. "They're stupid."

"Not nice to leave you alone," he agreed.

"Oh, who cares?" She raised and lowered her shoulders in an exaggerated show of unconcern. "They're just kids."

"Did your parents leave you in charge of them?"

"Nah, they're off at the Casino. They gave me money, but I spent it all." She gestured at the crane, cradling the Kewpie.

"Are you hungry? Would you like an ice cream?"

Her eyes narrowed and he quickly added, "Only if your parents give permission."

The girl snorted. "They don't care what I do, long as I don't smoke."

He smiled. "I promise, I won't let you smoke. Come on, let's find the ice-cream cart."

They walked along the Pike, the girl toying with her prize and seeming disinclined to pay him much attention, though she smiled obediently whenever he caught her eye. He took care to weave through the heart of the crowd, to not get too close to her, to affect the pleasant, detached expression of some benign male relative, an uncle or her father. If necessary, within seconds he could lose himself in the mass of Sunday visitors.

But they passed no one the girl knew. And while there might well be people here who knew him, he felt safely hidden behind the anonymity of his hat brim, tipped to shade a face that was utterly unremarkable, save for those occasions when it needed to be. Thousands of men—tens of thousands—surrounded him, each clad almost exactly as he was, in seersucker, white shirt, celluloid collar, bow tie, gun-metal calfskin shoes. He slipped among them like an eel, his gaze seldom leaving the girl beside him.

As they drew near the ice-cream cart, he gave her a dime. "You go and get whatever you want," he said, lifting his head just enough to reveal his smile beneath the hat's brim. "I'll be in the shade over there."

He gestured to a stand of rhododendrons, watched her run to join the line. He felt as though he stood on a cliff edge, leaning over so as to feel the air rushing up at him from that black place where he could dive and never be followed. Not yet, anyway, not this minute or the next: he would capture as many as he could until time ran out for all of them, himself, too, but he would pluck a garden's worth of girls before it did.

He headed to the rhododendrons and stepped into the thicket, removed the heroin cordial and a tin of lemon drops. He opened the tin and let a few drops of cordial fall onto each lozenge, closed the tin and shook it, then repeated the process. When he finished, he pocketed the tin, sucking his fingers to remove the sticky residue. He glanced around to make sure no one had seen him, and strolled back to the Pike.

The girl ran up to him, grinning, the Kewpie in one hand and a cone of strawberry ice cream in the other. "Thanks!" she said breathlessly.

"You're very welcome," he replied with a smile. "Now, how about a movie?"

She nodded, her mouth full, and they joined the mass of people heading toward the Hippodrome.

Chapter 44

THE ROBEY STREET station house was filled with reporters when Francis arrived. After leaving Cue's, he'd walked around the neighborhood, mulling over what he'd learned. Could it possibly be true?

The barman had no reason to lie. Dr. Holmes had committed atrocities right here in Chicago during the 1893 exposition, and elsewhere for some years before that, and gotten away with them until his capture. Francis had been a thirteen-year-old boy at the time, utterly captivated by the exposition; one of the few things that made his ignominious transfer to the Riverview force palatable. Riverview was much smaller and, despite Baumgarten's insistence that it reflect his own clean Lutheran values, quite a bit seedier than the exposition, yet it stirred an echo of the wonder and delight that Francis had partaken of at the White City.

Now he felt the same sick terror he'd felt reading about Holmes's crimes as a boy: men and women interred alive, then incinerated in the furnace Holmes had installed in his mansion, or their skeletons flensed and sold to medical colleges.

And this was not the first child murder in Chicago in recent years. In 1911, when little Elsie Paroubek disappeared, Francis had joined sergeants and volunteers in one of the biggest manhunts in the city's history. After a month, her body was discovered in a sewage canal thirty-five miles from the city. The coroner's report attested that she had been "mistreated," then smothered, and tossed into the canal in or near Chicago, probably the same day she'd been abducted. No water was found in her lungs, and the official cause of death read *Unknown.*

Various suspects were questioned. Two committed suicide afterward. Another, a lunatic, fled into the woods. The real killer had never been found.

And two years ago, an Italian child had disappeared from Little Sicily, and after that a Gypsy girl. Both were a bit older than Elsie, but could they possibly be connected to the Riverview murder, and the one Cue had just told him about? Boston was a thousand miles from Chicago, but what were the odds of the same bizarre crime occurring twice within a few years, at such a great distance? He pushed open the station door and stepped inside, trying to make himself as inconspicuous as possible.

Most of Robey Street's force had been sent to Riverview, so the crowd was chiefly made up of reporters who swarmed around the duty sergeant manning the front desk. Francis found a space by an open window to get some fresh air.

"Is that Francis Bacon? How are you, man?"

Francis turned to see a gangly young man in a snappy, if rumpled, checked suit and brown fedora, pencil tucked behind one ear and notebook in hand, a dog-eared magazine poking out of his jacket pocket. "Bennie. You're looking well."

Bennie grinned. "Can't say the same for you, Bacon."

Francis grimaced wryly, and the two shook hands. He'd known Bennie Hecht since the kid was a picture chaser for the *Daily Journal,* sneaking onto crime scenes to nab photographs of the victims or their families. Francis had chased him off a few times himself, and once saved him from a beating from another cop, when Bennie tried to make off with the wedding photo of a guy who'd committed suicide upon discovering his wife was actually a man named Waldo Timmins.

Bennie returned the favor. He covered the Black Hand story for the *Daily Journal,* sharing the names of a few informants with Francis before everything had gone south with Francis's investigation. Francis hadn't seen him since.

"It's been a while," he admitted. Bennie still looked like a kid, with his floppy dark hair and scruffy mustache. He couldn't be more than twenty or twenty-one. "You still at the *Journal?*"

"Nope. *Daily News* now. This story's kept me busy since last night. Did it happen on your watch?"

Francis eyed him measuringly, then nodded.

"How's Baumgarten dealing with it?"

"As you might expect. He's not."

Bennie glanced around. "Hear anything new?"

Francis made a noncommittal sound. He stepped closer to Bennie, lowering his voice. "You got the girl's name, right?"

Bennie glanced at his notebook. "Maria Walewski. Polish girl from St. Hedwig's parish, the funeral's Wednesday. She was an only child, her mother saw an ad in the paper saying Essanay was looking for child actors. Only the second time the kid had been at the studio. Not sure if there's any connection to the movies, but I'm gonna play it up—Chaplin was at the studio yesterday, did you know that? Everyone knows he's a creep with young girls. You didn't happen to see him around the park yesterday, did you?"

"Not me. But this is a bum rap—you know that, right? Hauling in Clyde Smithson for this?"

"He's the colored magician?" Francis nodded. "You know him?"

"Seen his act a few times. Few years back he did a stunt when he buried himself underground in a coffin and got dug up three days later."

"That could come in handy. You don't think he did it?"

"I'm sure he didn't. He was working that ride—between visitors and employees, thirty, forty people must've seen him around the time that girl got killed. But no one can identify him because he was wearing a rubber mask."

"So how come you're so sure?"

"He's got a wife and kids. A respectable man. Even if he was a lunatic, which he's not, why would he commit murder in a place where everyone knows him? He's hired Roscoe Nelson to represent him, so if he's got a chance in hell, he might get off. In the meantime, Baumgarten doesn't want a panic, so Cabell arrests a Negro, and everyone's happy."

"Unless it happens again."

"What if it's happened before?" countered Francis.

Bennie raised an eyebrow, grinning. "You know something?"

But before he could continue, the door to Cabell's office opened, and the Robey Street captain strode into the room. He surveyed the room, pointedly ignoring Francis.

"Thank you all for waiting, gentlemen." Cabell clapped the back of the man from the *Herald* as he passed him. "It's a hot day, and I know you're eager to jump, so I'll make this short. As you've heard, yesterday afternoon a young girl was found murdered in one of the rides at the Riverview Amusement Park. She was—"

"Which ride?" someone shouted.

Cabell raised a hand. "I'm getting to that. She was found inside the Hell Gate attraction. We're still waiting for the coroner's final report and autopsy, but it appears that she was smothered. Thanks to quick work by the fine men here at Robey Street, a Negro man has been taken into custody and will be charged with the crime."

A din of shouted questions rose, then ebbed as Cabell once more raised his hand. "The suspect's name is Clyde Smithson, that's S-M-I-T-H-S-O-N. He's a resident of the freak show. From my understanding, paperwork's being drawn up now. That's all I know and all you need to know at this time."

Some of the reporters turned and dashed from the room. One who remained called out, "Do we know who the girl is?"

"Her name is Maria Walewski. W-A-L-E-W-S-K-I. Her parents are Polish, I don't know more than that."

"A Polack." A man near Francis shook his head. "Figures."

Someone else yelled, "Who discovered the body?"

Cabell pulled out a cigar and rolled its tip between his fingers. "A boy, another employee of the amusement park."

"Will Riverview Park remain open?"

Smiling, Cabell turned to point at Francis. "There's your man! Ask Mr. Bacon, he works at the park. You can also ask him how to beat the lines for the Shoot-the-Chutes."

With a laugh, Cabell headed back toward his office, stopping to chat with the man from the *Daily Tribune*. A few reporters wandered over to Francis. He assured them the park was open and there was every intention for it to remain so. The men scribbled in their notebooks before hurrying to the door.

Francis glanced at Bennie, who'd remained silent during Cabell's blather. "It's like Elsie Paroubek all over again. And that Italian girl two years ago."

Bennie shrugged. "Yeah, but we got a body this time."

"We had a body with the Paroubek girl."

"You think there's a similarity?"

A shout of laughter rang through the room. "You'll be the first to know if she does, Malcolm!" Cabell slapped the *Tribune*'s reporter on the back and waved his unlit cigar. "I'll make sure of that."

The man grinned. "Thanks, Rusty."

Cabell let loose another raucous laugh and walked the reporter to the door. His slack mouth twisted into a smile when he spotted Francis. "Got any free tickets for the freak show, Francis?" he yelled as he headed to his office.

"Let's go," said Bennie, and he started for the door. Francis stayed put.

"Captain Cabell." Francis's voice echoed in the now-nearly-empty room. "Are you aware that four years ago, a twelve-year-old girl was found murdered inside the Hell Gate attraction at Wonderland Park in Boston?"

Bennie halted, and Cabell, too, stopped in his tracks. The desk sergeant looked up, startled.

"Deirdre Monahan, twelve years old," Francis went on. "She had been defiled and her clothing removed. They've never found her killer."

Cabell twisted the cigar between his fingers. "Well," he said. "We'll have to ask Smithson about that, won't we?"

"I think you'll find that Mr. Smithson was here at Riverview at that time."

Cabell blinked. "This is a police matter, an open investigation—"

"An open investigation, Captain Cabell?" Bennie called out, and the two remaining reporters turned to him. "Yet you're telling everyone that a colored magician will be charged with the crime. Is that correct?"

"We need to confirm everything before we—"

"I stood here and heard you tell a roomful of reporters, and I quote, 'A Negro man has been taken into custody and will be charged with the crime…From my understanding, paperwork's being drawn up now.'"

Bennie looked up from his notebook. "Those are your words, Captain Cabell. Every man in this room heard you say them."

"I'm not denying that I said them." Cabell's voice dropped. Francis recognized this as a far more dangerous sign than if he'd started shouting. "Mr. Bacon, if you do anything to interfere with this investigation, I'll have you brought in for tampering."

"Is that what it's called?" broke in Bennie. "I'd think you might be more concerned with negligence on the part of your staff—twenty sergeants at this station, and not a single one made a connection between this murder and one in Boston?"

"Boston is a very long way from here."

"So it is," said Francis. "I suggest you check with Mr. Smithson as to his whereabouts at the time of the Wonderland murder. I bet he has a very good alibi, just like he does now."

Cabell strode toward him, his moist cigar pointed at Francis's throat. "Don't you tell me how to do my fucking job."

"Someone's got to," said Francis, and left the station.

Chapter 45

HE STOOD IN the crowd outside the Hippodrome with the girl Gilda, fuming. He'd forgotten they'd held over this Italian movie, rather than premiering Chaplin's new comedy. Who wanted to see a moving-picture version of Dante's *Inferno,* anyway?

Everyone in Chicago, apparently. Just past the ropes at the theater entrance, a machine pumped out clouds of steam. Red gel lights bathed the lobby in crimson. A huge poster depicted naked men and women who gazed imploringly at two figures being ferried across a reach of black water:

THE GLOBAL SENSATION!
CROWNING ACHIEVEMENT OF THE MOVING
PICTURE WORLD
POET'S JOURNEY THROUGH HELL SEEN THROUGH
HUMAN EYES

Gilda nudged him. "Kids aren't allowed."

He peered over the sea of hats at the ticket booth:

ADMISSION 50 CENTS
NO UNACCOMPANIED CHILDREN

Fifty cents! He'd never heard of a theater charging so much for a flicker. "It says 'no unaccompanied children,'" he said. "That means you can't go in alone. Still want to see a movie?"

She nodded. "Sure."

"It's a bit scary, I think." He pointed at the figure of a devil waving a pitchfork.

She rolled her eyes. "I'm not scared."

"All right, then. If anyone asks, tell them I'm your uncle Arthur."

The girl giggled as the crowd began to move at last. Inside, he guided her through the packed lobby and up a narrow stairway. "We'll be able to see better from up here," he said.

At the top, a uniformed usher took their tickets, raising an eyebrow at Gilda. "Picture's over an hour long. Might be kinda spooky for a kid."

"She goes to Sunday Mass," he replied. "She's used to sitting still. And devils."

This, the uppermost level of the Hippodrome, wasn't as crowded as those below. The last dozen rows of seats were empty. The rest were occupied by younger couples, all purposefully sitting a good distance apart from one another. A group of high-school boys perched at the edge of the balcony, their feet on the brass railings as they smoked and tossed candy wrappers into the audience.

He led the girl to the center of the last row. From here he could see everyone in the balcony, and no one could see him, not unless someone sat in the same aisle. But he knew that older adults tended to avoid the balcony seats, which attracted young couples more interested in each other than in what was on the screen.

To his relief, no one else ventured into the balcony. Fifteen rows in front of him, several couples had already sunk into their seats, the tops of their heads barely showing. The high-school boys sniggered, but no one took notice of him, or the girl.

It was stifling up here. The walls were the color of a rare tenderloin, the horsehair seats upholstered in red velvet. Electrical lights glimmered behind ruby-glass shades, as a pall of rising tobacco smoke settled over them.

"Can you see?" he asked the girl, pointing to the screen far below. A small figure sat in front of a huge pipe organ and began to play Bach's Fugue in D Minor.

"I can see just fine." Gilda slumped into her seat, the celluloid doll in her lap.

After a few minutes, the organist walked backstage. A line of women marched into the orchestra pit and played "Paragon Rag." He reached into his jacket pocket for a tin of lemon drops, opened it, and popped one in his mouth before holding it out to her.

"Care for a lemon drop?"

She took one, her gaze fixed on the Ladies' Orchestra, and crunched it greedily. "Can I have another?"

"Help yourself."

She took two more and stuck them in her mouth as he loosened his tie. She yawned and mumbled, "When's it gonna start?"

"Soon."

The Ladies' Orchestra struck up a lively rendition of the overture to *William Tell,* finishing to loud applause. The electrical lights dimmed as a bright square appeared on the movie screen below. The music swelled into something ominous and unfamiliar, eerie piping, strings that sounded like human voices. The high-school boys fell silent and leaned over the rail, staring raptly as the screen filled with the image of a beautiful woman floating above a field, her hand extended to a black-clad man.

He glanced at the girl beside him, her glassy eyes only half open. The doll had slipped beneath her armrest. He picked it up and set it back in her lap.

The orchestra's accompaniment grew louder. He watched as the phantoms on the screen journeyed among the damned, many of whom were indeed naked. As the orchestra's playing grew louder and more feverish, he let himself sink down in his own seat, one anonymous shadow among many, as beside him the girl breathed heavily, and then not at all.

Chapter 46

Is it true?" Bennie asked Francis when they were a safe distance from Robey Street. "About that other killing?"

"How could I make that up?"

"How'd you find out?"

"I'll tell you—but what about filing your story?"

Bennie laughed. "I already did—it'll hit the streets in half an hour. But maybe I should've waited. How the hell did you know about that murder in Boston?"

"Someone who used to live there told me about it, not more than an hour ago."

"Is he trustworthy?"

"I believe him."

"Think he'd talk to me?"

"No."

"And they never caught whoever did it?"

"Not as far as I know."

They waited at a corner to let a streetcar pass. Francis jangled the keys in his pocket, a habit when he was concentrating.

"It can't be a coincidence, Bennie," he said as they crossed the street.

"Two girls, two murders inside the same kind of dark ride—what are the odds?"

"Not good," admitted Bennie.

"Have you heard of any other girls disappearing?"

"Girls are always disappearing. Especially in Little Sicily. And Gypsy kids. They run away, or their families marry them off when they're twelve or thirteen years old."

"Those girls don't show up dead in amusement parks."

"They don't show up at all. That's my point. Maybe your two girls aren't a coincidence, but you can't prove that. And there's only two of them. Two crimes, what was it—four years apart?"

"It's queer, Bennie. You can't argue with that."

"Of course it's queer. That's my job—following every bit of queer news I come across, and making it up when I have to."

Francis laughed. It was true: a few years back, Bennie had faked a story about an earthquake in Lincoln Park, and another about pirates on the Chicago River, paying a tugboat captain to dress up like a buccaneer. "But really," he said, "can you think of another crime like this? It could be a big story."

"It already is."

Francis halted. "The *Daily News* is a big paper. Do they keep records of crimes like this? Not just in Chicago—other cities."

"Like Boston?'"

"Boston, Minneapolis, New York—anyplace that might have an amusement park."

Bennie shook his head. "You're not a detective anymore, Francis."

"Doesn't mean I stopped thinking like one. Do me a favor—look through your paper's records, see what you can find and let me know."

"And? Can you get me a copy of the coroner's report?"

"You know I won't get close to that, Bennie."

"What about photos of the dead girl?" Francis scowled. Bennie went on, unruffled, "Okay, so how's about that kid who found the girl's body? You know who he is, right? All you need to do is point him out to me, I'll do the talking. What time's your shift start?"

"I should be there now. I appreciate this, Bennie."

"Beats counting corpses—that's what I was doing a few weeks ago with the *Eastland*." Bennie stuck his notebook into a pocket and turned toward the streetcar stop. "If I find anything, I'll track you down at the park. This could be a great story, Francis. Like Dr. Holmes."

Francis gazed at the Hippodrome's angel gleaming in the summer haze. "I sure hope not," he said.

Chapter 47

SHE PASSED THE Wild West Show, Henry a dozen yards behind her with his head bowed, talking to himself. Pin kept an eye on him, increasingly unnerved.

The more she thought about it, the more convinced she was that there could be only one reason he'd have newspaper clippings of Elsie Paroubek and Iolanda Vasilescu and her sister, Abriana. Once news broke about the girl she'd found in Hell Gate, he'd add her picture to his wallet as well. She'd been stupid, thinking she could trust him, imagining that the two of them might find a murderer. He wasn't some harmless weird little man: he was crazy, a chester.

He scared her. She should go back to the Riverview station and warn them—while they were congratulating themselves on locking up Clyde Smithson, this guy was lurking around the Infant Incubators.

She began to walk faster. After a minute, she looked back to see that she'd momentarily lost Henry in the crowd on the Pike. She darted forward, ducked behind the back of an arcade and held her breath, listening; heard the sound of running feet.

Damn. He'd seen her. As she turned to race farther down the alley, someone punched her in the ribs. She collapsed to the ground, clutching her stomach.

"You fucking little sneak." Ikie stared down at her, his fist raised. "You son of a bitch."

"Fucking fairy," Mugsy spat. He glanced around, then slammed his boot into Pin's side. She cried out, tears filling her eyes.

Mugsy laughed and kicked her again. "Goddamn sissy. What'd I say? He's a punk."

Pin tried to gasp out a retort, but her lungs wouldn't work. She turned onto her side, reaching for the shiv in her pocket.

"Why'd you say that about Clyde?" Ikie's loathing was tinged with hurt. "You punk."

"Fairy," Mugsy repeated. He reached into his pocket for a switch-blade knife, clicked it so that the blade sprang out.

Ikie reached for his friend's arm. "Mugsy, don't."

Mugsy elbowed him away. He bent, sweeping the knife down toward Pin's jaw, and with a grunt went sprawling onto his back. A blue-clad figure sat astride him, hands locked around his throat. Pin pushed herself onto her knees as Mugsy's face turned purple and Henry stared down at him with impassive eyes.

"Henry," she croaked, trying to stand. "Henry, stop..."

Like a mastiff grabbing a terrier, Ikie flung Henry aside. He dragged Mugsy to his feet.

"Come on, man!" he cried, and Pin realized Ikie was frightened of Henry. "They're pansies. We gotta go." He turned to cast one last glance at Pin.

"How could you?" he asked, and dragged Mugsy down the alley.

Pin staggered to her feet, wiping her eyes as she fought to catch her breath. Ikie, the one person she'd thought of as a friend, thought she was a fairy. He believed she'd betrayed Clyde—she *had* betrayed him, even if she hadn't intended to.

And what was she? Not a girl, not a boy. Beneath her shirt, the elastic truss dug painfully into her skin. She tugged at it, overwhelmed by a wave of yearning as she thought of girls she'd seen walking hand in hand around the Lagoon, laughing as they whispered to each other, their summer dresses blown against their legs. She'd never wear a dress again if she could help it. Yet she felt almost sick with a longing to see Glory in her teddy bare, the peach-colored silk against her tanned skin and her red mouth that tasted of sugar.

It hurt to think of Glory; her eyes burned, but she wouldn't cry. Next time she'd use her shiv to kill Mugsy; she'd kill them all before letting them see her cry.

"He was a bad man." She could barely hear Henry, whispering as though to himself. "I killed people before."

She refused to look up, just stared at the ground with her hands clenched. Henry babbled on, now trying to get her attention.

"Pinhead. Pinprick. Pin Drop. Pin…"

He filled her with disgust, despite the fact that he'd just saved her from a beating, or worse. She'd seen the man at the Ten-in-One who bit the heads off chickens—not a gaffed freak but the real thing, they called him a geck or geek. He'd stare at the wriggling bloody creature in his hands, as though wondering how the headless thing got there. Henry reminded her of the geek. So what did that make her?

Ikie was right. She was just a dirty little punk. A real girl would have screamed upon seeing that body inside Hell Gate, and Clyde would have run to investigate, along with everybody else working the ride. Everyone would have known Clyde wasn't the killer. It would be her fault if he went to the gallows.

"Pin!" Henry's voice grew more urgent. "Pin, *look*."

She looked up to see him clutching a paper sack stained with grease.

"Here," he said. He set the sack beside her foot, along with an open bottle of sarsaparilla from the arcade. Pin hesitated, then grabbed the sack and opened it. She jammed a potato wedge into her mouth, barely chewed it before swallowing, took a gulp of sarsaparilla, and wolfed down the rest of the potatoes. Henry stared at her, his head cocked and brow furrowed.

"*Armes einsames Kind, armes einsames Kind,*" he murmured in German. "*Es is so verloren…*"

She couldn't understand him, but the tenderness in his tone cut her like a whip. She turned so he couldn't see her face. After a moment, she heard him move beside her.

"Do you want to see the Black Brothers Lodge?"

Her gaze remained fixed on the ground. "The what?"

"The Black Brothers Lodge. Where the Gemini have our Destiny Meetings."

She couldn't help it—she laughed. Henry stiffened: what she saw in his eyes froze her. He backed away and lashed out at the air in a rage. "You are not to mock!"

"Stop!" she hissed. "They'll toss us!"

But she and Henry might have been atop the Blue Streak: no one gave them a glance.

"Not to mock, not to mock!" Henry mumbled his nonsense, agitatedly rocking back and forth. "Ticktock, laughingstock…"

Pin stared at the now-empty sarsaparilla bottle and paper sack at her feet. Henry had fed her; he'd protected her from Mugsy. Why? He might be a chester, but he'd made no move to touch her. She could barely imagine him touching anyone; he acted like his fingers would be burned if he tried.

And his voice still echoed in her mind, repeating those German words she couldn't understand, as though soothing a sick child. Clyde hated her, and Larry and Ikie. Mugsy might have killed her if Henry hadn't stopped him. She took a deep breath.

"Are you having a meeting tonight?" she asked. "The Gemini. At the lodge?"

He shook his head, still upset. "No, no. Willhie's away—only when both Gemini are there with the Black Sack of Destiny."

She bit her lip to keep from laughing again. "The Black Sack of Destiny?"

Henry stopped rocking on his heels. "Yes! But if we do this"—he lowered his voice—"no one can ever know. Bad for business. Do you swear?"

She didn't respond, thinking.

I killed people before.

Detectives killed people. In stories, anyway. Maybe they were real, the Gemini. Maybe he really was a detective—that was why he kept all those newspaper clippings in his wallet. Maybe together they could find the Hell Gate killer. Maybe he knew who killed her sister.

At last she nodded. "Where's your friend? Willhie?"

"In Decatur, until later. Visiting his sister, mister. If you come with me now," he said in a hoarse whisper, "I'll show you."

Without waiting for her reply, he turned and walked away.

Pin let her breath out in a low whistle. He was crazy as a bedbug. But would he lure her off someplace to kill her, after saving her from Mugsy? Probably not, but she touched her shiv for reassurance, just in case. And she could always just run.

She left the arcade. She didn't catch sight of Henry again till she reached the main gate. A crowd had gathered by the Hippodrome, even more people than usual for a late-afternoon showing—three policemen held them back from the theater's main doors.

Pin shaded her eyes from the blinding sunset. Was a new Chaplin movie opening tonight? *The Inferno* had been held over, and Pin still hadn't seen it. Maybe now she'd missed her chance.

She hurried through the exit gate to meet Henry at the streetcar stop. From farther down Western Avenue came a grinding shriek, as the trolley raced toward Riverview. As it slowed in a shower of sparks and the smell of hot metal, a woman outside the Hippodrome began to scream.

Chapter 48

He shut the door behind him and leaned against it, waiting until his heart slowed. The little bitch had attacked him. Like a rat springing from its nest, not asleep at all, not silent. He'd had to cover her mouth with both hands, and still she'd fought. Strong as a grown woman, how was that possible?

He licked his lips. His mouth tasted foul: a shiver of nausea passed through him as he remembered the bottle of cordial he'd finished. He dug a hand into his pocket and withdrew the Kewpie doll. The nausea became a spasm. His legs buckled and he knelt, retching.

After a few minutes he got unsteadily to his feet. The room's stifling late-afternoon air was alive with dust motes. He recalled images from the movie: arms waving like underwater plants, the eyeless faces of the damned. A title card.

Hope not ever to see Heaven. I have come to lead you to the other shore; into eternal darkness, into fire and into ice.

He stared at the red half-moon imprinted on the back of his hand, where she'd drawn blood. He'd misjudged the amount of cordial in the lemon drops. It was the first time one had put up a fight, the first time he'd gazed down into eyes that were not a doll's, glazed and placid, but those of a terrified child.

He squeezed his eyes shut. The orchestra had been loud enough to drown out any sounds, and that imbecilic usher hadn't shown his head during the movie. The other couples scattered across the balcony had been engaged in their own skirmishes in their own velvet seats. No one had noticed his own.

But the girl's struggle had made it impossible for him to maintain either illusion or excitement—all his energy had gone into silencing her. Her dress had been torn in the tussle; he'd taken it anyway, but it was spoiled, everything was spoiled.

He walked to the closet and unlocked it, pulling the torn calico dress from his pocket. It had been threadbare and patched to begin with. Now it was nothing but a rag. He couldn't clothe her in that, couldn't take the photographs he'd so meticulously planned in his head. He tossed the dress aside.

He'd have to develop the negatives he'd already shot—a waste of the remaining film on that roll, but he'd already been deprived of one pleasure back in the theater. Now, with her dress spoiled, he'd have no joy in dressing the doll again, and no joy whatsoever in giving her the bitch's name. What had it been? Gilda.

He pushed it from his memory. He would find another girl to-morrow.

Maria waited inside the closet, arms held stiffly at her side, her blue glass eyes gazing straight ahead. Her bisque fingers would be cold to the touch. She had no teeth to bite.

He stared at her, turned, and walked to the bed. He knelt to re-trieve the camera and film tank and light apron where he'd hidden them, picked up the doll, and set her on the mattress. He spent several minutes posing her, shooting what remained of the film.

When he was finished, he turned his attention to the film tank. He measured out the grains of pyro, sulfite of soda, and soda carbon-ate into five ounces of lukewarm water in the cylinder, added cold water. He repeated a similar process with the acid bath, dissolving the fixing powders in warm water he poured into a washbasin. He proceeded with the intricate transfer of the film cartridge from his camera, carefully lowered the reel into the cylinder, set it on a plate.

He got out his pocket watch, and every three minutes turned the cylinder, until twenty minutes had passed. He brought the cylinder to the sink, removed the transferring reel, and set it into the fixing bath; washed it five times in another bowl, changing the water each time. Last of all, he hung the filmstrip from a dowel to dry. Later, he would examine the negatives and make the prints in the same closet where he kept the doll. He used a flashlight for this, which gave the final prints a misty, dreamy quality.

He washed his hands, cracked a window to disperse the acrid scent of the chemicals, and returned to the closet. The familiar ritual of developing the film had calmed him, but as he gazed down at Maria in her yellow dress, he felt that ease dissolve. Her vacant gaze seemed focused on something in the room behind him: it took all his effort not to look over his shoulder to be sure he was still alone.

He stared at her, unable to look away. A black abscess burst inside him, the sickening horror of what he'd done, not once but over and over again, more times than he could count. He could no longer sense his own breath, hear the wind in the leaves outside, or feel the heat of the afternoon air upon his skin. Whatever thin membrane had held him intact within the void had dissolved. All that remained was the knowledge and the realization that he would do it again, without ceasing, until he died.

Chapter 49

ENTERING RIVERVIEW, HE found himself missing the noise and squalor of Coney Island. Here, the rubbish bins didn't reek of discarded seafood luncheons left to rot in the afternoon sun. The gravel had been neatly raked, the grass watered and trimmed. The entrance gates resembled those of a medieval castle in a movie, banners flapping. The candy colors and fairy-tale buildings reminded him of a spun-sugar egg he'd received one Easter as a boy: he'd smashed it with a rock to better see what was inside, swallowed the sweet splinters, and made himself ill.

A flicker of that sickly desire overcame him as he navigated the thronged midway. He'd visited Riverview only once, shortly after it opened for the season in May. He'd been curious about the heavily wooded picnic area known as Fairyland, its name ironical considering the activities reputed to take place there. That day he saw no one at Fairyland save a young mother with her children, and he left the park feeling disappointed.

Now he meandered along the Pike, scanning the crowds and carnival workers for a face that might spark a story idea. He ignored the Ten-in-One—people with obvious scars or deformities interested him less than those whose eyes betrayed an inner disfigurement, perhaps one that mirrored his own. But it was early enough in the day that most of the people he passed seemed cheerful and expectant. Families, courting couples, small gangs of boys racing along the Lagoon.

He drew up short when he reached the Hell Gate pavilion, momentarily confused by the sight of policemen everywhere, guarding its entrance and dredging the canal, poring over piles of refuse.

Of course—the murder! The queasy excitement he'd felt earlier flared into delight. *Here* was a scenario for a movie! And they might even be able to film right here at the park! He took out his notebook and scribbled *Hellgate,* stood, and watched until a policeman walked over.

"I'll have to ask you to leave, sir." The cop gazed at him with distaste; contempt, even. Or perhaps he just imagined that? But no, the man fingered a billy club in a manner that seemed both suggestive and threatening.

Unless he imagined that, too. He nodded at the policeman and hurried off, and didn't stop again until he reached Fairyland.

Not far away rose the abandoned smokestacks and kilns of Bricktown, but here the air was fragrant with loam and decaying leaves, last year's sprouting acorns and golden dropseed. Trails crisscrossed the forest floor, left by rabbits or foxes and coyotes. Vagrants used these trails to reach the railroad bed.

So did men looking for anonymous assignations. He peered through the leafy patchwork but saw no signs of human traffic, not even the remains of a campfire. He wasn't sure if he felt disappointed or relieved.

He tapped out a hashish cigarette, lit up, and smoked in rapid puffs, hoping he was downwind from any unseen picnickers. When he was done, he popped a lemon drop to mask his breath, and unsteadily retraced his steps, his thoughts pinwheeling from Hell Gate to actors who might be enticed to play a murderer.

A figure stepped from the trees in front of him. Older, white, with a carefully trimmed mustache and grey hair beneath his fedora. He froze as the man raised a finger to his hat brim and gave him a nod.

"Looking for a friend?" the man asked, his tone offhand and amiable. His mouth went dry as he stared at the man and remembered other encounters like this at Coney Island, grunting and sometimes a bit of blood, the memory of splintered sugar exploding into a sour hot taste. He shook his head, bolted past the man, and crashed through the trees until he found the path again and emerged near the band shell.

He walked breathlessly past rows of chairs filled with people taking a break from the rides, his heart beating so hard he thought he might keel over. The hashish. He shouldn't have smoked so much. To calm himself, he bought some hokeypokey and settled on a bench to eat it.

When the ice cream was gone, he took out his little notebook and began scribbling ideas for his story. A child's murder in an amusement park—it was ghoulish, but look how many people were here today, just hours after a real murder had occurred! He underlined the word *Hellgate,* scrawled a few other words—*girl, rope or knife?*

If Spoor turned this one down, he'd take it elsewhere. He finished writing and sat for a few minutes before heading off to explore more of the park.

In several minutes he found a fortune-teller—a real person, not one of those automatons:

MADAME ZANTO ORACLE OF THE AGES
WHAT DOES YOUR FUTURE HOLD?
25 Cents

He pulled aside the shabby velvet curtains and walked in.

The dim room was hardly bigger than a closet. Joss sticks smoldered in a corner. A frayed Persian rug covered the floor, caked with dirt. At a table set with a china teapot, two cups, and saucers sat Madame Zanto, clad in a red shawl, black shirtwaist, a skirt that ended only a few inches below her knees.

"You come to know your future?"

She looked up at him, much younger than he'd expected—twenty-seven or twenty-eight, several years younger than he was. Small and very thin, her dark curling hair held in place by two combs. Delicate features, swarthy complexion, her face more piquant than pretty. Italian, he thought. A genuine Gypsy wouldn't be permitted to work here.

She gestured at the chair opposite her, the silver bracelets on her arms jingling. "Have a seat. Twenty-five cents."

She held out a hand as he sat, searching for his coin holder. He removed his notebook, set it on the table as he emptied his pockets.

"Here it is." He extracted a quarter and dropped it into her palm. She set it aside and reached for the teapot, poured tea into one of the cups, and pushed it toward him.

"Drink that. Every drop."

It was tepid and tasted of jasmine smoke, but he downed it. She set the cup upside down on the saucer and turned it three times, tapping it as she gazed at him.

Looking for tells, he thought. He held up his hands so she could see he wore no wedding band. She gave him a tired smile, turned over the cup, and leaned forward to stare at the sodden mass.

"These here—these are tears," she said, dabbing a finger in the saucer. "And this—"

Her finger hovered above a small mound of tea leaves. "This mountain signifies you have a powerful enemy."

"An enemy?" He laughed.

"Yes." She tipped her head. "You have no enemies?"

"Not that I know of."

"Well, it means trouble, anyway." She narrowed her eyes. "You won't marry," she said, lifting her head to see his reaction. He tried to manage an expression that combined diffidence and disappointment, instead felt himself blushing under the woman's intense stare.

"What else?" he asked, hoping to change the subject.

"What else," she murmured. "I don't see anything else."

"That's it?" he said in mock dismay. "A powerful enemy and I won't marry? You're not even trying!"

She made a face and prodded the tea leaves with a fingernail. "You might consider getting a dog."

"A dog?"

"For companionship. And to protect against your enemy."

He snorted. "For a quarter I should get a good omen."

"You want me to lie? The dog's not a bad omen. It's a piece of advice. Usually I charge extra for that."

He stood and tipped his hat. "Thanks for the advice. I'll take it up with my landlord."

He pulled aside the velvet curtain and left. Neither he nor Madame Zanto noticed that he had left his notebook on the table.

Chapter 50

It was after five o'clock when Francis returned to the Riverview station house. Magruder manned the desk, chin propped on one hand as he read a newspaper. At the sight of Francis, he held up the front page so Francis could see the headline:

Vicious Murder at Amusement Park: Colored Magician Arrested

"It's everywhere." Magruder pointed at a stack at his elbow. "O'Connell brought these in. Cabell met with all the reporters, he—"

"I was there," said Francis.

He found the Riverview captain slouched in his office chair, puffing ruminatively at a cigar. As he entered, Hickey sat up heavily and stubbed out the cigar in a marble ashtray.

"Francis. Where've you been?"

"Robey Street, like you asked me."

"I know that didn't take three whole hours."

"I did some catching up with a man I knew there."

Hickey regarded him through bloodshot eyes. The creases in his jacket suggested he'd tried to get some shut-eye here in the office. "Anything new?"

"Not a thing."

Hickey poured a scant inch of water into a glass, opened a packet of analgesic powder and tipped it in, gulped down the murky liquid without bothering to stir it first.

"Christ, this is all we need." He reached for another cigar. "You still don't think Smithson did it?"

"He says he's been here since opening day. I can vouch for that, and so can a thousand other people."

"Can he account for every single day?"

Francis dragged over a chair and sat. "I know I saw him around here last month—I saw his show twice. It's a good show," he added.

"I don't give a tinker's damn how good his show is."

Francis's jaw tightened. "Goddamn it, Bill. You know he's innocent, and so does anyone else who knows Clyde Smithson. That boy who saw the man going into the ride with the girl says he was a white man. If you don't release Clyde, there's going to be trouble. Remember those kids last summer? You want that on your hands?"

Hickey's face darkened. "You sure there was nothing new at Robey Street?"

"Not a word other than what the Maffucci boy told us right here in this room."

"That kid—he could have told us anything. For all we know, *he* could've done it."

"Now you're just being obtuse." Francis shook his head. "He's a scrawny kid, you saw him. This was some kind of crazed sex fiend. That girl was—"

"I know what she was," Hickey broke in angrily. "I have three daughters. It's unspeakable. And all we have is a description of a man who looks like every other man. You think we're going to question every dude in Riverview wearing a boater and an ice-cream suit? People are going to read the papers and scream about closing the park. Baumgarten's going to have a heart attack."

"Elsie Paroubek's case didn't affect business here."

"Elsie Paroubek wasn't murdered in summer at an amusement park." Hickey heaved himself from his chair, walked to the window, and raised the shades to stare at the crowds outside. "I bet there's a hundred thousand people here today."

He turned back to Francis. "Well, not much we can do but wait. Cabell give you any guff?"

"What you would expect."

"Well, there's no reason you should spend the rest of the day here," Hickey said. "We have enough Chicago men on duty to hold a parade. Report tomorrow as usual."

Francis clapped his helmet back on his head and stood. As he turned to leave, Hickey said, "What do you think the odds are of this killer attacking again?"

"Not good. It would be like lightning striking twice. And he would have to be a fool. He could be in Minnetonka by now."

Francis headed for the door. He hadn't won a bet since 1906, when he'd wagered that the Hitless Wonders White Sox would win against the Chicago Cubs in the World Series. He'd considered telling Hickey that, but had thought better of it.

Chapter 51

THE BLACK BROTHERS Lodge turned out to be a weathered barn behind a sprawling white house on Roscoe Street. A nice part of town, not the sort of area where she'd expect to find a secret society holed up.

"This is it?" Pin gave Henry a doubtful look as they hurried down the sidewalk. He'd had to pay her streetcar fare—she was flat broke.

"Yes," he said. He kept glancing stealthily over his shoulder, in a way guaranteed to draw attention if anyone happened to notice a very short, scruffy-looking man and an even-scruffier boy walking in a respectable neighborhood early on a Sunday evening. "We need to get inside before anyone sees us."

Pin wondered if they were doing something illegal. She began to look around nervously as well. On the streetcar, Henry had stared at her with such a strange, intense expression that she began to feel frightened.

Goddamn sissy. What'd I say? He's a punk.

What if Henry was a fairy? She'd contemplated hopping off the streetcar and running back to Riverview, but next thing she knew he was gesturing at their stop.

There were no streetlamps here, only large old trees and green lawns in front of houses all but hidden behind rhododendrons and azaleas and hydrangea bushes. The air smelled different from Riverview's—no trace of river-bottom stink or dust raised by the passage of thousands of feet. The wind stirred the trees, and their branches made a sound like people whispering overhead. Lights glimmered in some of the houses, but not at their destination.

"Is anyone home?" she wondered.

"I told you, he's gone to Decatur. Traitor."

"This is Willhie's house?" She looked at him in surprise. "Do you live here, too?"

Henry shook his head. "I told you, I live by the hospital."

"But before that, was this your house?"

"Before that I lived in the asylum."

"The asylum?"

"Till I was seventeen."

"How old are you now?"

"Twenty-three. They sent me there when I was twelve. I only escaped six years ago. They called it the crazy house."

"Were you—" She almost asked if he was crazy. "Why did you live there?"

"I burned a building. Many buildings. A peddler cheated me and I snuck into his yard and set his crates afire. It burned to the ground—an entire building. I was a very dangerous boy. I burned up a picture of Jesus Christ. I hit a boy on the head with a brick, and blood came out his ear. Once I pushed a baby down the stairs. I killed a man, too, but nobody knew about that. And I threw hot ashes on a little girl. She went into the hospital, my father had to pay for it."

Pin stared at him, repulsed yet also fascinated. "Why'd you do all that?"

"I just hated babies." He shook his head in remorse. "Not now. Now I love and protect them. My little sister disappeared when I was four."

Pin's neck went cold. "Your sister? What happened?"

"Nobody told me."

"What about your father?"

"Father, bother." Henry cut across the lawn toward the house. "He made good pancakes. I cut a teacher with a knife, her arms and face, what a place. They put me in the home for boys. Awful noise. People did bad things. I watched the snow..."

He threw an invisible snowball. "Blizzards. People froze standing up. I saw a cyclone pick up a barn with cows in it. There were cows hanging in the trees. You had to climb to get milk."

"That's not true."

"Who said it was?"

"Where was your mother?"

"Dead. Dead in bed. My sister murdered her. I went to an outside school until Dr. Stegman sent me to the asylum. A big tunnel where we walked in the winter, under the snow. That was where the people froze to death, in the fields by the asylum. They turned to icicles. Men put them in their mouths and sucked on them. Five years I kept running away. Finally I escaped."

Pin rubbed her arms, trying to dispel the chill that had overcome her at the words *My little sister disappeared when I was four.* In the near dark, Henry looked younger and tougher than he had back at Riverview. Twenty-three wasn't so old, really. She would have felt safer with someone older. She looked up at the dark house and trees in front of them. She would have felt safer if she hadn't come at all.

Chapter 52

THE SUN WAS low when Francis left the station, the park even more crowded. Bennie's story would have hit the streets by now: People who'd never been to Riverview, or who might have been there the day before, would stream through the gates and make a beeline for Hell Gate to gawk at the site of a child's murder. The ride hadn't reopened yet—the commissioner had quashed that—but the minute the police detectives completed their investigation, Francis knew there'd be hundreds of people lined up, gaping at the devil guarding his gimcrack palace.

He wandered in that direction, brooding. There was no way Clyde Smithson could have killed that girl, but the park employed nearly a thousand men who might have—groundskeepers, carpenters, mechanics, concessionaires, performers, animal trainers, ticket takers. It was likely the murderer was someone who'd specifically visited the park to commit his crime—Cue's account of the Wonderland killing suggested that.

But what if it was a man who worked here, someone who'd familiarized himself with the rides, so he'd know precisely when and where he could defile a child, then disappear into the crowd? No one who worked at Hell Gate would be so stupid, but someone from one of the other dark rides might easily have figured out the precise place and timing in the canal tunnel.

Yet it didn't need to be someone from a dark ride, or any ride: everywhere he looked, he saw men in boater hats with money to spend, and little oversight as to how they spent it. Just a month ago, two policewomen from the Chicago force had been assigned to Riverview, specifically to arrest men who came here to pick up girls no older than fifteen, plying them with alcohol at one of the beer gardens, then spiriting them off to a nearby hotel. After two weeks, the policewomen were detailed to the beach, and the mashers resumed their pleasure as before.

Francis passed Hell Gate, where sawhorses and a makeshift rope fence kept the rubberneckers at bay. He wandered along the path toward Fairyland and the Woodland Cabaret: the shadowy side of Riverview, with its booths selling seedy postcards and the ragged hootchy-kootchy tents.

But he saw no policemen here: once Clyde was taken into custody, there was no need to question anyone else. Francis sighed in frustration, elbowing past a line of men who watched the Dancing Dolls, young women in skimpy dresses who flounced around pretending to be life-size toys.

A few yards away stood the She-Male's tent. Usually there'd be a crowd by now, though Max kept an unreliable schedule, especially on Sundays. Francis knew he had a woman somewhere—Max had made a point of telling him that. So Max wasn't a fairy, and Francis had never heard of him molesting Pin, or any of the other boys. He pushed aside the tent flap and peeked inside, wrinkling his nose at the reek of mud and urine; dropped the flap and walked over to Max's shack. He rapped at the door and, when he heard no reply, turned the knob. The door opened, which was odd.

But inside he saw nothing worth stealing. A half-full bottle of whiskey and some dirty postcards, a stained cloche hat, and a tattered silk skirt, tinsel drooping from its hem. A table scattered with cosmetics and some empty cigarette packets. A gaffed freak's dreary props, all dusted with cigarette ash and a melancholy air that made Francis quickly return outside.

He headed back to the Pike, wiping a trickle of sweat from his cheek. He hadn't eaten since breakfast. He considered getting a hot dog, decided to wait until supper. His landlady, Mrs. Dahl, served a decent pork chop. He walked toward the exit gate, pausing to tip his helmet at a young woman in a smart new military-style frock. "Very nice," he said, admiring her hat, a regimental turban in bright pink.

The woman's cheeks pinked. He started to ask if she was in need of directions, but she turned and ran toward a man waiting beside the Lagoon.

Francis watched her go, the flicker of desire fading into the more familiar pang of loss. Maria Walewski; his sister, Ellen; Maura; that girl in Boston…Women and girls, they were all destined to disappear.

He flinched, thinking of Maura. The abortionist had stolen three lives that afternoon—Maura's, their bastard child's, his own. Yet maybe it wasn't too late for Francis to steal back the kind of life that should have been his. He did an about-face and headed to the arcade on the far side of the park.

Three high-school girls stood in front of Gina Maffucci's booth. One, pretty and plump in a dotted-swiss dress and straw Panama, burst into laughter when she saw him.

"There's the next man you see! Hey, Mister, want to marry our friend here? That's what her fortune said!"

Francis tipped his hat at each of them. "I could, but then what about the rest of you? I'd hate to leave anyone disappointed."

The girl they were teasing stuck her tongue out at him. "I ain't marrying no old man," she announced. "Who says I'm marrying ever? Maybe I'm a suffragette."

Her friends doubled over as she stalked off, nose in the air.

"Yay, you ain't so old," the plump girl said to Francis. "But my fortune says I'm gonna marry someone from across the sea. So unless that's you…"

"Um, no. I'm from right here in Chicago."

She made a show of sighing in disappointment and ran after her friend, the third girl at her heels. Francis stepped to the fortune-teller's booth and read the sign pinned above the velvet curtains:

MADAME ZANTO ORACLE OF THE AGES
WHAT DOES YOUR FUTURE HOLD?
25 Cents

He hesitated, then entered, removing his hat. "Mrs. Maffucci?"

The slight figure at the table looked up, a flash of panic in her eyes. "My God, is it Pin? Did something happen to Pin?"

"No, no! Or, well, I wouldn't know." He stood awkwardly, the heat rising in his face. "I'm—well, I'm off duty, I just thought I'd see how the boy was doing. And you."

"Have you seen him?"

"Pin? No. Big crowds today. And I've been busy."

"Of course." She sighed, and he saw how drawn she looked, her eyes deeply shadowed beneath a dusting of face powder. "I can't bear to think about it. And Pin...I can't make him stay put."

"If I had a daughter, I'd be inclined to keep her at home. But I'm sure Pin can take care of himself." Francis tried to smile reassuringly, and glanced at the objects on her little table. A teapot, two dirty china cups. "I never had my fortune told. Figured I'd try it out."

He set down a quarter. Gina slid it toward her and dropped it into a small red pouch. He continued to stand, hat in hand and unsure where to look in the tiny space. Gina Maffucci's black shirtwaist revealed only a demure décolletage, but her skirt was short enough that he could glimpse her legs, crossed at the knee and sheathed in black stockings. Skinny legs, skinny arms, peaked face. Like her son, she looked like she could use a few hot dinners.

"You looking for an answer to a particular question, Sergeant?"

"Francis," he said.

"Francis," she repeated. For the first time, she smiled, revealing a tiny gap between her front teeth. "Have a seat."

He did, trying not to stare at her. But there really was nowhere else to look.

She set a velvet pouch in front of her and removed a deck of cards so creased and worn he couldn't imagine shuffling them, but she did so with ease. She had small delicate hands, long fingered, with silver bracelets around her thin wrists. A ring winked from her left hand, the gold plate slightly tarnished.

He should have known. He wrenched away his gaze, pretending to show great interest in the cards. After a moment he asked, "Does your husband work here at the park as well?"

Her reply was terse. "He's dead."

"I'm very sorry to hear that."

"I'm not. He was an evil man."

Francis blinked at her vehemence. "Do—do any of your predictions come true?"

"What makes you think they all don't?" With a loud *snap* she set the cards down in front of her. "Well, there's your answer. You get one question."

"That wasn't my question!"

"No?" She burst out laughing. "Well, what is it?"

Without thinking, he blurted, "Would you care to have dinner with me?"

She blushed and shuffled the cards again, set them back down. "I already had some hard-boiled eggs. But thank you."

"That's not much of a dinner."

"I'm not a big eater."

He leaned across the table. "Well, would you like to go out dancing?"

"Dancing?" Her eyes widened. "What, now?"

"Well, no. But the Casino Restaurant's open for a few more hours. We could go dancing after supper. Or we could go somewhere else. Sadowski's, they have a good band plays ragtime."

"It's a busy time of day for me."

"Or the Idle Hour Café, that's right across the street. I can come back later to pick you up."

She stared at the cards. "I shouldn't be out late. Not after last night. My son, Pin…"

"Pin knows how to find his way across the Pike."

"Oh, I don't know." She bit her lower lip, reminding him of when he'd questioned Pin in the station house. Finally, she said, "I'll do your fortune. Give me your hand."

He hid his disappointment but obediently put his hand on the table. She took it in both of her own, turning it over to examine it. Frowning, she extended her finger to trace the lines of his palm.

"How many times a day do you do this?" he asked, hoping to break the mood.

"Hush." She bent over his hand for a long time, at last sat back. "I'll go with you to the Casino for dinner."

"What?" He stared at her, confused, and she grinned.

"I just wanted to be sure you weren't married. Some men, they take off their wedding rings, but you can always tell—"

She tapped the base of his ring finger. "There—the sun never reaches it. So if they wear a ring, you can see where it was, 'cause it's white."

She sat back in her chair, pleased with herself. Francis laughed.

"Well, that's very clever," he said. He stood, relieved. "Should I come back, say at half past?"

She nodded. "I'll close up early. Like you said, big crowds today. I've been busy. That poor girl…"

Her voice trailed off, and her expression grew strange—not frightened but vacant. It unnerved him, and he stared at her, tongue-tied, until she blinked, the spell broken. She withdrew a small pouch, heavy with coins, turned her back to him, and made some adjustment to her blouse. When she turned back, the pouch was gone.

"I keep it with me," she explained. "Even at night. If anyone's going to steal it, they'll have to kill me first. I have this, too." She twitched her hand and held up a shiv.

Francis tried to hide his shock. "Well, I know where Pin gets his moxie, I guess."

Once again her face grew masklike. She set the deck of cards on a small shelf, alongside a notebook and a hurricane lantern, and froze.

"Oh, God! I forgot all about this!" She picked up the notebook and shook her head. "A customer left it, I meant to go after him and give it back, but someone else came in right away."

Francis glanced at the little book—the sort of notebook reporters like Bennie used. "I can bring it to the station house tomorrow—we have a lost-items box there, he might come to reclaim it."

"Oh, could you? Thank you."

She handed him the book. He slid it into his pocket and pulled aside the velvet drapes in the doorway. "I'll secure us a table at the Casino," he said. "After, we can do whatever you'd like—dancing, I hope."

"I'd like that," Gina replied, and smiled.

Chapter 53

WHEN HE ARRIVED at his apartment, Lionel hung up his jacket and hat, removed his collar, and exchanged his shoes for his house slippers. He poured himself a glass of whiskey, set it on his desk beside the typewriter, and went to retrieve his notebook from his jacket. He'd begun writing the scenario in his head on the way home. If Essanay refused to let him make it into a photoplay, he'd turn it into a story and sell it to one of the adventure magazines. Someone was going to cash in on this Hell Gate killing: Why not him?

But the breast pocket of his jacket was empty. He found his handkerchief and coin purse in one of the other pockets, along with a toothpick. But the notebook was gone.

He cursed under his breath, pacing the room as he struggled to reconstruct the last few hours. His thoughts were still slightly blurred from Max's hashish. When had he last had the notebook? In Fairyland? Yes, but it was after he'd left the woods that he'd seen all those cops at Hell Gate and realized that was where the murder had occurred. He'd written a note to himself, and then gone—where?

In an instant he remembered: the fortune-teller. He'd searched his pocket for a quarter to pay her and set his notebook on the table. Then forgot it just minutes later.

He swore again, more irritated now than genuinely upset. Surely she would have held on to it. Though if she happened to look inside, God knows what she'd make of his scribbled notes. He'd go back first thing tomorrow, drop by to see if Max was around to buy another few cigarettes. Make a few sketches of Hell Gate. Maybe he could even go inside, if they'd opened it again.

He sank into his desk chair and stared at his typewriter, feeling a frisson of mingled fear, desire, expectation: the emotion he experienced writing or reading a tale of forbidden things, walking after dark along the Manhattan docks or sitting in a dim Bowery saloon where men gathered to meet others with the same furtive thoughts. The world held a secret—many secrets—and he didn't need a notebook to uncover them.

Flushed with excitement, he thought of the tunnel beneath Hell Gate, the mysteries it held that he might re-create on the page. He rolled a fresh sheet of paper into his Royal Upright, and began to type.

Chapter 54

THE BARN WAS tucked into a weed-grown yard behind the house, surrounded by old elms. Henry lifted the latch and pulled the heavy door back, revealing a single long room cloaked in shadow. He stepped over the threshold and was immediately swallowed by the darkness. Pin hesitated, then went in after him.

The barn smelled of dirt and neat's-foot oil, chicken shit, and straw. After a few seconds her eyes began to adjust, and the outlines of unknown objects gradually became recognizable. A scythe, hoes and rakes and shovels, a wheelbarrow. A hay rake, twice as long as she was tall, hung from the rafters like a huge many-taloned claw. Sawhorses had been pushed against one wall, along with a wire frame that contained a small chicken coop.

Pin knelt in front of the coop and peered inside. She heard soft inquisitive clucks as the hens stirred in the straw where they slept. She poked a finger through the chicken wire, trying to touch their fluffed-up feathers.

"Here's a rabbit," Henry called.

She stood and joined him in front of a hutch. A large grey rabbit lay pressed against the front of the wire cage, hind legs outstretched like one of the leaping targets in the shooting gallery. Henry slipped his fingers through the wire and stroked its fur. Pin stared at it with longing and trepidation. "Will it bite me?"

Henry shook his head. She warily slid a finger through a gap in the chicken wire and touched the rabbit's long ear, feeling it quiver beneath her touch. She stroked it gently, the velvety fur softer than anything she could have imagined. "Can I let it out?" she asked.

"Foxes would kill it. Small things aren't safe."

He walked to the back of the barn, where not even the dim light from the door reached. She continued to stroke the rabbit, crooning at it, until Henry called to her again.

"The lodge is here."

She leaned her forehead against the hutch. "Goodbye," she whispered.

She picked her way carefully to the back of the barn. She could barely see Henry, though she heard him moving things around. Then there was a *ppffft,* and a blue-white flare appeared an arm's length away. The match moved through the air like one of Clyde's magic tricks, lighting votive candles in blue and red glass holders.

She turned, letting her eyes again adjust. When she looked back, she saw a sort of altar, made of two sawhorses with planks laid across them, its back flush against the rear wall. Black cloth covered the planks, not quite long enough to reach the floor and hide the coils of rope stored underneath. Arranged on the makeshift altar were numerous pictures, like the oversize cards her mother used to tell fortunes. Pin stepped toward the table and picked up one of them, peering at it in the candlelight.

A newspaper picture of a young girl had been pasted to a piece of shirt cardboard. Not Elsie Paroubek—Pin thought at first it might be Lillian Wulff, the girl who'd escaped from the Gypsies. But while this girl had braids like Lillian, she was thinner, pale and unsmiling. Pin squinted to read the caption beneath the photo:

Alice Porovsky, who has been missing since Thursday morning, was last seen walking from…

The rest of the words were missing. Lightning bolts had been inked above the girl's head, with colored flowers cut from seed catalogs scattered above them.

She glanced around for Henry, spotted him in the shadows. The flickering candlelight glinted in his eyes: he was watching her. She set the picture down and picked up another card. This, too, had a photograph clipped from a newspaper, a towheaded girl with a huge grin and several missing front teeth:

Parents bereft by Sonya Castillo's murder. "Who would rob us of our precious angel?" mother cries before fainting.

Stars had been drawn in a circle around the girl's picture, zigzag lines and a row of *X*s. Words were printed at the top in childish block letters:

ALL GIRLS WILL AVENGE THEM!

Pin replaced the card and picked up the next one, and the next, moving around the altar as the candles guttered in their votive glasses.

Every picture showed a different girl's image, cut from a newspaper. Sonya Castillo, Alice Porovsky, Katy Wilder, Dolly Trent, Lucia DeMarinis, Gunella Edmundson, Irena Novak. Each picture had been glued to a square of cardboard decorated with stars and lightning bolts, flowers clipped from catalogs, along with bunnies and kittens and baby chicks. Some of the girls had their eyes crossed out. One had a line of *X*s drawn across her mouth, as though it had been sewn up.

All the girls had been kidnapped. Two had never been seen again. The rest had been murdered.

She set the last card down. Her hand trembled as the candles flickered, blue and red. She counted the cards, searching for her sister's face among those of the dead or missing. But Abriana wasn't there.

Her sister had been too old, she realized. None of the girls pictured here were more than six or seven. She looked at Henry.

"In your wallet—that picture of another girl, her name was Abriana. Why isn't she here?"

His head moved quickly, the pinprick light in his eyes darting like fireflies in the darkness. "Not here, so queer," he said, his hoarse voice rising anxiously. "Can't save them all. So small…"

Her stomach flipped: he did know of her sister. Or did he? He might just have saved the article. Or he might have killed her.

She wanted to run, but it was too dark. She swallowed, a bad taste in her mouth. *Don't let him know you're scared,* she thought. Like with dogs, pretend you don't care. And don't look them in the eye.

Behind the row of candles, a larger piece of cardboard leaned against the wall. As she reached for it, she heard Henry behind her, breathing hard.

The cardboard was painted midnight blue and covered with gold-foil stars, like you got in school for good behavior. In the center was a photograph of Elsie Paroubek, the same one that had appeared everywhere the year she died. Her hair had been colored with orange crayon, her eyes dotted with midnight-blue paint. Her lips were bright red, and yellow lines squiggled from her hair and face. Pictures of the other girls surrounded her, a halo of children beneath words in yellow paint:

ANNIE ARONBURG
CHILD OF GREAT SOUL
PROTECT US ALL

"You did these," Pin whispered. She looked at Henry, and he nodded.

She stared at the picture of Alice Porovsky. She would always be missing since Thursday. Pin's heart beat hard, but she felt calm, so calm, as though her head had detached from her body and floated above it like a balloon, attached by a thread.

This is how those girls died, she realized. *This is the man who killed them, and now he is going to kill me.*

Bright blots sparked in front of her; she heard a sound like when she'd listened to a conch shell back at Lenore's place. *That's what the ocean sounds like,* her mother had said, but now she'd never hear the ocean. She wanted to see her mother, and now she never would. He would kill her like he'd killed those other girls.

But she wasn't a girl. She was Pin, a fourteen-year-old boy. She dropped the poster and turned to flee, reaching for the shiv in her pocket. Henry grabbed her wrist.

"It's part of the Ceremony," he explained, so close that she could feel his warm breath at her temple. "I protect them. So we don't forget."

Still grasping her, he stooped to pick up the fallen poster, set it tenderly on the altar, then reached beneath the altar. She watched numbly, too terrified to scream.

He straightened and held out a shapeless, dark mass—a burlap sack. He let go of her wrist, pushing her against the sawhorse so she couldn't run, and dug into his pocket to produce a pencil nub. He set it on the altar, then pulled something from the sack and handed her a small square of cardboard.

"Sign your name," he commanded.

"No."

"You have to—it's part of the Ceremony! All brothers of the Black Brothers Lodge have to sign their names!"

Pin blinked, confused. Maybe he wasn't going to kill her—maybe it really was a ceremony. She picked up the pencil stub, glanced aside to see Henry nod eagerly. Carefully she wrote *Pin Maffucci* at the bottom of the square. "So—am I a Gemini now?"

"That is never for you to say that!" Enraged, he snatched up cardboard and pencil, tossed them into the burlap sack, and kicked it back beneath the makeshift altar. *"Never!"*

He gestured wildly at the poster of Elsie Paroubek. "You are not to have touched her! You are not to speak her name! You—"

"Henry!" Light slashed through the darkness, blinding Pin, as a man's heavily accented voice called out in alarm. "Henry, who in hell is this?"

A tall figure moved behind the flashlight's beam. Henry's friend, she realized—the night watchman, Willhie. The man who'd gone to Decatur.

"Willhie!" cried Henry. "You're back. Sack," he added, glancing at the floor.

"Who is he?" demanded Willhie, and Pin flinched as he drew closer, pointing the flashlight at her face. "Who are you, boy?"

"A friend, Willhie," Henry insisted, "he's—"

She whirled and bolted out of the barn, the sound of pursuing footsteps echoing across the plank floor behind her.

Chapter 55

T HEY HAD SUPPER at the Casino Restaurant, where Gina made short work of a Wiener schnitzel. Francis had hurriedly returned to the station house, where he kept a change of clothes suitable for an evening out. But after dinner, Gina didn't want to go to the Palace Ballroom.

"I work there some nights," she said, and made a face. "Showing people with two left feet how to do the fox-trot."

"You're a dance teacher, right?"

"Not really a teacher. I demonstrate new dances, show them the steps. Sometimes men get a little fresh, but they're usually there with someone."

"Animal dances?"

"That's right. Grizzly bear, bunny hug, fox-trot, turkey trot. Dime a dance. Anyone gets frisky, Mr. Schneyer shows 'em right out."

Francis nodded, unsure what to say. He would have thought she'd be too embarrassed to admit such a thing. Or, at the least, that she'd blush while making the confession. Instead, she went on as though she'd been the one to ask him to dinner.

"Let's go to the cabaret," she said. "The girls I work with, we go all the time. They have a good singer, Sunday night's a piano player, but he's good, too."

Back out on the Pike, they might have been any couple. Francis hesitated to offer her his arm, but Gina took it on her own. He smiled down at her. A few more good German dinners would put some meat on those bones.

The Woodland Cabaret was on the far side of the park, near the arcade and minstrel show. It was managed by a colored woman named Bella Bynum, who kept a pistol in her pocket and had patented a system of alarms that made her a pile of money. "If I had ten men like her on the force, I could retire," Hickey often said. When Francis and Gina entered, Bella sat at a table, reading *Popular Mechanics* magazine.

"Gina! You got a date." Bella set aside her magazine. She was a few years older than Gina, clad in a stylish blouse with a Ritz collar. "Or this another student?"

"Just a friend," said Gina.

As Bella turned to Francis, her expression cooled. "I know you."

Francis shrugged. "I'm off duty now."

"You stayed on the job long enough to arrest Clyde."

Francis blushed as Gina raised a warning hand. "I'm sure he had nothing to do with that. How is he, Bella? Did he get hold of Mr. Nelson?"

"He did. That lawyer charges like he's the king of Sweden." Bella's gaze returned to Francis. "Only right thing to do is release an innocent man."

Francis took Gina's elbow. "Why don't we call it a night?"

"'Cause I don't want to," she snapped. "And we all know Clyde's innocent. We came here to dance—will that be a problem, Bella?"

"I guess not," she said, and waved them inside.

The dance floor wasn't crowded. The Negro pianist he recognized from the minstrel show, where he performed in blackface. Without his makeup he wasn't much darker than Gina. He wore an elegant jacket and trousers, rather than the garish stripes and gambler's hat he sported in the show.

"He looks snappier dressed like that," said Francis, steering Gina across the room.

"What, did you think he dresses in those loud duds when he's not on the stage?" She glanced at the piano player, who acknowledged her with a nod and broke into "Peacherine Rag." Gina turned to Francis. He offered her his arm, and they stepped onto the dance floor.

Francis was a good dancer. Gina feigned surprise that he could fox-trot. After a few songs she asked, "Do you know the Texas Tommy?"

Francis shook his head. She peered over his shoulder to catch the pianist's eye. Without missing a beat, he began playing "King Chanticleer."

"Like this," proclaimed Gina. "Watch me."

Francis followed her lead, stooping to set his chin on one of her shoulders and his hand on the other. She did the same, standing on tiptoe to reach him, and segued into a two-step, moving faster than he would have thought possible. She pulled him close and began to spiel, whirling so that her hair tumbled around her face. Francis caught flashes of the other dancers watching them, their expressions ranging from disapproval to shock.

When the song ended, Francis loosened his tie, grinning as he walked her toward a table. Gina sat across from him, breathless and flushed, as Francis ordered two schooners of beer from a passing waiter. Gina raised her glass to him. "You're a pretty good dancer, Francis."

"Not so fleet with the newer styles. That Texas Tommy's a hot one."

"You learned fast."

"If I learned slow you would've trampled me! Where'd you learn to tough dance?"

"That's not a tough dance. A girl I worked with at the milliner's used to live in San Francisco. She taught me." She took a long swallow of beer. "It's fun, isn't it?"

The pianist launched into a slower melody, and the couples on the dance floor arranged themselves into tipsy approximations of a waltz. Gina set her glass on the table and stared at it, as though divining something there. At last she looked up.

"Why aren't you married?"

Francis found himself too tongue-tied to respond to such a question. Unperturbed, she asked, "What about a sweetheart?"

He shook his head. "I had a girl, but..."

"She broke the engagement?"

"No. She died."

"Oh!" Gina's arch expression crumpled into dismay. She covered Francis's large hand with her small one, gazing at him with such heartfelt pity he felt ashamed.

"It was three years ago," he said, hoping he didn't sound diffident. "No—four, I think."

"Was that before you left the Chicago police?"

He let his breath out in a long *whoosh*. He'd hoped that, as a newcomer this summer, Gina might have been immune to Riverview gossip. But why should she be? Her job on the Pike would make her privy to more secrets than he knew himself. "It was," he said at last.

"Do you miss it?"

"I do. Very much so."

He gazed at Gina curiously. How odd that she didn't ask, *Do you miss her?* The truth was he didn't miss Maura, not really. She was an ache that flared up sometimes, after too much drink or not enough sleep, then subsided with sunrise. But his detective work had been so deeply ingrained that its loss felt like losing a part of his body, like the strange pains that amputees were said to experience after an arm or a leg was removed in surgery.

"What sort of policeman were you?"

"A detective sergeant. An investigator."

"You were the man who investigated the Black Hand. That was why you lost your position. That's what I heard."

He shrugged, avoiding her gaze. For an instant her fingers tightened around his, and then she withdrew her hand. "We lived in Little

Hell before we came here, me and Pin. Those men do the work of the devil. I wish you had been able to murder them all."

"I wish they'd been brought to trial. And that I'd kept my position."

"It must have hardened you, that work."

He looked at her in surprise. "I would hope not. Why would you think that?"

"You're here…" She opened her hands to indicate the room around them, the half-dozen drunken couples on the dance floor, swaying to the melancholic strains of "Solace." "Not a day after that girl's murder."

Francis gave another awkward laugh. "It does sound hard, when you put it like that," he admitted. "I guess I just don't give much thought to things when I get off duty."

Gina laughed. "I'm flattered."

He downed the rest of his drink, flustered. "That wasn't what I meant to say. I just—I thought you might enjoy doing something sociable. As a distraction after last night. I'm very sorry your son was the one who had to see that."

Gina said nothing. Francis finally asked, "Would you like another beer?"

"That would be very sociable," she said, and smiled.

He signaled the waiter. They sat without speaking until he returned with their beers, listening as the pianist played another wistful tune. Francis raised his glass to Gina. He tried to think of what to say. "Have you—have any of your predictions ever come true?"

"No. I've never done anything like this before. I was a frock-hitcher, but girls don't want fussy plumes and silk peonies anymore, not unless it's for a garden party. A friend worked here last summer and said I could make money pretty easy."

"And is it? Easy money?"

"It's money. Never enough, but that's nothing new." She sipped her beer. "Mostly I worry about Pin. After last night…"

As her eyes welled, Francis broke in, "It's a terrible thing—but it would seem much worse if you had a daughter, instead of a son."

Gina's mouth twisted. He wasn't sure if she was fighting a sob or trying not to laugh.

"Maybe I should see you home," he said gently. He glanced at his pocket watch. "It's getting late. May I see you home?"

The Pike seemed strangely deserted when they stepped back outside. The Hippodrome's angel shone brilliantly, but the other attractions had gone dark.

"That's odd." Francis stared at the coasters, black and skeletal in the hot night. "It's too early for them to shut off the lights."

Gina remained silent, and Francis kicked himself for ruining the evening by talking about his past. Still, in for a penny, in for a pound.

"Do you think you might enjoy doing this again one night?" he asked.

Gina tilted her head to look up at him. "I might be persuaded. Under the proper sociable conditions."

Francis let his breath out. "I'll see if I can arrange for that."

They had reached the Great Lagoon, where the angel's reflection broke into fragments as wind stirred the dark water. Gina glanced in the direction of her shack. "I hope Pin's back home."

"He's a brave kid—I know some sergeants would have gone faint if they'd seen what he did."

"Clyde," she said without looking at him. "You know he'd never do such a thing."

"I do. But my word doesn't count for much."

"Still, couldn't you—"

"Bacon!"

Francis turned to see Anton Magruder running toward them. "There's another one," he gasped.

"Another what?"

"A girl. Murdered." Gina cried out as Magruder pointed at the angel. "The Hippodrome. Some kids found her in the last row of the balcony."

"Does Hickey know?"

"Everybody knows." For the first time, he noticed Francis was out of uniform. "Except you, I guess." He turned to Gina and lifted his hat. "Apologies, ma'am. Francis, you better come along with me."

Gina stared at him wide eyed, one hand covering her mouth. Francis firmly grasped her arm, glancing at Magruder. "Go ahead—tell them I'll be right there."

Magruder seemed about to protest, but thought better of it and ran on toward the Hippodrome.

Francis could feel Gina trembling as he drew her close. "Are you sure you have no one you can stay with?"

She shook her head frantically. "No. And Pin—what if it's Pin?"

"You heard him—it's another girl. If Pin's not home now, he will be soon. Look around—they've cleared the park. Come on…"

They hurried down the alley to the shack. Francis took out his billy club. "You stay right there," he ordered. "I'll check everything first."

He entered the shack, struck a match, and lit the lantern hanging inside. Three strides and he'd crossed the entire room. There was no possible place to hide. Nothing but a small trunk and a mattress on the floor. He turned and beckoned Gina.

"It's safe. I hate to leave you, but I need to go."

"Pin," she said.

He took her hand. "If Pin doesn't show up by morning, you're to let me know. Here…"

He gave her his billy club. "I hope you won't need this. But if you do…"

She stared at him and whispered, "Thank you, Francis."

He clasped her hand, and left.

Chapter 56

PIN! PIN!"

She heard Henry shouting after her, then Willhie's alarmed voice, but she didn't look back. She didn't slow until she reached Bosworth Avenue, half a mile away. She doubled over, coughing as she fought to catch her breath, checking to see if she'd been followed.

She saw no one behind her, or anywhere else. The shops were all closed, the streets and sidewalks deserted except for a Model T that chugged past. The gas lamps hissed—no electrical lights here—and bats flitted around the halos of yellow light, chasing moths.

She began the trek back to Riverview. She felt as though some poison swam around inside her, a terror that could not be separated from her body, from herself. She'd felt like this when Abriana disappeared, but that fear had been attached to her sister. This fear seeped from someplace inside Pin, like the blood that trickled from her every month.

Who were those girls? Henry's pictures made the missing girls look like dolls. But they weren't dolls: they'd been alive, like she was now. Why would Henry—why would anyone—set up such a crazy display?

She could think of only one reason: he'd killed them, and he was proud of it.

Yet he hadn't gloated over the images. And he hadn't killed her. But what kind of grown man would cut pictures of murdered girls from newspapers and decorate them with crayon and pictures of flowers clipped from seed catalogs?

I lived in the asylum... They called it the crazy house...

She shuddered. Beneath the elastic band her chest burned, the skin chafed raw by heat and the filthy fabric. She unbuttoned her shirt, tore off the truss, and flung it into the dark, a disgusting stinking rag. She longed to rip off her shirt, too.

But then *she* would be crazy; not as crazy as Henry but close. If someone saw a fourteen-year-old girl walking the streets late at night shirtless, never mind the heat, they'd arrest her for a whore. Or lock her up like they'd done to Henry. She fastened up her shirt and kept walking, thinking of Henry's pictures.

It's part of the Ceremony. I protect them. So we don't forget.

Were there other Gemini? She doubted it now. The Child Protective Society and the Black Brothers Lodge were some kind of game that Henry had made up. He claimed to live at the hospital, but he could be lying about that, too. He might have escaped again from the asylum, with Willhie protecting him by going along with his crazy game.

But if Willhie knew Henry had murdered those girls, why would he help him? Unless Willhie was a murderer, too. Nothing made any sense.

By the time she arrived back at Riverview, the cuckoo clock was crying ten forty-five. For some reason all the lights were out, save the glowing angel. She saw no people except for a small crowd by the Hippodrome. Too exhausted to investigate, she continued on to her shack.

Chapter 57

W<small>ILLHIE WAS TOO</small> tired to listen to Henry's explanation for why Pin had been in the barn.

"No more!" Willhie held up a warning hand as Henry excitedly reached into the Black Sack of Destiny, searching for the secret card that Pin had signed. "You must go home now! My sister is tired, that boy frightened her when he ran away."

So Henry trudged back to Workingmen's House, sweaty and hot and still excited by the night's events. He entered his stuffy room as quietly as he could, removed his shoes and heavy canvas jacket, and sat at his desk, brooding.

Why had the boy run off when Willhie arrived? Was he guilty of some crime? Could *he* have been the one who choked the girl to death in Hell Gate?

Henry knew this was impossible. He'd seen Pin with his own eyes, standing outside Hell Gate after the murderer and the girl entered the tunnel. Pin scarcely looked older than the girl, and he was skinny as a rat. She would have fought him off easily. People never thought of girls as good fighters, but they were.

He opened his desk drawer, took out the votive candle, and lit it, then withdrew his manuscript and bundle of pictures. Tenderly he removed the newspaper photograph of Elsie, placing it where only she could see him.

"Dearest one," he whispered.

Tears stung his eyes. He'd wanted only to protect her, and yet she had come to great harm. He squeezed his eyes shut and prayed for forgiveness, touching Saint Dymphna's scapular beneath his shirt.

I firmly resolve with the help of thy grace to sin no more...

When he opened his eyes, Elsie's face moved in the candlelight, smiling at him. He got out his stub of pencil, found a blank sheet of paper, and began to write:

Elsie Annie Aronburg struggled against General Arnold Patsfry his hands clutched around her neck. The other girls watched in awestruck terror...

Hours later, the candle burned out. He looked up to see the slit of window above his desk tinged with gold. Hurriedly he bound up his manuscript, hid it and the votive candle back in the desk, darted to his bed, and slid beneath the blanket, still fully clothed. It seemed his eyes had only just closed when Sister Rose pounded on the door, clanging the handbell that woke the entire corridor at five each morning, so they could attend six o'clock Mass.

"Mr. Darger!!"

He waited until she moved down the hall before jumping from bed, and changed into a cleaner shirt. He ran his fingers through his hair, forcing thoughts of Elsie and the others from his mind. There would always be more dead girls. Time to go to work.

Chapter 58

THE BODY HAD been discovered by a high-school boy who'd been sitting in the uppermost balcony with his friends. When the movie ended, they'd laid low in their seats, hoping to sneak into the next show, then began roughhousing, running back and forth between the rows. His shouts drew his friends, and then Sergeant Paterno, on security duty at the theater entrance.

"There wasn't an usher there?" demanded Captain Hickey, who'd raced back to the station house from his home in Hyde Park. There'd been no time to change into his uniform, and his jacket and trousers didn't match. Francis could smell roast beef gravy on his breath.

"It's a passion pit," said Paterno. "The usher admitted he didn't clear the balcony between shows, or even poke his head in. Claims he's a churchgoing man and he can't stand to know what goes on in there."

Hickey shook his head, disgusted. "He must have taken their tickets—could he describe the man who went in with her? What the hell was she doing there in the first place? It's not a goddamned kids' show."

The three of them were back in Hickey's office—Francis, Hickey,

Paterno. Through the closed door, they could hear the girl's mother screaming in the next room.

"Parents bring their kids sometimes. The high-school kids, they sneak in all the time." Paterno glanced anxiously at the door. "Has someone called a doctor for her mother?"

"The coroner's bringing a sedative," Hickey said tersely.

The body of the child, Gilda Belascu, was laid out on a table at the back of Hickey's office. Someone had covered it with a uniform jacket, and Hickey had closed the window blinds.

Francis felt numb: he'd been here when the parents had first glimpsed their daughter. Their anguish made him feel as though the flesh had been peeled away from his scalp. He was starting to believe he could use a sedative himself.

Paterno tapped his knees nervously as he sat. "What were they thinking, leaving the girl to run wild while they were out dancing?"

"You think this was their fault?" demanded Francis.

"I do, if—"

"Shut up!" Paterno blanched as Hickey continued, "Cabell's men are questioning all the ushers and the projectionist, anyone who might remember seeing a man and a girl."

"What about the ticket seller?" asked Francis.

"Him, too." Hickey rubbed his forehead, glancing at Francis. "Jesus Christ almighty, look at you, man. This is enough of a mess without Cabell seeing we're all run down to the bone. Go home, sleep for a few hours, then come back. I've called in Anton Magruder and Tom Haller."

"They haven't been involved with this investigation. I have."

"Investigation?" Hickey's voice rose angrily. "You're not a detective sergeant anymore, Bacon. Go home. *Now.*" Hickey pointed at the door. "I don't want to see you in uniform before sunrise. And get a proper shave, you look like you've been on a bash. Paterno, finish your statement and you go, too."

Paterno gave Francis a sympathetic look as he grabbed his hat and stalked out the door. The outer room was crowded with Chicago police sergeants, several men in usher uniforms, and half a dozen high-school boys who looked equal parts scared and excited to be part of the fray. Anton Magruder stood over a figure slumped in a chair—Miriam Belascu, the girl's mother. Her husband, Werner, knelt beside her, his face transformed by grief into a gargoyle's. As Francis approached, Werner Belascu looked up at him imploringly. Francis held his gaze, his own eyes filling. He felt as though he were being strangled.

"My sympathies," Francis muttered, and pushed his way to the door.

Once outside he stood for a minute, sweating as though it were noon. He reached into his pocket for his blackjack, remembered he'd left it with Gina. His fingers brushed something else.

The notebook from Gina's booth. He'd forgotten he'd promised to bring it to the station's lost-and-found. He opened it, squinting as he skimmed the pages.

Bury her in coffin as in EAP. When she's found only skeletal remains + her long beautiful hair.

Realizes too late that she is not an automaton but live person. Gasping w horror he drops her body to the ground. Leader: THE END

He continued flipping through the book until he reached the last written page and stared at a single scribbled word.

Hellgate

"My God," he exclaimed.

He shoved the pad into his pocket, glanced over his shoulder at the station house, then hurried toward Gina's shack.

Chapter 59

Gina!" Francis called her name urgently, hoping she wasn't already asleep inside, hoping he didn't wake the boy. "Mrs. Maffucci, it's Francis Bacon, can you come out, please?"

The door cracked open and Gina stared at him, clutching a silk kimono around her thin frame. "Sweet Jesus, now what is it? Pin?"

"No! I mean, I don't know. I haven't seen him. But I need to speak with you, Gina, can you please step outside?"

She peered down the dark alley, disappeared back inside and returned, holding the hurricane lantern. "What's happened?"

"This." He held up the notebook. "How did you come by it?"

"I told you, a man came in. I told his fortune, and he left it behind."

"Can you describe him?"

"Describe him? Why? Where's my child? Where's Pin?"

"I have no idea where he is," snapped Francis. "Listen to me, Gina. What do you remember of the man who left this book?"

He reached for her arm, but she slapped it away. "What man? I've told you what I know!"

Francis drew a deep breath. "Gina, take a minute and think on it. This notebook…"

He opened it and held it up so she could read the word *Hellgate*. She stared at it blankly. "*Hellgate?* What does it mean?"

"I think it belongs to him. The murderer. Almost surely it does."

"What? How would you know?"

"There are...other things, written inside."

"What other things?"

"Things you don't need to know, Gina!"

"Who are you to say what I need to know?" Her voice grew shrill, furious and also despairing. "What are you keeping from me?"

"Nothing!" His frustration veered into anger. "Damn it, Gina—I have to bring this notebook to the station house! It's evidence and they'll need to question you. I'm trying to help you. So please, tell me now—do you know this man? Do you know anything about him?"

Gina shook her head, ashen faced. "No. I never saw him before, he just walked in like everyone else."

"Was he with anyone?"

"I don't know. No, I don't think so. He came in alone."

"Do you remember what he looked like? Anything he said? Was he a colored man?"

"No!" She set the hurricane lantern on the ground and began to pace, arms tightly crossed against her chest. "I can't think, let me think."

She stopped and stared at the lantern. "He was a white man, in a light-colored suit. Seersucker. And a straw hat, a boater hat."

Francis groaned softly. Was he the only man in Chicago who wore a derby? "Do you remember what color stripes?"

"No."

"What else? How old was he, what color hair?"

"Thirty or thereabouts, I'd guess. His hair..." She rubbed her arms, thinking. "I believe he had dark-colored hair."

"A mustache or beard?"

"No, I'd remember that."

"What about a wedding ring?"

"No. I always check."

"What kind of accent did he have?"

"Accent?" She hesitated before replying. "Not from here. Somewhere back East, I think. Philadelphia?"

"Anything else?"

"Nothing, really. I did most of the talking. He didn't have any questions, not that I recall."

"What did you tell him?"

"The usual nonsense. That he had a powerful enemy, and he'd never marry."

"Why on earth would you tell a man that? A complete stranger?"

"It's what the tea leaves said," she retorted. "There's a book that you have to memorize, it tells you how to read the omens. His said he'd never marry."

"And that he had a powerful enemy?"

"Yes."

Francis didn't know whether to laugh or toss the notebook at her. "Do you think it upset him? What you said?"

"Maybe." She seemed disquieted. "Some people are angry if they don't hear what they want to hear, but usually they just pay for another reading. Do you think he got so angry he killed someone?"

Francis sighed. "No. I was just hoping you might give us something more to go on."

"Well, he'll come back for it, right?" She leaned against the shack, pulling her kimono tight. "If he notices it's missing."

"Maybe." Francis's tone was doubtful. "Once he realizes it's gone, he's not likely to come looking for it at the station house."

"I could keep it at the booth, and notify you if he shows up."

"Too risky—once he has it, he'll run off."

He tucked the notebook back into his pocket, removed his derby, and fanned his face, his hair gold in the lantern glow. "This heat, I'm surprised more people aren't going nuts. Tell you what..."

He tapped the derby back onto his head. "You keep an eye out for this man. I'll have a sergeant in plain clothes standing close by your booth tomorrow—I'll tell him to come by early. It'll probably be Morgenstern, do you know him?" She nodded. "Good. You two work out a signal, if your man comes back, let him know, and we'll get someone right on it. Cabell's men will be crawling all over the park, we won't be lacking for policemen."

"You don't think they'll close the park?"

He gave a sour laugh. "Not if Baumgarten can help it. Every day this place has to shut down, he loses a fortune. The police commissioner would have to order him to close it, or the mayor or governor. They're all in each other's pockets, and none of 'em wants to lose a dime. Everyone's going to make money off this—the newspapers, Baumgarten, the guys who run Hell Gate and the Hippodrome. Everyone but those dead kids and their families."

Gina looked away, and he sighed. He'd offended her by being so blunt. But he was too exhausted to apologize properly. And he knew that everything he'd said was true.

Chapter 60

PIN DRAGGED HER feet as she approached the alley by the shack. The faces of the murdered girls on Henry's altar still floated behind her eyes, as sweetly fanciful as drawings in the Sunday funnies or picture books. And she was no better than him—in the tunnel, she'd mistaken a murdered girl for a doll or balloon.

The memory sickened her. The girl wasn't a toy, she'd had a name—Maria—a mother and father, maybe a sister. She leaned for a moment against the side of the empty Kansas Cyclone building, trying not to think that Henry might be a murderer, trying not to throw up.

Outside the Cyclone's utility room she paused again before ducking inside. She made her way past mops and stacks of empty film cans, until she found the metal sink that occupied most of one wall. She turned on the cold-water tap—there was no hot water—and grabbed the sliver of harsh carbolic soap she kept hidden. She stripped and hauled herself into the sink, which was deep enough to serve as a bathtub. She covered the drain with one foot, gasping at the cold water. When it reached her knees, she crouched and washed herself, trying not to lose the bit of soap. Her chest stung where the awful elastic truss had chafed it, but the water felt wonderful against her sore skin. She let the dirty water drain, filled the sink again, and washed her hair.

At last she clambered out. She retrieved her once-white shirt, scrubbed it vigorously with the soap, and did the same thing with her socks, which were so filthy she was glad she couldn't see them.

Finally, she wrung out her shirt and socks and stood, dripping, to savor the novelty of being clean. With a sigh she pulled on her trousers, grabbed the wet shirt and socks and her shoes. She nudged the door open and stood warily, listening, before stepping back into the alley.

For a few seconds she stood there, bare chested and exhilarated, all the tiny hairs on her arms stirring. Her nipples tingled where the warm air touched them, and for the first time she was aware of her breasts not as cankers that ached and burned beneath a filthy elastic band but as part of her body, as bound to her as her hands and feet. She touched one nipple, half expecting lightning to jolt from it as punishment. But of course nothing happened.

What would it be like to live like this? Boys and men did it every day, swimming or stripping off their shirts if they were workmen. They never needed someone else to button them into their clothes, never needed someone to peel off their dresses like dead snakeskin. Their heads didn't ache beneath straw nests heaped with plumes and fake flowers and entire dead birds. They didn't have to pile their hair atop their heads like another hat, clamped in place by metal combs.

Men could shave their faces and even their heads as often as they pleased—twice a day in New York City, according to Max. They could shuck their clothes as easily as they shucked their jobs. Even a Negro man could do up his own clothes, except when he had to do up some white man's first.

She started at the sound of voices—male voices, somewhere near the Lagoon—and quickly headed for the shack. Her exhilaration faded: All she wanted to do was sleep. All she wanted was to be back on the horsehair sofa in Lenore's apartment with Abriana's arms around her as they huddled beneath the scratchy wool blanket and their mother whispered at them to hush, she still had work to do, she couldn't hear herself think why couldn't they just...

"Pin!"

Her mother stood in the doorway, her face pale and eyes red, lips stained by the patent medicine she drank when she was restless. "Pin, where in God's name were you? Are you—"

"I'm fine, Ma. I'm just fine," Pin yelled, and pushed past her into the shack, so her mother wouldn't see she was crying.

Chapter 61

Francis was relieved to see that Gilda Belascu's parents were no longer among the crowd inside the station house. He saw no sign of Cabell or any reporters. *Thank God for small favors,* he thought. Most of the Riverview force was there, along with at least a dozen men from Robey Street. At the desk, O'Connell looked up wearily.

"Bacon. Thought you went home."

"I need to talk to Hickey." O'Connell sighed and cocked a thumb toward Hickey's office. "Are the girl's parents with him?"

"Nope. Someone from St. Procopius came for them, that Bohemian church on the South Side. But the coroner's in there—"

Francis thanked him and hurried down the hall, where several of Cabell's men stood chatting in a cloud of cigar smoke.

"Sergeant Bacon," one of them called. "How's the freak show?"

Francis ignored him. He rapped at Hickey's door, didn't wait for a reply before entering. Hickey was slumped behind his desk, with Dr. Phipps, the Cook County coroner, seated across from him.

"Francis," said Hickey, bleary eyed. Rusty stubble shaded his jaw; he appeared more haggard than Francis had ever seen him. "Why the hell are you here?"

Francis held up the open notebook and set it in front of Hickey. "Read that."

Hickey glanced at the page. "'Hellgate.'" He looked up. "What is this?"

"Go to the beginning," Francis urged him. He turned to acknowledge Dr. Phipps, a melancholy, reedlike man with a wispy mustache, black hair parted neatly in the middle, and small keen eyes behind tortoiseshell glasses.

Dr. Phipps nodded in response. "I remember you from the city force. We met after that row at the Shamrock when the Irishman took a knife to his brother's throat. You were a detective then—Bacon, right?"

"That would be correct," said Francis.

Hickey started thumbing through the book. His expression grew even more grim. "Shut that door," he ordered Francis. "And lock it."

Francis pulled a chair up alongside Phipps and watched as Hickey continued to flip through the notebook's pages. The room was unpleasantly warm, air and furniture alike permeated by the smoke from Hickey's cigars, one of which smoldered in the large marble ashtray on the captain's desk. It was not until Francis removed his derby and ran a finger beneath his collar, loosening it, that he noticed the small form, now covered with a white sheet, still laid out in the back of the room.

"Francis." Hickey held the notebook at arm's length, as though it were on fire. "Where did you find this? What is it?"

"The Gypsy fortune-teller on the Pike. One of her customers left it yesterday."

"How did you come by it?"

"I dropped by her booth this afternoon to ask her out to dinner. I noticed it and said I'd bring it by here, to be kept with the lost items."

"And you waited till now to do that?"

"I didn't read it until a few minutes ago. I returned to question her, then came here straightaway."

Hickey scanned the pages again. "Who is this woman? How do you know it's not hers?"

"Her name's Gina Maffucci. She never looked inside it."

"How do you know that?"

Francis's jaw tightened in irritation. "Because she would have told me if she had."

Hickey stared at the notebook. "Maffucci. She's the mother of the boy who found the body?"

"The boy had nothing to do with it. She said the man who left it was white, thirty-five or thereabouts. Boater hat and seersucker suit, clean shaven. He sounds like the same man her son described going into Hell Gate with the Walewski girl."

"May I?" broke in Dr. Phipps. At Hickey's nod, he leaned across the table, picked up the notebook, and slowly read through it. Francis sank back in his chair, regretting that he'd mentioned Gina at all.

"He's describing various murders." Dr. Phipps looked at Francis, then Hickey. "But the man who wrote these—he sounds quite calm. Businesslike. There's no frenzy."

Hickey frowned. "Meaning?"

"I don't know." Phipps spoke with care. "I would say that he has a very disordered mind—it's like he's writing a grocery list, describing the order in which these events occurred. He seems preoccupied with burying people alive. Not just people—"

He licked a finger and turned several pages. "Here he mentions walling up a cat. He sounds quite demented."

"Who's to say the boy didn't write this?" demanded Hickey. "He claims to have discovered the Walewski girl's body, but he may have killed her. The mother might be trying to protect him."

He turned to Francis. "I'll need her address—Cabell will want to question her. He'll want the boy in custody, too, no doubt."

Francis's face darkened, but before he could reply, Dr. Phipps broke in.

"What about Mr. Smithson? He's still being held at Robey Street, am I correct?" He waved his hand, indicating the sheet-covered body. "This proves his innocence."

"One would think so," said Hickey. "But what if we have two killers now, and not just one?"

Dr. Phipps winced. "God forbid."

Hickey held out his hand, and Phipps returned the notebook. "Show Mr. Bacon what you found."

The coroner stood and walked to the back of the room, motioning for Francis to join him. The girl's underclothes had been neatly folded and set on a chair beside a black leather medical bag.

"I told the undertaker I'd oversee delivery of the body myself when we were finished." Dr. Phipps gently pulled down the white sheet, as though unwilling to awaken a sleeping child. "I wanted to compare it with the Walewski girl."

There lay Gilda Belascu, black hair fanned around her face. Her skin had the bluish pallor of skim milk. Her lips had a darker, purple tinge. Francis glanced at Dr. Phipps. "Did she—was she killed the same way as the other girl?"

"Yes. Or, well, in a similar manner. She was suffocated, probably by a hand or piece of cloth, but also there are signs of strangulation. The other girl didn't put up a fight. Gilda Belascu did."

"Why?" Francis frowned. "I mean, why wouldn't the other girl have fought, too?"

"I'm not certain. For whatever reason, Maria Walewski doesn't appear to have struggled. She was asphyxiated—smothered—and in both cases, the girls' outer clothing was removed. Their dresses and pinafores. But Gilda—"

He picked up the girl's pale hand, turning it so that Francis could see what looked like dirt under her ragged fingernails. "She scratched him. Quite badly, I imagine—this is blood."

Francis grimaced as the coroner pulled a slender metal rod from his pocket and pointed at one of the girl's nails. "I wouldn't be surprised if she bit him, too. She put up quite a fight, this brave little girl," Dr. Phipps murmured. "That's why there's more evidence of trauma to her windpipe and throat."

"Yet no one heard this?" Francis shook his head. "Where the hell was Paterno?"

Captain Hickey bristled. "One sergeant in a theater that accommodates a thousand people? Paterno's job is to keep kids from sneaking in. The usher might have prevented this, if he hadn't been shooting craps in a storage room."

"This is what I find most interesting," said Dr. Phipps.

He opened his medical bag and withdrew a small, flat wooden box, opened it to remove a pair of tweezers, and reached into his pocket for a stoppered glass vial. He prized the cork loose and tilted the vial, using the tweezers to grasp something inside it.

"Here." He moved to the end of the table where Gilda lay, and from another pocket removed a small square of black cloth. He smoothed this onto the table and beckoned Francis to come closer. "Take a look. I've already shown the captain."

Dr. Phipps opened the tweezers, and something dropped onto the cloth. Francis stooped to scrutinize what resembled a bead of hardened pine resin, murky yellow, the size and roughly the same shape as a beetle's carapace. He looked up at the coroner.

"What is it?"

"A lemon drop. I found it lodged in the back of her throat." Dr. Phipps used the tweezers to pick it up again and held it out to Francis. "Smell it."

Francis complied. It smelled of lemons, but also something he couldn't place. "Do you think she might have choked on this?"

"No." The coroner dropped the lozenge back inside the vial and corked it. Turning to Gilda Belascu's corpse, he pointed at her lips.

"See how her mouth has turned purple? I thought at first that was because she'd been smothered. Blood pooling in her lips and face. But after I found the lemon drop, I checked again, and..."

He lowered his head to sniff delicately at the dead child's mouth, then gestured for Francis to do the same. "You're a detective. Tell me what you think."

Francis leaned down until his face almost grazed the dead girl's. A distinct odor of something sweet hung about her mouth. It reminded him of cherry compote. He looked at Dr. Phipps. "Another kind of candy? Ice cream?"

"No. It's some kind of anodyne syrup. The government's outlawed them, but they still end up on the market because some pharmacists refuse to pull them from their shelves. The chemical agents are always a form of opium—codeine, morphine. Sometimes chloral hydrate or chloroform."

"You think she was poisoned?"

"I think she was doped, and Maria Walewski as well. I noted the same purple hue in her lips, but I mistakenly attributed it to the fact that she'd been in the water. Maria's parents have already taken possession of her body, so there's no way for me to be certain now. But I think the killer did the same thing with both children—gave them candy treated with some kind of opiate elixir."

"Were they both—" Francis looked away from the girl's body. "Were they interfered with?"

Phipps nodded. "He kept their dresses. Perhaps he feared they could be used as evidence. He may not have intended to kill them—he might have panicked. I've seen that before. Women killed by their husbands, what starts out as one thing ends as something else."

"He's not panicked." Francis turned to Hickey. "Haven't you told him about the other? The girl in Boston?"

Hickey shook his head. "He's only just finished his examination. And it still seems too odd a coincidence."

"You need to tell him now."

Phipps tugged the sheet back over Gilda's face, pulled out a chair, and sat. "You tell me, Mr. Bacon."

Francis did. When he finished, Dr. Phipps tapped a cigarette from a silver case and lit it. He smoked thoughtfully, at last said, "Two young girls murdered at the same attraction at two different amusement parks, hundreds of miles apart. You're right, Mr. Bacon. This certainly doesn't sound like someone operating out of panic. And the notebook doesn't suggest that, either. Is Captain Cabell aware of this other killing? The commissioner?"

"I informed Cabell," said Hickey. "I have no idea whether he told the commissioner yet. I doubt it. He sure will tell him now that there's been another murder. But you know they'll do whatever they can to keep the parks open. Not just Riverview, all the parks—White City, Bismarck Garden. They don't want a panic."

"Amusement parks." Dr. Phipps made a face. "I can't stand them. All that noise! And they're the perfect vectors for disease, especially for children."

"The streets aren't safer," said Hickey. "In summertime, with two hundred thousand kids out of school? Vagrants everywhere, and half those kids' parents don't know what they get up to. Look at the Paroubek girl. And that other one last year—the Gypsy girl. And there was another girl the year before that."

"Perhaps this would be a good time to reopen those investigations," suggested Phipps.

"There's nothing to investigate. Gyppo girls run away, and I don't blame them. What's waiting for them if they stay?"

"One of those girls was Italian, not a Gypsy," said Francis.

"Does it matter?" Hickey ground out his cigar in the ashtray. "Here at least the children have some supervision. And a twenty-man police force."

Phipps exhaled a plume of grey smoke. "Better train them to do more than watch for boys sneaking into the nickelodeon. These murders are in Cabell's jurisdiction, so God help us all, we may be murdered ourselves." The coroner's disdain for the Robey Street captain was well known. He leaned over to tap his cigarette against Hickey's ashtray. "How's Mr. Baumgarten taking this?"

"As you might imagine," said Hickey. "But I agree with him—closing the park will do more harm than good. Panicky mothers, bad publicity...remember Holmes and the world's fair?"

"Like it was yesterday. I was still in medical school, I assisted on several of the examinations of the victims. Worst thing I ever saw, until *Eastland* last month."

Hickey nodded. "Another reason we don't want to close the park—there's been enough terrible news this summer. Working people need someplace to enjoy themselves."

"Yes, but someplace safe," countered Francis.

"Safe?" Hickey gazed at Francis as though he were a truculent boy. "What's safe, Francis, when you have a lunatic strangling children? Last night Baumgarten told me to go ahead and hire up to twenty independent security men. Bring in the Pinkertons if we can. Wasserman was here, too—Baumgarten's agreed to put up a thousand-dollar reward."

"Who's Wasserman?" asked Phipps.

"The park's press agent—James Wasserman." Hickey leaned heavily back in his chair. "Tomorrow we'll open and operate as usual. Baumgarten wants enough men on patrol that people feel safe, but not so many that it keeps everyone from enjoying themselves. So there'll be new hires here at Riverview, and a rotation of plainclothesmen from the city force. And some overtime for you, Francis, and everyone else."

He turned to the coroner. "I hope the same won't be true for you, Dr. Phipps."

Francis fought to keep his voice even. "If the park's open, Captain, you'll be inviting the fox right back into the henhouse."

"I'm well aware of that. But who's to say he hasn't already moved on?"

"He may well have," agreed Dr. Phipps. "Two killings within two days? It's unusual in my experience. If this is the same man who murdered that girl back East, he waited four years before killing Maria Walewski and the Belascu girl. He may have committed other murders during those four years, but if he did, they weren't in amusement parks. If they had been, we'd know about them.

"And he's not necessarily a vagrant," Phipps continued. "He might be a professional man, like Dr. Holmes. Or a salesman who could arrive and leave town without attracting notice. He could be someone who works in this park. A member of the police force, for instance," he ended dryly.

"I know for damn sure that is not the case," said Hickey. He stood. "Mr. Baumgarten pays my salary, and yours, too, Bacon. You're not a detective anymore, no matter what Dr. Phipps might believe. You need to do your job. Make the visitors feel safe. Wasserman's meeting with the newspapers in the morning. He'll tell them about the reward and the plainclothesmen. Surely that will be enough to scare off this madman. Or capture him."

"No doubt," said Dr. Phipps.

Hickey gazed expectantly at Francis, who remained silent as he stared at the motionless white form in the back of the room. "I hope you're right," he finally said. "But I don't believe you are."

Chapter 62

NEXT MORNING, PIN woke to the sound of her mother getting dressed, then grunts of annoyance as Gina brushed her thick hair and pinned it up, and finally a *thunk* as her mother tossed the hairbrush onto the trunk.

"Get up." Gina prodded her shoulder as Pin feigned sleep. She smelled of cherry elixir and Sen-Sen. "I know you're awake."

"Your breath stinks." Pin rolled over. "What time is it?"

"Getting on to eight."

"Jesus! It's so early!"

"Watch your mouth." Her mother swatted her. "It's Monday. You need to do me up."

Pin rubbed her eyes, sat up, and clumsily began to button her mother's clothing, shirtwaist first, then the cheap metal buttons that ran down the back of her skirt. Pin did this every day, morning and night, and never got any better at it. Or any faster, it took at least five minutes. When she finished, she flopped back onto the mattress and noticed an object on the rumpled sheet where her mother had lain.

A billy club. She picked it up. "Why do you have this?"

Her mother looked over her shoulder. "Put that down."

"It must weigh ten pounds." Pin turned it back and forth. "Maybe fifteen."

"I said, put it down!"

Pin dropped it to the floor with a loud thud. "Where'd you get it?"

"Mr. Bacon loaned it to me."

"Mr.—Fatty Bacon? The cop?"

"His name is Francis." Her mother stooped to gather her bag and fortune-telling cards. "Why do you call him by that idiotic nickname?"

"Why do you think?" Pin nudged the weapon with her foot. "Why'd he give you a billy club?"

Gina straightened. She stared at Pin with an odd expression. "Someone else was killed last night," she said. "He wanted me to be safe. Us."

"Someone else?" Pin looked at her stupidly: Was she still asleep, and dreaming? "You mean here at the park?"

Gina nodded.

"Who was it?"

"A girl, I don't know her name."

"At Hell Gate?"

"No. The Hippodrome." Her mother plucked at her blouse. Her hands were trembling. "I don't know any more than that."

"But how did you find out?"

"Francis. He walked me home, one of the other policemen ran up and told him."

"He walked you home?" Pin echoed her, stunned. "From where? What were you doing?"

"Stop it!" Her mother whirled. "I said that's enough!"

Gina sank onto the mattress and pulled on her shoes, fumbling with the buttons. Pin crossed to the door, cracked it open, and retrieved her shirt from where she'd hung it to dry on a nail on the outside wall. It was still damp. So were her socks. She dressed, stiffening as her mother took her by the shoulders and pulled her close.

"I want you to listen to me." Gina's hands still shook, but her voice remained steady. "I want you to come by the booth today."

"I'm not staying there."

"You don't have to stay. Just come by so I'll know you're safe."

"They won't open the park if it's not safe!"

"Do you really believe that, Pin?" Disdain and despair warred in her mother's gaze. "Do you think Baumgarten cares for anything except how many people he can crowd in here every single day?"

Pin flinched as her mother strode to the door and kicked it open, the flimsy wood splintering beneath her shoe. "See that?"

She pointed down the alley, to where two men on ladders adjusted a banner on the Cyclone building. "Everything as usual. Girls are murdered, but nothing changes. Nothing ever changes. No one is safe. Come by the booth, or..."

Without a goodbye, her mother left. When she was out of sight, Pin yanked the door closed, but it wouldn't shut properly—a hinge had loosened when her mother kicked it. Pin kicked it herself, and left it hanging.

She slumped on the mattress and stared at the two photographs she'd tacked to the wall, the room's sole decoration: Clyde and Harriet Quimby.

To Pin, with regards, Lord Clyde.
Vin Fiz! The Sparkling Grape Drink.

She traced the outline of Harriet's beautiful face, the aviatrix smiling as she stood proudly alongside the aeroplane she'd died in. Next to Harriet, Clyde gazed out at Pin with a strange half smile, as though some secret kept him safe.

She knew that wasn't true. Her mother was right: no one was safe. Her stomach roiled as she recalled the newspaper photo of her sister that had fallen from Henry's wallet, all those other photos in the Black Brothers Lodge.

We keep them safe. Girls. Because.

She bunched the thin sheet in her hands, torn between fury and fear. Henry was lying, he had to be. If he hadn't killed those girls, hadn't killed Abriana, he knew who did. Willhie, probably. She should go to the police, but then what would happen? She'd be questioned again, longer this time and not at Riverview but one of the city stations. She'd be searched and exposed as a girl, maybe even arrested and sent to the detention home.

She felt under the mattress for her shiv and slipped it into her pocket, turned onto her side, and stared at the two photos. Her mother's words repeated in her mind like Red Friend's bally.

No one is safe, no one is safe...

Not Clyde, not brave Harriet, who was remembered only because she'd been filmed, flying and dying. Would anyone remember Clyde if they hanged him?

No one remembered Abriana except for her and their mother. People only remembered you if someone took your photograph or painted your picture, or used your face to sell soda or magic tricks. Everyone else was forgotten. Everybody else just died.

Chapter 63

THE TRAIN ARRIVED half a day late into the Niles station. Chaplin passed the time reading and gazing out the window as the California desert crawled past, a vast waste of scrub and cactus punctuated by settlements that looked as though they'd been constructed by bored children deprived of anything except the most rudimentary blocks and tools. When the porter finally rapped at his compartment door and announced they were approaching Niles, Chaplin blew him a kiss. Then he stood, gathered his hat and valise, and peered out at the platform.

A good-sized crowd waited to meet the train—the *California Limited,* first class only. He'd grown accustomed to being met by fans and reporters, but surely only the most stalwart of his fans would have braved the afternoon heat of an August day to catch a glimpse of Charlie Chaplin. So he was mildly surprised as two men, one lugging a camera, rushed toward him as he stepped onto the platform.

"Mr. Chaplin!" The other man flapped a newspaper in Chaplin's face. "Care to make a comment on this?"

Chaplin glanced at the front page of the *Los Angeles Times,* where the photo of him and that adorable little girl from Essanay took up several columns. He shook his head and smiled. "That's yesterday's news, fellas. I was just there for a visit, I'm—"

"This is last night's edition, Mr. Chaplin—our paper, we're all from the *Los Angeles Times*. What do you have to say?"

"Not much to say, is there?" He flashed the photographer a smile as the man fiddled with his camera. "Other than I'm glad to be back in California. And I'll be starting work on *A Night in the Show* this week."

The reporter gave him a quizzical look. "Haven't you heard, Mr. Chaplin?"

"Heard what?"

The reporter thrust the newspaper into his hand, pointing at the headline:

Child Actress Brutally Murdered in Chicago Amusement Park

Chaplin stared blankly at the words. "I know nothing about this. Who is she?"

The reporter jabbed his thumb at the girl in the grainy photograph. "'Maria Walewski, twelve years old,'" he read, "'meeting the star Charles Chaplin at the Essanay movie studios in Chicago a few hours before her death.' How did you know her?"

"I don't."

He pushed past them toward the entrance to the station, the reporter shouting after him as Chaplin yanked the door open and hurried inside.

"Mr. Chaplin?" Another man rose from a bench and walked toward him. A policeman. "How was your journey?"

"My journey was fine." Chaplin looked over his shoulder to see the newspaperman racing toward them, the photographer at his side fumbling with his camera. "What the hell's going on? Have those men lost their minds?"

The policeman strode past him toward the reporters. Chaplin considered bolting but thought better of it. Moments later, the two men were headed for the exit, the photographer walking backward as he snapped a photograph.

"The train station manager said we could use an empty office here," the policeman said as he returned, his tone apologetic. "I'm with the Niles police. This way, if you please, Mr. Chaplin."

Chaplin started to protest, then saw that people were gathering to stare at him. Without a word he followed the policeman into a small unfurnished room at the far end of the building.

"Captain Farina, police department," the man said, closing the door behind them and extending his hand. "I apologize for this inconvenience, Mr. Chaplin, I know you're very busy. I've seen a number of your movies—my wife loves them. I do, too," he added, "though I work with some men who hate how the police always look so stupid."

"Tell them it's Sennett's fault." Chaplin forced a smile. He felt a buzzing in his ears; his hands had gone cold. Panic—he'd experienced it as a boy, when his mother sent him to the workhouse, and later when she entered the Cane Hill Asylum. He removed his cigarette case and offered one to Farina, who accepted it. "What's going on, Captain?"

"You probably haven't heard. I know the train was delayed out of Wichita, so you won't have seen the papers."

"Not since yesterday morning."

Farina stroked his mustache. "Well, a girl was killed back in Chicago. Young girl, smothered to death inside an amusement park ride."

Chaplin recoiled. "Jesus Christ! How horrible."

"It is. A young Polack girl. She was only twelve. Chicago police say she was at the studio with you on Saturday, working on a movie." He drew a notebook from his pocket and studied it. "S and A Studios, they said."

"Not with me, she wasn't." Chaplin took a quick drag from his cigarette. "I'm not with Essanay anymore—not in Chicago, anyway. I dropped by only because Spoor wanted to hire me back. But I'm very happy here at their Niles studio."

He flashed Farina another false smile. "I met the girl for only a minute, she and another girl were extras in a movie that was being filmed," he explained. "I happened to be in the room and the publicist wanted a photo with her. A Wallace Beery movie. He's got a reputation for young girls, maybe you should talk to him?"

"Police in Chicago already have. No one thinks you're a suspect, Mr. Chaplin. Just, you left town that same day, and they're trying to get as much information as they can. The other girl, she said you'd whispered something to Miss Walewski that made her blush. Like maybe you and her had met before. Can you remember what you said to her?"

Chaplin felt his face grow hot. "No," he lied. "Probably I said the same thing I say to every girl I meet—that she's lovely as a bluebell. That's an English flower. I don't think you have them here."

"No, I expect not." Farina dropped his cigarette to the floor and ground it out. "So, nothing else comes to mind?"

"I'm afraid not."

Farina clapped his hands on his knees. "I told them this was a wild-goose chase. I'm sorry for taking your time. Where are you staying? I'll help you get a taxi."

"That would be very kind."

They walked back through the station and into the burning gold of late afternoon. People milled around, porters heaving trunks onto carts, women wilting beneath their hats. Chaplin saw the men from the *Los Angeles Times* grabbing a smoke by a telegraph pole. He turned to Farina and made a show of laughing and shaking his hand.

"Thanks for being so congenial," Farina said. He squinted at a black taxi pulling in from the main street and raised a hand to summon the driver. "Here's one now. Before you go, would you mind…?"

The policeman pulled out his notebook and a fountain pen. Chaplin grinned. "I thought you'd never ask."

Chapter 64

HE SLEPT DEEPLY, and woke early to grey light. His hand throbbed painfully where the girl had bitten him. Someone would have discovered the body last night, but he wouldn't have been recognized. One man in a crowd inside a movie palace? He'd seen no policeman, no indication that the usher had noticed anything awry.

That would change now. People, not just policemen but men and women, even children in the streets, would be looking for a man who preyed on young girls. And because there was nothing, absolutely nothing, to distinguish him from other men, he realized with growing horror that he would now have to share his private theater—his dolls, his photographs—with all those others.

Not literally, of course. But he would never again be able to think of his carefully constructed tableaux, the dolls with their limbs and sleep-glass eyes and flowered pinafores, as being his alone. The fact that any man might be suspected meant that any one of them might be inspired to replicate his passion. Like a bad actor stepping into the role made famous by a great one, an audience of leering swine gazing with envy at and longing for what he alone should possess. They were all out there now, watching.

Desperation seized him, coupled with hunger. And rage. If he fled immediately, he might well be pursued and captured, but without the satisfaction of having those final moments with the doll lying silently beside him.

Yet he had no reason to believe the two Riverview killings would be immediately connected with those in Dreamland and Wonderland. The girl in Gary would be more problematic. Having heard of this weekend's murders, the Indiana police might well have contacted their counterparts in Chicago. The similarities would be clear. The body wouldn't need to be exhumed for them to determine the same person had killed all three.

On the other hand, the corpse of the slow-witted dago girl from two years ago would never be found. He'd disposed of it close to the amusement park. He'd passed the site often, and there was no reason to think the spot might not be useful to him again now, as long as he didn't hunt too far from it. There was no shortage of slums in this part of Chicago. If he was lucky, he might be able to take more photographs this afternoon.

He rose, washed up, and dressed. He examined the scratches on his chin where the little bitch had attacked him, touched them up with a styptic pencil. If anyone noticed, he'd say he'd cut himself shaving. He prepared himself a boiled egg and coffee, ate quickly, then grabbed the remaining tin of lozenges and bottle of cordial.

He started for the door, after a moment's indecision returned to the suitcase. Inside he found the leather wallet that contained the photographs he'd developed two nights before. He gazed at that calm smooth face, lips parted in an expression that held both a promise and a secret. He slipped the photos in his pocket, along with the leather wallet, tipped the boater onto his head, and left. Just another man out for a morning stroll, that was all, just another man.

Chapter 65

Hᴇᴄʜᴛ ᴄᴏʟʟᴀʀᴇᴅ ʜɪᴍ as he stepped off the streetcar at Riverview's entrance.

"Bacon!" Bennie ran up, dressed in the same checked suit as yesterday, now even more rumpled, and carrying a battered leather satchel. "Can we speak for a few minutes? Alone?"

Francis looked over at the park gates. A policeman stood there, along with men he recognized as reporters. It was not yet seven, hours before Wasserman would meet with the newspapers, but already they smelled blood. He nodded. "Yes, but not here. Come with me."

They walked a few blocks to a small German restaurant that Francis knew opened early. Inside were a half-dozen tables, only one of them occupied, by a man whose bloodstained overalls identified him as a laborer from Packingtown. Francis and Bennie took a table in the back.

"Just coffee for me," Francis told the waiter, and set his helmet in his lap. "I've already had my breakfast."

"Not me." Bennie perused the blackboard menu, ordered white sausages and beer. "And a pretzel. And strong black coffee. And some iced water, please. I haven't slept since Friday."

Francis winced. "Good thing you're young."

"I feel a lot older than I did three days ago. You were right—I was able to confirm that account of Deirdre Monahan's murder. It checks out as your man told you it did. This is what else I found."

He unlatched his satchel, withdrew a large envelope, and set it on the table. Inside was a copy of the *New-York Tribune*, dated the last week of July. Its front-page headlines blared news of the *Eastland* disaster, which had occurred less than a week before.

"Page seven," said Bennie. Francis scanned the columns until he found a brief item:

Skeleton Unearthed in Dreamland Ruins

A human skeleton was uncovered by a railway worker at Coney Island, on the grounds once occupied by the Hell Gate boat attraction at Dreamland amusement park. The skeleton is said to be small, that of a child or resident of Dreamland's Midget City, though no one was reported missing in the conflagration's aftermath. It is requested that anyone who might shed knowledge upon this macabre discovery contact the Coney Island police.

"There's one more," said Bennie, and handed another newspaper to Francis. "This is from May."

Gary Register

The body of a twelve-year-old girl was discovered in a drainage canal near Simons Road on Tuesday evening. Police are seeking information as to the child's identity and as to whether local people have sighted any vagrants in the vicinity. Any individual who has witnessed suspicious behavior or has any other information to impart, please contact Constable Musick.

Francis looked at Bennie. "Did they ever identify her?"

Bennie nodded. "I telephoned the Gary police captain yesterday. Gypsy girl, she and her family were camping in a field about ten miles from town. They arrested the father, but turns out he'd been working on a farm nearby for some months, and the farmer said he'd been there the day the girl disappeared."

Francis replaced the papers in the satchel. He thought for a minute before speaking.

"So. A girl's killed at Dreamland four years ago." He moved aside the water glass, drew an *X* in the condensation left on the table. "Then one in Wonderland that same year."

He drew a second *X,* and a third, and two more. "Another girl in Gary. And another here in Chicago, still missing from two years ago, presumably dead. And now two more at Riverview."

He dabbled a finger in the moisture and drew a six-pointed star connecting the *X*s. "Dreamland, Wonderland, Riverview…that's four girls killed at an amusement park, three of them murdered in a Hell Gate ride. How can they not be related?" Francis stared intently at the star. "What was the cause of death in Gary?"

"The captain says it was asphyxiation. Partially clad body. Which sounds like the same killer." Bennie took a long swallow of his beer. Despite his exhaustion, he looked exultant. "What do you think? Sounds like a vagrant to me, traveling between here and the East Coast."

"No," said Francis. "A vagrant wouldn't be so organized. The amusement parks—they're too far apart. And there's four years between those first two murders and the ones this weekend."

"He could be a hobo, riding the trains," insisted Bennie. "And those murders are only the ones we know about. There might be others. Dr. Holmes's killings, some of them weren't discovered for years."

"I don't think so. A hobo can ride the rails for free, but he'd have to be awfully committed to his crimes to travel so far." Francis rubbed his chin. "It's someone who has an affinity with amusement parks. Or maybe just with the Hell Gate ride. Or water—the rides, the girl in the canal in Gary."

Bennie cocked his head. "What about Elsie Paroubek? She was found in a sewage ditch."

"I don't think so," said Francis slowly. "For one thing, she's the wrong age—five. A twelve-year-old, she's still a girl, but she's starting to look like a grown-up woman."

"Not to me, she doesn't."

"Of course not. But think about it—Blanche Sweet, Mary Pickford, Gladys Egan, those Gish girls—they're all grown women, but in the movies they make them look like kids. Some of them *were* kids when they started, twelve, thirteen years old."

"So, what? You think this is someone who watches the movies, gets titillated, then goes out looking to murder a kid?" Bennie polished off one of his sausages and started in on the other. "I don't buy it."

"All I'm saying, it's not necessarily crazy that someone might look at them as women, not girls. I mean, it *is* crazy," Francis quickly added, "there's no doubt about that."

Bennie sipped his beer. "Well, maybe," he allowed. "I heard they're going to question Charlie Chaplin—he was with the Walewski girl before she was killed, did you know that? And everyone knows Chaplin likes young girls. Not this young, maybe, but fourteen, fifteen. And you've heard the rumors about Beery? There've been complaints about him and underage girls at Essanay for a while now. He may have to leave the studio and head west."

"How do you know all this?"

Bennie grinned. "That's my job."

"So you think it's a movie actor?"

"Nope. I think it's probably a vagrant. Or a Gypsy. Gypsies travel, and a caravan can cover a lot of ground in a year. Some of them join sideshows for the season—whoever this is, he could have worked at Dreamland, then Wonderland, and now Riverview. I heard there's some Gyppo fortune-teller working there now."

"It's not goddamned Gypsies," Francis said heatedly. "And it's a woman working at Riverview, not a man. And she's not really a Gypsy."

"A sensitive point, I gather," observed Bennie. "Well, there you have my contribution. How about introducing me to the kid who found the girl's body?"

"I have another bit of news." Francis leaned across the table, lowered his voice, and told Bennie about the notebook. When he finished, Bennie whistled softly.

"Did you copy down the contents?"

"No. I had to turn it in as evidence."

"Too bad. Can you remember what was in it?"

"Records of horrible crimes. Decapitations, women being buried alive."

"Anything specific about young girls? Or amusement parks?"

Francis nodded. "The word *Hellgate*—it was the last thing he wrote in the book."

"And you found it in the fortune-teller's booth? The same woman whose son came across the body in Hell Gate? The evidence seems to point straight at him, Francis."

Francis struggled to keep his temper. "The boy's so underfed, he couldn't strangle a chicken. His mother says he's starting high school in a month, but he looks about twelve. And others can vouch for his whereabouts at the time."

"Who?"

"A man associated with a detective agency called Gemini, who also claims to have seen a man entering Hell Gate with the Walewski girl."

"Is he a suspect?"

"No. We haven't questioned him. But the boy spoke to him and—"

"The boy *claims* to have spoken to him," said Bennie in exasperation. "This notebook—would a murderer really keep a record of his crimes, then leave it in a fortune-teller's booth? Can you remember anything else he wrote in it?"

"No! But what kind of person writes about killing a woman, then stuffing her down a chimney? Or sealing up a cat inside a wall?"

Bennie stared at him, then burst out laughing. "Edgar Allan Poe, for one. There's a cat walled up with a body in 'The Black Cat.' And an ape kills a woman and hides her down the chimney in 'Murders in the Rue Morgue.'"

Francis flushed. "Are you joking?"

"I am not." Bennie wiped his eyes. "Sounds like that notebook belongs to someone aping Poe—forgive the pun."

"Are you certain?"

"I'm certain Poe wrote the stories I just mentioned, and a few others about women being buried alive. Look, there's no way of knowing whether this notebook belongs to our man. If it does, he's extremely careless. Maybe he's getting reckless as time goes on."

Bennie gulped a mouthful of coffee. "I'm betting it's a vagrant, Francis, and that notebook belongs to some kid who spends too much time reading ghost stories. Maybe the boy who found the body."

"It's not him," Francis snapped.

Bennie shrugged. He tipped back the rest of his beer, retrieved his satchel, and stood. "Thanks for the tip about the Monahan girl."

"What will you do with those?" Francis pointed to the satchel.

"Sell a million papers." Bennie grinned again, then grew serious. "Look, unless someone comes forward and reports a child missing in Dreamland the day of the fire, we can only speculate about what they found at Coney Island. Girls get killed all the time. It's the way of the world, Francis. Nothing we can do about it."

He tossed some change on the table for his breakfast. Francis did the same, and the two returned outside. The grey early morning had grown dark, the sun obscured by bruised clouds that portended storms.

"I'll be in the park soon as it opens," said Bennie as they walked back toward Western Avenue. "So point that boy out to me, will you? Just a few words with him, that's all I want. I'd like to talk to his ma, too."

He gave Francis a sidelong glance, but the policeman said nothing.

Chapter 66

Distant thunder rumbled as he walked along the North Branch, the stagnant air bearing a faint scent of offal from the stockyards miles away. At the crook of the river, tramps had set up an encampment cobbled together from planks and moldering canvas. Four of them crouched around a smoky fire, Gypsies or unemployed brick workers who'd wandered down from the Sicilian ghetto. They watched him pass, their unshaven faces silent and suspicious, as though he was the outcast.

A gaunt mongrel pawed at something on the path—a dead smaller dog, he saw as the larger one slunk off. He sidestepped the lump of flesh and scrambled up the embankment, followed a derelict fence until he found an opening and slipped back onto the street.

He fumbled in his pocket for the box of lemon drops he'd doused with heroin syrup, took two, and chewed them. He needed calm in order to think, to act, to work. The cordial helped, but he'd emptied the last vial, and only a few lozenges remained. He needed to find a druggist.

He'd chosen this part of town because of its proximity to one of the poorer Irish neighborhoods. But even poor people needed a drugstore.

He passed saloons and pawnshops, a knacker's and countless stoops where old women sat and stared into the street, before he finally spotted a faded placard sporting a mortar and pestle.

Inside, a wizened man in a white coat stood on a stool, fiddling with a light fixture. "They promised me these bulbs would burn for a year," he said, looking down accusingly at the newcomer. "This is the third one I've had to toss this month." He stepped down from the stool, still scowling. "What would you like?"

He eyed the shelves behind a scuffed wooden counter. "Do you carry Sydenham's syrup?"

"I do. Jadway's, too—my daughter gives that to her little boy." The druggist removed a small box, squinted at the label, and set it on the counter. "That's Sydenham's."

"I'd like two, please. Twins," he added. "And, well, as long as I'm here, I'd better buy three."

"Twins! I would think so." The druggist placed two more boxes beside the first. "Anything else?"

He picked up one of the bottles and pretended to read the label. "Yes, now that you mention it. Some lemon drops—I'll take three of those, too, if you have them."

The druggist reached under the counter and produced three tins. He set them down and gave the other man an inquisitive look, his gaze lingering on his chin. "Now, don't you think that's very odd? Not half an hour ago, a policeman was here, and he asked about those very things."

His body went cold. Quickly he lowered his head and pulled out his wallet. "A policeman with twins?"

"No. He was—"

The druggist's gaze flicked from the other man's face to the items on the counter. "It was about those murders. The girls in the amusement park." With a shrug, he drew out an account book, a pencil attached to it by a piece of filthy string. "But these aren't the first infant remedies I've sold today. Mrs. Halloran's kids got the colic. Not the only lemon drops, neither. Just not all to the same person. Anything else?"

"That'll be all."

The druggist totted up the items, took his money, put everything into a paper sack, and pushed it across the counter. "I hope this helps your twins. Boy and girl?"

"Two girls."

"Ah, the girls. I have three of each. Girls are more trouble. Then they grow up and cause a whole new set of problems."

He took the bag and hurried outside, right into a woman toting a laundry basket. Its contents spilled to the sidewalk as she shrieked.

"See what you've done! All clean and now look! That's my wages!"

He looked over his shoulder to see the druggist stepping outside.

"Mrs. Rooney? What—"

"That bastard knocked me over and never even saw me! He needs a clout to the head, that one!"

He kept tight hold of his hat, racing down the first alley he saw, kept running until he reached a busy street.

Chapter 67

"Francis!"

Hickey called across the station's crowded main room, waving him over. Francis made his way to join him beside the reception desk, past a number of Chicago policemen along with seemingly everyone from the Riverview force. Paterno stood off by himself—reprimanded, no doubt, for his failure to prevent yesterday's murder.

"Glad you're here." Hickey rolled an unlit cigar between his fingers. "Wasserman's due any minute. Baumgarten wants him to meet with us first, before Cabell and the reporters arrive."

Francis removed his helmet, swiped a hand across his forehead. "Sweet Jesus, it's hot in here."

"Baumgarten wants everyone on duty from now till closing."

"Anything new?"

"Not a goddamned thing, except for these." Hickey grabbed several newspapers from the desk and shoved them at Francis. "Baumgarten says they're reporting it in San Francisco and New York City."

Francis scanned the screamer headlines on the front pages of the *Tribune,* the *Journal,* the *Evening Post:*

Second Girl Murdered at Riverview
Child's Death Shakes City
Amusement Park Killings Continue

"There's more." Hickey jabbed him with a copy of the *Daily News,* folded open to a long article:

Slaughter of the Innocents

"Read it," ordered Hickey. Francis only had to glance at the first paragraph to know it had been penned by Hecht.

"And you'll want to take a look at the advertisement Baumgarten's placed in those papers as well," Hickey went on, his tone ominous. But before Francis had a chance to do so, the station door opened, and James Wasserman, the park's press agent, strode inside.

"Here we go." Cursing, Hickey bulled through the crowd to meet Wasserman. Francis tossed the papers back onto the desk and angled for a better view.

"You all know why we're here." Hickey's voice boomed through the room, and everyone fell silent. He pointed at the park's press agent. "Any questions, please direct them to Mr. Wasserman."

James Wasserman rose and nodded. Rosy cheeked and blond, he would have benefited from a stool to stand on, also a megaphone.

"This will be brief," he announced in a piping voice. "I know you're eager to get to work. Mr. Baumgarten asked me to thank you for everything you've done to maintain Riverview's safety during this trying time."

He glanced around as though expecting applause, instead met several dozen baleful gazes. The press agent's face grew pinker. He cleared his throat and continued.

"Mr. Baumgarten has offered a one-thousand-dollar reward for the capture of this madman. I'll share this news when I meet with reporters at ten, so I'd appreciate it if you kept it under wraps until then.

In addition, Mr. Baumgarten has arranged for a special entry today, with all families with children to be admitted free."

Francis stared at him in disbelief, as other sergeants began yelling angrily. Hickey raised both hands to command silence.

"Hear him out!" he shouted, but his expression mirrored those of the men around him. Wasserman's head bobbed up and down like a tin duck's in the shooting range.

"That's right," he said, his voice cracking. "You all know how Mr. Baumgarten arranges free days throughout the season—Newsboy Day, the Milk Drive. He wants everyone to know that Riverview is open for business, and that our business is people enjoying themselves, especially children. He will personally make up the difference in whatever revenue is lost, and add that to the amount of the reward."

"That's crazy!" a man shouted above the angry chatter. "You're encouraging parents to bring their kids here while there's a murderer loose?"

"People need no encouragement—do you know how many visitors we had yesterday? Nearly seventy thousand. It's probably safer here today than it's ever been." Wasserman's quavering voice steadied, as though emboldened by his own words. "Forty Chicago sergeants will be on patrol, most of them in plain clothes, and that isn't counting all of you. Commissioner Deneen is arranging to meet with several Pinkerton agents, and if needed they will be called into the park as well."

"How come they're not here now?" someone demanded.

"It takes time to get here. And it takes money, too," Wasserman said. "Our resources are not unlimited."

"This isn't the Milk Drive," broke in O'Connell. Every summer, Riverview donated admissions from a single Saturday to buy milk for the city's poor children. "It's a stunt, pure and simple."

"It will reassure the public." Wasserman's tone grew heated. "Make them feel safe. Advertisements are in all this morning's papers, and we have snipers putting up posters across the city. Both Mr. Baumgarten and I believe that whoever committed these crimes has hopped a train out West, and if he has any sense, he'll stay there. If he doesn't, well, we have the resources to take him on. Now, unless someone has an urgent question, I'll leave you to your duties."

Wasserman swiftly made his way to the door as Chief Hickey raised his voice above the fracas.

"Enough, gentlemen! If you have any questions, you can direct them to me—and I mean questions, not complaints."

"Christ," muttered a man beside Francis. "Even if our man's in Denver, we're going to be ass over teakettle with kids and crazies."

Francis nodded in agreement. He waited till nearly everyone had dispersed before approaching Hickey. The chief shook his head.

"Don't! Cabell spoke to the commissioner last night—asked him to shut the park down, at least for a few days. Deneen refused. So don't waste any more of my time or your own."

Hickey thrust his cigar between his teeth and removed a box of matches from his breast pocket, a signal that Francis was dismissed.

Chapter 68

IT WAS FAR too early for Max to have arrived at the park, but Pin went by his dressing room anyway. The door was still unlocked. Inside, there was no sign that he'd been there. Mondays she did her studio run: she prayed he'd show up soon and send her off with a packet for Lionel. She was starving and had been able to scrounge only a nickel from the shack before she left. And she yearned to see Gloria again, to hear her sly laugh and tell her everything that had happened since they'd last met.

But there was no point waiting for Max. He kept his own hours. So she continued on, and drew up short when she saw a freshly painted banner flapping above the entrance to the Ten-in-One:

**BACK BY POPULAR DEMAND
LORD CLYDE, THE HOO-DOO KING
PRESTIDIGITATOR SUPREME & ESCAPE ARTIST
NO BARS CAN HOLD HIM!**

"You have a fucking nerve, boy."

She turned to see Clyde staring down at her, his eyes bloodshot and his usually immaculate white shirt soiled and rumpled.

"Clyde." Her voice came out in a croak. "Clyde, you're free?"

"Say what, boy? Speak up." Clyde stooped to bring his face close to hers. "Didn't have any trouble speaking up to the police, did you?"

"What? I didn't—"

Without warning, his hand clipped her ear, and she went sprawling onto the ground.

"I didn't tell them nothing," she gasped, rolling onto her back. "You can ask them, what'd they say?"

"They said you're a little dago punk. What the hell you doing where you're not wanted? Get your skinny ass out of here before I kill you. Go on now!"

Fighting tears, she grabbed her cap, staggered to her feet, and ran toward the park entrance.

The giant cuckoo clock was hooting ten. The roller coasters clattered as they completed their safety runs, Ballmann's band played the screamer march. The smells of scorched sugar and roasting wienies turned her stomach as she looked up to see the first wave of people come through the gates, some of them holding flyers.

"Don't do us any good now," a woman flanked by four excited children complained as she balled up a piece of paper and flung it aside.

Pin picked up the crumpled flyer and smoothed it out:

RIVERVIEW AMUSEMENT PARK
MONDAY ONE DAY ONLY!
ALL PERSONS ADMITTED FREE
SPECIAL FIREWORKS AT DUSK!

Her breath caught as she read the smaller words at the bottom of the page:

A REWARD OF $1,000 IS OFFERED FOR THE CAPTURE OF THOSE RESPONSIBLE FOR THE RECENT CRIMES AT RIVERVIEW.

Pin dropped the flyer as someone called her name.

"Pin! Wait there!"

She froze, fearful of Clyde's fury, then spotted a slight figure racing toward her from the gate.

"Pin!" Glory ran up alongside her, her cheeks flushed. She wore a skirt and jacket of lettuce-green linen, a Panama hat with a matching ribbon. "I was scared I wouldn't find you!"

"Glory." Pin grew hot, and stared at her feet. "What are you doing here?"

"Lionel sent me."

"Lionel?"

She looked up, and Glory nodded. "He was going to come himself, but they've got him on the stage, writing a new scene for Wally's bathing-contest movie." She gave Pin an odd look. "You okay? Your face is awful red."

"I'm fine. Just hot. You—you look pretty swell."

"Thanks." Glory twirled and held out her arms to show off the dress, her hair a dark cloud trapped beneath her straw hat. "My mother made it—she makes all my clothes. Mr. Spoor wants me to wear it in a scene they're shooting this evening. I get to play a judge at the beauty contest. First time they're letting me play someone who's not a married lady."

She measured up Pin through narrowed, blue-crystal eyes. "Lookee here. Lionel was here yesterday and lost something. A notebook. He knew you'd be coming to the studio later, but he can't get away, so he sent me to ask if you could get it and bring it to the studio later, along with…"

Her voice dropped to a whisper as she leaned in closer, her breath tickling Pin's ear. "Along with what I'm *not supposed to know about. Dope.*" Glory laughed and drew away.

Pin grinned sheepishly. "Sure. Did you check at the lost-and-found at the station?"

"Nope. Just got here. He says he left it at a fortune-teller's. Madame somebody."

"Madame Zanto?"

"Yup, that's her name. Madame Zanto. Know her?"

Pin closed her eyes. "Yeah, sure," she said at last. "I know where she works. But she won't be in yet," she lied. "I can look for it later. What kind of notebook?"

"Just a notebook, he said. Where he writes down ideas for scenarios and dialogue. Spooky stories. You've seen it, he's always carrying it with him."

"I'll find it and bring it when I come by later. Max isn't in yet, either."

"Promise?"

"Promise." Pin raised her hand, palm out. Glory regarded her seriously, then nodded and pressed her palm against Pin's.

"Okay. But if you forget, he'll get mad at me."

"I won't forget."

Pin shifted from one foot to the other, trying to think of some way to prolong the conversation. Glory, too, seemed disinclined to leave. She removed her hat and fanned her cheeks, squinting up at the dark sky. "Looks like it'll storm later."

As if in response, thunder mumbled in the distance, the sound immediately drowned out by the roar of the Jack Rabbit coaster. Glory shuddered. "I hate thunder."

"It won't rain—too far off. You want to see the Comique? That's what they call the nickelodeon here."

"Sure."

They started walking. After a few steps, Glory linked her arm through Pin's. "What do you do here all day?"

Pin's heart beat faster, feeling Glory's touch on her arm. "Not much," she admitted, trying to keep her voice steady. "I help out sometimes at the Kansas Cyclone movie—it breaks down all the time. I know how to fix it, but they won't let me. I wish I could work where you do. At the studio."

Glory made a face. "What, be an actor? Don't tell me that."

"Not an actor. A cameraman. Billy Carrera's taught me some

things, but I could learn more. I just wish someone'd give me a job there."

"Well, you're kinda young."

"I'm fourteen. Old enough to work."

"Maybe. But you look younger. No offense intended."

"I'll be in high school next month. I've seen guys at Essanay aren't any older than me. Well, maybe a year."

"But most of them are actors," said Glory. "You could be a joiner, if you were a girl."

Pin had seen joiners at the studio: a room full of young women holding up ribbons of film, trying to determine where to match one frame to another with no obvious break in the action. Every frame had to be checked, marked with a wax pencil, then carefully attached with gummed tape. Seamstresses were supposed to be good at it—many joiners came from dress-making factories.

She shook her head. "I'd rather be a cameraman. Or a cutter."

"Cutters do the same thing as joiners."

"Except cutters decide how to put the story together. I'd still rather be a cameraman."

"I'll say something to Mr. Carrera."

"He won't listen to a girl."

"He'll listen to *me*," Glory retorted.

She slid her arm from Pin's and adjusted her Panama hat. Pin kicked at the gravel underfoot. "Well, thanks," she said.

Another, louder rumble of thunder sounded. Glory looked at the sky in alarm. "My dress!"

Pin pointed to a large wooden building. "That's the Comique. C'mon—" They began to run as the first fat drops spattered against the ground.

Chapter 69

He never noticed when the busy thoroughfare fell away and he entered a street of tenements. Overhead, ash-colored clouds filled the sky, seamed with heat lightning. Earlier he'd seen a distant twister form before it fragmented into grey ribbons. He paused beneath a tree, opened the first bottle of cordial, and proceeded until he'd dosed all three tins of lemon drops. He finished what remained of the cordial and replaced the tins in his pocket, kicked the empty bottles into the underbrush, sucking his fingers to remove the sticky residue, and ducked out from under the tree.

The road here wasn't much more than a path, deeply rutted and coated with brick dust and soot. The cordial made him feel not languid but anxious, his earlier desperation sharpened. The world around him seemed harshly lit, as if battalions of electrical lights had replaced the sun. He cast no shadow on the cracked earth at his feet; when he knuckled his eyes, strange sparks flew out. His eyes itched, and his arms. His tongue. An image of the doll came to him, her glass eyes threaded with tiny black cracks and her mouth parted to show a black slit. No teeth, no tongue. He thrust the image from his mind, but another took its place: the girl struggling in the theater as he covered her mouth and her teeth sank into the ball of his thumb. She had died but still escaped him. The next one wouldn't; he shoved his hands into his pockets, finding a twist of soft fabric in one and shredding it between his fingers. No, she wouldn't get away, not her, not ever.

"Hey, Mister!"

A shrill voice disturbed him: he looked up, startled to see he wasn't alone. On either side, people stood or squatted on the stoops of ramshackle buildings, the women's hair hidden beneath dark kerchiefs, men's faces shaded by wide-brimmed hats as they puffed their cheroots. Huns or Czechs or refugees from some country he'd never heard of before the war in Europe.

"Hey, Mister, Mister, you lost?"

A row of small heads gazed down at him from a rooftop. Seconds later, something smashed into the road, and he hopped sideways as a bottle burst, spattering him with urine. Some of the people on the stoops laughed as a woman screamed angrily at the children. Cursing, he stumbled on, peals of high-pitched laughter echoing behind him.

Chapter 70

Push push, up and down, down and up, damn the mop. Pay special attention to the third floor, someone vomited by the window, they said. Spit, dirt, shit, hurt.

Damn the mop.

He pulled the ropy part through the mangle, sloshed it into a metal pail with cleaner water, then pushed it back and forth across the floor. Faces stared up at him from the wet linoleum, men with beards and gaping mouths, evil generals, evil men. Inside the wards people moaned and wept; he could hear them whispering behind his back.

Henrico Dargero he saved all those girls! So brave. Grave. Dead, head, bled. He saved them all. Don't fall!

Damn the mop.

The doctors never spoke to him, or the nurses in their white uniforms with the stains under the arms. The wards smelled of mentholatum, carbolic soap, and antiseptic. Mop mop.

He reached the end of the long hallway, where one broad flight of stairs led up, another down. An immense laundry cart stood on the landing. Sometimes he searched inside to see what he might find among the soiled sheets and bloody bandages. Sister Rose saw him once and punched his ear so hard he heard bells for a week. Bells hell. Oh well. .

Beside the laundry cart stood a trash barrel. Push the metal bucket on its squeaking wheels, drag the mop, stop to make sure no one saw. Look inside the barrel quick before they come. He hoped the boy found his message. Newspapers, sometimes a ladies' magazine or *The Little Girl's Sewing Book*. *St. Nicholas* magazine on the children's floor, they didn't like him to dally there, not since what happened. Not his fault.

Damn the mop, he slipped and nearly fell, caught himself and looked around, no one saw. He reached inside the trash barrel, grabbing what was closest. A newspaper, oh damn. He started to drop it, like playing the fishpond game, try another fish, you could win next time, a Kewpie, a celluloid doll. Something nice. Then he saw the headline:

Amusement Park Killings Continue

And the advertisement:

ALL CHILDREN ADMITTED FREE!

He looked over his shoulder. From downstairs came voices, Dr. Wiggins making his rounds. Rounds, hounds. Zounds. Quickly he read the article.

...police remain baffled. Riverview owner Karl Baumgarten has put up a $1,000 reward for capturing the killer...

A reward! Nothing rhymed with that except award. He'd never had one. He stared at a photo of a girl in confirmation robes, standing in front of a church:

GILDA BELASCU

His eyes watered: so pretty. Who would leave their precious child alone, someone might push her down the stairs. Set her on fire.

He tore off the picture and put it in his pocket, reached down again, and pulled up an issue of *Pearson's* with an advertisement for Pears' soap on the back: an infant with golden hair, her chubby hand reaching for a soap bubble.

Joy!

He curled up the magazine and stuck it down his trouser leg as someone shouted from the ward, then clattered up the steps, one of the nurses. She raced by him, knocking the metal bucket so that filthy water spilled everywhere and he cried out in a rage.

Damn the mop!

Chapter 71

He continued to swear, enraged at the pock-faced children, but they had already disappeared. He hurried on, the poverty of the slums trailing him like a bad smell. Twiglike girls nursed bundles of rags. Men pissed in the street, drunk through the morning. All of them foreigners, chittering like insects. They should never have outlawed wooden structures here, better it all went up in flames.

Another quarter hour and he reached a block where every building had been razed. Boards and twisted metal, heaps of rubble and rotting wood. He wrinkled his nose at the odors of charred brick, horse dung, river bile, and sewage. The North Branch wouldn't be far off. The tenement block must have abutted a brickyard, now demolished.

But people still lived close by. He craned his neck to see yet another row of dilapidated tenements. Between here and there stretched a wasteland of abandoned kilns and warehouses, a freestanding brick archway that opened onto nowhere.

Lightning lanced the horizon. The humid air played tricks with distant noises. The groan of an unseen freight train seemed to come from only a few yards off, along with snatches of a man singing "Can't You Hear Me Callin', Caroline." Yet when he turned, no one was there.

He walked on, after a few minutes stopped again.

Shrill voices echoed from the ruined brickworks. He heard laughter and then a shriek, followed by the sound of an argument.

His hands trembled with anticipation. He shoved them back into his pockets and continued at a brisker pace, picking his way through broken glass and boards riddled with nails, until he reached the phantom arch, the name FELLISON's carved into its bricks. He stood there, hidden from view, and watched the scene in front of him.

Children played in the ruins, all girls. He counted seven, clad in a patchwork of drab plaid dresses and pinafores. One girl, blond and taller than the rest, stood atop a pile of bricks, hands on her hips as she surveyed her kingdom. Two smaller girls crouched at her feet, whispering to each other and holding hands. The others remained a safe distance away and warily circled the mound. No one seemed to have spotted him.

A girl broke from the circle to shriek imprecations that the tall girl ignored. Another girl, stout and red haired and wearing a grimy gingham dress, clambered up the brick hill and reached for the two girls who crouched at the blond's feet. They bellied onto the rubble and stretched their hands out to her.

"Save us, Brigid! Save us!"

"Mother Witch, Mother Witch, have you seen my baby?" the redhead, Brigid, cried as she skidded back down the pile.

The blond girl playing the witch straightened. Sharp featured, she looked as though she'd blacken the eye of anyone who'd dare approach her. She stooped to grasp each of the smaller girls by the collar. The two captives laughed. The redhead again scrambled up the bricks, shouting, "Mother Witch, Mother Witch, have you seen my sister? She's the one still wets the bed!"

"I do not!" one of the captives yelled.

The witch sprang at the interloper, and the girl fled with a shriek. The others collapsed with laughter as the witch raced down to grab an unwary girl's arm. As she dragged her up the brick hill, Brigid turned to smack a smaller girl with russet plaits like her own.

"Shit! Una, why weren't you watching?"

Una, skinny and freckled, lunged at her. The two fell and tussled until the smaller girl began to sob. Brigid stumbled to her feet, screeching, "Whyn't you just go home?"

"I'm telling Ma!" Una pushed herself up, face crimson. "You're supposed to be watching Danny!"

"If you tell Ma, I'll kill you, you little brat!"

She pushed Una down again and rejoined the game.

Una wiped her nose and shrieked, "I hate you!" She struggled to her feet and stalked off, picking up chunks of brick and throwing them at the others.

Still hidden in the brick arch, he watched her pass, counted to sixty, and began to follow her. At first he stayed a good distance behind, but as the sounds of the game grew fainter, he hastened his steps. The girl walked aimlessly past the slag heaps, her pace slowing as she approached an abandoned warehouse. She picked up a rock and threw it at a window, nodding in satisfaction as the glass shattered.

He sidled toward the warehouse, staring at his feet as though deep in thought, even as he gazed from the corner of his eye to make sure the girl hadn't seen him. When he saw her stiffen, he stopped short.

"Oh my goodness!" His eyes widened as he took a step back, hands raised in alarm. "You gave me a start, I didn't even see you!"

The girl edged away from him. He took another backward step.

"I think I'm lost," he said, looking around. He avoided her eyes; that would spook her. "I'm looking for Emma Street, do you know where that is? The bakery, I'm supposed to pick up a white loaf for my wife."

He shot her a puzzled smile. She didn't smile back. But she didn't run, either. He allowed himself to relax slightly. Feigning interest in the warehouse, he approached its open doorway. "Was this a bakery, do you think?" he asked.

"Bakery?" the girl replied scornfully. "Not unless you eat bricks. This's the brickworks. Was."

She hefted a brick and heaved it. He blinked as it smashed through another window. "Good aim," he said.

For the first time she looked at him. Her braids had come undone, and she swiped her hair impatiently from her face. She had mistrustful blue eyes and appeared older than he'd first thought—thirteen at least. His fingers clenched and unclenched as he stared at her blue gingham dress, dusty and ripped from the fight with her sister. The torn bodice would be easy to stitch up, once he was back in his room.

"That wasn't very nice, what your sister did," he said.

She looked at him sharply. Then she laughed. "What are you, after Brigid? She's with Lester now, you'll be wasting your time."

"I hadn't heard."

"I seen you before, I think." She yawned, raising her arms so that her dress slid up, exposing a fringe of torn petticoat and scabbed knees. "At McKracken's there."

"That's right." He nodded, withdrew a tin of lemon drops. He popped one into his mouth, closed the lid, and made to replace it in his pocket, before hesitating to glance at her. "I'm sorry—I should have offered. Care for one?"

"What is it?"

"Lemon drops."

She made a face. "I don't like 'em."

"Me neither, usually," he said. "But these are very good."

Her eyes narrowed as she scrutinized the tin. "All right, I guess I'll try one."

She plucked out a lozenge and put it in her mouth. "Tastes like cherry," she said, "not lemon."

He offered her another. She chewed it and said, "This one's nicer."

"Please, help yourself." He held out the tin.

"Don't mind if I do," she said, and grabbed a fistful.

Chapter 72

DESPITE ITS FANCY name, the Comique wasn't a movie palace like the Hippodrome, or even a nickelodeon like the Kansas Cyclone, with its piano accompanist and movie projected on sail canvas, but a long barnlike structure with a screen door that banged every time someone entered or left.

"Won't be anyone here this early," Pin said as she held the door for Glory. "Except for Gus."

At a table sat a fat man with a scruffy beard, visor pulled low on his forehead as he read a newspaper. He barely looked up when she dropped a nickel on the desk.

"Heya, kid. Here ya go." He grunted and handed her twenty-five pennies from a metal dispenser. "Don't make trouble."

The long windowless room was dim and cool as the inside of a church. Mutoscope and Kinetoscope machines lined the walls. An odd, not unpleasant smell hung over everything—burnt dust from the peep-show lanterns, tobacco smoke, sawdust. Tattered posters advertised one-reelers, few of which could be seen in the Comique.

Glory surveyed the room, brows knitted. "Wow. I didn't know they still had places like this."

They walked over to inspect a Mutoscope. Handwritten cards stuck to the machines had titles like *Oh! What She Did!* and *What She Couldn't See.* You put a penny in a slot, then peered through a lens while you cranked a handle that turned a spool holding eight hundred and fifty black-and-white photo cards. The cards flipped over one at a time, and if you cranked fast enough, you saw a flickering movie that lasted a minute or two. If you cranked slowly, you got a better look at the individual photos of naked ladies.

But the Comique had other movies, too. Most featured girls in trouble, like *The Broken Doll, Lonely Villa,* or *The Adventures of Dollie.* Pin pointed to another Mutoscope.

"Have you seen *The House with the Closed Shutters?*"

Glory nodded. "That was a good one!"

"I love it," Pin said in a reverent tone. The heroine was a girl who dressed in her cowardly Confederate brother's uniform, ordered her mother to cut off all her long hair, then rode off to deliver an important letter to General Lee. Afterward she was killed while trying to raise the Confederate flag on the battlefield. Pin hurried over to the machine.

OUT OF ORDER

"Damn, it's busted."

"Don't swear," chided Glory, swatting her with her straw hat. "Lookee here. Harriet Quimby." She gestured at another Mutoscope:

THE ENGLISH CHANNEL FLOWN BY A LADY AVIATOR FOR THE FIRST TIME

"That's my favorite!" exclaimed Pin.

"Me too."

Pin jammed a penny into the slot. Heads touching, they leaned over the viewing lens. The brilliant light inside the machine flashed on as Pin turned the crank, title cards flickering.

263

HARRIET QUIMBY PREPARES HER BLÉRIOT AEROPLANE

And there she was—beautiful Harriet, standing beside her monoplane in her leather trousers and aviator's cap. She adjusted her goggles as a man looked on and another man spun the aeroplane's propeller. Smiling, she waved at the cameraman.

NEVER BEFORE HAS A WOMAN ATTEMPTED SUCH A THING!

Harriet stepped inside the open cockpit. The wind grabbed the end of her scarf as the Blériot began to move across the field on its little wheels, rocking back and forth as it gained speed.

Then, magically, the aeroplane lifted into the air, wings tilting one way, then the other, as it went up, up, up, shrinking until it might have been a bird, or an insect, and then not even an insect but something in Pin's eyes that made them water.

NEVER DONE BEFORE! THE WORLD'S FIRST LADY OF THE AIR

The end titles flickered. The screen went blank. Pin opened her mouth to say she'd gotten a cinder in her eye, but Glory moved closer, her lips soft against Pin's cheek as she whispered, "It makes me cry, too."

Pin turned her head, and for an instant their mouths touched. Through slitted eyes she saw Glory staring back at her, smelled her sugary scent mingled with that of burning dust as Glory's lips pressed against her mouth and Glory's tongue flicked against Pin's lower lip.

"Hey! None of that, you kids!"

Glory drew back, cheeks aflame, while Pin laughed, giddy and confused.

"I mean it!" Gus pounded on his table so the coin changer jingled.

Pin knew he wouldn't bother to heave his bulk from his stool, but she nodded.

"C'mon," she said, and took Glory's hand.

They hurried out through the back door, the leaden sky blinding after the Comique's cool darkness. The rain had stopped, but the air felt dank as a wet sponge. Glory looked at Pin and started to laugh. Pin began laughing, too, the two of them doubled over like they were at a Chaplin movie.

Finally, Glory caught her breath. "Lookee here, I need to get back. And we never even went for that book…" She appeared crestfallen. "Aw, Lionel will kill me."

"I'll find it, don't worry," Pin said. "I'll bring it when I come to the studio for—you know."

They both burst out laughing again. Then, "You better not ever get caught," Glory warned her. "They'll send you to Detention House."

"I won't get caught. Besides, it just looks like a packet of cigarettes."

"Not if you smoke 'em."

"Well, who's smoking 'em? Not me."

Glory gave her a smile that seemed equal parts admiration and worry. "I suppose you're just braver than me, Pin."

When they reached the park's exit, Glory stopped. "Lookee, I'll be working till late tonight, doing that bathing-contest movie. So if I'm not in the costume shop when you come to see Lionel, just come find me on the stage."

Pin nodded, unsure what to do now. Shake hands? But Glory had already turned to race for the streetcar, one hand raised in farewell, the other clutching her hat.

Chapter 73

HE WATCHED HER chew the lozenges, waiting for his chance. It came when a thin curtain of rain descended across the trash-strewn lot. The girl stared stupidly at the sky, rain spotting her gingham dress.

"Let's stay dry!" he exclaimed, taking her hand to pull her into the building.

"Feels good," she said, resisting, and he let go. "Been so hot."

His limbs felt suspended in honey. He'd continued to eat the lozenges himself, so as not to make the girl suspicious whenever he offered her another. She tipped her head back so the rain ran down her face.

"It's just a sun shower," she said. "I got to get back, my ma told me to watch my brother."

Without another word, she turned and broke into a run.

He'd been expecting this: he lunged, grabbed her arm, and dragged her into the warehouse. She screamed, not in fear but fury, and elbowed him in the chest. He grunted but didn't let go, clamping his hand across her mouth. It was as though he'd tried to silence a rabid dog. She bit down on his fingers, kicking him as she twisted away, screaming.

"Brigid! Brigid!"

His knees buckled as she landed another kick; her fist connected with his eye as he fell, catching himself against the doorframe. He clutched his face and dazedly watched her run off. When he heard the answering chorus of girls' alarmed voices, he turned and lurched through the warehouse, searching for the door. It was locked, but he kicked it open, pushed his way through the rotted boards, and fled.

He stumbled until he reached a railroad track, scrambled down the embankment, and followed it until he saw a break in the fence. Back on the street, he retraced his path to a streetcar stop and hopped the first car he saw. He rode it to within a few blocks of where he lived and staggered home, locked the door behind him, and raced upstairs to pack.

Chapter 74

BY EARLY AFTERNOON Francis felt like he was playing a bit part in one of those one-reelers popularized by the temperance movement—*The Drunkard's Curse, Satan in a Bottle.* He'd never seen so many drunks, men and women both. *This is what you get for giving away free tickets for the kiddies,* he thought. That much more money to spend on beer.

And of course the weather only made it worse. Something about the threat of a storm made people act like their days were numbered. Couples stumbled from the Woodland Cabaret, the women's skirts rumpled and the men's collars askew. A man held a woman's hat as she vomited near the Tickler's exit. Outside Hell Gate, a girl comforted her sobbing friend.

"He told me—he told me it couldn't possibly *be him..."*

Because of course they'd opened the dark ride again. How could they not, on what would almost certainly be Riverview's biggest day of the season?

Then there were the lost kids, at least two or three an hour, judging from how often the station bell rang. So far, every child had been reunited with his or her family.

His heart still contracted every time he saw a young girl on her own. By the time he returned to the station house for his break, it was after three o'clock.

Magruder was at the front desk, smoking as he bent over a logbook. The open windows let in a stifling breeze and the midway's racket. Magruder looked up and leaned across the desk to motion him over.

"There's been another one," he said in a low voice.

Francis stared at him. "Are you joking?"

"Not here—that Irish slum south of Division. Irish girl, there was a group of them playing in a vacant lot. She wandered off and said a man approached her. He offered her candy and tried to grab her, but she fought him off and escaped."

"Where is she now?"

"Chicago Avenue station. Her mother brought her in, Deneen's supposed to be questioning her."

"Could the girl describe the man?"

"Said he was white, light-colored hair. Younger, not grey hair. A mustache.

"And listen to this—" Magruder stubbed out his cigarette. "A drugstore man went to the police this morning. He said a man came into his shop early this morning to buy lemon drops and laudanum cordial. Three boxes of each. Said they were for his twins, but the druggist says he looked suspicious. Cuts on his face, and when he noticed the druggist staring at them, he ran off like he was on fire and knocked over a laundress in the street."

"Where was this?"

"Ashland Avenue. Same general vicinity as the girl."

"West Town." Francis stared out the window, thinking. "He lives nearby," he said at last. "He's too smart to try it again in the park, but he doesn't want to go too far away. Are they searching the slum?"

"Yeah. But the girl said he wasn't from there. She would have recognized him if he was. She said he was too well dressed. Not Irish. Not Italian or Polish or Czech, either. And not a Gypsy."

"Hell," said Francis. "He could be anywhere by now."

"They're watching the train station and steamboats. Baumgarten's pressuring the Bavarian Society to kick in another thousand to the reward money."

Exhaustion hit Francis like a sudden chill. "I need to get something to eat," he said. "You got enough men?"

"Oh, sure." Magruder ran a finger down the log in front of him. "Hasn't been too terrible. Mostly the heat, and a buncha drunks."

"How many lost kids?"

"Seventeen so far. But they've been brought in pretty fast. Last one, Baumgarten was here and gave him a pass for the rest of the summer. Kid nearly fainted, he was so excited."

Francis's smile didn't reach his eyes. "Good for him," he said.

Chapter 75

Lᴏᴜᴇʟʟᴀ Pᴀʀsᴏɴs ᴡᴀs driving Lionel crazy with her rewrites. For a matronly lady who dressed like she was meeting her friends for a rubber of bridge, Louella intimidated as many people at Essanay as Spoor or Anderson. He didn't know what was worse: being forced to churn out his own drivel for the studio, or enduring endless revisions on marginally better material written by someone else.

Now he and Parsons stood watching Carrera set up a new scene that Lionel had rewritten at her urging, but Lionel had already decided this would be the last time. When he saw Spoor, he'd pitch his idea for a movie inspired by the Riverview murders. If Spoor turned it down, he'd buy a train ticket and try his luck at the Niles studio.

Then a messenger burst into the scenarists' room.

"He's done it again!" he cried, waving a special noontime edition of the *Pilot,* a broadsheet emblazoned with one-inch headlines. Billy Carrera grabbed the paper as cast and crew crowded around him.

"Jesus," Lionel muttered as he read over Louella's shoulder:

Girl Narrowly Escapes Killer's Hands

Una O'Harran, thirteen years old, recounted how she was snatched from playing a game with other children in a vacant yard near Division Street early this morning. The young girl managed to escape but her adductor fled…

An actor pushed his way past Lionel, blocking his view. But he'd read enough. It would be impossible for anyone to focus on *A Truckload of Taters* until after lunch.

Someone tapped his shoulder: Louella. "I'll need you here this afternoon for *Bettie's Bathing Beauty Boast*. That Valerie can't remember her own name. You're going to have to simplify her lines."

"What time?"

"Three o'clock. Don't be late again."

Lionel wouldn't be late. He was done taking orders from Louella. He'd get his notebook, talk to Spoor, and take his chances.

He headed down the hall to Glory's dressing room. Glory sat inside, curling her hair in front of the mirror.

"Did you find it?" he asked.

Glory carefully freed the curling iron from a ringlet. "I didn't have enough time. But I saw Pin and asked him if he could bring it with him with the…you know."

"Well, I haven't seen him here," snapped Lionel. "Have you?"

"Not yet. I expect he'll be along soon."

This is what he got for trusting a kid. "I guess I'll just go myself, then. Did you hear that guy tried to kill another girl?"

"No! What happened?"

"Somewhere in an Irish slum, the girl got away. You better be careful, Glory—when Pin comes around, maybe you should ask him to stay and protect you."

He meant it as a joke. But to his surprise, Glory's cheeks pinked.

"I can protect myself," she retorted.

She sure could—Glory had just ratted out Wally Beery for flirting with a thirteen-year-old extra. But Lionel had seen the way Glory and Beery looked at each other. That girl's beautiful blue eyes sure could turn green fast. He touched his hat. "I'm going to Riverview to find my notebook. Don't want anyone stealing my ideas."

"Fat chance." Glory sniffed.

Chapter 76

AFTER GLORY LEFT, Pin had made her way back through the park, sleeves rolled up and hands slung in her knickerbocker pockets, head thrown back to stare raptly at the grey sky. She sauntered past Red Friend, grinning like she hadn't heard his bally a thousand times— *"Happened right where you're standing, friend—that very spot!"* She didn't even pause to watch the crowd outside the shuttered Hippodrome, where policemen chased away photographers trying to sneak in.

She felt pixilated, like one of those pictures from the funnies that showed someone with bluebirds flying from their eyes. She could hardly bear to think of Glory's mouth pressed against hers: the memory made her so happy she was afraid she might wear it out, the way film reels decayed after being played day after day.

Yet she couldn't keep it from her mind, or the thought of Glory's hand in hers, how she'd cocked her head and gazed at Pin with that sly half smile.

I suppose you're just braver than me...

No one had ever thought she was brave. *She'd* never thought she was brave. Girls never were, unless they were martyred saints, like Joan of Arc.

But Pin wasn't dead. And Glory's kiss proved she would never be a saint. The longing to be with her again made her feel restless, frantic even. She needed to get Lionel's notebook from her mother's booth. Once she retrieved it, she'd hit up Max for Lionel's delivery and streetcar fare, and head to Uptown and Essanay.

But that meant waiting for Max to show up. Maybe she could cadge the fare from her mother now. Then she could make two trips to the studio: one to deliver Lionel's notebook, the other after she saw Max and got Lionel's cigarettes.

The arcade was thronged with boys and girls her own age. Of course: kids were admitted free today. Pin tugged down her cap to hide her face. She didn't want to chance running into anybody from one of her old schools.

She squinted at the boys snatching hats from shrieking girls who were obviously delighted to be picked on. No sign of any kids she knew, though she recognized the beefy man who stood a few yards from the arcade, watching the goings-on with a detached expression, like he was pretending he was somewhere else. Sergeant Morgenstern, one of the Riverview cops, though he wore a natty brown suit and derby rather than his uniform. She skirted him, annoyed. She wasn't doing anything wrong, but she still didn't want to be recognized.

Why had Lionel even visited her mother's booth? First Fatty Bacon, now Lionel, who always spoke of Riverview with contempt, like he'd never be caught dead in an amusement park.

So why had he come here? Probably had some crazy idea for a movie, the way he had about fires a month ago, and that story about the black cat in the wall. He'd gone through four notebooks so far this summer. Now what?

The murders, she realized with a sick feeling. *He was here because of the dead girls.*

Chapter 77

Lionel edged through the crowds, hot and out of sorts and apparently the only person uninterested in joining an endless line for the Tickler or Witching Waves, Shoot-the-Chutes or the merry-go-round or—well, any of them. All he wanted was to be back in his own apartment, with a tumbler of whiskey and one of Max's hand-rolled cigarettes and his Royal Upright, "The St. Louis Blues" playing on the gramophone. Instead, he was wasting his afternoon, retrieving his damn notebook.

Overhead stretched a threatening line of anvil clouds. The near-constant rolls of thunder had grown indistinguishable from the coasters' roar. The wind carried a whiff of acrid smoke from Bricktown. Policemen were everywhere: he spied a brawny fellow with a walrus mustache and a pair of opera glasses, obviously a plainclothesman. The Hippodrome theater remained closed, but the line for Hell Gate stretched all the way to the Velvet Coaster. Even with tens of thousands of free admissions, the park's owner would make a killing today.

He avoided the stretch of midway in front of the freak show, where foot traffic had come to a standstill. Craning his neck, he spied a tall figure in formal wear and a top hat, holding aloft a birdcage as he threaded his way through the wall of rubberneckers. That black magician they'd arrested for the first girl's murder, out of jail and obviously back to playing to full houses.

Ahead of him the Pike curved toward the Miniature Railway and balloon sellers, Merry Ann the mechanical pony and the duck pond. Beyond were the Woodland Cabaret and burlesque stalls, Max's She-Male tent, and the booth that sold French photographs. Past those was the penny arcade where Madame Zanto held his notebook hostage.

He slowed as he neared Max's tent. From the shouts and taunts from inside, he must have just opened. Lionel halted beneath the lurid banner:

ADMISSION 25 CENTS NO ONE UNDER SIXTEEN ADMITTED.
NO WOMEN, NO CHILDREN
NOT FOR THE FAINT OF HEART

The wind had loosened the cords that held the canvas flaps closed during performances, leaving a gap that Lionel peered through.

A wall of men blocked his view of the stage. Even from here he could smell their rage and arousal, bodies packed like spoiled oysters in a barrel. He'd witnessed Max's show only once before, on his first visit to Riverview not long after they'd met at a supper club on the Stroll. He'd been impressed by the performance: Max knew just how to tilt his head and widen his eyes slightly, part his lips with a sideways glance; then turn so that the illusion of a youthful flirt was upended as a snappy dude challenged the audience, stroking his mustache with a salacious grin.

Now Lionel wondered if he'd somehow come to the wrong tent, or if Max had been replaced by another performer. Instead of Max's blond good looks, the actor resembled a roughneck, his hair black with a greasy sheen. Thick white powder covered his entire face, not just the woman's half. The powder didn't hide a cut on his chin with blood seeping from it, or the raw look of his upper lip, as though he'd been shaved with a dull razor. A scarlet bloom surrounded the iris of one eye. He hadn't even bothered with a wig, just a Panama hat. It looked as though he'd been at the losing end of a fight, his face knotted with such barely contained rage that he appeared deranged, like the poor soul who howled at the crowds in the freak show.

Yet Max was utterly silent, utterly still, refusing to move or speak despite the epithets and taunts shouted at him by the crowd. Like them, Lionel couldn't look away. Until, with a jolt of horror, he saw Max's gaze shift with the dreamlike slowness of an automaton's, until it focused on the rear of tent, and his bloodshot eyes riveted on Lionel's own.

With a gasp Lionel backed away, turned, and sprinted toward the crowded path. He let himself be carried along until he spotted a grassy patch at the edge of Fairyland where he sat, struggling to catch his breath, struggling to find words for what, exactly, he had seen in Max's eyes, and why it had terrified him.

Chapter 78

LIONEL WAS FASCINATED by murders; everyone knew that. The Riverview killings would make exactly the kind of story he loved, gruesome but also peculiar, like that scenario he'd written for the Sweedie movie with the dolls. Pin thought it was funny when Wally Beery played it, but she'd overheard Lionel pitching the original version to Billy Carrera. Dolls that came to life in the toy shop at night, dolls that the toy maker mistook for real girls. She was glad that Spoor had put the kibosh on that one. It gave her the willies.

The giant clock sang a solitary *cuckoo*. Already afternoon. If she didn't hurry, she'd miss her chance to get the book to Lionel at the studio, dash back to the park, and make a second run for Max. Glory had said she'd be around all day, but Pin knew how quickly things changed at Essanay, entire movies rewritten and reshot within a few hours. She hopped onto the arcade's wooden walkway and pushed her way through a group of girls milling in front of her mother's booth.

"Hey, we're next!" One of the girls squared her shoulders to block Pin's way. "Wait your turn."

"Yeah, get in line, buster." A girl with glasses grabbed Pin's hand and peered at it. "Phew! Says here, you need to take a bath."

Pin shoved her aside. The girl gasped, yelping, "Didn't your mother teach you not to hit girls?"

The black velvet drapes flew open. "Who's next? What's going on out here?"

Her mother stood in the doorway, frowning. After a moment, her eyes widened—in recognition, Pin realized, though not of her daughter but of someone behind Pin. Gina raised her eyebrows and quickly nodded, signaling to whoever it was. Pin glanced around but saw no one she recognized.

Yet when she looked back at Gina, her mother's gaze *did* fix on her, now in alarm. She made a shooing gesture, urging Pin to leave. Confused, Pin again turned to scan the Pike.

Morgenstern had removed his derby and was waving it. Standing on tiptoe, she could just make out another Riverview cop, this one in uniform, pushing through the crowd toward the arcade. She glanced back at her mother, who shook her head vehemently and mouthed the word *Go!* Without a sound, Pin left.

Chapter 79

SWINE. THEY WERE all swine. If he had a knife he'd pry that one's eyes out like a nutmeat.

And that one in the front, spit spewing from his mouth whenever he opened it. If he tried anything, he'd gut him. Slit their bellies like pigs' carcasses, expose their organs while they still breathed. Only a matter of time till nightfall. Catch the train, packed already, leave behind what can't be carried. Always another, that softness between his fingers. Never again would he allow one to strike him back. Take them to a dark place, hold them in your hands. The silence. The way they never blinked.

Chapter 80

THEY GRABBED HIM in front of the fortune-telling booth. Two men, one wearing a shapeless dark suit and derby, the other in uniform.

"Excuse me, what are you doing?" Lionel asked as they drew up alongside him.

"Shut up."

The policeman smacked his billy club against Lionel's ribs. He doubled over as the two men took his arms and bullied their way through the crowd.

They dragged him to the park station house, down a hallway and into an office where a barrel-chested man stood behind a desk, a police captain by the look of him.

But not a real policeman, Lionel thought, his desperation growing, surely he wouldn't have the authority to make an arrest. Someone must have seen him in Fairyland yesterday—that man, the one who resembled a banker. He could have been a plant, put there to entrap inverts. Yet Lionel had done nothing!

But he could still go to prison—he would be ruined, even murdered.

No, he would not, he thought. Think of it as a story, how would the hero escape? He drew a few deep breaths, focused on the details of the room around him. The smells of sweat that clung to the men's woolen uniforms and stale cigar smoke. The light scent of his own Lilac Vegetal cologne—they'd find a way to use that against him. Scattered newspapers. The carnival clamor from outside the open windows, air heavy as wet fleece.

"We found him, Captain Hickey." The man in the suit glanced in disgust at Lionel. "I spotted him by the booth and signaled Mr. Doylan."

"Looks like he put up a fight." Captain Hickey turned to Lionel. "What is your name, sir?"

Lionel stared the captain full in the face. "I didn't fight."

"I asked your name."

Hickey's eyes narrowed. He gestured at the two men, who released Lionel. For the first time, Lionel saw that the plainclothesman held his straw boater, now crushed flat. He set it on the desk in front of Hickey with a flourish.

The captain pushed the hat aside irritably. "If you please, sir. Your name."

"Lionel Gerring."

"Mr. Gerring, what is your employment?"

"I work at the Essanay motion-picture studio. I'm a scenarist—a writer. I write photoplays."

"A writer." Hickey shuffled through the scattered newspapers until he found a small object. "Would this be yours?" He held up a notebook.

Lionel laughed in relief. "Yes! That's mine—!" He stepped toward the desk but was restrained. His elation wavered. "Why have I been brought here?"

"How long have you known Mrs. Maffucci?" asked Hickey.

"Who?"

"Regina Maffucci. She works at one of the arcades as a Gypsy fortune-teller, Madame Zanto. Her given name is Regina Maffucci."

Lionel frowned. "I never set eyes on her before yesterday. I didn't know her name until you just told it to me."

"But this is your book?"

Reluctantly, Lionel nodded. "Yes. But—"

Hickey signaled silence. He opened the book and turned its pages, his face registering disgust. "You describe some revolting things, Mr. Gerring. 'Large stone pressed upon his chest till he expires.'" He turned to another page. "'All that remains afterward are her charred shoes.'"

"Those are notes for scenarios I'm working on. Stories."

"A moving-picture story?"

"Yes."

Hickey grimaced. "No one in their right mind would choose to watch a moving picture like that, Mr. Gerring. Just as no one in their right mind would write about something so reprehensible as the murder of those two girls."

"Is that what you think?" Lionel gaped at him. "That's ridiculous! Ask Mr. Spoor—call him now, damn it! I've pitched every damn one of those stories to him."

"Enough of that!" commanded Hickey. He continued to flip through the pages. "You have a diseased mind, Mr. Gerring. Who would imprison their cat behind a wall?"

"It's a *story*! And it's not even my story! It's by Edgar Allan Poe, 'The Black Cat.' The others are from 'The Pit and the Pendulum' and 'The Murders in the Rue Morgue.' They're very well known, ask anyone."

Hickey scowled. "I've never heard of them. Mr. Morgenstern, have you? Mr. Doylan?"

The plainclothesman, Morgenstern, nodded. "I have. Couldn't tell you the writer's name, but I read that story about the morgue and the ape who kidnaps a lady in France."

"France." Hickey pronounced the word as though this in itself might be proof of guilt.

Morgenstern nodded. "Don't know if he's the killer, but he definitely stole those stories."

"Everyone does it," Lionel protested weakly.

"What about this?" Hickey indicated a page with a single word scrawled on it. "'Hellgate.' Is that from one of your magazines?"

"That was a note for a different scenario, about the killings here at the park—"

"*How dare you?* Those children aren't in their graves and you'd defile their memories with this?" Hickey looked as though he might throw the notebook into Lionel's face. "Can you account for your whereabouts for the last two days?"

"I can. Yesterday—"

Someone knocked at the door.

"Captain Hickey?" A sergeant peered inside. "Detective Berens is here to question Mr. Gerring."

"Thank you, Sergeant Paterno. You can show him in. Mr. Morgenstern, Mr. Doylan, thank you."

As the plainclothesman headed to the door, he paused to leer at Lionel. "Your next story, you should use *The Man in the Iron Mask,*" he said.

Chapter 81

BEHIND HER, MORE and more people swarmed toward the arcade, shoving one another in their efforts to see…something. Pin cursed. Why had her mother warned her off? Now she'd missed whatever was happening, and there was no point trying to fight her way back.

She headed for the path by Hell Gate. A line snaked around the dark-ride pavilion, petering out where people stumbled laughing from the boats. In the ticket booth, Larry was handing out wooden tokens as fast as he could. She walked by, her eyes half closed, trying to re-capture the moment when Glory had kissed her. Her longing grew so intense she felt like she might pass out.

If she could only tell someone how she felt—not just Glory, any-one—that might help, like when you pierce a balloon to let the air out. Even Henry had a friend in Willhie. She had no one, other than Henry, and how could she trust someone who might have killed her sister? How could she even think about it?

Her mother's voice echoed in her head. *Stop feeling sorry for yourself! Your sister's the one who's dead.*

She heard the cuckoo clock chime and counted its notes. Still too early for Max, probably. She glanced up at the knoll, from where she'd seen the killer enter Hell Gate, let her gaze drop to the stand of poplars where she'd first met Henry, not even two days ago. It felt like centuries. What if she hadn't met him? Would she feel worse now, or better?

Her head ached from the heat, the heavy air fizzing like the electrical lights in the Ten-in-One. She touched the shiv in her pocket, its blade warm as her own skin, and wandered toward the poplar grove. Something moved in the green shadows, and she felt a stir of excitement: Henry had returned! But it was only a squirrel scurrying in the grass.

Still, she could pretend it felt cooler here. The leaves rippled in the hot wind and touched her bare arms as she slipped between the trees. Something caught her eye in the long grass, a scrap of trash or lost handkerchief. She stooped to see what it was.

A rock—two rocks, one atop the other—had been placed on a square of cardboard as big as her two hands. She looked around to see if anyone was watching her, then picked up the cardboard. It was stained and wrinkled, the torn flap of a carton, she guessed, folded to form a makeshift envelope.

Nothing was written on the outside, but as she carefully unfolded it, a smaller piece of cardboard fell out. White shirt cardboard, cut into a tidy square. One side was blank. She turned it over.

Three small pictures had been pasted on this side to form an arc. The first was a picture of a rolling pin from a magazine advertisement. The center was the photo of Maria Walewski from the newspapers, the photo that had been taken at Essanay with Charlie Chaplin. Maria's dark hair had been scribbled over with black ink, her mouth dabbed with red crayon, and her eyes made to look like the eyes of the crazy old man in the Polly comic strip.

The last picture was an illustration torn from a magazine story—a drawing of a rabbit lying on the ground, its long ears sleeked back and a peaceful expression on its face. Someone had meticulously shaded in its white fur with a pencil, so the fur looked grey, like the rabbit she'd seen in the Black Brothers Lodge.

She sank onto the grass and touched each of the pictures in turn. The rolling pin—that would be her, one of Henry's crazy nicknames. Maria. The rabbit. Last of all she traced the wobbly words at the bottom of the homemade card. No one had ever given her a card before.

MR PIN
    SORRY I SCARED YOU LAST NIGHT
SINCERLY YRS, H DARGER

Chapter 82

She put the card carefully into her back pocket and stood, feeling a flutter of the happiness she'd experienced with Glory. She'd go see if Max was in. If he wasn't, she might just head up to the studio anyway. She'd wait by the Blue Streak and look for coins that had fallen from someone's pocket on the coaster—as many people as were here today, surely someone would lose a few nickels for streetcar fare.

Near Max's tent, the ground was littered with cigarette butts and squashed stogies, the way it always was after a performance. The door to his dressing room hung open, and she could hear movement inside.

"Hello?" She knocked hesitantly, ready to take off if Max wasn't in the mood to be seen. "It's me, Pin…"

The sound of movement stopped, after a few seconds started up again. She knocked a second time. Still no reply. Not a good sign. She started to turn away when the door opened wider.

"Pin."

For a moment she didn't recognize him. His hair was black, not blond, his face damp and his upper lip raw, as though recently shaved. Patches of white covered his cheeks and forehead, as though she'd caught him removing his makeup, or just putting it on. He wore

Maxene's black kidskin gloves on both hands, not just one, and a clean white undershirt over dark trousers. Blood bloomed in the white of one eye, which resembled a spoiled plum.

He said, "You're early, boy."

Pin looked away, unnerved. "I can come back later."

"No, come in. Shut the door behind you."

Inside, the room had the same sense of calamity as Max. The big trunk was shut, some of its contents spilled across the dressing table alongside pots of cosmetics and shoe polish. Socks, another pair of black gloves. A glassine envelope containing the human hair Max used to make mustaches and eyebrows for his act. His seersucker jacket and pants dangled from a wooden hanger by the door.

"I figured I'd head up to the studio," Pin said awkwardly.

Max sat back at his dressing table and dipped a comb into a jar containing black liquid. A fringe of false eyelashes curled beside it like a dead spider. He drew the comb through his hair, spattering his shirt-front with black. When he remained silent, Pin said, "I didn't know if you wanted me to go down to the Stroll sometime."

"Not this week." Max picked up a hand mirror and inspected his hair. He dabbed at a trickle of black with a frayed bit of gingham cloth, picked up the comb, and applied more dye. "Colored folks aren't too happy about what happened to Clyde."

Pin swallowed and looked around, increasingly uneasy. French postcards lay across a side table: A girl on her stomach, wearing a corset trimmed with ribbons, head raised to smile at the camera. She had no arms or legs. Another girl, a midget, wearing only a chemise and straddling the lap of a man with a handlebar mustache and bowler hat, his stare vacant as a cat's.

"I wasn't—it was a mistake," Pin said. "All I said was I seen Clyde at Hell Gate."

"But that was enough, wasn't it?" Max's tone was low and insinuating. "I've seen them hang men for a lot less."

"It was a mistake."

He turned, his pupils pinpoints in the gaslight. There was a streak on one cheek; she'd thought it was hair dye, but now she saw it was a fresh scratch, oozing blood. She jumped as he snapped his fingers, and he laughed.

"You stay away from the Stroll, kid. Here."

He reached into a macaroon tin and tossed her a Helmar cigarette packet. She stuck it in her pocket, waiting for instructions. He picked up the mirror again, turning it to reflect Pin's own face.

"Go now," he whispered.

Chapter 83

SHE MADE IT as far as the park exit before she realized Max hadn't given her streetcar fare. She turned and went back, a heaviness in her chest. He'd be mad that she returned for the money. Might refuse to give it to her, might even smack her. She'd poke her head inside, and if he seemed angry, she'd run.

A cardboard sign hung under the drooping She-Male banner: NEXT PERFORMANCE 3 o'CLOCK. The door to his shack was closed. She stepped up to it and knocked softly.

"Max?"

She knocked again. "Max? It's Pin. I, uh…"

She let her voice drift into silence, pressed her ear against the door, and listened. She heard nothing. He might have hurried off to lunch, or for a drink at the Woodland Cabaret. Probably he just went for a smoke.

She tried to calculate which would be worse: To wait for Max to return, which could take hours or minutes, and she might not get her nickel, either.

Or she could go inside—easy if the door was unlocked, not much harder if it wasn't. She grasped the doorknob and turned it. Locked.

She knew what to do. Mugsy had shown her, when they broke into the building where the carved wooden carousel horses were stored all winter. Padlocks could be picked with a pin or nail: this wasn't a padlock but a cheap tumbler of soft metal. She kept hold of the knob and wrenched it back and forth, not exerting too much pressure as the knob met resistance, until the tumbler gave way, and she slipped inside.

The dim room was permeated by the rancid smell of old cold cream and kerosene from the lantern, now extinguished. Max's makeup and the French postcards had been cleared away, along with the false eyelashes and other remnants of his stage act. The Hotel Buckminster ashtray where he tossed his change held a single quarter.

She hesitated before taking it. She'd never seen the ashtray when it wasn't full of coins. Maybe he'd taken them to the bank, the way her mother did. But why leave a quarter?

It must have been intended as her streetcar fare. Max had set it aside, and they'd both forgotten about it.

Yet a quarter was far too much money. What if it was a mistake, what if he hadn't left it for her but only forgotten it?

She rocked from one foot to the other, tormenting herself with indecision. A quarter would be enough to get there and back; she'd bring the change to Max. He'd understand; he'd know she hadn't stolen it. Even if he didn't, she was fast. She'd be gone before he could strike her. She grabbed the coin, stuck it in her pocket, and darted back to the door.

A man stood there. When she ran into him, he fell, and she struck out wildly, her arms enfolded by something soft as she jerked backward, stumbling against a chair.

It was not a man, but the seersucker suit that had been hanging by the door. Panicked, she replaced the trousers on the hanger, then fumbled with the jacket. Something dropped from one of its pockets, a large leather envelope that spilled its contents onto the floor. A deck of playing cards. She stooped and frantically gathered them up.

Only when she got back to her feet did she see that they weren't playing cards but photographs, like the ones you got at Riverview's photo gallery, four poses for a quarter. She turned them, one by one, until they all faced the same way. She felt as though something sharp pressed against her from the inside, like an awl punching through her breast.

They were photos of the girl from the movie studio. The girl in the yellow dress. The girl she'd found in Hell Gate. Lying on a bed, her arms and legs akimbo like those women in the naughty Mutoscopes. *Oh! What She Did!* She recognized the long-waisted dress with its rows of embroidered daisies, the girl's long dark hair. No hair ribbon, no socks or shoes. Her eyes stared blankly at whoever was taking the picture. *What She Couldn't See.*

Only as she scrutinized the photos beneath the grimy window did she realize she wasn't looking at a girl but a large doll. Its face gave it away: vacant eyes always staring in the same direction, mouth parted in the same almost-smile, as though it recognized the person behind the camera. The hem of its dress was uneven where part had been ripped away.

She shuffled through the pictures again, checking the back of each one to see the same name written there in pencil.

Maria.

Black specks flew in front of her eyes. She couldn't breathe. She pinched her nose, gulped deep breaths until the room stopped spinning. Stared at the floor where the oversize leather wallet lay, open so she could glimpse what was inside. She knelt, her fingers thick as sausages, her head one of those floppy balloons in Hell Gate. She picked up the wallet, so much heavier than it looked, so heavy she didn't see how she could hold it.

Photos were stuffed inside like wads of cash. Girls, dolls, she couldn't tell which: no, not girls but dolls, not dolls but the same doll, its clothes different but its face always the same, those horrible staring eyes and long dark hair, sometimes tied with a ribbon, sometimes covered with a hat much too big for its head. A name written on the back of each photo.

Alice. Katy. Christina. Iolanda. Dolly. Rachel. Irena. Deirdre. Faith. Daisy. Rose...

Abriana.

The black specks in her vision bloomed into faces lined up on an altar, burning candles. She felt as though she were back in the tunnel, the world's true face revealed as she touched that of the dead girl. She heard a soft *huh huh huh,* realized it came from deep in her throat. From outside she heard voices, a man shouting.

How could she have not known?

She shoved the photos back into the wallet, began to thrust it into the jacket pocket, and stopped. She opened the wallet, fumbling for the photos on top, the photos that had first fallen out, of Maria Walewski, took one, and stuffed it in her pocket.

She peered out the front window but saw no one. She locked the door, crossed to the back of the room, to the window. At first it wouldn't budge, but finally she got it open and climbed back outside. Thunder cracked, the Blue Streak's cars shrieked overhead as she ran past the coaster, past a man who cranked a hurdy-gurdy, past a child wailing for a lost balloon. *How could she have not known?*

Chapter 84

THE STREETCAR WAS only half full: people were pouring into Riverview, not away from it. She clutched her arms to her chest, shivering, pushed open the window beside her, and curled up on the wicker seat.

She felt like she had a live wasp in her pocket, not a photograph. Maybe it wasn't his. Maybe he'd bought the photos at one of those places in the arcade that sold pictures of naked women.

She knew that wasn't true. The photos belonged to Max. That was why he'd looked so crazy, that was why he'd dyed his hair black. He knew he was being hunted. He had killed Maria Walewski and Gilda Belascu; he'd killed the Gypsy girl. He'd killed her sister, Abriana, and all those others, and maybe Elsie Paroubek, too. Then he'd dressed a doll in their clothing and taken pictures of them, like...

Like Henry, she thought, dizzied, *it's like what he does with those pictures of the dead girls.*

But Henry didn't kill Maria. It was Max, it had been Max all along. She'd been in the same room with him, she'd taken the money he gave her...

She wiped her hands on her knickerbockers. When Max returned to his dressing room, he'd see the quarter was gone. He'd realize she'd been there. And when he noticed that his photos had been disturbed, he'd know that she had seen them. He'd find her and kill her, snap her neck, then hide her body inside his dressing room. By the time it was discovered, Max would be long gone.

She would have to give the photo to the police and tell them what she knew. They would question her. They would learn who she really was, not a boy but the sister of a murdered girl. She would be stripped of everything she was, everything she had made herself into.

She felt in her pocket for her shiv. There was another way, there had to be another way. What?

She stared out the window as the streetcar headed north, threading its way through old brickyards and tenements, beneath the L and far from the new canyons of towering brick and steel that loomed closer to the lake. She thought dully of the heroine of *The House with the Closed Shutters,* disguising herself as her cowardly brother only to be killed in battle. Pin had always loved that movie—but why did the girl have to die? Why hadn't she been the one to kill that soldier, instead of some man?

And why didn't the girl have a name? She was known only as *the sister.*

Something moved on the floor at her feet, a discarded newspaper. She picked it up and read a headline:

$1,000 Reward to Any Man Who Captures the Hell Gate Killer

The reward. She'd seen it on the flyer that morning, then completely forgotten about it.

...to Any Man...

Her thoughts began to wheel.

Max wouldn't know that *she* had seen his photos. He'd believe that

Pin had seen them. A skinny kid in knickerbockers and beat-up boots. A skinny boy who'd betrayed him.

But Max wouldn't recognize *her,* not if she were dressed in her old clothing. Not if it were dark. He'd never be threatened by a girl. He sought them out. They were nothing but toys to him, like the cheap celluloid dolls given as prizes that broke if you tried to play with them. Her mouth went dry; she hardly dared to let her thoughts slow, lest she lose track of them. She'd need help, she couldn't do it alone, but maybe she wouldn't have to. She couldn't tell Glory the truth; it would be far too dangerous for her to know about Max. And if Glory knew who Pin really was, what she was…

Pin squeezed her eyes tight. She could do this. It was dangerous, but she'd have someone with her, someone who'd be in on her plan. Not Glory, it couldn't be another girl. And she would never let Glory come to any harm. No: she knew who would help her.

She reached in her back pocket for the homemade card she'd found in the poplar grove, the one with the pictures of a rolling pin, a murdered girl, a sweet grey rabbit.

Sorry I scared you last night. I was a very dangerous boy. I killed a man, too, but nobody knew about that. We keep them safe. Girls. Because. I protect them. So we don't forget.

She would find Henry. He was crazy as a bedbug, but he wasn't afraid. She got off at the stop for Essanay and walked to the studio, entered the enormous building, and hurried to Glory's dressing room.

Chapter 85

VALERIE'S NAME HAD been removed from the door and only Glory's remained. She could hear Glory singing to herself, moving around the tiny cubicle. She knocked and went inside.

Glory looked up as she entered. She was wearing another silk teddy bare, blue and trimmed with tiny bows. When she saw Pin, she yanked a dressing gown from a hanger and pulled it on, her cheeks reddening.

"Pin! You should've knocked!"

"I did," Pin said. She stared at the floor, but Glory had turned her attention to a pair of stockings. After a moment she looked up, beaming.

"Pin, I've got my own dressing room! I mean, it's the same room, but now I have it to myself. How's that?"

"That's swell." Pin cleared her throat. "Glory, listen. I—I need your help with something."

"Is it Lionel?" Glory examined one of the stockings for ladders. "Because he's not here, I checked when I got back. Do you have his book?"

"No. I couldn't—there were too many people at the fortune-teller's. And, well, no, it's not about Lionel. It's something else. It's— I need to borrow some clothes."

"Clothes?" Glory set down the stocking to stare at her. "What clothes?"

"Well, your clothes. Ladies' clothes."

"Ladies' clothes? What're you talking about? For what?"

"For a—for an act. At the park."

"An act? Like a minstrel show?"

"Sort of. If it works out, I can make a lot of money. We could—if you'd like, we could go to the movies. Afterward. Tomorrow or whenever you'd like."

"So, you want to borrow ladies' clothing for a show," Glory repeated slowly. "Like what Wally does? When he dresses up as Sweedie?"

Pin nodded. Her throat hurt, like the lie was stuck in there. "Yeah," she croaked. "That's what gave me the idea. It doesn't have to be anything fancy…"

"That's good, because I'm not giving some boy anything fancy. Especially you—it'd just get ruined." Glory continued to stare at Pin, bewildered. "They won't give you a costume?"

"No. They want you to bring your own. It's just an audition. I swear, I won't let anything happen to it."

"I'm still not giving you anything fancy."

Glory stepped over to the rack of dresses and began to examine them in a businesslike manner, glancing over her shoulder to size up Pin. As Pin watched, she felt again that tightness in her throat, though now it was a dry yearning, not the fear of being caught in a lie.

Glory would never look at her again the same way. Her admiration for Pin's recklessness, for her desire to work as a cameraman—all that would disappear the second she knew Pin wasn't a boy. Girls didn't deliver drugs; they didn't grow up to become cameramen, or even want to. Girls didn't trick other girls into kissing them by pretending to be a boy. Not even a thousand-dollar reward would change that.

"Okay, how's this?" Glory held up a middy dress, white blouse with navy-blue trim on its sailor collar and cuffs, attached navy-blue skirt. "It's boyish, so it'll suit you."

She tossed Pin the dress. Pin held it up in front of her, trying to measure its length.

"It'll fit," said Glory. "We're the same size, pretty much. But you'll need different shoes," she added, gazing at Pin's battered black boots. "And your hair..."

She reached to pluck at Pin's tangled curls, and Pin tried not to flinch. She wanted to pull Glory to her and at the same time to push her away, to run and to kiss her, all at once.

Instead she stood, mute and miserable, as Glory fussed with her hair. "I can borrow a pair of shoes," Pin said, finding her voice. "Or just wear these."

"Maybe. But we still need to do something about this." Glory tugged hard at a matted curl.

"Ow!" Pin pulled away. Glory crossed her arms and regarded her with those scarily blue eyes, then passed a delicate hand across her own carefully arranged hair.

"Wait here," she said. "Don't let anyone in, I'll be right back."

Pin sank into a chair and stared at the sailor dress in her lap. The blouse had been carelessly mended, and one striped cuff was stained. It stank of mildew. The thought of actually wearing it made her want to tear it into rags.

But that was why she had to borrow a dress in the first place. Her own few pieces of girl's clothing had been reduced to rags by hard wear and neglect.

"Here!"

Glory swept breathlessly back into the room and threw something at her—it looked like a cat. Startled, Pin dropped the middy dress.

"That's what I mean!" scolded Glory.

She snatched up the dress as Pin bent to retrieve what Glory had tossed at her. A tawny blond wig, its ringlets brittle as straw. Pin poked at the stiff curls. "Who wears this? What's it made of? Hay?"

"Flax and horsehair. Lookee..." Glory took the wig and set it on Pin's head, tugging it as Pin fidgeted.

"Ouch! Stop it, that hurts. Jesus—it's too tight!"

"Be quiet!" Glory pressed a hand against Pin's mouth. "Whoever needs it, wears it. It's for the extras. I borrowed it from the wardrobe shop—if you lose it, they'll kill me."

Pin took Glory's wrist, gently pulled Glory's hand to her, and kissed her palm. "Thank you, Glory."

Glory smiled. "You look cute."

They both jumped as someone knocked at the door and yelled, "Glory? Louella wants you to come look over your new lines this minute!"

"Be right there," Glory called, and pulled the wig from Pin's head. "Bring them back as soon as you can," she said in a low voice. "Here."

She handed Pin a brown paper sack, and Pin stuffed the wig and dress inside. "Tomorrow," she promised Glory, though that was probably another lie. "Oh, and wait…"

She dug into her pocket and withdrew the Helmar packet Max had given her. "Can you give this to Lionel?"

Glory hesitated, then nodded. "Okay."

She took the packet, opened it, and tapped out one of the cigarettes. Sniffing it, she pinched the end so that golden-brown flakes rained down on her open palm. Brow furrowed, she tore the cigarette paper and tipped its contents into her palm.

"Well, lookee here." She extended her hand to Pin. "It's not dope at all—it's just plain old tobacco. I wonder why he'd do that?"

Pin's heart raced. *Because he doesn't care anymore what happens next.* She tried to memorize everything she could: Glory's hair, her eyes, her smooth hands; the way she appeared so tall for someone who was barely five feet.

"Thank you again," she said. "Glorious."

Footsteps echoed from the hall, heading in their direction.

"Good luck, Pin," said Glory, and pushed her toward the door.

Chapter 86

Francis took a brief dinner break, alone at a table in the Casino Restaurant. He had little appetite for his pork chop and potatoes, but was grateful for the second cup of coffee that the waiter brought him without being asked.

He'd looked for Bennie on his rounds of the park but hadn't yet seen him, and he'd gleaned little additional information from the other policemen or newsmen he'd spoken to. No one seemed to believe that Lionel Gerring was guilty, but no one seemed in a hurry to see him released, either, not until another suspect was brought in, or another murder occurred. The newsmen were content to wait, at least for another day or two, and embellish the facts in the meantime.

The police, on the other hand, were increasingly exhausted and irritable, prone to sudden angers. It was a mood Francis recognized and feared, not for himself but for visitors to the park. Drunks were an easy target. So were colored people, and anyone whose accent or appearance identified them as a newcomer to the city. He waved away the waiter's offer of a free dessert and returned to his rounds.

For the last few hours he'd avoided the area near the arcade where Gina Maffucci worked. He knew she'd been brought into the station for questioning, then released. Now he saw a long line in front of Madame Zanto's booth, fueled by rumors of the arrest there earlier.

He heard mutters of protest as he pushed through the line, but those quieted when they saw the interloper wore a uniform. When the curtains parted and a middle-aged woman stepped out, Francis entered the booth. Inside, Gina had her back to him, cleaning a teacup.

"Please sit, I'll be right with you," she said. She turned and nearly dropped the cup. He put a finger to his lips, sat at the little table, and motioned for her to do the same.

"I heard what happened at the station, Mrs. Maffucci," he murmured.

He expected her to tell him to call to her by her first name. But she only stared at him. Francis cleared his throat nervously and went on. "I'm sorry I wasn't there. I would have—"

"What would you have done, Mr. Bacon? The detective asked if I could identify the man who owned the notebook. Which I did. Could you have done that for me?"

"No, of course not. But—"

"Then there's nothing to apologize for. It was the same man, I recognized him. He didn't deny the book was his. I only wish they hadn't made such a scene when he came back here for it. But now it's done."

She shook her head. "I wish I'd never told you about that damn book. I should have tried to return it to him directly."

"But that's ridiculous! You did the right thing, it was evidence—"

"Evidence of what? He works at the movie studio! That notebook contains ideas for movies, Mr. Bacon."

"Well, that's what he claims."

"Would he be so careless, if it contained evidence he intended to murder those girls?"

"He might be," Francis replied, with little conviction. "Men sometimes record imaginings of crimes they intend to commit."

"Do they? Then someone will have to prove it." Gina's dark eyes glittered. "Mr. Gerring knows Pin. Did you know that?"

"Did he say how?"

"No. But he looked shocked when he heard my last name. He asked if I was Pin Maffucci's mother." Her voice broke. "I—I said I was, and he just seemed…confused. Upset and confused."

"But don't you see, this could mean something, too?" Francis tried to choose his words with care. "A grown man, why would he know a boy?"

"From the movie studio. Pin goes there, I'm not sure why. Maybe he was looking for work." She picked up the teacup, set it back down. "I thought we would be safer here, at least for the summer. We come from Crosby and Oak—Little Hell. I thought this would be a better place."

Francis stared at her thin face, the bangles on her arm, and her sunken eyes. One would have to come from a terrible place to imagine living in a shack at an amusement park as an improvement. But then Little Hell was such a place. He slid his hand toward hers, waiting to see if she would remove her own. When she did not, he gently rested his atop it.

"I'm sorry" was all he could think to say.

"I'm sorry they're holding a man who's innocent."

"You don't know that, Gina."

"I do. I can see evil in men, and this man had none."

"You told me your husband was an evil man," said Francis. "Did you see that?"

"No. Not at first. That's how I learned to see it. After." She withdrew her hand from his, as unhappy mutterings came from outside. "I have to return to work."

She stooped to retrieve something from beneath the table and handed Francis his billy club. "Thank you for lending me this, Mr. Bacon. I don't need it anymore. I have an aunt in Indiana, I'm going to ask her to wire me the money so that we can go and stay with her."

"But why?" His voice rose plaintively as she stood.

"Because I want to. This is not a safe place for us. It never has been."

Chapter 87

Pin sat in the streetcar, hugging the paper bag to her chest. She didn't know which stop was closest to the hospital, but a woman in a freshly pressed and starched nurse's uniform had boarded at Montrose. Pin kept an eye on her as they rattled on. When the woman stood, Pin followed her to the rear door, waited for the streetcar to jolt to a stop, then hopped out, following the nurse as she crossed the street.

An ice cart rumbled past, its horse shying at a roll of thunder. The mottled sky looked like a shiner, sickly green and purple. A few yards ahead of her the nurse dodged horse apples in the road. Pin had to run to keep up. By the time she saw the hospital, vast as a castle, she was sweaty and out of breath.

St. Joseph's covered an entire city block, five stories high with corner turrets. An ugly castle. Pin watched the nurse hurry up the steps to the portico, where she greeted two other white-clad women and disappeared inside.

Pin looked down at her shabby knickerbockers and shirt. What if they didn't let her in the hospital? Henry had said he worked at St. Joseph's, but she didn't know where. There must be hundreds of people in there, nurses and doctors and patients. Her hand slid into her pocket to touch the photograph. A doll wearing a girl's clothes. A dead girl's clothes. Her sister was dead.

A bolt of lightning fizzed through the sky, followed by a deafening thundercrack and the hiss of rain on the hot pavement. She ran up the hospital steps to the portico and stopped, shaking her wet hair. An orderly stood by the door, smoking a cigarette. He gave her a sympathetic look.

"Cats and dogs," he said. "Stay dry, kid."

He stubbed out his cigarette and went inside. She smoothed her wet hair, then the front of her grubby white shirt, and took a deep breath. She pulled open the heavy door and entered the lobby.

It smelled like the Infant Incubators, of carbolic soap and Bon Ami. Everything was very brightly lit. Voices echoed from upstairs, the clatter of footsteps and the rattle of typewriting machines. Pin stood up straight and marched toward a long desk in the center of the room, where a tall nun stood behind a spectacled man who sat writing in a registry book. He raised his head at Pin's approach.

"Can I help you, son?"

"I'm looking for someone," Pin said. The nun's thin lips pursed disapprovingly.

The man blotted his pen. "A patient? It's not visiting hours, I'm afraid."

"No. He works here. Henry..."

"Henry?" the nun broke in. "A dozen Henrys work here. Who is it?"

"Dargero. Or no, Darger."

"Henry Dargero? Don't know him." The man turned to the nun. "Do you know him, Sister Rose?"

"Darger?" The nun squinted at Pin. "Henry Darger. Is that who you mean?"

Pin nodded. At the man's blank expression, the nun snapped, "That crazy janitor."

"Oh! Right." He nodded at Pin. "Yes, he works here. Why do you need to see him?"

"I have to give him a message."

The nun stepped forward to peer suspiciously at Pin. "Who are you?"

"His nephew."

"Is that for him?" The nun pointed at the package. "You can leave it here with me."

Pin shook her head. "This is mine. I only need to see him for a minute."

"You can't do that. Visiting hours aren't till five." The nun's black eyes burned into Pin like she wanted to set her on fire. "And that's only for patients, not employees."

The deafening buzz of an electrified bell rang out, signaling a shift change. Doors slammed as a white-clad army surged down the stairs and emerged from behind countless doors. Scores of nurses and orderlies hurried toward the desk.

"Good night, Mr. Gregorson! Good night, Sister Rose!"

"Sister Rose, Dr. Hudson asked if you'd sign this, I'll run it back upstairs before I go."

"Mr. Gregorson, here's the bandage request for West Four-A."

"Sister Rose, I lost my time punch card."

"Mr. Gregorson..."

"Sister Rose..."

Pin backed away, breaking into a run when she reached the staircase. By the time she reached the second floor, the corridor was almost empty.

This floor seemed to be all women patients. Rooms full of hospital beds, few of them empty. Crucifixes on the walls and holy-water fonts by the doors. She saw no sign of a janitor, no mops or buckets, no wheeled cart for hauling off trash. She stopped at a door that read CUSTODIAL CLOSET, but it was locked.

She climbed to the third floor, where all the patients were men. Still no sign of Henry. On to the next floor, where a sign read MATERNITY WARD: QUIET PLEASE.

It was much warmer here. Two nurses stood in the corridor, chatting. One laughed, adjusting her cap before she disappeared through a doorway. The other nurse walked in Pin's direction. When she caught sight of Pin, she cocked her head questioningly. Pin remained motionless. The nurse pushed open a door that led into a long glass-fronted room and went inside.

Pin let her breath out and continued down the hall. Behind the glass wall, babies lay in rows of identical cribs, like Christmas oranges nestled in paper at the grocer's. There must have been a hundred, tended by nurses who adjusted blankets and the tiny knitted elf caps on the babies' heads. In the hall, a solitary man and several women in hospital gowns stood with hands pressed against the glass, staring inside. Pin might as well have been invisible. No one took any notice of her whatsoever. At the end of the corridor, she opened the door to continue upstairs.

"You don't want to go up there, young man."

Pin turned to see a plump nun shaking a finger at her, black rosary beads dangling from a cord around her midsection.

"That's where the very sick people are," the nun went on in a soft Irish burr. "Not a place for boys."

Pin bit her lip. "Oh," she said.

The nun smiled, her blue eyes nearly disappearing in a face like rising dough. A rose-pink birthmark covered most of one cheek. "Are you looking for your mother, dear? Visiting hours for the babies aren't till five o'clock."

"No. I'm looking for Henry Darger."

"Mr. Darger?" The nun looked as though Pin had asked for directions to the moon.

"Yes. He—he said he works here."

"Well, he does, of course he does." The nun smiled again, but she still appeared startled. "Although his shift's just ended—he'll have gone back to his room, I suspect."

"Are you sure?" Pin's hands tightened around the paper bag. "I really need to find him."

"Are you a relation?"

"No. I'm a, a friend. He's expecting me, he'll be really upset if I don't see him."

The nun's mild blue eyes gazed probingly at Pin's face. Pin felt herself grow hot under that intense inquiry: not suspicion, not anger, but something fierce all the same. After a few seconds, the nun's hand dropped to the rosary at her stomach. She fingered the jet beads, then slipped her hand into the folds of her robes to withdraw a brightly colored slip of paper.

"Do you know Saint Dymphna?" She handed a holy card to Pin. "My name saint. She's the patron of girls in distress."

The card showed a red-haired girl, light streaming from the small crown on her head. Pin touched the embossed gold lettering. *Saint Dymphna, Protect Me in My Hour of Need.*

"Thank you," Pin said, and tucked the holy card into her pocket.

The nun folded her hands across her stomach. "Mr. Darger lives at Workingmen's House. Do you know where that is? No? Over there—"

She tipped her head to indicate the stairway at the opposite end of the hall. "There's a fire escape on that landing—if you follow it downstairs, it will take you directly outside, and you won't have to walk back through the hospital lobby. When you get outside, you'll see another big building right behind this one. That's Workingmen's House. The men live on the third floor. The nurses live in the rest of the building, and men aren't allowed there. Even young boys," she said, and gave Pin a strange look. "There's a separate stairway to the men's floor, you'll see it on the left once you're inside. I believe that Mr. Darger's room is number thirty-two."

Pin started to thank her, but the Irish nun raised that gently chiding finger again. "Tell Mr. Darger that Sister Dymphna gave you permission to see him. He doesn't have many visitors. I think he's lonely. How do you know him?"

"I know his friend Willhie, and Willhie's sister. I've been to their house."

"I have met Mr. Schloeder. His sister, that would be Elizabeth?"

Pin nodded. Sister Dymphna turned, robes swishing, then stopped to look back. "What would your name be?"

"Pin. Pin Maffucci."

"Pin." Sister Dymphna savored the word, then smiled. "Your nickname? Because you're bright as a pin, I reckon."

"Yes," said Pin, and met the woman's sharp gaze with her own. "That's right."

"Goodbye then, young man," said Sister Dymphna. "Good luck to you." To Pin's shock, she winked at her before turning away.

Chapter 88

Workingmen's House was a quieter, smaller shadow of the hospital, its dim hallways smelling of floral colognes, clean linens, the Murphy oil soap used on the slippery wooden floors. Two young women walked arm in arm past Pin, talking happily.

"He took me to the Movie Inn, we sat by the picture of Mary Pickford! Can you believe it?"

"He's a keeper, Eloise," said her friend.

Pin found the stairway to the men's quarters and went up to the third floor. The hallway was very plain, with white walls and windows that overlooked the street. Each wooden door had small brass numbers on it. A print of Jesus with a crown of thorns hung at one end of the hall, a crucifix at the other.

She walked along, counting each door until she reached number 32. She didn't know what she would do if he wasn't there. She barely knew what she would do if he was. She knocked quickly and loudly, before she could change her mind.

The door cracked open. One pale blue eye stared out at her from a sunburned sliver of a face.

"It's Pin," she said.

The door closed and she heard rustling. For an endless moment she thought he wouldn't return. Then the door opened just enough for her to step inside, a hand waving at her frantically.

"Get in."

She entered cautiously. Henry poked his head out into the hall, closed the door, and locked it.

What was he so worked up about? When she looked around, she saw nothing but a small room as plain as the hallway. A bed covered with a brown blanket; a deal desk, chair, and night table; a single closet. The only window faced an air shaft. Above the bed, yet another crucifix.

"Why are you here?"

She turned to see Henry watching her from the corner of his eye, like a cornered dog.

"I need you to help me."

"You ran away. Why did you run away?"

"From the barn? I was scared."

"Why were you scared? You missed the initiation! There were many Gemini there. General Jack Evans came! Willhie's sister was so alarmed. That you ran off. It gave her a start. Her heart." He looked accusingly at Pin, then said in a softer tone, "I said I was sorry. The secret note—did you find it?"

She nodded, set down the paper bag, dug through her pockets for the crumpled flyer, and handed it to Henry. "There's a reward for whoever finds the killer. A thousand dollars."

"I already knew that."

"Well, I know who it is. I have a plan to capture him."

"You're lying."

"No, I'm not." She took out the photograph of the doll. "Here's proof. Be careful!"

Henry took the photo, frowning. "What is this?"

"It's a doll. She's wearing the dead girl's clothes. Maria Walewski, the girl who went into Hell Gate."

Henry scrutinized the photo for a long time. "You're right," he said slowly. "It is a doll."

"It's also *her clothes*."

He continued to gaze at the picture, finally nodded. "The yellow dress. She was the one with the yellow dress. Can I…have this?"

"No, damn it! Give it to me!"

He returned the photo without an argument. "What is your plan?" he asked.

She sank onto the bed. "I need you to meet me at Riverview tonight. Say, eight o'clock. You and Willhie, too." She hadn't wanted to bring someone else into it. But now, seeing Henry…she'd forgotten how small he was. Willhie was tall. Even if he wasn't strong, he looked like he was.

"Willhie can't come. He's the night watchman."

Pin felt like crying. "It'll have to just be us, then."

"What are we going to do?"

She stared at the dark air-shaft window. "I'm still figuring it out."

What if Henry betrayed her? He could go to Willhie, or the police, or someone else—General Jack Evans, if he was real and not another of Henry's wild stories—and claim the reward himself.

But she couldn't do it on her own. She had no friends, no one she could trust but a crazy person who used to live in an asylum and believed in something called the Black Sack of Destiny. She wondered dully what would happen if she threw herself down the air shaft.

"Pin tuck. Pinwheel. Pin knife."

She glanced up. "What?"

"I'll come," he said, and quickly looked away.

It was settled, then. She plucked at the brown blanket, then noticed a sheet of paper on the desk. She leaned over to pick it up.

It was a drawing of an animal—not a real animal, something as fabulous and strange as the painted creatures on Riverview's carousel. This one had a dragon's scaled body and a snake's tail, antlers like a moose, and huge fantastically decorated wings, a cross between a butterfly and a Japanese fan. Its head was turned so she saw only one sky-blue eye, and its teeth were bared, though not in a threatening way. More like it was smiling. A smaller figure sat in the corner of the page, a girl whose hair and body were all painted the same shade of mustard yellow. She too had a curved scaly tail and batlike wings—blue, yellow, and red, like a flag.

Pin felt something, something entirely unfamiliar, rise in her. She was so captivated by the drawing that she forgot Henry was there until she heard him clear his throat. She looked up, afraid that he might fly into one of his rages, but he said nothing.

"Did you draw this?" At his nod she whistled, impressed. "It's really good. What are they?"

"Blengins. They protect the children. It's part of my book."

"You're writing a book?"

He opened the desk drawer and pulled out what at first looked like a soiled butcher's parcel. Instead, it was a bulky, misshapen manuscript tied with string. He set it down, untied the string, and pointed at the title page:

THE ADVENTURES OF GENERAL HENRICO
DARGERO,
OF THE GEMINI AND THE BLACK BROTHERS,
AND OF THE GIRLS ARMY THAT FOUGHT BESIDE
THEM
IN THEIR BATTLE AGAINST THE CONFEDERACY OF
THE CLAN OF THE AGIVECENNIANS

By Henry Joseph Darger
The author of this exciting story

She turned a few pages. The manuscript was entirely handwritten, not typed like Lionel's scenarios and photoplays. There were lots of crossed-out words and splotches of spilled ink. "What's it about?"

"It's an adventure story. Very thrilling. You can read it if you want." He pointed at the chair.

"Maybe another time," said Pin. "It looks pretty long."

"I'm going to be very famous. When the editors see it."

He rummaged in the desk drawer and pulled out several large sheets of butcher paper. Each was filled with brightly colored figures—girls, mostly, but also men in gold-and-purple military uniforms, and many, many flowers. Some of the girls wore dresses, purple, yellow, red, but others were naked, with very white skin and black or yellow hair. Many seemed to belong to the same family—their faces matched, their dresses and shoes matched, even their hair. The girls always seemed to be running: from giant flowers that had legs, from a tornado, from a sofa falling from the sky. But mostly they ran from the men in uniform.

Strangest of all, some of the girls weren't girls, but boys dressed as girls, or girls with boys' bodies, ram's horns, and rainbow wings like butterflies or bats. Staring at them, Pin clutched the bed beneath her, as though it had started to move.

They looked like her, or she looked like them. Something in between, something she didn't know the name of but recognized. A lightness filled her, the way it had when her mother had cut her hair and she'd first put on boys' clothes. She opened her mouth and let the lightness escape, almost surprised not to see a bubble or a balloon floating away from her, like in the pictures in front of her. How could one feel like this and not be flying? Like the Aerostat or a balloon; like Harriet before she fell.

Pin set the pages on her lap to examine them more closely. She recognized many of the faces—they all had the exact same features, those of one of the Teenie Weenies in the comic strip.

"Do you trace them?" she asked Henry.

"It's allowed." He sounded offended.

"I know. I just meant—they're so good."

She pored over the next sheet, and the next. More Blengins. A boy traced from Buster Brown. A cave that looked like the interior of Hell Gate. Balloons with eyes and teeth like piano keys.

Pin stopped at a picture of a pair of gigantic hands choking a girl with a grey face. Liquid spilled from her mouth, and her eyes were wide with an expression Pin had never seen on someone who was alive. She quickly pushed it to the bottom of the stack.

There were other drawings like that one—girls being strangled, girls on fire, girls tied up with string. She avoided looking at them, instead searched until she again found the picture of the dragon and the girl with rainbow wings. She stared at it, mesmerized by the dragon's strange half smile, the way the girl's arms appeared open to receive something from the sky. All the pictures seemed to tell a story that didn't quite make sense, unless you maybe knew the man who'd drawn the pictures.

Yet just because it was a story didn't mean it wasn't true. It had only been two days since she'd met Henry. Everything had changed since then. *She* had become part of a story, a different story from her sister's, which had been almost the only story she'd told herself for the last two years.

"Did you make them up?" she asked.

"It's a story."

"But it's your story, so you made it up, right?"

Henry nodded, then smiled without looking at her, a small strange smile like the dragon's. "I don't have to make it up."

She looked back down at the drawings, shuffled through them one last time, and handed the unwieldy stack back to Henry.

"I like them," she said. "Most of them."

She shook her head, dazed, and remembered why she was here. She'd thought she could trust Henry—but she'd seen those drawings of the girls being strangled or set on fire. She withdrew her shiv.

"Look at me," she ordered.

Henry stared at the floor, his mouth a stubborn line.

"Look at me," she repeated, holding up the knife so he could see it. If he attacked her, she'd stab him and run away. Everyone knew he was crazy. "I want you to swear to me you didn't hurt those girls."

He snorted angrily. "I did no such thing."

"What about Abriana Onofria?"

"Don't know her."

"You're lying." She tightened her fingers around the blade's handle. "You had her picture, I saw it. *Look at me.*" His head twitched, but he still didn't raise it. "The Italian girl, Abriana, she was in the papers two years ago. She followed an organ-grinder and disappeared. She was my sister."

"The girl." His hands opened and closed. "Your sister. Which one?"

"You know which one! You had her picture in your wallet. Did you hurt her? *She was my sister.*"

He lifted his head, so slowly it didn't seem he moved at all. Then he was staring straight at her, his face twisted like a rag.

"I swear," he whispered. "By the Gemini. By Elsie Paroubek. I never knew her."

"Did you—"

"No." For a full second their gazes held. His head jerked violently, as though the effort of looking was too much, and he turned away.

Pin let her breath out and slipped the knife back into her pocket.

"Remember the place near where we met by Hell Gate?" she said. "Where you left the note? Meet me there tonight, at eight o'clock. Don't tell anyone. Not even Willhie."

"Willhie's the night watchman."

"You already told me that." She unlocked the door and stepped into the hallway. "And bring your knife."

Chapter 89

IT WAS TWILIGHT when she returned to Riverview. Max might already be gone. But Pin didn't believe he was, not yet. He wouldn't rush off. It was so easy for him to change his appearance—fake mustaches and different color hair, different hats. A man who could turn two faces to an audience, and they would believe each to be his real one.

No, he was still here. He needed something. Money from the rubes. Another girl. Her fingers brushed the shiv for the thousandth time. She'd never used it, not seriously. Now it felt like a sixth finger.

Inside her shack, she pulled the filthy curtains and pushed the room's sole chair against the door, still hanging on its hinges. A useless precaution: a few good kicks and the entire shack would fall down around her in pieces. It still made her feel safer.

She set down the paper sack and sank onto the mattress, staring at the pictures of Lord Clyde and Harriet Quimby. She removed them from the wall, searched her pockets for the photograph of the doll dressed in Maria Walewski's clothes, the holy card that Sister Dymphna had given her, and last of all Henry's card. She set them in a row on the floor beside the mattress, leaning against the wall, then went to the trunk in the corner.

When she and Abriana were young, the trunk had been big enough for them to hide in, something their mother repeatedly warned them not to do. "Children die from being trapped inside trunks," she'd said, adding to her list of things that children died from. Lice, consumption, broken glass, chewing tobacco, falling off roofs, freezing to death, eating toadstools. Not hurdy-gurdy men, not dark rides, not watching a movie with a stranger.

Pin dug her fingers under the latch and prized it open, releasing the smell of camphor. Inside were her mother's few items of winter clothing. Ugly clothes, all moth-eaten. A boiled-wool jacket, much repaired. Worsted stockings, a long wool skirt. Also, the linen handkerchief that Abriana had painstakingly embroidered with wobbly red *X*s as a Christmas present for their mother, and a crushed straw hat that had been her sister's.

Pin kept digging, until she came to her own things. A tiny pair of white leather shoes. A chewed-up flannel nightgown that stank of mice. Her own winter jacket, scratchy red wool and far too short. A plain white cotton shimmy and some heavy black wool stockings.

She picked up the shimmy, and several items fell from its folds. Baptismal certificates, her own and Abriana's. And a photograph.

It was the Easter Sunday photo of her sister at Assumption Catholic Church. Abriana smiled at the camera, pretty as a girl in a soap advertisement, in her Easter hat and dress. The newspaper photographer must have given the photo to her mother after Abriana had disappeared. Why had her mother kept it hidden all this time?

She tried not to cry. After a minute, she put all the clothing back into the trunk, except the cotton shimmy and her wool stockings. She set the picture of her sister alongside those of Harriet and Clyde, Saint Dymphna and Maria's doll, Henry's card. Then she opened the paper sack and dumped its contents on the mattress. She unbuttoned her shirt, tossed it on the floor, picked up the middy dress, and felt a spasm of anxiety—what if it buttoned down the back?

It didn't. It had no buttons at all—it was designed to be pulled on and off quickly. A costume, not a real dress.

The thought reassured her. She tugged her old cotton shimmy over her head, then pulled on the dress. It fell just below her knees. A child's dress, intended for someone younger than Pin. It felt tight around the bust—flat chested as she was, Pin still had breasts. She ran her hands over the front. The fabric was thick enough that, with the shimmy beneath, she couldn't feel her nipples. She wished she had a mirror.

She tied the ends of the sailor collar in a clumsy bow, kicked off her boots and socks, and pulled on the hated black stockings, too heavy for summer though everyone wore them anyway. Her boots went back on, boys' boots but maybe no one would notice.

All that remained was the wig. She picked it up with a grimace: a cap of stiff blond ringlets, long enough to cover her ears, topped by an enormous cornflower-blue bow. The color almost matched the faded blue of her middy dress. Pin smiled: Glory must have selected it on purpose.

The wig's hair and flax had been glued to a flexible burlap form. A loop of string dangled from each side, to go over her ears. She tugged it on, stuffing her own dark curls beneath the blond ringlets.

It fit, barely—like the dress, it was designed for a younger girl. She slipped the two loops over her ears, did her best to hide them beneath the stiff ringlets, and glared at her discarded clothing on the floor. She still had no idea what she looked like. She stepped to the window and pulled aside the grimy muslin curtain.

Outside, the sky had darkened to the scummy pea-soup color that preceded a twister. The window reflected a girl, gangly, with bony knees, blond ringlets, and a floppy blue bow that matched her dress. No longer herself but a stranger. She picked up her knickerbockers and removed her knife from the pocket, instinctively reached for her thigh, and swore.

Her dress had no pockets. Girls' clothes never did. And she was wearing stockings, so she couldn't even tuck the knife into her sock. She fiddled with her boot until she figured out a way to stick the knife in there without stabbing herself. She practiced pulling it out, poking a hole in her stocking in the process. It was awkward, but she'd be able to grab it when she needed it.

Other than that, the details of how, exactly, she was going to attack Max were fuzzy. Maybe Henry would have a plan of his own.

She gathered up the pictures and set them on top of the trunk, got the hurricane lantern, and put it in front of them. She knew better than to leave a lantern lit when no one was there to tend it. But if she didn't come back, maybe someone would see the pictures there, and understand.

After a few seconds, she picked up the photo of the doll. She couldn't leave it here—it was the only proof they had of what Max had done. She realized then that she should have taken the entire wallet. A single photo proved nothing. No one would believe her. Even if they caught Max and questioned him, he would lie. She'd have to go back to his dressing room to get the other photos.

Chapter 90

AFTER THE BOY left, Henry straightened the pages of his book and put everything back in his desk. He was disappointed Pin hadn't read it. He'd written more than two hundred pages. But the boy was right. It would have taken too long, and the Gemini would be busy tonight.

He didn't own a pocket watch, so he stepped into the hall and listened until he heard the bells from St. Vincent de Paul. A quarter past six o'clock. He'd missed supper, damn it. *Bad luck, fuck!* He ducked back into his room, locked the door, and slapped the air in frustration. Slapped himself for thinking a bad word. Dressed in a clean shirt and trousers, clean socks, his dark jacket, and bowler. Pried up a baseboard and found his knife. They'd taken it from him when he arrived, but he bought another. It had a leather sheath, so he wouldn't cut himself when he tucked it down his socks.

When he was ready, he stood in front of the air-shaft window and looked at his reflection in the dark glass. *General Henrico Dargero steadied himself for the struggles ahead. Only his brave young companion knew of the risks they would soon meet. An evil man, perhaps some bad generals. Maybe death!*

But not for him. That would make a bad story. He knelt beside his bed and said one Our Father and two Hail Marys, one Glory Be to the Father, and the prayer to Saint Dymphna. He withdrew the scapular with Saint Dymphna's picture and kissed it, tucked it back inside his shirt. Time to face the evil generals.

Chapter 91

SHE HAD MISSED the moment when Riverview's thousands of electrical bulbs blazed on. Now the lights looked harsh and garish, the shadows they cast longer and blacker. Pin stood at the edge of the midway, feeling small and unprotected. Her disguise was not a disguise. It revealed her for what she really was: a girl, alone at night.

She forced herself to step out onto the Pike. Immediately she was buffeted by the passing crowd. People knocked into her without even noticing. If someone did notice, their eyes looked right through her. When she was a boy, they'd have reacted with anger or annoyance. But as a girl, she was too skinny and plain to look at twice, too young for any man to take an interest in her.

She prayed Max would be different. He *was* different. She prayed he would notice her, without recognizing her.

She longed to run, but she knew better. Girls didn't run unless they were being chased. Her instinct was to keep her head down, but she was afraid the wig might slip off. So she walked and stared straight ahead, trying to look like a girl who knew where she was going. She wasn't so young as to appear lost, the way a seven- or eight-year-old would. Still, as she passed the line for the Shoot-the-Chutes, a grey-haired woman reached out to grasp her sleeve.

"Are you on your own, young lady?"

Pin started to yank her arm away. But the woman's face was kind, and two girls about Pin's age flanked her in the line. Her grand-daughters. Pin shook her head.

"No. My family's waiting for me over by the Wild West Show. I was just getting a drink of water."

The woman smiled. "All right, then. Have a nice time."

The photograph of the doll grew limp between her fingers as she walked. She switched it to her other hand, wiping her sweaty palm on her dress. The thought of running into Ikie or Mugsy made her stomach hurt. She scanned the crowd but never saw them.

Beyond the glare of electrical lights, the sky had grown black. Thunder rolled, but the holiday mood and enormous crowds re-mained—it might have been the Fourth of July. She let the crowd carry her past the Wild West Show and the Ten-in-One, where people lined up five-deep for Armstrong's Freak Show.

"Happened right where you're standing, friend—that very spot!"

She pushed her way to the front of the crowd, to see if Red Friend recognized her. But he stared right through her. She was one of the line lice now, of no interest to him unless she was shelling out a dime.

The giant cuckoo clock started to call the hour, stopping at eight. Henry should be waiting for her near Hell Gate. She was late. She broke into a run as she neared Madame Zanto's booth. But the arcade was so mobbed, not even her own mother would have recognized her.

Past the arcade, the crowds began to thin. No families here. These were grown-up entertainments—the minstrel show, the Woodland Cabaret, and run-down burlesque stalls.

And Max's tent. There were more crushed cigars and cigarettes on the ground than earlier. The hand-lettered sign now read NEXT SHOW 10 o'CLOCK. He would wait till after that performance, she thought, and leave before the park closed at midnight.

She gnawed her lip, trying to steel herself. Max usually took a break around eight. He'd retire to his dressing room to remove his makeup, have a few pops of whiskey, then duck into the Woodland Cabaret for a quick dinner and a few glasses of beer. Afterward he'd wander down to Fairyland, smoking a cigarette under the trees. She'd seen him there several times when she'd returned from a delivery and hadn't found him in his dressing room.

Her heart pounded as she drew closer to his dressing room. Would he have gone to the cabaret this evening? If he was in his room and saw her now, her plan would be ruined.

She stopped ten feet from his door. Through the window she saw a flicker of lantern light, the shadow of someone moving. She turned and slipped into the shadowy trees beside the path, crouching behind them. Waited.

Minutes passed. At last the light inside the shack went out. Pin held her breath as a tall figure in a white shirt and dark trousers emerged. No jacket, his boater pulled low to hide his face. He closed the door behind him but didn't lock it, and walked in the direction of Fairyland, a glowing cigarette in one hand.

Pin watched until he disappeared into the woods, the yellow glow of his cigarette extinguished by the night, then sprinted toward his shack and slipped inside. The white suit hung where she'd last seen it beside the door. She reached into one pocket of his seersucker jacket—empty—then the other. The wallet holding the photographs was gone.

Chapter 92

HE KNOWS, SHE thought. *He knows it was me.*

She felt as she had felt back in the tunnel, the world peeled away like a mask to reveal a horror that had no words, dead girls indistinguishable from abandoned dolls. Quickly she pushed aside the jacket and stuck her hand into a pocket of the trousers that hung beneath it.

Inside was a first-class train ticket for the *Capitol Limited,* departing that night at eleven-fifteen from Chicago's Grand Central Station and bound for Washington, D.C., along with a chit for a trunk being held at the station. She began to stuff the tickets into her pocket, then remembered she had no pocket.

And it would be stupid to take the tickets. He'd discover they were missing and flee immediately. And Max would be too clever to hop on the train. She and Henry would lose their chance. She stuffed the tickets back into the trouser pocket and slipped outside.

Girl or not, she broke into a run. In the near distance, the huge devil embraced the Hell Gate pavilion, leering in the floodlights. The line stretched almost all the way to Fairyland. A bolt of lightning flared across the horizon, and for a second illuminated a small figure standing atop the knoll. Henry. As she started up the hill, the small figure waved at her excitedly.

Idiot! What if someone saw him? If anyone looked up, they'd spot a man on top of the rise, gesturing like a lunatic. Lightning pulsed like the flash pots inside Hell Gate as she joined Henry where he stood, feinting at invisible attackers.

"Henry, no!" She tried to grab his arm. "Stop! It's me—"

He froze and gaped at her. "Pin?" he said.

Chapter 93

HAD THE BOY forgotten? He'd been here for fifteen minutes, no, longer, twenty minutes at least, that damned clock! Damn the clock, damn the boy, he should have followed him! Stuck him with the knife, pushed him down the stairs and stabbed—

Oh, there he was.

Henry waved at the brave boy scrambling up the hill. *See, I am here, General Evans! Just as you ordered, awaiting your commands!* His sword flashed through the air: together they would defeat their enemy!

"Henry, no!" Someone grabbed his arm. "Stop, it's me—goddamn it, Henry, *stop*." Pin's voice, but it wasn't Pin. His hand dropped to his side.

"Pin?"

A girl stood in front of him. Pin's height and skinny like Pin, but with yellow hair and a big blue bow, wearing a sailor blouse and skirt and clutching something to her breast. What the hell was she doing here?

"Are you lost?" he demanded.

The girl stared at Henry. Her anger gave way to a grin.

"It's me," she said. "Pin. This is the rest of the plan. I'm in disguise."

Disguise! He shook his head in astonishment. "Pin? Pin? It's you, really? Pin basket, pin box, pin…"

"*Stop it!*"

The girl slapped his hand, and he recoiled, eyeing her with suspicion. She could have murdered Pin, tortured him to learn of their plan.

"Prove it!" he shouted over a peal of thunder. "Prove it!"

She held up a small photograph. "Look at this. Henry, it's me."

He took the photo—the same one Pin had shown him in his room, of a doll wearing a girl's dress that was too big. You weren't supposed to do what the doll was doing. It was supposed to be secret.

He looked back at the girl, the real girl, not this curious toy. She was biting her lip, the way Pin did when he was angry or frightened. And her voice…

It *was* Pin. He laughed and held the picture up in triumph, hopping up and down.

"Pin! Skin, twin—!"

"Damn it, Henry," the girl begged, "*please stop acting crazy.*" She ducked behind the biggest tree, motioning him to follow.

"Do you want someone to see us?" she continued in an urgent whisper. "There are cops everywhere down there. I said I'd tell you the rest of the plan when I got here, so—stop doing that! Just *listen,* damn it!"

He forced himself to remain still. Stared at the doll photo so as not to gaze at her—his—that other face. Pin yet not Pin. It was hard to think of him as a boy, or a girl.

Pin took a deep breath. "Now you have to listen to me."

He—she—told him everything.

"The She-Male!" he exclaimed. "Willhie and I saw him—he belongs in a museum!"

"He belongs in jail."

"Where is he now? Hell Gate? Fate!"

"No. The woods—Fairyland."

"I can pounce on him and wrestle him to the ground!"

"No." The girl not Pin shook her, his, head emphatically. "This is the plan. I'm going down to find him in the woods. I'll…entice him."

"What if he tries to hurt you?"

"I have my shiv."

"Is it poisoned?"

"No."

"Too bad, too bad."

She gazed at his hand, the one that didn't have the photo. "Your knife—I told you to bring your knife."

Without a word he pulled it from the sheath in his sock and slashed at the air. Light shone from his blade like fire, like lightning, like—

She grabbed his arm and forced it to his side. "Not now, you idiot! Wait until you follow me and he shows himself. That's when you attack him, we both will—I have a knife, too. We'll shout for the police, and if they don't come, we'll force him to go to the station house with us."

He shrank from her touch, shuddering. But he put the knife away.

"I need to go." She looked down toward the picnic grounds. "He has a ticket for a train tonight at eleven-fifteen. We need to capture him now."

"Can I keep the photograph?"

"No. We need that to show the police. They won't believe us otherwise. If we have to kill him…"

"I killed someone before."

"Was it—was it hard?"

He shrugged. "Not as hard as dying."

The girl nodded. "Wait till I reach the bottom of the hill, then come after me. Don't act crazy. And don't take too long."

Pin stared at him. Henry opened his mouth to tell her—him—to wait, they should go together, maybe they should tell the police. He had the photograph. They might believe them.

But it was too late. Pin was gone.

Chapter 94

SHAME FILLED FRANCIS after he left Gina Maffucci. He'd said or done the wrong thing, misunderstood something crucial. Yet what had he failed to comprehend? What had he said that was so wrong?

Steady rolls of thunder rode on a wind that carried the bitter smell of smoke from the nearby brickyard. The Black Hand must be there, burning God knows what, or who. As if things weren't terrible enough. As he drew near Hell Gate, he wished the sky would open and wash it all away to Lake Michigan.

"Francis!" Bennie Hecht pushed his way through the crowd toward him. "I've been looking for you all day, couldn't find you."

Francis felt a small spur of relief. He lifted his chin to indicate the shouting throng around them. "No? Are you surprised?"

"Nope. See any sign of him?"

"Not a thing. He could be twenty miles away. Or on a train to Wichita."

"Do you think he is?"

"No."

"Why not?" Bennie stared at him eagerly—not the way Riverview's patrons did when asking for directions to the washroom, nor with

Hickey's impatience, or the other park sergeants' veiled contempt for a man who'd been sent down from the city force. Bennie looked at him like he had back when Francis had been detective sergeant at Robey Street, and the two of them had met at Barney Grogan's saloon to hash out the particulars of a fink's murder, or the suspicious suicide of a man known to owe money to the Black Hand.

"I think he's here, right now," Francis confided as they passed the packed entrance to Hell Gate. "That Irish girl attacked him and escaped. He'll be thinking of that—how he failed. He could have left Chicago after he killed the girl in Hell Gate, but he didn't—he murdered another girl the next day. He's like a trophy hunter, only he collects children.

"And today they're all here," he went on, looking around them. "He knows we're looking for him. But he won't be easily recognized. Another man in a suit and boater hat..."

"Well, he may have changed his clothes, Francis," Bennie said. He cocked a thumb at the dark-ride pavilion. "Think he's in there?"

"I doubt it. There're plainclothesmen all over it, and around the Miniature Railway and the duck pond. He'll know that—he's smart. If he's at Riverview, I think he'll go there—"

He raised his billy club to indicate the woods, then craned his neck to scrutinize the small rise overlooking Hell Gate. "We could go up there, catch a view..."

Bennie nodded, staring at the knoll. He frowned. "What's that?"

Francis halted to see where he pointed. Atop the rise stood two figures—a man, not very tall, and a girl. The man held some kind of knife, its blade catching the light as he parried at the girl. She gestured frantically, he lowered the blade, and she fled downhill, toward the woods. Francis grabbed Bennie's arm. "It's him."

They raced up the knoll, Bennie outpacing Francis until they neared the top. Night had taken the girl, but the man remained where he was, staring after her until, with a start, he saw them and bolted.

They nabbed him as he ran down the hill. Bennie grabbed his jacket; the little man shook him off and stumbled away until Francis tackled him, pinning him to the ground. He reached past the man's writhing arms to pull a long-bladed knife from a sheath in his sock.

Bennie whistled. "I'll be damned. That's a Solingen."

"Not yours!" the man shouted. "My father's! My grandfather's!"

Francis stood and yanked the man to his feet. He recognized him now—the weird stunted fellow who stood outside the incubators, watching little girls traipse in and out. He was a good head shorter than Francis and, despite his deep voice, appeared no older than Bennie. He thrashed and babbled like a lunatic, raving about a general, knives, a reward.

"Enough!" Francis shook the man violently. To his relief, he fell silent, though he continued to mouth words as he stared, wild eyed, down at the woods. "Tell me your name."

The man grew rigid but said nothing.

"What were you doing with that girl?" prodded Bennie. "Who is she?"

"Not a girl!" The man lunged, nearly slipping free. "Pin. That's Pin!"

Bennie grabbed his other arm as Francis held up the man's knife. "I saw you threatening her, we both did."

The man's gibberish rose to a howl. *"I—did—not!"*

"I said *enough*!" Francis yanked the man toward him. "You need to come with me, sir. What is your name?"

Abruptly the man grew still. "General Henry Dargero. I'm from Brazil."

"Oh, for Christ's sake," said Francis. "Just tell me your name."

"Henry," the man said sullenly.

"Who's the girl?"

"Not a girl!" The man trembled in agitation. "It's Pin! *Pin!*"

"You may need to use that," Bennie said to Francis, indicating the billy club. "He's deranged."

Francis didn't hear him. He stared at Henry. "What did you say? *Pin?* Did you say *Pin?*"

"Yes, of course! Pin! He's in a dress—a mess, a disguise. Lies! The killer, we—"

"Pin?" repeated Francis. "You mean Pin Maffucci? In a dress?"

"Yes! I am telling you! The boy knows the man, he went to trap him, we have a plan, but you are *preventing us*—"

He gazed down to where Fairyland's trees tossed in the wind and lightning spiked the haze of smoke from Bricktown. "Oh, damn you!" he shouted. "He's alone there now, he'll be murdered!"

"Forget this nonsense, Francis," Bennie broke in. "The girl's gone, she's safe. Let's take him and go."

"Wait." Francis looked at Henry. "Are you saying that was Pin we saw you with? The boy named Pin Maffucci?"

"Yes, Pin! We are great friends."

"And he was, what—in a costume?"

"He is dressed as a girl. His idea."

"And Pin knows the murderer?"

"Yes!" Henry cried. "I just told you!"

"Who is he, then? Tell me!" Francis urged him. "The killer."

"The man with two faces."

"Two faces?" Bennie frowned. "Someone in the freak show?"

Henry shook his head. "No, the She-Male."

"Good God." Francis stared at Bennie. "He means Max—the actor who dresses as a woman. Half woman, half man."

"He's a fairy?"

"Obviously he's not, if he's killing girls," snapped Francis, and turned back to Henry. "Where's Max gone, then? Do you know?"

"To Fairyland, Pin says he goes to the woods every night. Pin's going to *entice* him. For the reward. I have to find them…"

Without warning, Henry butted Francis's head, twisting to kick Bennie in the groin. Bennie doubled over as Francis staggered backward, and Henry sprinted down the hill.

"Henry!" Francis yelled as the small figure grew even smaller in the distance. "Henry, wait!"

"Pin Maffucci—that's the same boy who found the body, right?" Bennie gasped. "And this fellow says that was him, disguised as a girl? Who the hell is Max?"

"I told you, a burlesque performer. That's why no one's recognized him—he wears a costume for his act. So one person says he has a mustache, the other says he's clean shaven. Fairyland's the name of the picnic area. It sounds like Pin's trying to trick him into thinking he's a girl, so they can claim the reward."

"If Henry's telling the truth," said Bennie, "the guy could've killed that kid by now."

Francis shoved blindly past him down the hill. All he could see was how Gina's face would look when he told her that her child was dead.

Chapter 95

SHE DIDN'T STOP running until she reached the dark copse of trees. Behind her, Hell Gate's recorded moans and screams faded into the sound of wind in the leaves. At the edge of the trees she stopped to catch her breath, suddenly mindful of where and what she was: a girl entering the woods, alone.

She held as still as she could. She could hear crickets and katydids, a nightjar buzzing in the low grass. The wind caught her white sailor collar so it flapped in her face. She slapped it down before it could catch the eye of anyone who might be looking in her direction and turned her as head slowly as she could, searching for the glow of a cigarette.

She saw him from the corner of her eyes a fraction of a second before he saw her. She knew the instant he did. Her gaze locked with his, she saw the red tip of his cigarette as he raised his head, so that his hat brim revealed his face.

"Why, hello," he said in a pleasant tone. "What are you doing here?"

Terror flooded her: she'd been recognized. But then he took a cautious step in her direction, and she realized no, he was afraid he'd spook her if he moved too fast. She cleared her throat—she had to make her voice sound different, higher.

"Hello." She stared at a glowworm crawling in the grass. What if he recognized her voice?

"Are you lost?" He tossed his cigarette, lit another. In the flare of the match his face was a skeleton's. "Do you need to find your parents? I can take you back to the midway."

His tone was gentle but also indifferent, as though he'd just as soon leave her alone. Her terror eased. What if she'd been mistaken? What if he just happened to have those doll photographs, for some reason she couldn't imagine? What if it was only an ordinary doll, what if the dresses just happened to resemble Maria Walewski's, and her sister's?

He shook the match and dropped it, took a drag from his cigarette, slipped his hand into a pocket, and withdrew a small tin. She heard the soft snap as he opened it. In the gloom, she saw him put something in his mouth, begin to close the box, then look up, remembering she was there.

"I'm sorry—would you like a lemon drop? They're very good."

She stiffened and almost said no—what, did he think she was an idiot?—but caught herself and nodded. "Yes, thank you very much."

He held out the tin and she picked up a lemon drop. It felt gummy, as though the box had sat in the sun all day. She forced a smile, daring a glance at the man, who smiled back.

As soon as she put it in her mouth, she knew the lozenge had been doped. She recognized the taste; it was the same horrible syrup her mother drank to help her sleep. So that was how he'd done it. Poisoned candies. With her sister, all he would have had to do was offer her candy, poison or not, and smile kindly, and Abriana would have followed him anywhere.

Pin blinked. He was watching her. If she spat out the candy, he'd know she was up to something. She let the lozenge slip beneath her tongue, tried not to swallow even as her mouth filled with sweet liquid.

"You can have another if you'd like," he said in the same offhand tone, and popped a second lozenge into his mouth. Were only some of them poisoned? But that wouldn't make sense. He was bigger, that was all, they would hardly affect him unless he ate the whole tin.

He continued to gaze at her with those shadowed eyes, so she nodded and took another. She clutched it, her palm sticky, sweat trickling between her breasts. The wind gusted, the tree limbs rustled like dry hands rubbing together. Lightning flashed and she steeled herself for the thundercrack that followed seconds later. It came, and she turned her head to spit out the lemon drop.

When she turned back, he was staring fixedly at her. Her hands and arms went cold, she needed to spit again, get rid of the horrible sweet taste on her tongue. She wanted to run, but she'd backed up against the tree, and he was suddenly too near, just inches away. The smoke from his cigarette stung her eyes, and she smelled his breath, lemons and whiskey and cherry cordial. She opened her fingers and the poisoned candy fell to the grass; inched her hand down toward the shiv in her boot, and made the mistake of glancing up.

His face had twisted; he gazed at her as though she were one of the freaks in the Ten-in-One, something disgusting. He knew she meant to fight. Abriana hadn't fought, it might be better not to fight. He was going to kill her. She was going to die.

Something snapped inside her chest and spun out of her like smoke: she saw herself from above, as though watching a movie, a small white figure pressed against a tree as a shadow engulfed it. She could no longer hear the wind, there was a seashell roar in her ears that drowned out everything except for something, something she needed to remember, someone…

"*Henry!*" she screamed.

He grabbed her throat and pressed his other hand against her mouth, choking her with a cloth as he pushed her to the ground. He hadn't needed poisoned candies, he was so much bigger than she was and stronger, much stronger; she had never imagined Max might be this strong. She tried to bite his hand, but he thrust the cloth deeper into her mouth. She gagged as she tried to scream Henry's name, she'd told him to follow her, he should be here by now he should be here *where was he where was Henry?*

But the man pinched her nostrils closed and it was like trying to breathe in a dream of dying; and then it was too late.

Chapter 96

THEY RAN DOWN the path past the arcade, past the minstrel show and burlesque tent and Woodland Cabaret. Three young men stood outside Max's tent, smoking.

"Hang on," Francis ordered Bennie. He pointed at the She-Male banner and called out to the three men. "Have you seen him?"

The men tossed their cigarettes and ran off. Francis cursed, pulling at the tent flap to look inside. No one. It was the same with the shack Max used as a dressing room.

"Look at these." Bennie thrust a handful of postcards at Francis. "Our man has peculiar taste. No kids, though."

Francis flipped through them—pictures of women missing arms or legs or both; an actress named Polaire, whose wasp waist must've made it nearly impossible for her to eat. A smiling girl in pigtails and a checked frock, sitting atop a haystack.

"What about her?" he asked Bennie.

"Nope. That's Peggy Driscoll, she's twenty if she's a day. Come on."

Outside, thunder drowned out sounds from the park as they followed the path into the woodland. There were no electrical lights here. As Francis's eyes adjusted to the darkness, he picked out familiar trails beneath the trees. Some led to glades where people would lay their picnic blankets, but most meandered off into tangled underbrush. He'd lost his way there even in the daytime, chasing pickpockets or truant boys.

Now it seemed an impenetrable forest, though he knew the Velvet Coaster loomed not far away, and the brickyard that bordered the woods to the north. He looked at Bennie, who nodded. They walked, silent, for about thirty paces. Then Francis raised his hand, signaling Bennie to stop. He cupped a hand beside each ear, listening.

Nothing but the rustle of leaves, the murmuring of the North Branch. How could that little madman Henry have disappeared without making a peep? Maybe he'd been in collusion with Max all along.

From within the trees, a girl screamed, *"Henry!"*

"That's her." Bennie pushed his way through a wall of brambles. Francis remained where he was.

"No! Listen. I think it came from there." He pointed to a coppery smear low in the sky. "Bricktown. The kilns."

They crashed through the woods until the undergrowth gave way to an expanse of sand and gravel. Stacks of wooden pallets littered the ground between abandoned buildings, enough fuel to burn for days. In the center of the lot a looming smokestack spewed bright cinders.

"Henry! Henry, help!"

The two men halted as a small figure emerged from the woods and ran wildly toward the kiln.

Chapter 97

SHE WOKE, BURNING hot and jostled as though she sat in the last car of the Blue Streak. Why was she sleeping? And where? Someone carried her, clutched against his chest like a sack of flour. Her windpipe ached. It hurt to swallow.

She remembered: Max.

She drew a few shallow breaths, afraid to move. If he knew she was awake, he'd choke her again. His shirt reeked of sweat and urine. She'd read about the stink of fear, of being paralyzed by terror, but she'd always believed those were things made up for the magazines.

She cracked her eyes open. Mostly she saw his shirt, but when she cut her eyes, she caught a glimpse of buildings, darkness behind them and a flare of heat lightning in the clouds. The rattle and screams from the Velvet Coaster echoed in the distance. The air had a red tinge like Hell Gate, but there were no lights, not even streetlights. The carnival riot of Riverview sounded the way things sound underwater. Smoke stung her nostrils, and she saw a sliver of gold shoot up against the black sky.

Not lightning. Embers. They were in the brickyard, the one her mother insisted had been dismantled; the one where the Black Hand burned their dead.

She bit down on her tongue to keep from screaming. Held her breath, straining to hear voices or any sound of pursuit, but there was only the grumble of thunder and Max's heavy panting, the slap of his feet on the ground. Her terror dulled into a numb heaviness.

Where was Henry?

He had gotten lost. Or scared. Or he had simply forgotten, distracted by his imaginary enemies rather than her real one. She would become a name, like Elsie, Maria, Gilda, her sister, and all the others. Only there would be no photo of Pin. No one would remember her except her mother.

Her thoughts spiraled back to where she was now, her face pressed against the folds of a man's reeking shirt. Her wig had come loose: she rubbed her head against his chest to keep the wig from falling off. *He still doesn't know who I am,* she thought, fighting another surge of terror. What would happen when he did?

Max's steps had slowed. His hold on her had loosened—he wasn't concerned about her escaping. *He's not afraid of being caught,* she realized. He hadn't bound her arms or legs; he probably thought she was still unconscious. But he couldn't carry her forever. He would have to set her down; at some point he'd stop.

When he does I'll run. I'll scream, someone will hear me. Henry will hear me.

I'll scream now.

"Henry! Henry, help!"

"Shut up, you fucking bitch!" Max squeezed her until she whimpered in pain, and he began to run again. If she struggled, he'd kill her. She had to stay calm, make another plan. Make another plan. Now.

He thought she was a girl. She moved her right leg, and something bit into her ankle. Her shiv. He hadn't taken it. He didn't know she had a knife.

She did what she had as a child when she didn't want to go to bed, and made herself into a dead weight, sagging in his arms. After a few seconds he slowed, his breathing so loud she could hear nothing else. A few feet in front of them was the base of the smokestack. That was where they brought the bodies. The Black Hand. And him, Max. She tried to writhe free as he kicked the door, kicked it again and again until she heard wood split and the roar of flames and an unbearable heat surrounded her. They were inside.

Chapter 98

He nearly dropped her as he battered at the door. Perhaps she was already dead. He didn't care. He wanted her dress; he should have smothered her back there in the woods and taken it.

He coughed at the stench of scorched stone and burning coal. In the back of the room the kiln's iron door glowed like those rivers of fire in *The Inferno*. Broken brick covered the ground, clinkers, coal dust. Smooth patches where sand had fused into glass. In a few minutes she'd be a twist of smoke eaten by the clouds, like the Italian girl. He'd be in time to catch his train.

He set her down, leaning her against the wall so as not to spoil her clothes. She sat there, motionless, and he felt a stab at his heart.

How beautiful she was—like his sister, with her blond curls and blue bow, her sailor blouse and skirt rucked up above her knees. Her skin like the Gypsy girl's, darker than any doll's he had ever seen.

But still: a doll, her eyes closed. A doll's sleep-glass eyes would open, if it were sitting up like this.

Her eyes did. Staring at him, not with fear or mindless dreaming, but fury. Before he could move, she'd pushed herself to her feet. Her head fell away from her body, and he gasped.

But it wasn't her head but a wig. A different girl stood there, cropped hair and unsteady on her feet, someone he knew, what was her name, how could he possibly know her, he had never—

"Pin?"

She raised her hand, and he saw something shining in the dark. A knife? He didn't understand, who was this? Why would a girl have a knife?

She flung herself at him, her free hand clawing at his eyes, his mouth, whatever she could reach. He shouted; his arm slammed against her as something cold, then hot, grasped his throat. Didn't grasp: slashed.

"Pin!"

She looked away as another voice shouted hoarsely. Max caught her arm, yanking her toward him as the knife plunged through his cheek.

"Henry!" she screamed.

Max wrenched her arm back as the knife spun into the air. She screamed again as he grabbed her and stumbled toward the glowing door at the back of the room. The other girl hadn't fought; he'd slung her into the kiln like a log. Why would a girl have a knife? Thunder roared behind him, too close to be thunder. A train, he thought wildly, he'd miss his train. A weight fell on him and he toppled to the floor. The girl rolled free. A small figure crouched there with a knife in its hand, the girl, her face twisting as she drove the knife down repeatedly and screamed a name, *Abriana, Abriana!* Pain exploded in his chest and erupted into flame, not light but dark, nothing but darkness, heat, an agony of time as he struggled to speak but his mouth filled with blood. *Why would a girl have a knife?* Then nothing.

Chapter 99

THUNDER PEALED; SHE saw a bright flash and heard someone shouting her name.

Pin! Pin!

Henry. She dropped the knife as Max's body fell alongside her, she tried to push it away, but she was too tired, so she just lay there, waiting. *Henry came, Henry came. I knew he would.*

Chapter 100

SHE'D ALWAYS THOUGHT a hospital might be exciting. It wasn't. At first she couldn't remember how she'd gotten there—Max, the brickyard, Henry. A knife. Fatty Bacon and another man, then many men, policemen mostly. A woman screaming, was that her mother? She'd heard Henry's voice, he'd been there with her inside the kiln. But where was he now?

In the hospital, they pumped her stomach. Even after her stomach was empty, they did things to make her throw up again, "to get the poison out," a doctor said, though she tried to tell them she'd spat out the lemon drop, she hadn't swallowed enough poison to kill a fly. The room smelled of disinfectant and carbolic soap, scents that reminded her of Henry. Someone had dressed her in a long shapeless linen shift that felt stiff and cool against her bare skin. After a long time, she heard her mother's voice.

"Pin." With great effort Pin opened her eyes, to see her mother leaning over her. "My brave girl. You're safe now. Go back to sleep. Everyone will talk to you in the morning."

Her mother's eyes were red, her face swollen. She looked the way she had after Abriana's disappearance.

But Pin herself was alive, right? She wondered again where Henry was. He worked at the hospital, he must be here somewhere. Someone placed a cool compress on her forehead, smelling of rubbing alcohol and antiseptic. She heard her mother speaking, but she sounded very far away. The room grew light, then dark. When she next woke, there was only a nurse in the room with her, and her mother, who jumped from her chair, no longer grief-stricken but angry.

"What in God's name were you doing? You could have been killed—you nearly *were* killed."

The nurse left the room as Pin struggled to sit up. "Aw, Ma." Her throat hurt too much to argue. She looked around, blinking in the sunlight, and spotted a newspaper on a small table.

Riverview Owner Says Reward Will Be Shared By Heroes

The reward! "Are the police here?" she rasped. "I need to tell them—"

Her mother nodded wearily. "They're here. They're waiting to talk to you. *Lots* of people want to talk to you," she added. "But not until you feel up to it."

"I feel fine. I need to tell them about the reward, we—"

But she didn't feel fine once they had finished questioning her. Policemen, doctors, the police captain from Riverview, and another man, the Chicago police commissioner, Deneen. More doctors.

They didn't believe her when she told them about her plan. They didn't believe her when she mentioned Henry and told them that he worked here at the hospital, even though they asked repeatedly about the second man and how she knew him. The second man wasn't a hero, they told her. He'd fled, almost certainly he was there to assist the murderer, then ran when he saw the policeman and the reporter. When they asked how she knew Max, she lied and told them she only knew him by sight, from the park. No matter how many times they questioned her, she repeated the same answer.

"Leave the kid alone," someone finally said in exasperation. "The fellow's dead. Let her rest."

But they wouldn't let her rest, even though she felt that, if she closed her eyes, she'd fall asleep right there, surrounded by all of them, detectives and the commissioner and some other coppers who sometimes interrupted to ask her a question. Fatty Bacon wasn't one of them, though she glimpsed him in the hall with her mother, who was not allowed in the hospital room while the policemen were there.

There were doctors, too, almost as many doctors as policemen, and they all seemed perplexed and concerned about one thing, though it took them a long time to bring it up. When they did, Pin refused to answer until yet another doctor was called in, along with her mother. The doctor was named Dr. Bergman. He was not very old and wore a suit, not a white doctor's coat, though he did have a stethoscope around his neck and carried a black leather medical bag.

"We know from your mother what you've been doing all summer," he said to Pin gently. "But the police would like to hear it from you."

"Why?" She sat up straight in the hospital bed. "You haven't even given us the reward! Why do you even have to know, it's none of your damned business!"

A man came back into the room then, the police commissioner, Deneen. A big white man, older, with small, mean eyes like a sow's. He pushed aside Dr. Bergman, placed his hands on the bed's metal rails, and stared down at Pin.

"We've had enough of this nonsense, young lady." He raised his voice loud enough for everyone in the hall to hear. "A great deal of effort has been put into making sure you're safe. It's time for you to cooperate. What is your Christian name?"

"Pin."

His face reddened. She'd seen men who struck their children: Commissioner Deneen looked like one of them as he bellowed, "You're not going to leave this room or see another person, not even your mother, until you tell me your Christian name."

Pin glared at him but said nothing. She stared at the closed door to her hospital room. Through its window she could see her mother's small face, gazing at her with mingled pity and fear and anger as she nodded and frantically mouthed the words *Tell him, tell him!*

Pin stared in disbelief until her mother turned away, her face in the window replaced by that of a policeman.

All of a sudden she understood everything. She was a fourteen-year-old girl in a hospital room—a prisoner, surrounded by men, policemen and doctors, none of whom would ever believe anything she told them about what had happened, even if it was the truth. No one would believe she and Henry had tricked a murderer. No one would believe she had stabbed a man to death with a knife. Not even her mother would defend her.

And Henry had forgotten her, or maybe they'd made him a prisoner, too.

There would be no reward. Everyone believed that Fatty Bacon and a reporter were the heroes: not her, not Henry. She looked up at the hospital wall and saw a crucifix there. She hated it, she hated God. She hated this world and those who made it.

She stared at Deneen, wanting to spit at him, to attack him as she had attacked Max, claw his tiny piggy eyes from his face and leave him bleeding on the floor.

Instead, she told him her real name. And then she collapsed on the bed, weeping inconsolably.

Chapter 101

THEY FINALLY ALLOWED her to leave early that evening. They brought her the clothes they'd found her in, the soiled sailor dress that Glory had loaned her. She almost cried again, thinking of Glory, who would surely never speak to her once she knew the truth. She begged her mother to bring in her own clothes, but Gina refused.

"That's all over, Pin," was all she said, and returned to the corridor.

Pin dressed in a silent fury, then went into the hall, where her mother and Fatty Bacon were waiting. Her mother tried to take her hand, but Pin pushed her away and walked on ahead of them without speaking.

Outside the hospital stood a dozen or so men, all holding notebooks. Several had cameras and took her picture. She glared at them, turning to where her mother and Fatty had halted behind her.

"Make them stop," she ordered.

Fatty looked at her, then nodded. He walked over to the reporters and spoke to them. She could hear them arguing, but after a few minutes they all left, except for one dark-haired man who stepped over to a tree, where he lit a cigarette and watched her as he smoked. She recognized him from inside the hospital: he was the reporter who would share the reward with Fatty Bacon.

Pin walked out onto the street. She didn't know where she'd go. She might run away, hop a freight car near Belmont and see where it took her.

"Pin! Pintail, Pinafore!"

She whirled to see a small figure running toward her. He wore his hospital work clothes, dirty overalls and a stained work shirt and work boots.

"Henry!" She ran to meet him, and he stopped, turning his head to avoid her delighted gaze. "Jesus, Henry, where were you?"

"I had to go to work."

She glanced back and saw her mother and Fatty whispering to each other as they watched her. She turned to Henry again, lowering her voice. "Did you talk to the cops?"

He shrugged, not meeting her eyes. "Tried to. They think I'm crazy. That policeman, too. He said it wasn't me, he said the second man was taller. He lied to them."

"I hate him," she spat.

"I think he didn't want them to arrest me, maybe. Because I had a knife. Life."

She stared at her feet. She could feel Henry's gaze, but when she raised her head, he looked away.

"They told me that you're really a girl," he said. "Is that true?"

She bit her lip, after a moment nodded. When she spoke, she no longer sounded defiant, just defeated. "They made me tell them my real name."

"What *is* your real name?"

She took a deep breath. "Vivian."

"Vivian?" He frowned. "Vivian?"

He repeated it several times, as though trying to find a rhyme. At last he shrugged. "Vivian is a good name. Boy, girl: same."

He fumbled through his pockets. Pin let her breath out, relieved he wasn't going to mock her as everyone else was sure to.

"Pin," her mother called. "We need to go."

Pin ignored her. She watched as Henry pulled out a small crumpled card and a pencil stub. He crouched, smoothed the card on his knees, and painstakingly wrote on it, pressing down hard for each letter, as though to make sure the words wouldn't blow away. When he was done, he stuck the pencil back in his pocket and stared at the card. At last, satisfied, he handed it to her. For a fraction of a second, his pale blue eyes gazed directly into hers and didn't look away.

"I knew you weren't really a boy," he said.

"How?"

"Because only a girl would be so brave."

"Miss Onofria! Miss Onofria!"

Pin turned to see someone walking toward her, the reporter who'd gone to smoke his cigarette beneath a tree.

"I'd like to have a word with you, Miss Onofria," he said, stopping to remove his hat. "A few words, to be honest. I'm Mr. Hecht, a reporter with the *Daily News*. I've already spoken to your mother, but I'd like to hear your side of the story. I suspect it's a very interesting one."

Pin thought, then nodded grudgingly.

"Yeah, okay," she said. "Just hold on a minute." She turned to say goodbye to Henry, but he was already shuffling back toward Workingmen's House.

Chapter 102

He reached his room, elated, locked the door, and hurried to his desk. He hadn't slept in nearly two days. Exhausted as he was, he felt wide awake, thrilled by the great events in which he'd taken part.

He had saved Pin before any of the others could reach his friend. *General Dargero!* they had all cried. *We await your orders!*

Stand by, I will kill him!

And so he had! He'd seen the man fall, but he'd had to retreat as those other two men came racing toward him. One was dressed as a policeman, but they might have been evil generals. He knew they would take him back to the asylum if they could. So General Dargero had quietly slipped away under cover of darkness, until next he was called upon to defend all girls against the powerful and wicked forces who so relentlessly pursued them.

Pin had fought so bravely! It was she who had slain that evil man with her blade, even though they claimed the policeman had done it. Brave Pin, brave Vivian! Was there a better name? Why had it taken so long for him to think of it?

He got out his manuscript, his pencil and votive candles, his sheaf of creased newspaper clippings, last of all the faded newspaper photograph of Elsie Paroubek. He pulled out Saint Dymphna's scapular and kissed it, sharpened the tip of his pencil with his knife. For a long time he sat and stared at the title page of his book. He reached into the drawer for a sheet of blank paper, smoothed it on top of the desk, and began to write:

THE TRUE ADVENTURES OF THE VIVIAN GIRLS,
WHO FOUGHT BESIDE THE GEMINI
IN THE TIME OF THE TERRIBLE WAR STORM,
CAUSED BY THE REBELLION OF THE CHILD SLAVES

By Henry Joseph Darger
The Author Of This Exciting Story

He turned to the first page, frowned, and crossed out a few words, then began to write.

It was dark and the Vivian Girls were still awaiting the return of Violet.

Even as the light paled and he heard Sister Rose's footsteps in the corridor outside the room, he continued writing. It would be a very, very long time before he stopped.

Chapter 103

PIN HATED SCHOOL. She hated everything. There had been no reward. Riverview's owner, Mr. Baumgarten, had given Fatty Bacon and that reporter five hundred dollars apiece. They were the heroes: she was only the one who'd needed to be rescued.

And when Baumgarten learned she and her mother had been living in the shack behind the Kansas Cyclone, he'd evicted them, though he didn't call it that. He gave her mother two hundred dollars and told her it was for new school clothes for her daughter, and any incidental expenses they might have. She and her mother now had rooms in a boardinghouse, the same one where Fatty Bacon lived, with a nosy landlady named Mrs. Dahl. Fatty was courting her mother, no doubt about that. Pin didn't speak to him unless her mother ordered her to.

To her relief, Fatty mostly left her alone. Pin seemed to intimidate him, which was fine by her.

It was just as well they'd left Riverview. Once Mr. Hecht's exclusive newspaper story ran in the *Daily News,* and everyone knew that the boy they'd known as Pin was actually a girl named Vivian, she'd been hounded by the boys in the park. Surprisingly, only Clyde was polite to her.

"I don't blame you now," he said a few days before she and her mother moved out. "You with your sister…it's a bad old world for young girls. I don't blame you one bit."

Now, in her freshman English class, she sat staring at a blank page in her composition book and waited for the bell to ring, signaling the end of the school day. At first, the other high-school students had boiled with curiosity over the girl who'd dressed as a boy who'd dressed as a girl, and escaped from a murderer.

But Pin felt shy and tongue-tied in her stiff new sailor dresses and shirtwaists. The other girls bored her, and the boys showed little interest, once she rebuffed their feeble attempts at flirting. Her classmates didn't taunt or torment her, as she'd feared. After the first few weeks of school, they simply ignored her.

She lifted her gaze from the page to the wall clock, watched as the second hand ticked along. The bell rang. The classroom erupted into a chorus of laughter and chatter, chairs being scraped back and people racing for the door. She gathered her textbooks, waiting till the room emptied before she stood.

"Vivian? Miss Onofria?"

Pin headed to the door, halting only when someone grasped her arm.

"Vivian Onofria, I'm speaking to you."

She looked up to see the school principal, Miss Weiss. Miss Weiss always dressed in sensible clothing, a plain dark-blue street dress and brogues. She wore her brown hair in a boyish bob, a recent fashion for women.

"Sorry, miss," Pin said, flushing. She still couldn't get used to being addressed by her given name.

"Someone's here to see you. In my office, come with me, please."

Pin followed her down the hall, avoiding the eyes of students who stared as she passed. She'd stayed out of trouble since arriving here; she was a mediocre student, but only one among many. Now she wondered if her continual failure to remember she was Vivian Onofria, not Pin Maffucci, had earned her detention.

"I'll be in my office," Miss Weiss said as she waved Pin into the waiting room. The school secretary, Miss Kingsley, glanced up at her and smiled.

"Here she is! Vivian, you have a visitor."

A tall, broad-shouldered man unfolded himself from a chair and stood, holding his hat.

"Pin," he said, and grinned.

"Mr. Carrera!" She grinned back, for what felt like the first time in weeks.

Billy Carrera looked her up and down, shaking his head, and sank back into his chair. He wore a suit jacket over his usual shirt, a celluloid collar curling from the heat. "Well, you surprised us all, I'll give you that, Pin. Vivian, I mean."

"Pin," she said under her breath. She glanced at Miss Kingsley, who had returned her attention to a stack of papers. "I prefer Pin."

"Well, that was quite a story, whatever your name is." Billy Carrera shook his head again, as though still not quite believing it. "Lionel helped me track you down. Almost got him in a lot of trouble, that notebook of his. He remembered the name of the policeman he talked to at the park, and when I told him I wanted to see you, he went to Riverview and spoke to Mr. Bacon and found out where you go to school. So here I am."

Pin bunched up her skirt, then smoothed it out again. She smiled nervously, uncertain what to say. It was impossible to know how to act now, especially around grown-up men.

"We miss you hanging around the studio," Carrera went on after a moment. "So I came to ask you, how would you like a job there?"

"A job?"

He nodded. "As a joiner—your pal Glory Swanson said she thought you'd be interested. What do you think?"

Pin bit her lip, trying to hide her disappointment. Why a joiner? Why not an assistant to Billy himself, or one of the other cameramen, out on the studio floor? When she said nothing, Carrera continued.

"That would be to start. We use a lot of girls, you know that. If you did it for a while, and you liked it—if you're good at it—then maybe you could be a cutter. There's some girls in the cutting room, along with the fellas. I'm thinking you could work maybe two, three days a week after school. Saturdays if you want. If it's okay with your mother," he added. "You're fourteen?"

She nodded.

"Well, that's young, most of the girls are sixteen. But I can vouch for you. I know you're a quick study, I've seen that. So if you want to think about it—"

"No, I'll do it," she broke in. "I can start now."

Carrera laughed. "Why don't we wait till Monday? That way I can tell the girls in the office and we can get you all set up."

He picked up his hat and stood, extending his hand. Pin took it and they shook. "Thanks," she said, and smiled again gratefully.

"One more thing." He dipped his hand into a pocket, withdrew an envelope, and handed it to her. "Glory asked me to give you this. She's gone out to California with her mother, to the Niles studio. Her and Wally Beery seem to be an item."

"Glory?"

"Yup. He's going to teach her to drive for *The Danger Girl* at Keystone. She dresses as a fella in that one. You'll have to see it," he said, and winked.

"I will." She clutched the envelope, resisting the urge to tear it open then and there.

"She's making quite a splash, that gal. Okay, I better go. You ask your mother to come with you on Monday, let's say four o'clock. How's that?"

"That's swell." She smiled at him. "I'll see you on Monday."

He grinned and tipped his hat to her—something else she had to get used to. "See you Monday."

She put a good five or six blocks between herself and the school before she opened Glory's letter. The neighborhood where they lived was quiet: she heard distant laughter from other students as they walked home, and dogs barking eagerly as they raced to the sidewalk to greet them.

She halted at the end of the street that led to Mrs. Dahl's boardinghouse. Pin's mother had gone to work at a lunch counter. Fatty Bacon had told her she no longer needed to work if she didn't want to. "But I do want to," Gina had retorted.

Pin ducked behind a tree that shaded the sidewalk, dropped her school satchel, and sat cross-legged in the grass. The envelope was pale blue, as was the paper inside, which had scalloped edges and smelled of carnations. Glory's small neat handwriting filled the page, black ink with a single blotch. Pin longed to think it had been left by a tear, though it was difficult to imagine Glory crying over anything.

Dear Pin,

I suppose I should call you Vivian but I can't! How could you tease me like that? I should be so angry! But I'm not, I only wish you had told me, perhaps I might have helped. But probably not.

Mother and I have decided to go to California, where I will take more singing lessons. I may also do some motion picture work at the Niles Canyon studio. Charlie Chaplin is out there, you will remember that I'm sure. Wally is there too now. Maybe you can come visit me.

I will miss our happy times at the studio, Pin—I don't think I'll ever be able to call you Vivian, I know I said that already but it's true.

Your affectionate friend,
Gloria Swanson

P.S. Please don't fret about that middy costume, I never told them at the studio and they will never miss it.

A lightness filled her, the same sense of freedom and anticipation as when her mother had cut her hair months ago, before they moved to Riverview; the same exhilaration she'd felt whenever she watched the film of Harriet Quimby's flight, or turned the crank on Billy Carrera's Bell and Howell camera. She slipped Glory's letter back into the envelope, stuck it inside her book bag, and stood, brushing grass and twigs from her skirt, then hurried home to tell her mother about her new job.

Chapter 104

New York City, November 1977

Pɪɴ! Aʀᴇɴ'ᴛ ʏᴏᴜ ready yet?"

Pin sighed and finished tying her shoe. "Where's the fire?"

"You were the one who wanted to go. Come on, slowpoke."

Pin stood, tugging at her trousers. They were a nice dark-blue gabardine, and worthy of nicer shoes than the Puma sneakers she wore. But other shoes hurt her feet these days.

"That's what you're wearing?"

She looked up to see Angela standing in the doorway of their bedroom. Pin shrugged. "Why?"

"It's Thanksgiving."

"It's dinner with your niece's daughter and her boyfriend."

"I want us to look nice."

"Nobody cares how a little old lady dresses."

"Two little old ladies," said Angela. "Only one of them very well dressed."

It was true—Angela always looked elegant, a carryover from her career as a stewardess for Pan Am. Angela had started there when Juan Trippe ran the company, and now, years after retiring, she could still fit into her uniform. She'd gotten her pilot's license and continued to give flying lessons in small aircraft, Cessna 150s. Pin had never seen her wearing trousers. Even for Francis's funeral a decade earlier, and her mother's a year ago, Pin had never worn anything else.

"Eh, I don't want to compete with you," Pin said, and ran a hand over her silvery curls. "Anyway, no one would recognize me if I was in a dress."

"At least put on some jewelry. That beautiful necklace I gave you three years ago for Christmas—I've never seen you wear it, even once."

Pin sighed. "I'm sorry. I just never—"

"Just wear it." Angela stepped over to kiss Pin's cheek.

Pin went to the bureau and began to rummage through the drawer where she kept odds and ends. Old photos from when she worked at the studio, old tax returns, a box of stray buttons and pennies. She didn't own much jewelry, a few things Angela had given her over the years that Pin had dutifully exclaimed at, then put away and forgotten. Where was that damn necklace?

She found it shoved into a shoebox full of yet more papers, receipts and ticket stubs from plays and movies, a newspaper clipping from when someone interviewed Angela about being a woman pilot. The necklace was still in its original plush velvet box. As Pin picked it up, a bit of cardboard fell to the floor. She retrieved it, sucking her breath in sharply when she saw what it was.

The handmade card Henry had shown her the first day they'd met, the same card he had given her the very last time she saw him outside the hospital, when he'd painstakingly written something on it.

"Pin?" Angela stepped beside her. "What is it, darling?"

Pin shook her head, eyes welling. She handed the card to Angela, who gazed at it, bewildered.

GEMINI CHILD PROTECTIVE SOCIETY
BLACK BROTHERS LODGE
HENRICO DARGERO AND VIVIAN PIN

"'Henrico Dargero,'" Angela read. "Was that someone you knew in Chicago? I've never heard you mention him before."

"Oh yes," said Pin, taking back the card. Very carefully, she set it on the bureau, beside the wedding photograph of her mother and Francis, stared at the card for a long time before she finally turned back to Angela. "We were great friends," she said. "Very great friends."

Acknowledgments

For three decades as my agent, Martha Millard steered me through the creation of dozens of books, and she walked every step of the way with me through the first draft of this one, before her retirement last year. None of my novels would have been written without her support, inspiration, and encouragement. I owe her more love and thanks than I can express.

Martha passed the baton to Nell Pierce, who has done an amazing job. My gratitude to Nell and everyone else at Sterling Lord Literistic.

Three years ago, Josh Kendall at Mulholland Books read the earliest version of this novel. Without his brilliant suggestions and guidance, and those of Emily Giglierano, this book would never have been written. I feel extremely fortunate to have worked with two of the best editors in the business, along with my publicist, Alyssa Persons, marketer Pamela Brown, and production editor Betsy Uhrig, and to have had the support of everyone at Mulholland who helped bring Henry and Pin's saga to life.

My copyeditor, Susan Bradanini Betz, did an exemplary job of catching those anachronisms that slipped past me. Her knowledge of Chicago and especially of Riverview enhanced every page she worked on—thank you!

The inestimable Steven Silver volunteered to authenticate and map my 1915 Chicago. He provided me with the names of streets, neighborhoods, buildings, businesses, and streetcars (many of them long gone), going so far as to create a Google map of Henry and Pin's journeys across the city. I owe him an incredible debt of thanks for sharing his remarkable knowledge of and love for a lost Chicago.

Many people assisted me by sharing or tracking down archival material, books, articles, and documentary footage—among others, Greg Bryant, Kristabelle Munson, Jason Ridler, David Shaw, my sister Barbara Legan, my brother Brian Hand, my sister-in-law Amy Hand, and Ken Barr, who shared his childhood memories of Riverview Amusement Park and Chicago.

Penn Jillette told me about the African magician Black Herman and provided an introduction to the legendary magician Johnny Thompson. Johnny, the Great Tomsoni, spoke to me at length about his experience of working at Riverview as a boy magician, sharing his insight into the park's history, the characters who populated it, and early twentieth-century magicians in the United States. His kindness and generosity toward a total stranger were exceptional but not at all out of character, as demonstrated by the outpouring of love for him after his death, at eighty-four, earlier this year.

Enza Vescera tracked down a rare copy of Ben Hecht's *A Child of the Century*. Robert Levy gave me a copy of *Henry Darger's Room: 851 Webster*. Ellen Datlow, Gemma Files, Jeffrey Ford, Callie Hand, Cara Hoffman, Carla Hufstedler, Robert Levy, Sharyn November, Bill Sheehan, and Gary Wolfe all read early drafts and gave suggestions for improvements.

Finally, my love to my partner, John Clute, who as ever read multiple drafts, year after year, offering editorial and moral support when it seemed that Henry and Pin's adventures would never see the light of day, or end. Most of all, my love and thanks to my mother, Alice Ann Silverthorn Hand, who shares my love for Henry Darger's work, and who thought he would make a good detective.

On Henry Darger

I've been obsessed with Henry Darger since 1979, when I heard a haunting and enigmatic song titled "The Vivian Girls," by the late avant-garde performer Snakefinger. A few years later, I learned the song was inspired by the self-taught Chicago artist Henry Darger. In 2002, I reviewed John M. MacGregor's groundbreaking *Henry Darger: In the Realms of the Unreal* and wrote at length about the similarities between Darger's work and that of J. R. R. Tolkien, another Catholic visionary artist and author. My notes below are excerpted from that article. You can read it in its entirety at https://www.sfsite.com/fsf/2002/eho210.htm, or visit my website, www.elizabethhand.com.

Born in Chicago in 1892, Henry Darger lived an impoverished life. When he was four, his mother died after giving birth to a girl who was given up for adoption. The infant's history remains unknown. After a stint in a Catholic boys' home, twelve-year-old Henry was placed in the Illinois Asylum for Feeble-Minded Children. The reasons: a propensity for aggressive behavior toward other children; setting fires; "acquired" self-abuse. He ran away from the asylum several times and escaped for good in 1909, walking to Chicago, where he found work as a janitor at a Catholic hospital. He spent the rest of his life as a menial laborer and seems to have had only one true friend, Willhie Schloeder, with whom he visited Riverview Amusement Park.

Darger was obsessed with the 1911 abduction and murder of Elsie Paroubek, a five-year-old Czech girl. The loss of a treasured newspaper photograph of Elsie threw him into the tumult of grief and rage that, in part, inspired his magnum opus. In 1932 he moved to 851 Webster Avenue, occupying a single large room until poor health necessitated his move to a Catholic nursing home when he was eighty.

In 1956, the Webster Avenue building was bought by the noted Chicago photographer Nathan Lerner. An extraordinarily compassionate landlord, Lerner never raised Darger's rent. Along with other residents of the building, he provided occasional meals and, as Darger grew increasingly frail, help with medical care. Darger, a furtive, slight man, just over five feet tall, always wore the filthy ruins of his army overcoat and spent hours poking through trash cans for refuse, which he then brought back to his apartment. His neighbors often heard Henry talking to himself, carrying on lengthy conversations in which he took on different voices. He was in fact engaged in the final stages of a lifelong battle with God.

Not long before Darger died in 1972, Lerner entered his room to clean it. There he found (among other works) fifteen volumes, totaling more than fifteen thousand pages, and hundreds of pictures illustrating a vast epic, *The Story of the Vivian Girls, in What Is Known as the Realms of the Unreal, of the Glandeco-Angelinnian War Storm, Caused by the Child Slave Rebellion.*

Modeled upon the books he loved as a child—L. Frank Baum's Oz books, Johanna Spyri's Heidi stories, *Uncle Tom's Cabin,* Booth Tarkington's Penrod series—Darger's epic follows the Vivian Girls through an endless relay of scrapes, plots, imprisonments, battles, tortures, escapes, and cataclysmic storms. Yet, as Darger himself admits, "This is not the land where Dorothy and her Oz friends reside." Art critics make much of Darger's luminous use of color and his genius for collage, and many of the paintings in the Henry Darger Collection at the American Folk Art Museum are breathtakingly gorgeous. But this is not Oz. *The Realms* is as excruciating and detailed a portrait of the human psyche as we have seen: brutal, banal, transcendental, with flashes of the divine. The timeless urge to create is what made the profoundly damaged, isolated, and lonely man named Henry Darger human. It is also what may make him immortal.

Selected Bibliography

Whenever possible, I relied on primary sources, including myriad period books, magazines, and newspaper articles in archives, online, and elsewhere. This is a very select list of the books I found most useful over nearly ten years of researching this novel.

1. Henry Darger

Anderson, Brooke Davis, editor. *Darger: The Henry Darger Collection at the American Folk Art Museum*. New York: Harry N. Abrams, 2001.

Biesenbach, Klaus, editor. *Henry Darger: Disasters of War*. Berlin: KW Institute for Contemporary Art, 2000.

———. *Henry Darger*. Berlin: Prestel Verlag, in cooperation with the American Folk Art Museum, New York, 2014.

Darger, Henry. *Henry Darger: Art and Selected Writings*. Edited and with an introduction by Michael Bonesteel. New York: Rizzoli, 2000.

———. *Darger: The Henry Darger Collection at the American Folk Art Museum*. New York: Harry N. Abrams in association with American Folk Art Museum, 2001.

———. *Henry Darger's Room: 851 Webster*. Introduction by John M. MacGregor. Tokyo: Imperial Press, 2007.

Elledge, Jim. *Henry Darger, Throwaway Boy: The Tragic Life of an Outsider Artist*. New York: Overlook Duckworth, 2013.

MacGregor, John M. *The Discovery of the Art of the Insane.* Princeton, NJ: Princeton University Press, 1989.

———. *Henry Darger: In the Realms of the Unreal.* Lugano, Switzerland: Fondazione Galleria Gottardo, 1996.

Yu, Jessica, dir. *In the Realms of the Unreal: The Mystery of Henry Darger.* DVD, 2004.

2. Early Film

Ankerich, Michael G. *Broken Silence: Conversations with 23 Silent Film Stars.* Jefferson, NC: McFarland & Company, 1993.

Brown, Karl. *Adventures with D. W. Griffith.* New York: Farrar, Straus and Giroux, 1973.

Corcoran, Michael, and Arnie Bernstein. *Hollywood on Lake Michigan: 100+ Years of Chicago and the Movies.* Chicago: Chicago Review Press, 2013.

Griffith, Mrs. D. W. [Linda Arvidson]. *When the Movies Were Young.* New York: E. P. Dutton and Company, 1925.

Kiehn, David. *Broncho Billy and the Essanay Film Company.* Berkeley, CA: Farwell Books, 2003.

Nickelodeon: The Director's Cut. Commentary by Peter Bogdanovich. Columbia Pictures, DVD, 2009.

Smith, Michael Golver, and Adam Selzer. *Flickering Empire: How Chicago Invented the U.S. Film Industry.* New York: Wallflower Press, 2015.

Swanson, Gloria. *Swanson on Swanson: An Autobiography.* New York: Random House, 1980.

3. Riverview Park and Chicago

Ellis, A. Caswell, and G. Stanley Hall. *A Study of Dolls.* New York: E. L. Kellogg & Company, 1897.

Gee, Derek, and Ralph Lopez. *Laugh Your Troubles Away: The Complete*

History of Riverview Park, Chicago, Illinois. Livonia, MO: Sharpshooters Productions, 2000.

Haugh, Dolores. *Riverview Amusement Park.* Charleston, SC: Arcadia Publishing, 2004.

Hecht, Ben. *A Thousand and One Afternoons in Chicago.* Chicago: Covici-McGee, 1922.

——. *A Child of the Century: The Autobiography of Ben Hecht.* New York: Simon and Schuster, 1954.

Hoffman, Adina. *Ben Hecht: Fighting Words, Moving Pictures.* New Haven, CT: Yale University Press, 2019.

Larson, Erik. *The Devil in the White City: Murder, Magic, and Madness at the Fair That Changed America.* New York: Crown Publishers, 2003.

Wlodarczyk, Chuck. *Riverview: Gone but Not Forgotten, 1904–1967.* Chicago: Riverview Publications, 1977.

About the Author

Elizabeth Hand is the author of more than fourteen cross-genre novels and collections of short fiction. Her work has received the Shirley Jackson Award (three times), the World Fantasy Award (four times), and the Nebula Award (twice), as well as the James M. Tiptree Jr. and Mythopoeic Society Awards. She's a longtime critic and contributor of essays for the *Washington Post,* the *Los Angeles Times, Salon, Boston Review,* and the *Village Voice,* among many others. She divides her time between the Maine coast and North London.